IN THE S
THE MC

The door was halfway open as Fletcher barged into the darkened living room. He shone his powerful flashlight around the rooms seeing they were empty.

"Jennifer!" he yelled. "Madame Von Bruen! Where are you? Jennifer!"

Hearing nothing, he quickened his pace down the hallway, stopping at the open doorway of the bedroom. He grimaced at the fading but still pervading stench of rotting flowers and smoke. Regaining his composure, he scanned the room with his flashlight, suddenly stopping to focus the wide beam on the lifeless body lying on the bed. *Oh God, no!* He put his hand on the wall and felt for the light switch, flipping it on.

He stepped back in shock as he saw Von Bruen lying there. Her long slender body was still and her head was propped up on a pillow. The drip-pan of the overhead girandole had been bent forward, allowing the molten candle wax to drip onto her narrow, ashen face. Her open, terror-filled eyes peered upward through the thin mounds of solid glistening tallow.

Tense, he looked around the room, seeing the small pools of nauseous slime giving off a vile, steamy vapor. He nervously aimed his flashlight into the shadows of the corners, fearful at what else he may discover.

Alarmed, he abruptly froze the beam on Jennifer's crumpled chain and crucifix lying on the floor. Stepping around the mire, he picked it up and firmly grasped the silver cross while looking upward with a silent plea.

As the laden moon sheds its platinum sheen high above the sea, casting a vast glade of shimmering silver ...and fate awaits ...

IN THE SHADOWS OF THE MOONGLADE

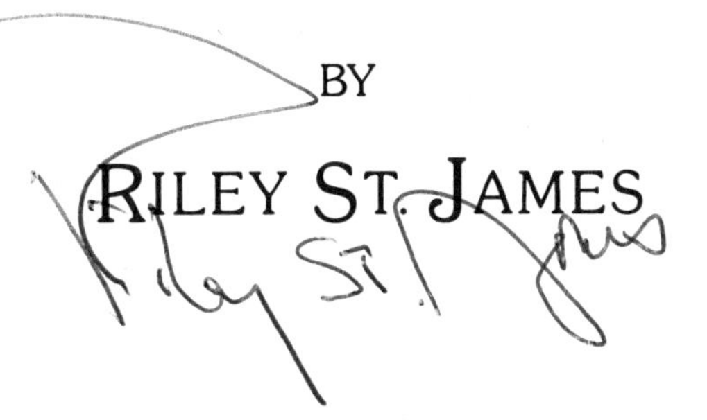

BY

RILEY ST. JAMES

SHADOWCREST
PUBLICATIONS

IN THE SHADOWS OF THE MOONGLADE
A ShadowCrest Publications Paperback
Post Office Box 1069
Tustin, CA 92781-1069 U.S.A.
Fax: 714-730-4008

www.shadowcrestpub.com

First Edition
May 1998

2nd Printing / Sept. 1998

ISBN: 0-9662612-0-8

Library of Congress Catalog Card Number: 98-90091

Cover design by Lynn Phillips, Ocean Avenue Design

Printed in the United States of America by:
Malloy Lithographing • Ann Arbor, MI 48103

Acknowledgements

While there are many people who deserve my utmost gratitude for the success of this novel, the greatest deal of appreciation is owed to my good friend and mentor, Ms. Linda Pinson, business author and owner of *Out of your mind...and Into the Marketplace*. Her wealth of knowledge and continual inspiration were instrumental in getting this book to the bookshelves. It would not have happened without you. This book is dedicated to you. Thank you, Linda.

Additionally, I offer my sincere gratefulness to my friends, Ed Kirkwood, Mark delaBretonne, Kay Sulzer, Michelle Rippe, Karen Olson and Maryann Riley. Their ongoing stamina while wading through my initial drafts was indeed a virtue in itself. I thank each of you for your help and support. It was invaluable.

I would also like to acknowledge all the gracious people around the U.S.A. and London who kindly provided me with the abundance of research data needed for the creation of this story. Thank you, All.

“The dead are conscious of nothing at all. Their love and their hate and their jealousy have already perished. They have no portion anymore to time indefinite in anything that has to be done under the sun.” — Ecclesiastes 9:5, 6

And so we are solemnly taught . . .

Chapter 1

Then

Late August of 1834, London

The rhythmic clomping of horses' hooves against the cobblestone carriageway cast a piercing echo into the foggy night as the sleek buggy-cab left the hushed city of London. Gaslights pitched only dim flickers through the mist as lamplighters maneuvered their long lighting poles, carrying out their evening duty.

Cautiously, the driver lumbered his way through the tumbling shroud toward the home-county of Middlesex, a lush countryside on the outskirts of London. Enriched with sprawling wooded terrain and a serene ambience, the setting was highly favored for the vast estates owned by the British highborn.

Inside the coach an entwined couple, wrapped in a heavy woolen quilt, chatted and laughed as they sipped rum from a leather-trimmed flask. Still buoyant from their late afternoon celebration at the bawdy Bartholomew Fair, they hardly noticed the long and bumpy ride.

Finally the driver pulled hard on the reins, halting the carriage in front of a tall, brightly-lit redwood gate. He peered through the carriage's small trapdoor and saw the couple writhing passionately under the quilt. Moaning softly with rapture, they hadn't even realized the buggy had stopped.

Uncomfortable over the couple's fervent display, the driver quickly turned away, saying quietly, "Sir Alec, if ye might be disturbed, 'tis your home, 'tis."

Sir Alec Drenton quickly withdrew himself from the woman's fiery clinch and struggled to sit upright while adjusting his trousers. He slurred, "Thank you, my good man. I shan't be more than a moment for my good-bye to Miss Quinton then return her to London." He reached up through the small opening in the roof to hand the driver a half-crown.

As the cabby pocketed the silvery coin, he stepped down from the driver's seat into the chilly summer air and anxiously walked to the gate. Knowing that Sir Alec's female companion was not his wife but a woman of questionable morality, the driver would not pull up any closer to the house. Sir Alec would have to walk up the long winding pathway leading to his home. With both hands, the driver tugged on the heavy steel latch and pushed open the gate, revealing an enormous country mansion standing majestically on rising wooded grounds that bordered a small sparkling lake.

Sir Alec Drenton tussled with the quilt, trying to free himself from the dispirited lady now nestled in the shadows of the cab. Straightening her open bodice, she suddenly grabbed for the quilt edge.

"Sir Alec," she whined through a flushed whisper, "make love to me again. I am aflame from your touch." She pressed his palm against her breast, covered only by a chemise of fine lace. "I cannot control my desire when you're near."

Sir Alec slowly drew his hand back and wrapped it around hers. "No, my dear Bernadette, we have no time left. And I am at my home."

Frustrated, she pulled away and began lacing up her bodice. "Oh, Sir Alec, when shall we be together forever, as we should?"

"My dearest, it shall not be long," he lied. "First I must finish some affairs of paperwork so that Lady Drenton can be free and taken care of for life. She is in agreement and waits patiently, as you must."

Turning toward him, she conceded softly, "'Tis sad, Alec, that she is cold to your touch. But you have me to keep you warm, you do. You're a good husband to care for her, even though she is the instigator of your grief."

"Yes, 'tis good I have you in my time of sorrow and loneliness," he said, sighing. "But now we must part. The driver shall return you to London."

Standing to step down from the cab, he wavered while attempting to adjust the silk top hat over his thinning gray hair. He sneered silently into the darkness, amused at her continuing gullibility.

She moved forward, grabbing the thick velvet cuff of his sleeve to steady him. "Sir Alec, you mustn't forget this," she said, handing him his black leather satchel. "Even an accomplished surgeon such as yourself is of no use without his tools."

"Ah Bernadette, my beautiful," he replied, turning to face her. "As usual, attending to my every need. It was a fortunate day when we met." He cupped her chin in his hands and brushed her lips with his. "I shall meet you my beloved, tomorrow at noon in Regents Park."

She nodded in silence as he took the bag, stepped down off the passenger rung onto the slate-covered roadway and strolled through the gate entrance. While closing and latching the gate behind him, he scoffed at the cab as it vanished into the coal-black horizon.

Sir Alec turned with a brazen scowl and began weaving through the shadows. A large cloud drifted across the full moon, blurring it to a pale white orb and heightening the growing eeriness. With a menacing leer in the direction of the mansion, he reached into the flap pocket of his heavy frock coat for the ivory handled dagger he always carried. He caressed the golden serpent embossed onto the smooth finish of its sheath.

Standing on the Veranda, a delicate and radiant lady had been alerted to his return by the opening of the gate. Lady Annabella Drenton, not quite twenty-nine, gripped the railing with trembling hands and peered toward the roadway entrance. With aid of the fence lamps, she had seen Sir Alec and the Quinton woman carrying out their ardent farewell.

Seeing Sir Alec stagger through the darkness toward the mansion, she became fearful of another vicious encounter. She swiftly turned and dashed inside, summoning her faithful maid from the kitchen.

"Margaret!" Annabella called nervously. "Avoid Sir Alec coming up the walkway and quickly fetch my sister Melissa from the neighbor Courtneys. Tell her she is especially needed. I shall wait for her in the drawing room."

"Yes, my Lady," the older woman answered worriedly, sensing the urgency.

Knowing that one of Sir Alec's dreaded moods was about to unfold, Margaret waited tensely to exit the side door as soon as Sir Alec entered the front.

Sir Alec stumbled into the entranceway, heaving his satchel at the foot of the hatstand. Wobbly, he removed his coat and hat, hanging them on empty hooks. With his eyes beady and suspicious, he looked around the darkened house to find Annabella. She wasn't in sight, but he knew where she would be. He removed the dagger from the coat and slipped it into the back pocket of his trousers. Teetering, he made his way down the hallway toward her favorite room.

As the door to the drawing room inched open, Annabella's eyes darted nervously toward the hearth of the fireplace where the expired blaze consisted only of charred embers. Sitting in her cushioned rocking chair, the soft glow of the dimmed oil lamp setting on the mantle produced a gentle shimmer on her long hair. She turned, seeing the imposing silhouette standing in the doorway glaring at her.

"Are you not happy to see me, my love?" Sir Alec asked sarcastically in a low tone.

She quickly returned her gaze to the floor. "Sir Alec, must you bring that Quinton woman to our country home?" she asked timidly, trying to put him on the defensive. "Haven't I suffered enough indignity by your desecration of our marriage? Melissa has told me that everyone knows about your scandalous liaison with that harlot."

Unmoved, Sir Alec approached her chair and stooped, breathing heavily close to her face. "My dear Lady Annabella," he seethed, "my dealings with frivolous pets should be of no concern to you or your meddlesome sister. Your spying on me is indeed unladylike."

Flinching, she stood up and tried to leave but he grabbed her arm.

She turned her head away from him. "You reek of stale liquor," she said, gasping, trying to free herself from his wrenching grip. "I appeal to you, let us talk tomorrow when you are sane again."

"Tomorrow?" he retorted with a chilled expression. "Ah yes, maybe you think I shall have forgotten what I heard at the King-O-Men pub in London. The mockery and sneers about that painter Wilkinson and you."

He reached up and slowly traced his finger through her thick golden hair. Pausing at the large plaited knot on the back of her head, he abruptly twisted his hand around the long braided ringlet resting across her shoulder.

Terrified, she cried out in defense, "'Tis not true, Alec! Whatever you have heard from the drunken mouths of the working class is false. My affections for you have always been true. You know well Christopher Wilkinson and I were together only for the purpose of painting our portrait. You were always there." Tears flooded her large blue eyes. She strained to turn away from his callous icy stare and rancid breath. "I beg of you to stop this attack," she pleaded. "Tell me what has transpired over the years to change you and your love for me. Why have you forsaken the ways of the Lord for those of Satan? Why?"

Sir Alec's head bobbed as he struggled to focus his empty, bloodshot eyes. Stubbornly ignoring her heartfelt words, he reached into the pocket of his trousers and fumbled for the dagger.

Lady Annabella's eyes opened wide in panic.

Yanking out the dagger, he unsheathed it with his teeth and dropped the cover to the floor. Tightening his grip on her ringlet, he forced her head back and sliced away the frilly collar of her dress. Exposing her neck, he pressed the jagged point into her skin just below the jugular. Blood trickled onto the razor-thin blade.

Annabella remained motionless in silent hysteria.

"You damned bloody bitch!" he raged, spraying her with spittle. "I shall seal your life forever if any man takes you from me. Your lives won't last a minute if your infidelity is discovered."

"Release her! Now! You hideous beast!" An infuriated female voice screamed from the doorway. "Free her and be gone! Return to London and fetch your floozy! Be gone, I say! Be gone!"

Withdrawing the dagger, Sir Alec released Annabella and turned to face a statuesque woman steadily aiming a derringer pistol at his head.

He froze, his eyes never leaving the gleaming barrel as she slowly cocked the hammer.

The servant, Margaret, hovered behind Melissa, nervously gripping her shawl.

Chortling under his breath, he stepped away and sluggishly bent to retrieve the sheath. Pocketing the dagger, he bowed and conceded defeat. "Calm my dear sister-in-law," he said quietly but sternly. "Once again, Melissa, I am indebted to you for an uninvited intrusion into our private life. Your widowhood has indeed rendered you a meddling nuisance."

"Just be gone! Now!" Melissa said again more firmly, glowering.

Melissa stepped aside as Sir Alec brushed past her, making his way for the staircase. "As you demand, I shall leave," he grumbled behind him. "But be sure I shall remember this night."

Melissa followed his exit with a relentless glare, then shut the door and quickly pocketed the small handgun. She rushed to her distraught sister who had slumped to her knees, weeping into her hands. "Oh, Melissa, you are so courageous," Annabella muttered.

Kneeling down beside her, Melissa gently consoled her, "Yes, the Almighty has granted me strength enough for both of us. Now dry your tears. Sir Alec's horrid acts are not deserving of your lingering grief."

Annabella wiped the tears from her face, but remained silent.

Pulling a handkerchief from her sleeve cuff, Melissa gently blotted the blood droplets from Annabella's neck and hair. Her anger only increased as she did so. She was unable to tolerate any more assaults on her younger sister. "Oh, Annabella, take leave of Sir Alec. He is going mad! He is cruel, without remorse. You must leave him. Why not live with me?"

"No," Annabella resisted, still trembling. "I cannot turn against the sacred vows that I made eleven summers ago." She collapsed against her sister's breast. "I cannot."

"But you have done nothing to deserve this brutal treatment," Melissa insisted, stroking Annabella's back. "Sir Alec has not aged gracefully. He is unsure of your love for him and fears he has lost his skills as a surgeon. All this causes him deep internal suffering that you cannot relieve. He takes his wickedness out on you. 'Tis of his own doing that devotion and warmth have been driven from this union. Even the dutiful cries from your youthful heart cannot restore it. "

Annabella lifted her head. "Yes, but he is still a capable surgeon and my husband with whom I must remain loyal and faithful as I always have."

Melissa grimaced. "But Annabella, his whole person is depraved, worsening by the day. You know yourself he blames God and has renounced him. It is widely known that he openly worships the devil."

Annabella bowed her head, still cradled in Melissa's arms.

Worried over Annabella's stubbornness of protecting Sir Alec, Melissa decided she would try another approach. "Annabella," she said in a mild, testing manner, "I saw Christopher Wilkinson at the London square market early the last morn. He asked me to greet you with affection. Though he is of the artisan social class, he's a fine young man. Sadly, though, he is wasting himself through sorrow and drink."

Annabella looked up sharply, her eyes suddenly shining. Then she looked down again, attempting to conceal her emotions. "Yes, he is a fine, upstanding gentleman and a wonderful artist," Annabella murmured. "But as I have told you many times he became only a fond friend while he painted our portrait."

"Annabella, end your masquerade!" Melissa ordered sternly, out of patience. "I have seen you stare endlessly at the painting in the upstairs gallery. It is not the portrait you see, but the life and love of Master Wilkinson through his work."

Annabella slowly looked up and asked, "Did Christopher indeed speak of me with affection?"

"Yes," Melissa answered, gently lifting Annabella's chin so that their eyes met. "And I could feel the adoration that flowed from his heart. 'Tis not possible for him to hide his passion for you, but he respects your wishes as the wife of another even though he knows well of your unhappiness with Sir Alec." Sensing Annabella's vulnerability Melissa finished softly, "He remains without comfort in his painful longing for you and offers no disguise of it."

Annabella hesitated, then lost all power to contain her passion. It had festered for too long. "Oh! My cherished sister! 'Tis true that I love Christopher Wilkinson! Let me confess!" Annabella gushed helplessly. "Allow me to open my heart to you. I am smothering from heartache and despair."

"Yes, Annabella, I will listen," Melissa replied, continuing to cradle Annabella in her arms. "Open up your heart and tell me all."

Annabella began weakly, "After years of Sir Alec's brutality my love for him had shattered. But I kept my feelings hidden and lived with my loneliness. Then Alec brought Christopher to our country home to begin his work on our portrait. Our affection for each other was immediate. Even though we had never met before it felt as though our hearts had always been close. As the days passed, I secretly longed for Christopher's loving attention." Annabella paused, holding back her tears, then continued as her sister listened intently, "I remember that dreaded day when the painting was finished and Christopher was going from my life ..."

Christopher, inwardly dispirited, carefully hung the large painting at eye level in the center of the wall. He then took out his pen, dipped it in heavy black ink and carefully signed across the bottom of the canvas:

For the distinguished Drentons, Christopher John Wilkinson, November 3, 1833.

Christopher inhaled and turned around to face a proud Sir Alec Drenton. He avoided any eye contact with Annabella, standing with her eyes downcast behind Sir Alec. She too was tormented with silent despair.

"I think it turned out as we planned, Sir Alec," Christopher said, soberly.

Sir Alec beamed as his eyes remained fixed on the portrait of he and Annabella sitting side by side in a formal pose. "Ahh, splendid, my good man," he said proudly. "Splendid, indeed." He then turned to Annabella. "Well, my love?"

Annabella quickly focused her eyes on the painting and replied, "Yes, Master Wilkinson, I am also very pleased with your work. 'Tis truly superb."

Christopher smiled as he slowly shifted his eyes toward Annabella. "And I am pleased that you are pleased my Lady," he said, stooping to pack his pen away with the other tools in his tanned leather bag.

"Oh, my Lady," Christopher said as he stood, picking up his bag. "Please assure that the portrait is dusted regularly with a fine cloth, preferably muslin. And it shall serve you both with years of happiness."

"Yes," she agreed. "I shall take pains to ensure its luster is maintained."

Together they slowly descended the long, winding oak staircase and stopped in the front entranceway.

Sir Alec put his hand on Christopher's arm. "Are you sure you won't stay longer, Christopher?" he asked. "For dinner, perhaps. Annabella and I would be most honored to have your company."

"No, thank you, I cannot," Christopher lied, feeling the need to leave before he unwittingly revealed his true feelings about Annabella. "I must travel to my studio in Stratford-on-Avon. The trip will be long and weary."

"And your commission, sir?" Sir Alec asked.

"Please dispatch your promissory note to my studio there," Christopher answered. "I shall not like to carry it with me."

"As you wish," Sir Alec agreed, offering Christopher his hand. "Good-bye, Christopher."

"Good-bye," Christopher responded, firmly shaking his hand. Then, at what was one of the most difficult times of his life, he turned to the woman with whom he had secretly fallen hopelessly in love. Masking his true feelings, he set his tools on the floor and reached for her hand. He bowed slightly, kissed her hand then straightened and looked deeply into her eyes, saying, "My Lady, it was my sincerest pleasure to serve you. The portrait indeed displays your beauty to the utmost."

Softly, as her gaze fell into his, she told him, "Thank you, Master Wilkinson. I shall cherish the portrait forever."

Christopher turned away to escape her tender web and picked up his tools. A sweeping darkness stole through his heart. Turning, he nodded at Sir Alec and quickly left.

As Sir Alec slowly closed the door behind the departing painter, he turned a piercing and angry stare toward his wife. “My love, I see you shall miss the painter,” he accused.

Her eyes widened with fear. “Oh, Alec, please. Let’s not quarrel about this again,” she begged, turning to rush up the stairs. “I am not fit today. My head aches and I am very tired.”

“Yes, flee my darling,” Sir Alec’s angry voice followed her up the staircase. “But I know of your concealed feelings for the painter! I know well! I know well!”

Annabella looked up at Melissa and sighed hopelessly, “Oh, dear sister, Sir Alec was right. It was at that moment I realized that a love between Christopher and I had been truly conceived within our souls.”

“Yes, Annabella,” Melissa answered. “I knew as much. I was only waiting for you to tell me.” Melissa hesitated. “And you never saw Christopher again?”

Annabella wiped her eyes. “No. Although soon after that day, I received his heart’s outpouring in a letter. I sent a letter back to his cottage studio in Stratford-on-Avon explaining that I was a faithful wife and, as such, could not submit to any form of infidelity. I assured him, however, that I would think of him always. And that we would somehow live within each other’s soul and love as only the angels do. I closed the letter with a request that we not communicate again, that we must not encourage our impulsive and sinful desires. He has respected my wishes.”

The silence in the room grew brittle before Annabella hugged Melissa tightly and gushed, "Oh, dear sister, I cannot go on … I cannot!"

"I understand, dearest," Melissa whispered. "You cannot go on fighting to save such a destructive marriage. And you cannot fight your feelings for a man as refined as Christopher." She slowly helped Annabella to her feet. "I shall not return to County Essex this eve. I shall stay with you through the night so that you will know there is someone close who takes pity on the plight of your heartbreak."

"Thank you," Annabella replied, drying her tears. "That would please me."

After lighting a new candle in the miniature torchère setting on the table, Melissa reached over to the mantle, extinguishing the oil lamp. Using the small flame from the torchère to guide them, they walked out of the room and through the darkened hallway.

Their arms locked together, they began to climb the staircase in solemn silence. Suddenly, as they reached the first landing, they saw the large-framed portrait lying askew in the shadows. Annabella gasped with shock and remained frozen as Melissa lowered the torchère to cast light on the two figures in the painting. Annabella's figure had been grotesquely sliced and mutilated. The signature of Christopher Wilkinson had also been slashed. Sir Alec's figure was untouched.

Melissa, keeping her wits, calmly picked up the portrait and set it against the side of the railing. She then firmly gripped Annabella's hand to finish climbing the stairs while keeping a watchful eye on the dark corners of the stairwell.

By the time they reached the top, Countess Melissa Grayson had decided that she would liberate her sister Annabella from this painful marriage, by whatever means it took. She would arrange a meeting with Christopher and devise a plan that would bring the two of them together.

Entering the guest bedchambers, Melissa closed the door behind them and bolted the lock as Sir Alec glared at them icily from behind the half-closed door of the master bedchamber.

CHAPTER 2

Early September, London

Torrential rain pounded at the hackney as it passed through the wealthy neighborhood of Mayfair and into the heart of London's market district surrounding Hyde Park. As the buggy slowed to a halt on Piccadilly Road, the passenger peered out to determine the quickest route to his destination: a large steeple-topped building nestled within a row of small shops.

The tall, trim man of thirty-one scooted from the cab's interior tugging the thin leather smock more tightly around him. He ducked his head and sprinted across the roadway, dodging the rippling puddles. Bounding the stone stoop, he abruptly stopped on a small covered entryway.

Removing his hat and waist-length smock, he shook them to rid the rain while he grimaced at the dreary weather. But his high spirits remained unchanged. Nothing could stifle his cheerfulness, he thought. Not on the day he was to meet with Lady Melissa and arrange his rendezvous with Annabella—the day he had waited so long for.

Leaning against the porch pillar, he read the painted lettering on the inside of the sidelight window, noticing it was beginning to fade.

WELCOME
KING O' MEN PUBLIC HOUSE
ALE, FOOD & TOBACCO
DANIEL DOHERTY, PROPRIETOR
ENTER 12:00 NOON

Needs repainting, he decided, as he pulled out his gold pocket watch and opened its crystal cover. Seeing that it was only half past eleven, he glanced up at the smudged fanlight window in the weathered archway and was relieved when he saw that it was open. Daniel was inside, readying for business.

He turned the brass doorknob. The weighty door opened easily onto a dim, almost empty room. There were only a few wooden tables and chairs scattered about. A long scruffy bar, lined with stools, encircled saloon doors that led to a supply room in the rear of the building.

Entering, he hung his soggy overgarments on the nearest chair and turned to look into the bar mirror. He checked his handsome clean-shaven face and smoothed his auburn, mid-length hair. He then looked himself over from head to toe. His white silk shirt was complemented by a wide apricot-colored cravat and a finely tailored mustard waistcoat beneath his forest-green morning coat. His formal and colorful attire was finished off with neatly pressed doeskin trousers, tapering sharply to patent leather Hessian-style boots. He was pleased with himself. Today, regardless of the early hour, it was important that Christopher John Wilkinson look impeccable.

Scanning the room, he glanced up at the painting hanging just below the center cross-beam of the high vaulted roof. The colorful canvas showing the building's warm interior and the roly-poly figure of his long-trusted friend seated on a bar stool, gladdened him as usual. It was signed:

To Daniel Doherty, In Sincere Friendship,

Christopher J. Wilkinson, July 15, 1833.

Pausing, he pondered today's unpredictable situation and sat down to reflect on that mid-summer evening last year when it had all begun. The night he'd hung his friend's portrait…

The King O' Men was crowded, but soundless, as Christopher stood on the tall bar stool held steady by Daniel Doherty. He carefully hung the newly finished painting off the lofty beam. He then stepped down and stood back to survey the set-up.

Daniel Doherty joined him, looking up with pride at the painting. Perspiration ran down his round, balding head. His oversized shirt, sporting a mass of superfluous frill, was tucked into baggy brown trousers, firmly drawn under his enormous potbelly with a ragged belt. The wrinkled trouser legs were stuffed loosely into scuffed knee-high black boots.

Suddenly a loud voice bellowed, "A spittin' image of ya Doherty, ya fat ancient Mick."

Doherty, a bluff man quickly turned his head from left-to-right amid the chorus of heavy laughter. "Who said that?" he snapped in mock anger. "Whoever it was has drunk his last in the King O' Men, he has. Now, who was it? Be gone with your arse, I say."

When no one confessed, he grinned widely as Christopher broke into a hearty laugh and firmly took hold of Doherty's shoulders. They strolled to the bar while the other good-natured patrons returned to their private circles.

"Bernadette," Doherty yelled to the barmaid who was in the back preparing the evening's specialty of mutton stew and bread pudding. "Please be kind e'nuf to set a supper place for Christopher and me at the bar."

"'Tis comin' up Daniel," she answered through the doorway, "'tis comin' up."

Christopher was relaxing after their dinner, sipping brandy and chatting with Doherty at the bar when he heard behind him, "Master Wilkinson? Master Christopher Wilkinson?"

Christopher and Doherty together turned to face a well-dressed professional man. His face was drawn and narrow, framed by full trimmed side-whiskers.

"Yes, I am Christopher Wilkinson."

The man removed his top hat. "My name is Drenton, Alec Drenton. 'Tis my pleasure to meet you, my good man." He extended his hand. Christopher shook it. "And you, Master Doherty," Sir Alec said, turning toward Doherty.

Doherty, silent, also shook Sir Alec's hand.

Christopher tipped his head quizzically and asked, "Sir Alec Drenton, the renowned surgeon?"

Sir Alec nodded. "Yes. It is I."

Christopher wondered why a man of Drenton's stature would visit a working class pub. He knew that Sir Alec was not only a famed surgeon, but also a member of a wealthy land-owning family of the gentry class.

Sir Alec reading Christopher's surprise, said, "Master Wilkinson, I see that you're baffled by my approach."

"Yes," Christopher answered. "I cannot restrain my curiosity."

"Of course, I understand," Sir Alec replied, turning toward the back room. "Well, as you know of me, I also know of your distinguished repute as a gifted artist. Bernadette speaks very highly of you."

All eyes rotated toward Bernadette, who stood smiling in the doorway. Christopher now realized that Drenton's connection to the pub must be through Bernadette.

Sir Alec turned his gaze upward, fixing on the new portrait of Doherty, saying, "Splendid, a splendid stroke of work." Turning back to Christopher he added, "And I can certainly see that you are a gentleman as well."

Christopher smiled, with a slight expression of humility. "My gratitude for your noble compliments," he said. "But if my craft is worthy of praise, 'tis because of total dedication to my toil." He paused. "And I know you are most aware of that same creed. The prominence you've earned from your professional toil is most worthy of your dedication."

Sir Alec bowed, acknowledging the mutual respect, then straightened. "Master Wilkinson, I am hoping to engage your services to paint a portrait of my wife and me. Of course, you would be generously rewarded for your effort."

Christopher responded quickly, "It would be an honor to bear the task, sir. It requires no further thought on my part."

"Excellent," Sir Alec answered, pulling a small address card from his pocket and handed it to Christopher. "If you please, meet with us at our Middlesex home to discuss the details. Would tomorrow afternoon about two be favorable? Over tea, perhaps."

"Agreed. About two, over tea," Christopher confirmed. "It will be my pleasure."

"And mine," Sir Alec replied, shaking Christopher's hand. "Indeed."

Sir Alec then bid the men farewell and made his way to the end of the bar where Bernadette stood. They talked quietly for a few minutes before Sir Alec left through the front door. Bernadette watched him leave with longing.

Christopher and Doherty observed the fervid good-bye and turned to each other.

"I haven't seen him before," Doherty said, looking puzzled. "He must have quite a spell over my wench."

"It is not our concern," Christopher quickly replied.

"I know, but, I must say it was a bit of a shock when the gentleman was here," Doherty said. "Do you know much of him?"

"Yes, Daniel. Sir Alec is upright and well regarded. The High Church has spoken notably of him. And he has a distinguished standing with the nobility as well."

Doherty raised his eyebrows. "The nobility class, you say?"

"Right, Daniel. When Sir Alec was a young Eton scholar, he laid the deed for a substantial plot of inherited Portsmouth land at the foot of the throne."

"Aye," Doherty interrupted, "from where the mighty frigates sail."

"Right again, Daniel, the most esteemed naval port of the Crown," Christopher replied. "He then went on to become a celebrated surgeon. I understand that during the Napoleonic wars he perfected the skill of swift amputations, greatly relieving the pain and suffering of the soldiers."

"Yc' gods!" Doherty exclaimed, grimacing. "What a way to gain distinction."

Christopher chuckled, then said, "Sir Alec truly proved himself a sterling patriot. He was most worthy of his knighthood. One of the first surgeons of our century to be so honored."

Doherty's eyes widened. "Christopher, you're a lucky bloke to be serving Sir Alec. And in his own home, even."

"Yes, Daniel," Christopher agreed as he finished his brandy, "most fortunate, indeed."

Christopher lowered his eyes from Doherty's portrait to the butt of a wine cask he had hung about six feet off the floor. He used it for his favorite sport of darts. The five target-circles, coarsely painted in different colors, were still distinct. The miniature middle circle was a bright cherry-red. He chuckled at the splintered holes surrounding the crude wooden disk. It was not uncommon for the players, often rowdy and drunk, to completely miss the target.

Across the room, heavy dark-green satin drapes concealed the snuggery where he would hold his long awaited meeting with Melissa this afternoon.

Removing a wooden object from his smock pocket, he stood and walked toward the bar. The creaking of the worn wooden floor echoing throughout the empty building brought the short, slovenly owner out through the backroom doors. He pushed a wooden dolly that supported an 80-gallon barrel of dark ale.

Looking up, he broke into a broad smile and hastily set the dolly upright. "Ye' gods, I can't believe my bloody eyes! Christopher!" he exclaimed in surprise, wrenching himself over the edge of the bar to shake hands. "Where've ya been kept? 'Tis not a fine day for trekking, 'tis surely not."

"Daniel Doherty, go slowly! 'Tis only been a Monday week since I was last here. I am still close in Kensington borough, so my travel today was quick." Christopher laughed, exchanging a hardy handshake. "How are you, friend?"

"Well, my arse is a bit stiff today, but 'tis still fit for business, 'tis," Doherty answered tiredly, pulling a stool close to the bar. "Now, friend what are ya doin' here this early? And in full regalia, I see."

"Ah! 'Tis of a very special reason for me to be here, actually," Christopher answered, sighing. "I shall explain in due time." He suddenly beamed, holding up a small, rectangular wooden case. "But first behold the handsome commission paid to me by the High Church for my recent painting I hung in St. Pauls Cathederal."

Christopher set the elegant case on the bar-top. Doherty admiringly read the inscription at the top edge of the glossy, red oak cover.

For a noble and God-fearing
Master Christopher Wilkinson
In fullest gratitude
Bishop Thomas W. Thornton
Church of England
September 1, 1834

Embedded beneath the inscription was a solid gold heraldic cross of the Fleury, buffed to a bright luster.

Doherty's eyes remained fixed on the box as Christopher opened it, revealing five magnificent long-point gaming darts. They were set into a bed of plush green velvet separated with black-hickory knuckle-bridges.

Christopher proudly lifted one out and handed the small missile to Doherty.

The dart's sleek silvery point melded into a slender polished torpedo-barrel made of metal. Three vanes of meshed golden eagle wing feathers had been flawlessly inserted into the wooden tapered stern shaft.

"Aye, 'tis of a kingly sight and of a perfect feel for a toss," Doherty marveled, rolling the dart between his chubby forefingers.

"Yes," Christopher boasted, lifting out another. "The body is crafted of the superb new Swedish alloy called Tungsten. 'Tis forty-three grams and of precise pitching balance."

Swiftly he whirled, cocked his arm and hurled the dart at the crude target. It spiraled straight and true before burying itself deep in the middle of the small red circle.

"Ye' gods!" Doherty gasped, awestruck. "'Twas a twenty pace toss, Christopher! 'Tis in dead center too! And without a moment's lingering to aim. Ye' gods!"

"I have practiced," Christopher confirmed smugly. "Daniel, my friend, accompany me to the Crown's tossing tournament in Devonshire this October."

Doherty bowed, grinned proudly and replied, "Aye, 'tis a journey for sure." He paused, then added, "Ya always did have a bit of a'venture in ya. Much to the sight of a cavalier at times. Though it mixes oddly with yer gentle artisan ways, it does."

Christopher laughed heartily as he walked to the target to retrieve his dart.

"Christopher, do ya laugh today cause of yer grand new bounty?" Doherty asked, carefully placing his dart back in the case. "Or does it involve the Drenton woman? It wouldn't take the town sage to figure it, I say," he chided with a smile and twinkling eyes.

Christopher silently walked back to the bar. He replaced the fifth dart, closed the case and looked up beaming. "Yes, Daniel, my spirits are high because of Lady Annabella. I'm meeting her sister Melissa here today, to at last arrange a rendezvous between Annabella and myself."

Doherty's eyes quivered nervously, asking, "But what about Sir Alec?"

Christopher turned solemn, taking in Daniel's worried stare. "Sir Alec has pushed the limits of their marriage vow to its end," he rasped. "It would be impossible for him to heal the vicious hurt he has caused Annabella. She will no longer accept his despicable behavior. It seems his armor has cracked."

Christopher stood against the bar thinking as Doherty rose to get two of his favorite polished pewter tankards. He flipped the lids back and filled both with frothy red ale from the spigot of the large barrel standing upright on the floor. He handed one to Christopher and sat back down.

"Aye, I've seen it with my own eyes," Doherty said, shaking his head. "Drenton entered here one day last spring and frolicked the evenin' away in the snuggery with my barmaid wench, Bernadette. Imagine, a married man of the gentry rank trifling with the working class, let alone the likes of a fallen woman." Doherty fidgeted with the handle of his tall mug before taking a drink. "And when I found out they were taking up with the devil himself, I briskly gave her a boot."

"Yes, Daniel," Christopher said. "'Tis called Satanism that they practice."

Doherty gripped Christopher's forearm with a concerned expression, saying, "You be careful, my bold friend. 'Tis talked around that the archfiend himself has cloaked Sir Alec with the powers of deviltry in return for Sir Alec's devotion."

Christopher stared down at the bar. "'Tis blather Daniel, drunken blather. Indeed, Sir Alec has turned to Satan. But that's of no matter to me. 'Tis only earthly powers that I concern myself with."

Doherty continued his worried appeal, "Aye, maybe. But Sir Alec shan't take his jealousy meekly. I say he shan't linger as a weeping wittol. The law of the land could cost ye a spell of public scorn, clamped in the town square pillory. Or maybe even lose yer life hangin' from the gallows." Doherty pointed his stubby finger at Christopher's neck. "Then both yours and the Lady's heart would be forever lost."

Christopher thought about it for a moment, then replied firmly, "Daniel, we are both well acquainted with Sir Alec's powerful social influence! But I cannot endure another moment without the treasure of Annabella's affection!" He slammed the full tankard down and smashed his fist on the bar. "I shall be deaf to his barbarous threats! And I will ignore the damn class difference between us!"

The old Irishman slowly nodded, laying his hand on Christopher's taut fist. "Ya might calm a touch, ya might. I know of your great love for the lady. If hers is as equal, I'm sure yer hearts will find their way to union."

Christopher, calmed by his friend's good faith, reminded himself of the happy state he'd arrived in. Poised once again, he swallowed some ale, then said, "Recall, Daniel, that during my initial acquaintance with Sir Alec last fall we got on quite well. I respected what I knew of him and his marriage to Annabella." Christopher took another drink of ale as Doherty sat listening. "But he has soured and failed himself as well as Annabella. I will not accept nor recognize their marriage union any longer." Christopher threw his head back and emptied his tankard.

"What do ya suppose bred his failing?" Doherty asked.

"'Tis well known that years of aging and drink have worked to ruin Sir Alec's ability as a surgeon," Christopher answered, setting his empty tankard down. "He ails from his loss of value and now a heart full of evil."

"Oh! 'Tis a too common, piteous tale," Doherty replied, "that a once fine man turns to a louse because he has now become full of years and the shield of youth has withered."

Christopher nodded as Doherty turned to the spigot to refill the tankard.

At that moment they were surprised by the squeaky turn of the doorknob. The profile of a woman appeared at the pub's entrance. Her attractive face, dignified and assured, was nearly hidden by a wide-brimmed hat, secured tightly under her chin with a silk ribbon. A dark veil on the back of the brim fell across her shoulders and down her back.

Loosening the ribbon, she removed the damp hat. Her thick, dark brown hair was pulled smooth and plaited over her ears, with a large knot just above the nape of the neck.

She glanced at the men, closed the door and removed her sodden shawl. She shook it vigorously and hung it under the hat on a wall-hook just inside the doorway. She then shook her black leather riding boots which were hidden by the full floor-length skirt. It was designed to fall properly in the interior of the cabriolet she had navigated alone on her long journey through the countryside.

Her stateliness produced a respectful silence from the two men. Yet she made it clear by simply showing up in such a place that it mattered little what her "nobility" demanded. She turned, smiled slightly and walked toward them.

Christopher relaxed and returned Melissa Grayson's smile while saying, "Melissa, my Lady. You are indeed of a striking appearance today." He bowed to kiss her smooth, slender hand.

"My gratitude to you, Master Wilkinson," she replied softly. She turned, cocking her head slightly to greet Doherty.

Still stunned by her presence, he clumsily began wiping off the bar and returned the nod. He then turned and slipped into the back room.

Amused by Doherty's nervous awkwardness, Lady Melissa and Christopher laughed as they walked to the snuggery to hold their long awaited meeting. Entering, they pulled the heavy drapes shut and sat opposite each other in the hard wooden booth.

Christopher looked up eagerly. "'Tis a priceless comfort to meet with you, Melissa. I have waited so long for this."

"Yes, I know Christopher," she replied solemnly. "Now we must hurry. I have to settle my late husband's land dealings with the London Court of the Magistrate today. Unfortunately, my stay with you must be brief, but most purposeful."

"I understand," Christopher replied. "I was sorry to learn of the Baron's unfortunate hunting accident."

"Yes, it was tragic. Thank you for your respects," Melissa answered. "Now Christopher, as I proposed in my message, this meeting is to arrange the bringing of you and Annabella together. She has consented to sacrifice her wretched marriage to Sir Alec and soothe the burning cries of both your passionate yearnings."

"Indeed," Christopher agreed impetuously. "In our eyes, and now surely in God's, our love cannot be denied! She must not change her mind."

Melissa smiled, reaching for his hand. "Christopher, despair no further. Annabella has been haunted by the memory of your adoration and princely manner. She longs to be with you. Her life will be deprived of happiness until she is by your side."

"Oh, Lady Melissa! I must be with her!"

"Be doubtless," Melissa whispered. "I shall deliver her to your sincere affections. Your separation shall not go on much longer."

Christopher clutched her hands, saying, "Lady Melissa, I shall be forever grateful."

"But heed, Christopher," she reminded him cautiously, "Sir Alec knows of your feelings for Annabella. He will never willingly take leave of her." Melissa sat back and inhaled. "Understand that Sir Alec is growing more ruthless by the day. If his suspicions are aroused and you are discovered with Annabella, he will wreak a hell upon you both."

"I know, my Lady. But, we must all take the chance."

Melissa moved forward. "Yes, Christopher. After giving it a great deal of thought, I agree. However, your rendezvous must be guarded with extreme caution. Our deception must not be uncovered."

Christopher listened closely as Melissa continued, "I have devised a plan. When the week ends, I shall fetch Annabella for an Essex holiday visit. However, instead, I shall arrive with her at your cottage outside Stratford, then take my leave, but stay close at hand back in the village inn."

He nodded enthusiastically, replying, "And your arrival shall be anticipated with honor and discretion."

"Christopher," she warned again, "you both must use this precious time to plot her escape from Sir Alec. You shan't have long. Do not delay, for I must fetch her early the next morn for our return journey to Middlesex. Sir Alec must not be alerted in the least by her prolonged absence."

"Yes, my Lady. 'Tis a firm plan. I shall engage a messenger boy to meet you at the church near the town common at sunset on Saturday. He shall guide you to my cottage where I will be waiting impatiently."

She smiled in agreement, then said, "However, after this rendezvous you and Annabella must move forward on your own wit and shrewdness."

"Lady Melissa, you must know I shall love and protect her forever."

"I do know," she replied. "And I shall be content with knowing Annabella is with you." She turned toward the draperies. "But now I must go."

Dashing from the snuggery, she bid farewell and exited into the sudden emergence of a brilliant afternoon sunshine. Hurrying toward her cabriolet, Lady Melissa was unaware that she was being eyed closely by the cloaked woman who had discreetly blended herself into the bustling crowd.

CHAPTER 3

Late September, Stratford-on-Avon

Dusk brought a cool breeze to the modest but picturesque village of Stratford-on-Avon. The flaming-red horizon was a scorching reminder of the sweltering day it had been. Yet the evening was charged with a new energy. The cobbled streets were alive with scurrying youngsters, barking dogs and cheerful marketers enjoying the unseasonable heat.

Melissa and Annabella calmly emerged from the quaint, lichen-covered church and climbed aboard the small cabriolet. While refreshing themselves at the inn, they had decided to briefly pause from their long trip to meditate before continuing on to meet with Christopher.

As she settled herself Melissa glanced about, careful to avoid worrying Annabella, yet constantly remaining alert to the possibility of Sir Alec finding them. Throughout the journey she had sensed something was wrong. Occasionally she'd thought she'd seen the same hansom carriage following them. But when she strained to get a closer look, she could only make out a driver and a lady sitting in the coach, both were dressed in black. The passenger was wearing a veil and the forked rein guide on top of the buggy's roof made it impossible to see the driver's features. They also kept their heads bowed like mourners. Melissa was unable to recognize either of them and was reluctant to drop back and investigate further. It would be awkward, especially if the people were truly mourners.

Turning her attention to the town common, Melissa shrugged off her fear, reasoning that she hadn't seen the carriage since they had arrived in Stratford. And that the mourners must have passed through while they were at the inn. Regardless, it was too late for caution, she decided. Sir Alec knew the whereabouts of Christopher's cottage and, if it was him, would know it was their destination. If he wanted to find Christopher and Annabella together he would.

Spotting Christopher's messenger boy mounting a large thoroughbred, Melissa confidently turned the cabriolet to the south and lined up behind him. With a silent gesture, the boy directed the women to follow him and prodded the horse into a mild gait. The cabriolet followed, skipping along the graveled roadway leading out of Stratford-on-Avon.

With a biting snap of the wispy buggy-whip, the mysterious hansom carriage abruptly emerged from the shadows of the tree-lined courtyard and began taking the same route as the cabriolet. The incensed driver fiercely gripped the reins while the lady passenger held herself steady in the coach.

Melissa was pleased that Annabella appeared calm as the cabriolet casually bounced along in a soft lope toward her new life of love and comfort with Christopher.

She remained silent, seeing that Annabella was entranced by the lights of the thatched-roof cottages and hilltop hamlets, filtering through the darkening serene Cotswold countryside. A chorus of chirping crickets' soon lulled the two women into a tranquil realm of joyful thoughts. Melissa glanced up and smiled at the new moon that had emerged. It was symbolic of the journey she was taking.

The hansom carriage relentlessly tailed the cabriolet as the driver kept a vigilant eye on the blazing lantern that bounced from the saddle-horn of the leading thoroughbred. Fueling his wrath, he caressed the dagger in his pocket.

The messenger boy slowed and motioned with his lantern that they had arrived and halted the cabriolet in the roadway, next to a graystone cottage.

Farther back, the hansom carriage came to a brusque halt and pulled off into the woods.

"Look, my sweet, as I suspected," the driver seethed through the trapdoor toward the woman passenger before stepping down off the driver's seat.

Bernadette noticed his skewered scowl and only nodded. She was worried about his growing fury but said nothing, seeking to avoid further provoking his anger. Why wasn't he pleased about his wife's infidelity, she wondered. It would surely quicken the divorce. Confused, she exited the carriage and joined him as they quietly crept toward the cottage.

In the cabriolet, Melissa turned to Annabella and said softly, "Dear sister, I will return to the village. But remember I shall arrive back for you immediately after sunrise. You and Christopher must use these brief hours wisely and decide what must be done to start your new life together."

"Yes, Melissa," she obliged. "I shan't squander another moment and will plan with Christopher on how to escape Sir Alec."

Melissa smiled, signaling that it was time.

Annabella clutched her hooded cloak to her neck and stepped down. Pausing, she watched the cabriolet depart to follow the boy back to the village.

Then Annabella turned to face the faint candlelight where the glimmering silhouette awaited, just beyond the partially opened front entrance. Full of wonderment, she stepped along the darkened footpath. Reaching the door, she pushed it open and froze, captivated by the man before her.

He was bent on one knee offering a single freshly cut cardinal-red rose from his open palm. With his thick wavy hair brushed back, he gazed up at her with a romantic aura of quiet confidence. His dark summer tan enhanced the ice-blue, fine silk shirt that hung loosely over his trim fitting cotton trousers. On his feet were deerskin slippers.

Seeing his expression of total adoration removed all of Annabella's earlier apprehensions. She released the grip on her cloak, letting it fall open.

Christopher slowly stood and came to her. Reaching for her hand, he led her inside and gently removed her cloak to expose a pure white summer muslin dress, bedecked by a frilly lace collar. Gathered in at her thin waist, the ankle-length dress fell easily over her petite but well-proportioned frame. Her pointed black satin shoes were each decorated with a yellow silk bow.

He delicately lifted her chin up to meet his and paused, capturing this precious moment. Her full head of luminous soft golden hair, knotted heavily on top, sparkled in the candlelight as it fell around her angelic face. He gingerly placed the fresh rose in her plaited knot and carefully stroked the full flowing ringlets that lay at the base of her neck.

Sensing her vulnerability, his every move was gentle and taken with care. He knew that she had not been touched like this before, not even in her most intimate thoughts.

Her resistance was fading, for she knew he truly loved her.

"I shall never know a more priceless moment," he whispered affectionately as he backed away, lightly placing his hands on her shoulders. "It would be even more cherished if you were to tell me that you feel the same."

Her curved, lightly painted lips easily confirmed, "You know I do."

As they looked at each other, her shimmering blue eyes beamed in amazement. She was overwhelmed and lost all ability to resist his soft yet commanding power. The deep harmony between them held more meaning than she had ever known with Sir Alec. Suddenly they both lost all control and began frantically clutching each other, both striving to end the loneliness they had lived with for so long.

Christopher reached behind her, closing the door, but failed to drop the latch.

The view of this passionate spectacle was now cut off from the two sets of eyes secretly peering from the dark of the garden.

Christopher and Annabella unclenched and moved to the sofa, sitting next to each other. Then Christopher kneeled to remove her shoes and lifted her feet so she could lie down. He gently lifted her shoulders forward and slipped a down-filled pillow behind her head.

Enchanted, Christopher sat quietly, clearly adoring her. Nothing in the world was as important as her. He had never before known anyone who gave him the sheer feeling of blessedness that she did.

Annabella reached for his hand to acknowledge their shared emotion.

The ambiance of the small cozy cottage was at last brimming with joy. Mellow candlelight from polished silver candelabra flickered about the room, creating a shadowy, gentle radiance throughout. On a table next to them a large basket of freshly cut flowers filled the air with a sweet flowing fragrance.

Clutching her hand, he said softly, "You must be weary, my darling."

"Yes, though it matters little next to my feeling of happiness, my beloved," she replied, smiling. Then her features quickly contorted into a dispirited look. "Oh Christopher! Whatever must we do to be free? To be together endlessly?"

He answered directly, "Sir Alec must be stripped of his power to deny our being together. He shall have to accept his own blunder of betraying you and squandering your faithful devotion."

"Yes, oh yes. Take hold of me!" she appealed desperately.

He reached down and drew her into his arms. They kissed passionately for the first time. Their longing for each other was uncontrollable. He slowly shifted to lie next to her, but restrained himself as she moved backward nervously signaling her disapproval. As their lips parted, he regained his composure and sat upright.

She leaned back against the pillow and looked up at him through a golden glaze. She had used everything within her power to deny his desires. She whispered delicately, "I am burning with passion and want your hungered touch. I too wish you onto me, into me, unending." She paused. "Yet we must take this time to plan our future."

He nodded, as he was in awe over her inner spiritual dignity as well as her external beauty. He couldn't and wouldn't breach that, he thought. He would wait. Again he drew her into his arms. "Yes, yes, my love!" he agreed. "We shall delay our time in paradise."

"Oh, Christopher," she whispered excitedly into his ear. "I have waited so long for this. We must find a way, quickly, to be free so that I am able to enjoy your beloved affections with peace of mind. Let us flee to enjoy life and love by the seaside. Maybe to Brighton, I have always fancied that thought."

"Yes, Annabella," he answered. "We shall soon flee to Brighton …"

Abruptly the front door burst open, slamming hard against the wall.

The wrathful Sir Alec stood in the doorway staring venomously through a teeming sweat. He gripped a double-barreled pistol with both hammers cocked.

Bernadette stood staunchly at his side.

Christopher bolted up and stepped backward toward the fireplace.

"Stay still!" Sir Alec boomed in disgust. "Stand fast in the light! I shall not tolerate another move!"

Annabella, speechless and horrified, remained motionless on the sofa.

Christopher stiffened against the mantle.

Sir Alec turned, directing a chortled sneer toward his companion as they slowly entered the room. "Ah, Bernadette, we have traveled in earnest to discover my wife's debauchery," he droned icily. "Look on as a witness."

"Yes, Sir Alec," Bernadette said. "You were correct about their illicit acts. Now the divorce can be carried out."

"Divorce!" Sir Alec retorted, his eyes narrowing in fury. "Damn the divorce! The parting of my deceiving wife must be final."

Bernadette quickly looked at Sir Alec, horrified by his increasing frenzy. She began to realize his capacity for cruelty. Her eyes darted around the room, from Christopher to Annabella, wondering if he was even capable of murder.

Leaning back against the mantle, Christopher glanced at the prized mahogany box he had received from the High Church.

"Let me speak, Sir Alec," Annabella tensely pleaded. "I shall grant you total freedom from your marital obligations. You have forsaken our union long ago and can't possibly care for me anymore. I beseech you …"

"Silence! Silence!" Sir Alec shouted. "Your charade about our marriage union is mindless!"

Christopher impulsively surged toward Sir Alec, but immediately confronted the pistol barrels glittering in the candlelight.

"Christopher!" Annabella shrieked.

Christopher stopped, grimaced, and retreated.

Sir Alec's obvious display of jealous viciousness still confused Bernadette. Now perceiving Annabella's innocence, she began to question her judgment of Sir Alec's real motives. She was now almost sure she'd failed to see his true depravity.

Deciding she must find out, Bernadette placed her hand on Sir Alec's forearm. "Sir Alec, shan't we be calm?" she appealed. "'Tis true, this discovery is shocking, but we mustn't twist it into a cruel suffering."

"My dear Bernadette," Sir Alec replied coldly, jerking his arm away. "I asked you to accompany me here to serve as a witness to my anguish over my wife's lover, not as my conscience. Now I shall also demand that you remain silent."

Bernadette backed away, stunned over Sir Alec's jealousy, a jealousy he had never revealed before. She stood wide-eyed, struck by his apparent insanity and insatiable drive for vengeance.

Christopher again lost his patience, bellowing defiantly, "Your anguish is caused by your own hand, Sir Alec!"

"Christopher!" Annabella cried. "I beg of you to remain peaceable."

The devoted compliance between Annabella and Christopher increased Sir Alec's rage. Crazed with jealousy, he cocked his head sideways, raised his eyebrows and faced Annabella.

"Annabella, your foremost concern for this artist is proof enough of your unfaithfulness," Sir Alec seethed. "I have no option but to deal with both of you at once!"

Sir Alec closed the door behind him.

Bernadette backed away pleading, "No, please Sir Alec, no…"

Annabella put her hands to her face.

Christopher turned toward the mantle in apparent cowardliness. He then inconspicuously reached for the oblong box, mentally repeating the inscription on the cover…*For a noble and God fearing …*

Sir Alec's eyes shifted wildly as he trained the barrel and squeezed the trigger.

Annabella's agonizing cry of "Oh, Christopher!" smothered the room.

All eyes turned to the jerking head of Annabella and to the spreading light red spot on her bosom. Her eyes blinked wildly in shock as her head fell back against the pillow, moaning in pain.

"Oh God in Heaven, no!" Christopher howled.

Sir Alec turned the smoking pistol toward Christopher.

Shocked by Sir Alec's savagery, Bernadette abruptly lurched at him and yanked on his arm. The pistol dropped to the floor, discharging the second shot on impact.

"You damned bloody whore!" Sir Alec yelled, yanking his ivory-handled dagger from his belt. As she fell backward, he swiped wildly at her, cutting her sleeve. Narrowly escaping his thrust, she scrambled toward the corner, Sir Alec close after her with the drawn dagger.

"Over here, you grisly bastard!" Christopher screamed at Sir Alec, as his beloved Annabella lay dying.

Sir Alec reeled toward Christopher and met a speeding dart that landed precisely between his eyes. He dropped the dagger and flailed at the protruding missile, but the slender point of steel had found its mark, penetrating his brain. Groaning, he fell back against the wall and slid to the floor as the blood stained his forehead, bubbling slightly around the silvery needle.

Sir Alec feebly pawed around the floor for the dagger. A second dart pierced his hand, securing it firmly to the wooden slat.

Squinting up at Christopher, Sir Alec mumbled, "You shall never know peace again, you fool. The reckoning of your soul shall be eternal."

Christopher bent down and picked up the dagger. Lifting Sir Alec's head, Christopher said icily, "And may your soul agonize forever in hell as I tread above your bones." He plunged Sir Alec's own blade, flush to the handle, into its owner's evil heart.

Bernadette remained motionless, gripping the wall, weak with terror.

Christopher quickly rushed to the fading Annabella. He knelt, gently lifting her small quivering hand to touch his wet eyes so she would know that his love for her was endless.

Her usual sparkling blue eyes were now barely open. She fought for breath and managed a final frail smile.

Feeling his strong grip, she murmured, "My love, I have long been with you, in both heart and thoughts. Do not mourn, for now no one can halt our being together. I have loved you dearest and shall be with you always."

Knowing his deep sorrow, she lightly brushed his moist cheek with her finger before closing her eyes in finality.

Christopher remained kneeling as he felt Bernadette's hand on his shoulder. He turned to meet her saddened eyes while she tenderly handed him Annabella's cloak. Wrapping the cloak around Annabella's lifeless body, he gently picked her up. He held her tightly and turned to carry her out the door.

As he disappeared with Annabella into the warm darkness, a soft rain began to fall, as though to cleanse the large crimson stain that had blemished the breast of her white muslin dress.

Bernadette, following behind, paused in the doorway. Looking down at Sir Alec slumped stiffly against the wall, she now knew he had been filled with hate and evil, driven to torment everyone, including herself.

Hurrying to catch up with Christopher, she quickly pulled the door closed behind her as the earlier warm and tender ambiance of the cottage was now ravaged, replaced with a chilled, demonic aura of death.

CHAPTER 4

Year's End, Newgate Prison, London

The melodious harmony of Christmas carols ascended the still darkness as the winter solstice embraced the east side of London with an icy grip. Swaying slightly and bearing small candles, the solemn carolers gathered beneath the scaffold of the lofty gallows, erected mighty in the stony yard of Newgate prison. They lifted their sweet voices upward, to where the condemned stared back at them through barred windows—packed with straw to ward off the penetrating cold. Grim and without hope, the prisoners prayed to themselves, knowing this was their final Christmas.

Christopher Wilkinson sat silently on the dank, stone floor with his back against the pitted wall. Motionless, his arms hung limply from the weight of the long shackles that chained him to the floor. Occasionally he would wiggle to deflect the crawling vermin that shared his cell. Rats scampered around his tattered moccasins, scavenging for scraps of moldy garbage. They often drank from his rusty saucer of stale water. Huge roaches boldly crawled in and around the piles of urine-soiled straw that covered the floor.

Christopher's shaven head was bowed, concealing his gaunt face. He had withered from the lack of food and no further will to live. The loss of Annabella and the unbearable conditions of his final bondage only increased his desire to be set free from this earthly decadence.

Suddenly his dismal solitude was shattered by the clanging of heavy metal rods and the opening of the rough wooden door. The burly jailer entered and placed tall pails of milky mush, mixed with scaly fish parts and rancid beef, amid the squalor in the middle of the cell. The half-starved inmates quickly abandoned the carolers and hurried toward their nightly gruel.

Approaching Christopher, the jailer stopped. "Wilkinson," he said gruffly, "as you wished, the Magistrate has hastened yer hangin'."

Christopher opened his eyes and looked up lethargically, remaining still and mute.

The jailer continued gruffly, "It will be held in privy at midnight on the eve of Christmas." He then turned and left.

Christopher again lowered his head and closed his eyes, flinching again at hearing the loud clanking of the metal bolts.

The staid clergyman stood outside the large cell as the jailer escorted the weak, but grateful prisoner through the doorway. Christopher straightened himself as he emerged with his hands bound behind his back. He proudly lifted his head and followed close behind the churchman who was leading him to his fate. Yet a destiny that Christopher eagerly awaited.

Reaching the gate, they paused while the prisoner was handed over to the brazen executioner. Proceeding through the prison yard, Christopher's face tightened when he saw the towering cross-beamed structure profiled ominously within the torch-lighted blackness. But he maintained his bold posture as he heard soft cries of "God be with you. God be with you." Christopher refused to even glance at the small somber crowd huddled in the public viewing square. He had already said good-bye to the few people who had remained his friends.

Lady Melissa Grayson, standing rigidly behind the restraining ropes, took her eyes off Christopher when she spotted an approaching, dispirited woman. Melissa met the woman's sorrowful gaze and gently touched her shoulder. Bernadette Quinton reached for Melissa's hand, clutching it tightly.

"Oh forgive me Lady Grayson," Bernadette said, weeping softly, "forgive me. I was so wrong about the lot of it. I have asked God to forgive me and have begged to be taken back into his fold."

Melissa answered with tenderness in her voice, "Miss Quinton, I am sure the good Lord has heard you and will respond favorably to your plea."

"You have my deepest gratitude, my Lady," Bernadette replied humbly.

Melissa smiled. "Christopher told me you visited him often."

"Oh, yes," Bernadette answered, sighing. "He was so brokenhearted during his spell in prison. We grew to be dear and loyal friends."

"Yes," Melissa replied, "I know your visits became very important to him."

The women turned back toward the gallows, locking arms to give each other support as they watched Christopher kneeling at the bottom of the scaffold.

The clergyman blessed Christopher and backed away as the executioner took a firm grip of Christopher's arm, leading him up the scaffold steps. When they reached the still-closed trap door, Christopher was halted and positioned upon it. Motionless, the condemned man looked straight ahead, determined to ignore the buzzing of the crowd.

The executioner pulled out a white, hooded mask from his side-pouch then hesitated, asking, "Do you have any final words, Master Wilkinson?"

Christopher slowly looked upward, whispering in prayer, "Please absolve me oh Lord, not for the fear of hell, but so that I may enter your kingdom and again be united with my Annabella." Christopher then lowered his head and closed his eyes, his last gesture in preparing for his final destiny.

The executioner slipped the mask over Christopher's head and laced it taut. Seizing the rope, he loosened the running knot and methodically placed the noose around Christopher's neck. Christopher stiffened, but managed the courage to remain still as he heard the executioner walk to the trap-release.

The crowd hushed as the executioner, waiting dutifully, studied his timepiece. When the hands struck midnight, Christmas eve, 1834, the executioner jerked heartily on the long, wooden lever. As the spectators gasped, the trap door dropped downward with a heavy thud. It was over quickly. The brutish executioner and the Newgate prison gallows had done their job well.

Melissa pulled hard on the wide leather strap and buckled it, securing the bulky saddle on the back of the large Chestnut. Pulling a carrot from the saddlebag, she fed it to the horse while stroking its neatly cropped mane.

She turned and looked out the stable door, observing the high moors of Dartmoor while thoughtfully planning her morning ride. The rugged trail through the rocky bluffs of the barren wasteland was partially obscured by a morning mist. Worse, heavy sea fog was welling up amid the strong gusts of wind. With the poor visibility she realized that she would have to alter her usual route if she was to find the wild ponies today. She would also have to avoid the treacherous marshlands and peat bogs while making her way to the grasslands.

Sighing, she slipped the bridle over the horse's head, adjusted the bit and grabbed the reins to lead the horse out of the stable. But she stopped, suddenly distraught over the recent deaths of Annabella and Christopher. Would the haunting aftermath ever leave her, she lamented, leaning her forehead against the horse's muscular neck. Tears of desolation fell to the dirt floor.

Feeling a light tap on her shoulder, Melissa turned to find Margaret—now her personal servant after the Drenton mansion was shut down and sold.

"My Lady," Margaret said gently, recognizing that Melissa was falling into one of her depressions. "I have brought you your lined riding habit. It will be needed with this weather." She handed Melissa the heavy outer garment.

"Thank you, Margaret," Melissa answered, wiping her moist cheeks as she slipped on the long coat. "I am grateful for your loyalty. And I know Annabella felt the same about you."

Margaret smiled, replying, "My gratitude for your words of kindness, my Lady." She then turned solemn.

Melissa noticed. "What troubles you Margaret?"

"My Lady," the servant said nervously, "this morning is not fit for a gallop. I'd hoped you wouldn't go."

Melissa reached for her servant's hand. "Margaret dear, I do appreciate your concern but do not fear for me. I will find and gallop behind the wild moor ponies. They will guide me and help me forget my heartache."

Margaret bowed her head. "My Lady," she said respectfully. "If I may appeal to your heart, you must stop blaming yourself for what transpired between Master Wilkinson and Lady Annabella. You must if only for the sake of the people you are close to. We need your strength again."

Melissa's face slowly brightened as she pondered Margaret's touching statement. She gently withdrew her hand from Margaret's tender hold. "Yes, Margaret, you are correct. And 'tis a brand new year. I shall begin afresh today."

Melissa then turned and led the well-groomed animal out of the stable with a positive change of attitude as Margaret followed closely behind.

Outside, Melissa hastily explained her intended route to Margaret as she became exhilarated by the damp ocean air. Turning, she stepped up into the stirrup, gripped the saddle-horn and gracefully mounted the exuberant animal. She probed the horse's belly, urging him into a mild trot. Soon, beaming excitedly into the onrushing wind, Melissa was at full gallop toward the high moors. Margaret stood and watched her disappear into the harsh brume to search for what she now needed most, the wild moor ponies.

After only a short trek into the brutal moors, Melissa was forced to dismount and walk the horse along the base of the tall rocky bluff. She thought about how she should have heeded Margaret's concern as she squinted to maintain her route. Her view was now limited and rapidly deteriorating, intensifying her precarious situation.

The wind howled menacingly, blowing immense and blinding plumes of gray mist about unpredictably. Melissa relied on her expert horsemanship to guide her safely. But she realized that even she was no match for the severe elements of the unmerciful moors. Still, she knew she must somehow remain on her planned course.

Why hadn't she listened to Margaret? From now on she would, she decided, fondling the butt of the rifle, holstered against the horse's rib.

Disappointed and fearful of the elements, she would forget trying to find the ponies for today. She mounted the horse and looked upward, deciding it was probably best to climb the hill and take a broad view of the countryside. It would help her regain her bearings for the return trip home. After turning the brawny animal, it obediently hoofed over the jagged rocks lining the steep ravine and carefully made its way to the top.

Reaching the crest, Melissa dismounted and held onto the reins as she scanned the desolate fog-shrouded wilderness. Alarmed over the poor visibility, she swallowed nervously while planning her next move. Suddenly, the wind abated and the horizon began to clear. The sun swathed a limpid shaft of light into a distant meadow. She blinked in wonder when she then saw the herd of short, stocky ponies whinnying and frolicking in the golden brightness. She became enthused, but hesitated, knowing the location was far off and not in her intended direction back to the farm. But her judgment faltered when the Chestnut, also seeing the horses, began snorting and pawing excitedly at the ground. Melissa then made her decision to reach the grassland and gallop among the wild ponies.

She eagerly mounted the excited stallion. The powerful animal was hardly able to contain his commotion. Melissa began the buoyant ride down the bluff, bounding the rocks and loping through the flowered heather and spiny gorse shrub. Then, slowing, she noticed it had grown eerily quiet. Gradually a shrill laugh-like cry began to fill the air. The wind, she thought, as she prudently stopped the horse on a plateau and fixed her gaze on the meadow. But what she saw made her gasp. The meadow, the warm spread of light and the horses had disappeared! The horizon was a solid blanket of gray once more.

Now uneasy, Melissa knew she would have to rely on the horse's strength and instinct to get them back to the stables safely. She anxiously jerked on the reins to turn the horse back. The horse, mysteriously unnerved, shuddered with fear and refused to follow her commands. She again attempted to urge the horse forward but he continued to balk and quiver. Impatient with the stubborn animal, she began to kick fiercely at his belly. Then, as the shrill noise grew louder, the horse reared wildly. The panicked animal bucked uncontrollably with such force that it flung Melissa into the air before vaulting off into the ashen horizon. Melissa hurtled down the hill through the wet heather and jagged rocks. Managing to stop herself, she lay stunned as the piercing shrill hung in the air.

Shaken, she began to crawl up the hill, blood dripping from a deep gash on her head. Dazed and scared, she suddenly noticed an overpowering reek carried on a waft of ice-cold air. Wearily she stopped and leaned back against a boulder, curling up for warmth as she looked around, frightened by the alarming shrill and putrid odor. Her eyes filling with fear, she saw a silhouette slowly emerge from the haze. Her heart pounded as she cowered in dread.

"Who are you?" she yelled tensely. "Who is there?"

The figure finally slunk into view. "It is me, my dearest Melissa," the voice responded firmly, filled with threat. "I am here to aid you …"

Petrified, Melissa's eyes gaped in horror. "It cannot be!" she shrieked. "It cannot be!"

Again she tried to rise and run but her legs had lost all strength and she slid back down the boulder.

Shocked and trembling in the chill, she stared upward at the figure, now reddish in hideous form, standing over her. The injured woman could only emit screams of terror, screams that were swallowed up by the sound of the fierce, shrill cry, still hanging in the air.

CHAPTER 5

February of 1835, King O' Men Pub

The winter onslaught on Saint Valentine's night in London was forbidding. Pelted by a wailing blizzard, the streets were desolate as people sought refuge in the warmth of their homes.

Inside the pub on Piccadilly Road, it was empty and dim. Charred candle stubs in the tarnished wall sconces sat unlit. The faded sign on the sidelight window had been scraped off for repainting, and the fanlight window boarded up for the winter.

Heavy-hearted, Daniel Doherty slowly removed his stocking cap as he stood in front of the blazing fireplace. Staring upward at Christopher's painting, he recalled that summer day when Christopher had last been there, bold and spirited with his new gaming darts and gladdened over his love for Lady Annabella. He turned to the scraggy dart board, regretting they hadn't been able to journey to Devonshire in October for the Crown's dart tossing tournament.

Deciding to leave, he began to extinguish the fire when he heard a knock and saw the front door slowly open, a gust of snow rushing inside on the wind.

A thin woman wearing a hooded woolen coat and a large furry muff appeared on the threshold and timidly looked around the room.

"Ye' gods, woman!" Doherty bellowed, "Come in, come in. Do hurry or ye'll catch yer death."

She bustled in and closed the door.

Squinting through the glimmering shadows she asked, "Daniel Doherty, is that you?"

"Aye, 'tis I," he answered. "Ya look frozen. Come closer to the fire and warm yerself, I say."

She stepped into view.

"Bernadette Quinton! How ya be?" he exclaimed with surprise.

"Daniel, 'tis good to see you again," she said, smiling. "Why is your place buttoned down? Where've you been? 'Tis been quite a spell to find you."

"Back in Ireland, Dublin city. Visitin' with my two brothers," he answered while dragging down two chairs that had been stacked on the one remaining table. He set them in front of the roaring fire. "I've just returned. I secured the pub and journeyed there durin' the Yul'tide."

Bernadette sat down across from him and laid her muff on the stony outer hearth to dry. "'Tis good you're back, you've been gone a stretch, you have."

"Aye," Daniel confirmed. "Now would ya care for some sherry to warm yer cockles? I don't have much stock left, some ale and sherry 'tis."

She nodded, rubbing her hands close to the crackling fire.

"Now what brings ya here on such a bleak night, woman?" His voice echoed through the barren pub as he walked to the bar. He poured some sherry into a small crystal glass and filled his tankard with ale. Returning, he handed her the sherry and sat down.

"Daniel, I saw Christopher many times during his jailing," she answered, sipping on her sherry. "We became fast friends as I mourned and repented openly for my wrongdoing and sins against Annabella and the Lord. Christopher understood and forgave me, he did."

Doherty remained silent as she set the glass down and reached inside her muff. She removed the polished oblong box containing Christopher's cherished darts. "At the end he asked me to fetch you this."

Doherty looked on in surprise. "I can't! I say I can't," he rasped, turning away.

"Daniel," she continued softly, "One of Christopher's final wishes was for you to have his proudest possession. He told me that he thought of you as a father."

Relenting, Doherty accepted the box and opened it, seeing that all the darts were there.

Bernadette smiled, saying softly, "Bishop Thornton has blessed the lot of 'em. They are sanctified. He asked the Lord to understand and pardon Christopher's woeful deed at Stratford on that dreadful fall night."

Doherty stretched upward and carefully laid the box on the fireplace mantle, saying, "Then the devil's claim has been removed. I shall treasure the gift, I shall indeed." Suddenly filled with sorrow, he sat back and lowered his head. "I only saw Christopher at the trial. I couldn't bear to see him in shackles marched to the bloody gallows, I couldn't," he lamented, rubbing his forehead in distress. "He would've been thirty-two full years tomorrow, he would."

Bernadette put her hand on his shoulder. "I'm sure Christopher knew of your pain, Daniel," she consoled. "Do not fret. He met the gallows without a tussle. He'd suffered greatly without Annabella. Now they're together."

"Ahh, yes," Doherty agreed, looking upward.

"And he didn't have to face Christmas," Bernadette continued. "Lady Grayson used her influence with the Justice hall to hasten the execution."

Doherty patted her hand. "My gratitude for the kind news," he replied, somewhat relieved. "I shall visit Lady Melissa and thank her for aiding Christopher at the end."

Bernadette appeared troubled, abruptly looked away and said, "Of course, you have been gone and couldn't have known."

"What is it, woman?" Doherty exclaimed. "Woman! Known of what, I ask?"

"Lady Melissa passed away soon after the new year. God rest her soul."

"Ye' gods! I say, it can't be! Ye' gods!"

"Oh yes, 'tis true all right," Bernadette answered soberly, turning to face him. "She never strengthened after that tragic night in Stratford. She blamed herself for the lot of it." Bernadette shook her head. "The Yul'tide was the worst on her. She was terribly lonely without Annabella."

Doherty sat stunned as Bernadette set her empty glass on the hearth and continued, "After Christopher was gone, Melissa journeyed with her servant, Margaret, to her horse farm in the moors of Dartmoor…"

"The moors! The bloody moors of Dartmoor?" Doherty interrupted, flabbergasted. "That God forsaken bog of screamin' gales and ghostly demons? What ever took the woman there, I ask?"

"For the solitude," she answered. "And to be among the wild moor ponies. Margaret says the lady would gallop into the wind, chasing the ponies. Lady Grayson loved the horses, ya know."

Doherty nodded and shakily offered Bernadette more sherry.

She declined, continuing, "One day, in the heavy rollin' mist, the lady's horse came back to the farm without her. Margaret, with the horse and a constable from Devon dashed and searched about the countryside until they came upon the spot where ..." Bernadette hesitated, grimacing.

Doherty patted her arm. "Go on woman, go on."

"Well, they figure that somethin' must have startled her mount that day and she was thrown viciously amongst the heather and rocks."

Doherty remained frozen as Bernadette's eyes widened.

"Strangely, when they found Melissa's body, her face was etched with a dreadful look of fright," Bernadette whispered. "She had died from a terribly bashed head and slashed neck. It was peculiar indeed. They say it was not rocks that had done the ghastly deed, but she had been done in by a gruesome hand. Yet they found no proof." She shrugged, concluding, "I know nothing more about it."

Doherty sat shaking his head as Bernadette reached for her muff. She stood and made her way to the door. "I must be leavin', Daniel. My gratitude for the warm welcome."

Doherty stood. "Bernadette, yer a good woman who only went astray. I shall be openin' up soon. Would you be pleased to toil at my pub again?"

She turned as she reached the door. "Oh, I can't," she replied.

"But wherever shall ya go, I ask?"

"I shall remain in Lambeth. I'm allowed to pray at the Abbey of St. Mary's with Bishop Thornton's blessing. I shall live there to keep the graves of our friends freshly flowered. I have no other wishes."

"Aye, Bernadette," he said with a wide grin, "you shall pass this world a forgiven woman, ya shall."

She smiled and turned for the door then hesitated and looked back at him.

"Daniel, should you care to pay your respects, Christopher, Annabella and Melissa are all buried in St. Mary's churchyard beside each other, facing east toward Jerusalem."

Doherty furrowed, asking, "And Sir Alec?"

Bernadette stiffened. "Ah yes, Sir Alec. Well, he's surely in the churchyard too, he is. But Lady Grayson saw to it that he was buried up on the north rising with the wicked." She paused. "But no matter where they are laid away, their souls will now rest in peace forevermore. Good-bye Daniel, and may the good Lord always be in your sight to protect you."

She slipped into the dark onrushing cold, pulling the door closed behind her.

Doherty turned toward the dying fire. "Aye, forevermore, they will rest," he murmured, glancing at the darts resting on the mantle. He lifted the shiny pewter tankard to his mouth as large tears rolled past the metal brim and down his pudgy cheeks.

CHAPTER 6

Easter Sunday, London

Bishop Thomas William Thornton appeared exalted, arrayed in his colorful attire of ceremonial vestments. His ruby-red flowing cape and purple mitered bireta produced a kingly aura as he stood in the expansive main entrance of St. Paul's Cathedral. He watched Bernadette, full of Easter spirit, scamper down the cathedral steps and past the cheerful gathering. He was pleased by her happiness and the rebirth of her faith in God.

"Bernadette," he called after her. "Do be at the park grounds on time. And remember, the picnic will be on the west side of the lake."

Bernadette nodded at him as she stopped at a street vendor and bought a large open bloomed daffodil. Removing her wide-brimmed sunbonnet, she carefully pushed the bright yellow flower into her braided hair, just above the ear.

She turned and lifted the hem of her stylish pink dress before climbing into the back of a carriage. Settling herself, she placed the bonnet in her lap.

"Lambeth, please," she happily told the driver. "Abbey of Saint Mary's."

The cabby carefully guided the buggy onto the busy street and down Ludgate hill, dodging the throng of carriages all struggling for the right-of-way.

Bernadette raised the side-window shade and basked in the glistening late-morning sunshine. Deeply inhaling the warm spring air, her mood was high as the carriage gently bounced its way through downtown London. The special Sunday mass the Bishop had performed had left her feeling virtuous. For the first time in her thirty-four years she felt cleansed and free of the burdens that had plagued her for so long. And the memory of the previous year's tragic events was rapidly fading in her new realm of spiritual joy. At peace with herself, she leaned back and closed her eyes. Her thoughts turned to the afternoon picnic as her ears drank in the sounds of chirping birds and noisy pedestrians dressed in their Easter finery.

Bernadette handed the driver his fare as he reined the carriage to a halt in front of the expansive high-walled monastic complex.

Stepping down from the buggy, she paused and stretched herself as she looked up at the graceful tower, surmounting the arched roof of the elegant chapel. She fixed her eyes on the golden cross of Christ placed atop the steeple, glittering against the deep blue skies and fluffy white clouds that floated in the soft breeze. *Thank you God*, she said inwardly.

Turning, she strode down the pavement and ducked into a covered opening set inside the building's thick wall. She quickly stepped through the passageway, making her way into the compound's interior. Reaching the garden cloister, she met two nuns carrying large wicker baskets of sandwiches, cookies and bottles of cold tea.

Surprised, one remarked, "Bernadette, my dear. Are you not picnicking with us? Everyone has left for Hyde Park. We're going there now."

Bernadette smiled. "Oh yes, sister Caroline, I'm going. But first I must tend to the graves of my friends while the day is so beautiful. I'll join you soon."

"Splendid," the nun replied. "Then we shall see you there promptly afterward."

Bernadette promised and bid them good-bye as the nuns walked past her.

Enjoying the solitude of the deserted complex, Bernadette swung her bonnet by the brim as she sauntered along the new flagstone walkway that encased the square garden-cloister. Proud that Bishop Thornton had arranged for her to live at the Abbey, she scanned the interior of the complex, admiring the appearance of the freshly painted buildings. The dark mahogany doors of the rectory and the church had been recently refinished, producing a silky sheen that gleamed in the sunlight.

Abruptly startled by a pronounced buzzing in her ear, she spun around to catch a curious hummingbird investigating her daffodil. It turned and zipped into the center of the cloister to indulge itself in the heavily scented garden.

Smiling, she paused to absorb the tranquility of the garden. Evergreens and flat shrubs lining the edge of the walk were cropped short, yet still flaunted a lush bristly growth. A profusion of leafy vines, precisely pruned and heavy with bloom, clung to wooden climbing-racks. Small laburnum trees, artfully spaced, were complemented by well-groomed beds of dahlias, chrysanthemums and roses. A hardy mat of emerald-green grass, edging the flower beds, completed the display of springtime splendor.

Bernadette sighed, stepped into the garden and picked three large roses. Kneeling, she closed her eyes and gently pressed the pinkish-red petals to her face, deeply inhaling the rich perfumed fragrance. She started to rise, then hesitated. *'Tis Easter,* she thought, stooping to pick one more rose for the fourth grave.

She set the roses in the deep crown of her bonnet and briskly headed for the pathway leading to the churchyard. Reaching the pathway, she slowly made her way toward the large wrought-iron gate. As always, she felt strange and sad when she saw the graves just past the entrance. Taking a deep breath, she tugged on the gate latch and let herself into the churchyard. She turned to the east and began to follow the thin trail leading to the graves of her friends.

The sunshine, cleaved by thick branches of a massive oak tree towering overhead, glanced off Christopher's headstone as Bernadette stood at the foot of his grave. She was pleased that the plot had remained orderly since she had been there last. Although the wild grass was yellowish-green from the lack of adequate sunlight, it was growing well. She then noticed a fresh bunch of flowers buried next to his and each of the two adjoining graves. She smiled, thinking Daniel Doherty or Margaret, the ladies' former servant, must have been here visiting.

She crouched down and plucked a few weeds that were spreading unchecked on Christopher's plot. Pausing, she leaned back on her heels and recalled the bravery and calm strength he displayed on the day of his execution. Then, shifting forward, she replaced the withered flowers in the small copper urn—attached to the headstone—with one of the roses she had brought. It would do until she came back next week and replaced it with a bouquet of some sort.

Rising, she moved on to Annabella's grave. As Bernadette quickly tidied up her plot, tears welled up in her eyes as she thought of that night in Stratford-on-Avon and recalled the brutal death of the innocent Annabella. "I'm sorry, my Lady," Bernadette mouthed softly as she placed another rose in the urn and continued on to Melissa's site.

As Bernadette placed Melissa's rose next to her gravestone she grimaced and shook her head, recalling the deadly encounter Melissa had met on the high moors. She wondered if the authorities would ever find any clues to her gruesome death as she stood and stepped back to view the three graves.

"Good-bye my friends, I shall see you again soon," she whispered.

Turning, she put on her bonnet and peered toward the distant north end of the churchyard. She glanced up at the sun. It's getting late, she thought, better be getting back for the picnic. *No*, it wasn't that late she decided, looking down at the final rose she clutched nervously. She realized she just didn't want to go up there. She quickly scolded herself, *'Tis Easter. And just because Sir Alec died a wicked man on earth was no reason she shouldn't visit his soul, a soul that was now surely at peace.*

She sighed and began making her way up the small hill. The closer she got to the site, the more ragged and unkempt the grounds became. The grass was parched and brown. Only a few scattered patches of wild flowers had survived the assault of wet decaying tree leaves and heavy swaths of weeds.

No one ever comes up here to maintain the area, she thought. It's no wonder the nuns had decided to discontinue burying anyone in the yard who didn't belong to the church. *Certainly not anyone who had roamed among the wicked.* Downhearted, she decided she would visit regularly and tend to the graves that remained. Someone needed to care.

As she reached the dilapidated perimeter of the enclosed burial area, the sun gradually slipped behind a massive dark cloud. Bernadette shivered and crossed her arms to ward off the abrupt chill as she scanned the neglected graves beyond the rotting rail fence. She shook her head in disappointment. The gravestones were filthy and covered with leafless, stringy vines. The borders of the plots were obscured by shaggy foliage and there were no flowers, even withered ones.

She lingered, slowly becoming aware of the eerie quietness, broken only by the dull whistle of the wind as it passed through the treetops. Although feeling strange and cold, the nip of the chill growing sharper, Bernadette was determined to finish her chore. Her pulse and pace quickened as she passed through the gateless entrance to hike the shady, dirt trail to the top of the rising.

When she came upon Sir Alec's grave, she paused in surprise when she saw it had been tended. The plot was weeded and teeming with flowers in full bloom. Shrubs neatly lined the fringe. The headstone was clean and free of growth. Perplexed, she wondered who would do this? As far as she knew, no one ever came up to visit him. She would question the nuns about this later, but now only wanted to finish her deed and get back to the complex to prepare herself for the picnic.

With growing apprehension, Bernadette stooped to lay the rose at the base of his gravestone then quickly got to her feet. With the strange sensation that she was being watched, she slowly turned around. Her anxious eyes darted from side to side as a shrill cry began to wail through the air. *Must be a loon,* she thought nervously.

Turning to hurry back down the hill, she stopped in wonder when she spotted large mounds of dirt extending behind some bushes just over the rising. Curious, she walked up beyond Sir Alec's plot to investigate the mounds. She bent over and felt the soil. It was moist and dark brown. Astonished, her eyes gaped as she abruptly blurted aloud, "A new grave!" Puzzled, she was unable to make sense of it. *No one would have prepared a new grave up here! Not any more!*

She stood and glanced around nervously knowing she should leave, but again, found she could not. She was mysteriously compelled to move closer to the newly-dug grave. She stepped to the edge of the long rectangular plot and, pushing her bonnet to the back of her head, cautiously crouched forward to peer into the deep cavity. Relieved, she saw only an empty coffin lying on the dirt bottom.

As she quickly stood up, the feeling that she was being watched intensified. It was then that she noticed a crude slate gravestone lying in front of the pit. She made her way around the mounds of dirt to read the headstone. Glancing down, she froze in shock as she read the inscription:

Bernadette Quinton
Born 1801 Died 1835.

Shuddering breathlessly, she jerked backward in panic. The air, growing colder, filled with a powerful stench. Bernadette tried to run but found her foot trapped under the gravestone, causing her to twist violently and fall heavily onto the ground. Stunned, she tried to raise herself, her bonnet slipping from her head and fluttering down into the hole. Her leg was paralyzed with a piercing pain. She was unable to move and, with shock on her face, rested against the mound.

"Please, God help me!" she cried out.

She suddenly felt a clammy grip on her shoulder and heard behind her, "May I be of help, my love?"

She turned to face a ghastly figure. Wrenching back at the sight, Bernadette felt jagged fingernails cut deeply into her back, drawing blood. Her screams of terror were drowned out by a piercing shrill while the stench grew stronger and the icy chill seeped upward from the blackened abyss of her own crypt.

A lingering drizzle from the early evening shower trickled steadily off the wire bridge of Bishop Thornton's horn-rimmed spectacles, bathing his craggy features. As he blinked away the dribble through a hard stare, he stood rigidly as the churchyard gravediggers worked vigorously in the enveloping darkness to complete their task.

Stone-faced authorities from the London Metropolitan Police struck up their lanterns and stood in ready as the coffin was finally unearthed and wrestled to the top edge of the muddy day-old tomb.

Bracing himself for the grim reality of their ominous discovery, the Bishop stepped back to allow the police more room to work. One of the inspectors quickly seized the coffin and held it in place while another anxiously wielded a stunted claw-bar to remove the lid.

The two nuns who had found the alarming site stood behind Bishop Thornton and grimaced with every screech of a yanked nail. They gripped each other's hands tightly as the coffin lid was at last pried off and heaved onto the ground. Gasping with shock, they abruptly looked away from the crimson remains of Bernadette, brutally illuminated by the blazing glow of the lanterns. Her still-open eyes were fixed and filled with horror.

Bishop Thornton winced and raised his gaze upward. He immediately sensed that this gruesome deed could not have been carried out by any human. It had all the savagery of a fiendish and evil act.

A hush fell over the gathering while the bishop whispered a quick prayer and blessed the mutilated corpse. He turned away as one of the inspectors carefully pulled the ivory-handled dagger from Bernadette's severed torso and dropped it into a cloth bag, pulling the drawstring tight. He then crisply instructed two bobbies to reclose the coffin and transport it to the Scotland Yard morgue.

A mournful Bishop Thornton slowly turned and walked over to the grief-stricken nuns. Putting his hands on their shoulders, he urged them to rise. Together the three began to follow the police, cautiously making their way down the darkened trail toward the abbey.

Passing by the grave of Sir Alec Drenton, the Bishop suddenly felt a startling uneasiness. And as he walked by the graves of Christopher Wilkinson and Christopher's dearest love, Annabella, the bishop pondered all of the events surrounding their pitiful fate.

While the somber procession filed out of the churchyard, Bishop Thornton lagged behind, the last to pass through the wide wrought-iron gateway. He paused as he turned to close and latch the gate. Leaning against the gatepost, he peered into the darkness to take a final look at the gravestones glimmering in the sweeping moonlight.

He did not need divine prophecy to know that the tragic saga of Christopher Wilkinson and the people he loved was not yet over. This most recent turn, the savage killing of Bernadette, worsened his fears that their departed souls lived on, and surely not in peace. For he knew their souls were eternally marked for satanic revenge.

Shaking his head, he latched the gate and made his way up the pathway, quickening his pace as he hurried to rejoin the dim light of the lanterns that floated distantly at the far end of the garden-cloister.

CHAPTER 7

NOW

Late June of 1997, Southern California

The silence in the cramped cockpit was brittle as the small, single-engine plane approached the scenic island of Santa Catalina, twenty-four miles off the Southern California coast. The high sun splashed brilliantly onto the soft-white beaches that bordered the steep rocks and gentle crystal coves dotting the shoreline.

The aspiring pilot stared nervously at the minute airport, which sat precariously atop a sheer seaside cliff a thousand feet below. The tension mounted as the plane slowly descended toward the obscure runway that gradually began to dip below the glared windshield.

Bob Chapman, the flight instructor, shook his taut index finger at the air speed indicator, demanding insistently, "Pick up the airspeed! Dammit, Fletcher!

"Lower the nose. You're losing it. We're close to stalling! Jesus!" Chapman yelled, "You're about to ditch us into the side of the cliff!"

Fletcher anxiously reached for the throttle.

"Goddammit! Don't touch that throttle! Lower the nose! You know that!"

Fletcher quickly let go of the throttle and tensely pushed the control yoke forward, aiming the nose downward. As the plane accelerated, he carefully backed the throttle down with his sweaty hand.

"Why the hell do I have to land here? It's not an FAA requirement!" Fletcher snapped, venting his pent-up frustration.

"Because if you can put it down here, you can put it down anywhere. Now pay attention. Reduce the airspeed, now you're going too fast!" Chapman barked as he lurched for the right-seat control yoke.

"Negative, Chapman! I've got control!" Fletcher hollered defiantly.

Even though Chapman feared a botched landing, he remained steady. Sitting back, he crossed his arms, conceding that it was Fletcher's plane to land, but ready to take control if Fletcher passed the plane over to him. *Fat chance,* he thought.

As the plane passed over the jagged cliff edge, Fletcher realized that he was slightly above the landing descent angle and still going much too fast. He was in danger of overshooting the runway and too low to pull up and make another approach. *This was one runway that can't be overshot*, he thought. Committed to landing, he abruptly raised the nose and backed the throttle down. First the main wheels, then the nose wheel struck the asphalt. Chapman's heart pounded furiously as the plane began to porpoise down the runway. But he knew he shouldn't interfere at this point; that might only make it worse.

Fletcher carefully eased the control yoke forward to lower the nose while reducing the power, bringing the plane to a safe lumbering roll.

Chapman, relieved, exhaled loudly and wiped his sweating brow. The middle-aged instructor lowered his eyes and leaned against the door. "Let's go home," he muttered, "we've had enough for today." Exhausted, he stared out through the windshield.

Fletcher nodded as he taxied the craft back toward the takeoff end of the runway. He picked up the radio microphone and announced his takeoff.

After confirming air clearance, Fletcher smoothly applied full throttle. The plane gradually picked up speed, bouncing easily down the runway. With the wind sweeping under the wings, he eased the control yoke back to lift the plane off the ground. The laboring engine of the Piper Warrior II whined as the plane soared safely over the far edge of the runway and maneuvered toward the ocean.

I'm lucky, Fletcher thought, looking down into the certain grave at the bottom of the barren rocky ravine a hundred and fifty feet below. You don't usually get another chance here. One mistake; no recoveries allowed. "Why put a runway on top of a fucking mountain," he mumbled to himself. He then thought, *Why not in the middle of a pasture? So this is why they call it the Airport-in-the-Sky.*

Chapman looked over at Fletcher. "I know we've talked about scheduling your test next month. But after that botched landing, I'm not so sure you'll be ready," he said before turning back toward the windshield.

"Bob, you've told me many times that even expert pilots sometimes screw up landings," Fletcher answered confidently. "You know I'm safe. Maybe not the best yet, but safe. C'mon, Bob, you know that I'm just worried about my decision over Lainey, that's all. Gimme a break, will ya?"

Chapman remained silent as Fletcher flew over the rich jade-green pastures of the island before turning northeast and climbing to an altitude of fifty-five hundred feet to begin his short cruise over the ocean. With a calm sea breeze at his tail, a composed Fletcher James McKeane headed for his home in Newport Beach. Bob Chapman, his friend and mentor, remained lost in thought, peering out at the ocean.

The sun was pale and sinking to the right as Fletcher brought the plane in for a smooth landing on the short general-aircraft runway of Orange County Airport. Ground clearance to Shelanary Aviation, a private terminal, was a welcome relief for both men.

After securing the airplane, Fletcher thought enthusiastically about testing for his license next month as he and Chapman walked to the terminal.

Stopping at the terminal entrance, Fletcher handed Chapman his flight log to fill out and sign, asking, "Well, Bob, what's the verdict?"

"Okay," Chapman replied. "I suppose you'll be ready. We have a few weeks to do some more practice landings. In the meantime I'll discuss your progress with Inspector Jaynes."

"Jennifer Jaynes? She'll be testing me? The new one from the L.A. district office?"

"Right," Chapman replied. "She's been testing everybody for weeks. Shelanary really likes her. Why?"

"I dunno," Fletcher said, shrugging. "I guess she just seems really young for that, and beautiful too. Is she a full-fledged FAA operations inspector or just an appointed examiner?"

"She's a pedigree. Full-fledged," Chapman answered. "I also know she's a hell'uva pilot. Her dad was an air force jet ace and trained her when she was just a kid."

"Impressive," Fletcher commented.

"For sure," Chapman agreed. "You ever been inside the office Shelanary gave her?"

Fletcher shook his head.

"Look in there sometime. The wall is plastered with her credentials. She's even got her masters in aerospace engineering from the University of Kansas. One of the best aviation schools in the country. She's really sharp."

"I did talk to her once," Fletcher said. "I had a few questions about emergency radio frequencies and stopped her in the hall when I noticed her FAA ID badge. Answered them right away. You're right, she really seemed to know her stuff."

Chapman nodded and lowered his eyes to record today's flight data in Fletcher's log. Fletcher took the moment to recall that one time he'd talked to Jennifer and how strangely familiar they'd felt toward each other. They even questioned whether they'd met before but decided they hadn't since she'd just transferred from the Pensacola district office.

Chapman handed the completed log back to Fletcher, asking, "How about if we go up again next Thursday? We'll try the Catalina thing again."

"Sure, sounds good," Fletcher agreed, glancing at his watch. "I gotta go." His face turned serious. "I have to start making arrangements for my move south. And I don't just mean the business end of it."

"Yeah, I understand," Chapman replied, turning toward the terminal hangar. "Good luck on both counts. Hey, but just remember, women like Lainey don't come along very often. She's a sweetheart. Anyway, see ya later, I have to meet a student for a pre-flight test."

"Okay Bob, see ya next week," Fletcher answered, his voice trailing as he turned for the parking lot. Walking slowly, Fletcher thought about what Chapman had said concerning Lainey. He also thought about their conversation concerning Jennifer Jaynes and again recalled his strong attraction to her. He told himself his interest in her was simply because of her beauty and unusual piloting talents. Regardless, the whole thing wasn't important right now. He needed to concentrate on Lainey and nothing else. He loved her. He pulled out his car keys as he reached his Jeep.

Inside Shelanary Aviation a woman stood in the spacious foyer looking through the plate glass doors toward the terminal parking lot. Appearing adept, slender and of medium-height, she was dressed in a yellow jumpsuit. It was unzipped to the waist, exposing a heavy cotton T-shirt. A colored plastic FAA ID badge hung around her neck.

FAA Operations Inspector, Jennifer Lee Jaynes, nervously tugged at her long velvet-black hair as she watched the man climb into the jeep and drive away.

CHAPTER 8

Fletcher's Town House, Newport Beach

Fletcher's frosty beer went down easily as he sat resting at his dining table. He was spent from the day's piloting challenges and the botched landing at Catalina. Overall, he felt confident but wondered why he'd ever become involved in something as humbling as flying just because it might enable him to become more flexible on his new photo assignments. *Flexible? Yeah, right! Hell, it'll probably get me killed!* he thought sarcastically.

Mellowing, he looked over at the lease papers for his new and bigger town house in San Diego. He was happy about moving closer to the home office of Geographic Unlimited and particularly excited about the upcoming wildlife photo shoot in South America. And he was eager to learn the details of the trip the following week, when he met with Tom Berkshire at his office. He smiled, thinking of how Berkshire had dangled that plum assignment as an enticement for him to sign a new contract.

His elation disappeared, however, when he thought beyond his career and of how he would miss

Newport Beach and, of course, his beautiful girlfriend Lainey. Whenever he felt the need for total closeness with a woman, she was always the one he wanted. He was proud that she had wanted him too, for both companionship and to love, especially when she was sought after by so many men who frequented the MoonGlade Lounge.

Fletcher opened a second beer and hoisted his feet to the chair across from him, recalling the night of his birthday early last year when he'd met Lainey for the first time. That night that had drastically changed his life from carefree to caring …

Newport Beach was captivating on that early evening of February 2. A crisp afternoon rain had left the air fresh and clear and the brimming moon lay reflected lustrously on the water.

Fletcher was full of good cheer as he entered the parking lot of the MoonGlade Lounge with his date, Marsha Cunningham. Just back from a long vacation in Mexico, he complemented his tanned body with pleated khaki slacks and a black cashmere cardigan draped over a light-blue, cotton pullover shirt.

He exchanged greetings with the lot attendant, George, then left him the keys to his jeep and swaggered through the door with the well-proportioned redhead on his arm. Frank Conklin, the owner, noticed them approaching the maitre d' stand. The men exchanged handshakes and Frank gave the woman a friendly embrace.

"Frank, you need a maitre d'. When the hell you going to hire one?" Fletcher asked glibly.

"As soon as I find someone worthy of you," Frank quipped with a chuckle.

"Good answer," Fletcher said as he exchanged a broad smile with Marsha. "By the way, there's only two of us."

"Okay, that'll work out fine," Frank responded, examining his reservation list. "I had to give up your favorite table to the Kent Fitzroy party. I hope you don't mind. Five of them arrived in a limousine, a bit smashed. It seems that he's very excited over the production of his new movie. I think I'll seat you at the small table next to the beachfront entrance."

Fletcher shrugged, replying, "No problem."

"Excellent," Frank answered. "Oh, by the way, we're breaking in a new server tonight. We hired her while you were in Mexico. She's friendly and appears to be very competent. She'll be serving your table, okay?"

"Like I said, no problem, Frank…whatever," Fletcher replied, playfully nudging his smiling companion. "Just let us eat, will ya? And I may bring you back a souvenir from Africa to hang on your wall. Over my favorite table, of course."

"Oh yeah, Africa, that's right. When you going?" Frank asked as he escorted them to their table.

"Next week," Fletcher answered as he and Marsha sat down. "I'm taking Marsha and her parents to a wild game preserve in Kenya then probably on to Ivory Coast for a little hunting. I'm going to do a layout for Geographic while I'm there."

"Sounds like a great time," Frank replied as he walked away smiling. "And I'll hold you to that new wall decoration." His words trailed behind him.

Fletcher and Marsha settled themselves at the table and began making small talk when a pleasant yet articulate voice interrupted their festive spirits.

"Good evening," she greeted with a warm smile, holding two menus. "My name is Lainey and I'll be your server tonight."

Fletcher looked up and did a double take. He had never met a woman who instantaneously captivated him in the way that she did. She beamed elegance and grace without the slightest effort.

She was slim and petite with long blond hair that fell loosely to her shoulders. Her skin was smooth and fair and her lips, painted a light shade of pink, were full and bow-shaped. Her large brown eyes were inquisitive and sparkling, her tiny hands meticulously clean with freshly manicured nails.

Fletcher sat still, staring at her, lost in her beauty.

"Sir, is everything all right?" Lainey asked, glancing first at him, then at Marsha, who appeared mildly irritated at his interest in the waitress.

Flustered by his awkwardness, he mumbled something about her beauty stunning him.

"Thank you, sir," Lainey replied modestly, remaining poised but appreciating the compliment. "May I take your drink orders before dinner?" she asked, handing Marsha a menu, the other to Fletcher."

"Just a carafe of the house Chianti, please," Fletcher answered, glancing at her while accepting the menu. "We'll order dinner when you return."

"Yes sir, I'll be right back with your wine and take your order," Lainey answered as she walked away.

Fletcher appeared staggered by his overwhelming attraction to Lainey. He couldn't hide it from Marsha.

"Well, I guess I take a back seat tonight, huh?" she fumed quietly through clenched teeth.

"Jesus, take it easy. She's beautiful, that's all. So are you," Fletcher offered, managing a smile while rubbing her hand.

"Sure. Right!" she retorted, yanking her hand away, glaring at him with her icy, violet eyes.

Although Fletcher's strong attraction to Lainey bothered him throughout dinner, he worked to mask it. Yet it didn't matter. Marsha had shrugged it off as she always did when Fletcher noticed another woman. She had no choice.

When they finished dinner and Lainey failed to bring the check, Fletcher glanced around the near-empty dining room for her when Marsha went to chat with Frank in the foyer. He spotted Lainey standing just outside the beachfront entrance staring at the ocean. Annoyed, he got up and went to get her, but couldn't help calming down when he stood before her and their eyes met. "Excuse me, Lainey…but…"

"Oh, sir," Lainey said surprised, cutting him off. "I'm so sorry. But before I arrived from Utah, I'd never seen the moon shine so beautifully over the ocean. I just love to look at the silvery trail shimmering on the water. It's so lovely I can't take my eyes off it. But I've delayed you, I apologize. I'll come right in."

When Lainey started for the doorway, Fletcher reached out and gently grabbed her arm, saying, "Wait, it's okay. I also like that scene." He looked toward the ocean. "When I was a small boy in Ireland my mother would take me on trips to Galway Bay. We used to see it on nights when it was clear."

She relaxed and smiled, saying, "I understand it's called a moon-glade and that's where the name for this lounge came from."

They looked into each other's eyes, both temporarily entranced before Fletcher answered, "Yes, that's true. Frank told me that one night Jimmy Conklin, his father, was sitting on the beach trying to come up with a name for his new lounge when he suddenly realized how extraordinary the sight was. That's when he decided to call the lounge, MoonGlade."

Lainey glanced back at the ocean, sighed and said, "And the name moon-glade makes the view so much prettier." She paused. "Thank you, sir, for understanding about the delay, I mean."

"Sure, I understand. By the way my name is Fletcher McKeane. So please call me Fletcher instead of sir, okay?"

"Yes, thank you, Fletcher," she agreed, beginning to feel more comfortable with him. "My full name is Lainey Cole. I moved here from Ogden, Utah about a month ago."

"I'm glad you did," Fletcher replied, slowly leading her toward the door. "I wish we could keep talking, but I don't think my date would understand. I see she's back at the table waiting. We'd better go inside."

Just before entering the dining room they hesitated and glanced first at each other, then again at the ocean and the moon-glade.

Fletcher tipped his beer and emptied the bottle as his mood turned sour over his frustrating situation with Lainey. He loved her, and had known it since that first night, but had constant doubts about committing to her completely. He knew that every time he grew that close to someone he truly loved, he lost them, usually to death. The inner turmoil, caused by that nagging sense of fate was always intense.

He recalled the foggy night and the mysterious car crash that took Ashley, the first woman he felt he really loved. And his best friend Leblanc, who faced a violent death fifteen years ago in Louisiana. Then his father followed, dying of a sudden heart attack soon after they'd arrived in America from Ireland. But there was the utter and most glaring loss that came early in his life. His mind wandered back to that dismal March day in Cork, Ireland, when he was only twelve …

Fletcher's small fingers tugged nervously at his curly brown hair as he sadly looked out the window at the vast array of dark green foliage, veiling the rolling Irish hills. The day had started softly with the gentle rain providing a mild warm curtain. Then it gradually turned dark when the menacing winds grew in force, blowing the rain hard and cold against the rocky coast of southern Ireland.

He reluctantly turned when he heard the faint calling of the desperately ill woman lying in the four-poster bed. The room seemed wide and barren as Fletcher crossed it to reach the woman that he didn't want to lose. He was heartbroken and had already braced himself for the greater grief he knew he would soon face.

He stopped at the night-stand and reached down to the Waterford crystal decanter, her most prized possession. He poured some water into the matching tumbler and pushed the bed's side curtain back to gently raise her head and give her a few sips.

She moved her hand slightly as Fletcher picked up the bony fingers and gently squeezed. He knew she needed to say something, and his tears mustn't distract her. He stood hushed and rigid, holding back the urge to cry out.

"Yes, Mom. I am here," he whispered.

She smiled weakly and spoke, gasping for each sentence, "Fletcher, I brought you forth and by the grace of God, you were born with Irish courage. Do not be afraid to face the pain of death. There is much suffering and joyous times throughout life. You will laugh and weep and you must know both." She paused and inhaled for breath. "Now please promise to stay strong for your father. He will need you."

Holding onto Fletcher's hand, she smiled and tilted her head toward the door. Fletcher knew he couldn't be selfish with her time. There was another person who must also see her once more.

He reached down and embraced her softly, letting a tear fall on her cheek as he made his last good-bye. He thought bitterly that twelve years was not enough time to spend with her. Picking up her hand, he gently laid it across her breast as he whispered the promise that he wouldn't ever fail her. He would carry her rich abundance of knowledge and strength with him forever.

With his eyes full of tears, he turned and walked toward the thick wooden door to the living room where his father waited. He didn't look back.

Silently, Shawn McKeane, a hardy but now exhausted man, slowly passed the small boy and entered the bedroom. His hair had grown long and white and his face was weathered and lined.

After a few minutes the bedroom door opened, allowing an ice-cold waft of air and a light smoky odor escape from inside. But in his sorrow, the old man hadn't noticed the strange elements as he walked to Fletcher, putting his arm around his shoulders.

"Fletcher, she is gone," he said, "and you must begin living without her guidance. You're all I have left. She asked that we go to America to give you the best chance at life. We will go."

Fletcher lifted his foot off the chair and sat upright. Rubbing his tired ice-blue eyes, he recalled his mother's last words: do not be afraid of death and suffering. There is much of it to endure in life. *Too much suffering*, he thought. Why was it, he lamented, that inner peace achieved through love and commitment seemed so elusive to him? Where was the true happiness? It never lasted, only ending tragically.

Therefore, even though he knew he loved Lainey and was hopelessly involved, he'd made his decision. He was strong, but not strong enough to handle losing her. He couldn't chance it. They would have to wait until he felt more secure about their being together. It shouldn't take long. Surely she'd understand. She'd have to; there was no other choice. But, damn, how he'd regret having to tell her.

Rising, he chucked the beer bottles in the trash, deciding that this might be a good evening to go out alone. Maybe he'd check out a few night spots by the pier. Shit, maybe on the way he'd even join the crowd for a little karaoke at the Beach House Inn. He could sleep in tomorrow and then do some more studying for his pilot's test in the afternoon. He lethargically walked upstairs to the master bathroom to take a shower.

After drying himself he wrapped the towel around his trim waist that he maintained through a moderate but earnest workout agenda. He stepped in front of the bathroom sink and looked into the three-paneled mirror, deciding to let his thick, sandy-brown hair dry on its own. He simply brushed it back, smiling as he was still able to cover the strands of gray that were beginning to creep in around his temples. Although aging didn't really matter to him. He had already lived an exciting life, and it was only getting better.

Discarding the towel in the clothes hamper, he entered the bedroom. Because of the heat, he chose loose-fitting clothing for his lean 6-foot frame. Hell, it would probably even be warm by the ocean.

As he slipped on his calfskin loafers, he tried to improve his spirits. But he remained confused by thoughts of Lainey. Might just as well begin getting used to not seeing her every day, he told himself while making his way downstairs. Walking through the kitchen, he took one more look at the lease papers for the San Diego town house before picking up his car keys and wallet.

The clear summer night was dimming as he drove down Pacific Coast Highway enjoying the tepid ocean breeze streaming through his open-air jeep. As he passed by the MoonGlade Lounge, he again became frustrated by his inability to be firm in his decision about Lainey. He wanted to stop in and see her but kept going. He decided to avoid her tonight. *Dammit! There was no other choice.*

Chapter 9

Mid-July, Tuesday, Shelanary Aviation

Bob Chapman casually approached the open door of the FAA satellite office located in the administration sector of Shelanary Aviation. Holding a cup of strong black coffee, he paused in the doorway to admire the strong-profiled woman staring at a large map of the airport complex taped on her back wall. At Chapman's soft knock on the door, she turned and broke into a broad smile.

"Hi, Jennifer," Chapman greeted her, sipping on his coffee. "I was just passing by and noticed you in here. Hope I'm not bothering you."

"Hi, Bob, C'mon in. You're no bother, you know that," she responded warmly, pleased at seeing her new friend. "How are you this morning?"

"Fine, thanks," Chapman replied as he walked in and sat down in a chair next to her desk. "Did you administer a test today?"

She sat down in her large swivel chair. "No," she answered, shaking her head. "Ever since the Shelanary family bought the terminal, they've wanted to convert the facility to support private corporation jet aircraft.

"So, I've been helping to define the required logistics. I've been touring their buildings most of the morning."

"Oh, I see," Chapman answered. "Anyway, just thought I'd stop and tell you that I'll have Fletcher McKeane's approval papers to you before his pilot's test on Friday. Gary Shelanary had told me you'd be here and available."

"Oh yes, Fletcher McKeane," she replied. "I confirmed the appointment with Mr. Shelanary after reviewing Fletcher's training records. It looks like he's ready."

Though acting nonchalant, she was interested in finding out more about Fletcher than his flying record. The strange attraction she felt for him had been constantly on her mind since they'd met. This might be her chance. "Any final reservations about McKeane?" She smiled, adding, "No pun intended."

"Well," Chapman answered haltingly, "he struggled with a few landings at Catalina, but he was always able to bring the plane under control and land it safely. Overall, I'm confident about his abilities."

Jennifer cocked her head teasingly, and asked, "But are you sure he's ready?"

Chapman chuckled loudly over her animation, then became more serious. "Yes, I'm sure. He's just a little confused about other things lately. If I didn't think he was really ready, I wouldn't go through with recommending him for the test."

"Hey," she said, "I can tell you really care about this guy. Is he a friend?"

"Yeah, a good one. I've known him for years. In fact, I'm the one who convinced him to go after his license so he'd be able to fly himself around on his work assignments. He's a professional wildlife photojournalist."

"Okay, Bob, you've convinced me he's ready to be tested. I'm just being careful that your judgment isn't colored by friendship."

"I understand," Chapman replied. "But like I said, he's safe. He's just a little mixed up right now over his move to San Diego."

He was playing into her hand. She asked curiously, "Why's he moving there?"

"He's works for Geographic Unlimited, an outdoors magazine publisher. Their headquarters is down there."

"Sure, I've heard of them," she said, then pried further. "So why is he confused about that?"

"Mainly because of his girlfriend, Lainey. It's decision time. You know, does he take her with him or not."

She frowned, then said, "Oh, one of those macho man-things I suppose. Like maybe he's afraid of a serious commitment."

Chapman furrowed his brow. "No, I don't think it's that, I mean in that sense of the word," he answered. "They're pretty much in love. He's just wrestling with the whole idea. Something about always losing the people he gets close to. He tried explaining it one day, but it gets really involved." Chapman shrugged.

"Hmm, interesting," she replied coolly, deciding to ease up on her questioning. "I somewhat understand what he's going through," she added. "I moved to L.A. from the East Coast with my boyfriend, Donald. At first I also wasn't sure. Although I love him, I admit that I'd had my doubts."

Chapman appeared surprised. "Really, what finally made you decide to come?"

She replied sadly, "Well, about the time I was having to make the decision, my parents were killed in a plane crash. I guess that's what convinced me to leave. There was nothing left of my life in Pensacola anymore."

Chapman lowered his eyes. "Oh, I see, umm, I'm sorry."

Jennifer smiled, saying, "Thank you." She quickly glanced up at the clock to relieve Chapman's sudden awkwardness. "Damn, I didn't realize it was that late. I have to attend a business luncheon."

Chapman looked at his watch, exclaiming, "Oops, and I'm late for a student session!" He rose, turning to leave but paused in the doorway. "Oh, incidentally, be careful on Friday. Fletcher's a smooth character. Don't let him get away with anything." He winked kiddingly. "He's potentially addictive."

"Gottcha," she quipped with a smile. "I'll be on my toes."

As Chapman left, Jennifer opened her bottom drawer to reach for her purse, but paused and sat back, pondering her conversation with Chapman. *So, this McKeane is addictive as well as easy to look at*, she thought, remembering the occasions she had watched Fletcher in the terminal. She then recalled the few times Fletcher had briefly chatted with her about his upcoming test over the last week. Now she wasn't surprised that he hadn't brought up his personal life, much less revealing his unusual reason for not wanting to take his girlfriend with him to San Diego.

She thought back to her move and the tragic events of that fateful day in Pensacola, the day that had drastically changed her life forever…

Jennifer sat silently, occasionally peering out the expansive picture window at the dark mountainous clouds rolling in from the Gulf of Mexico, obscuring the northwestern Florida coast. *It's turning into a dreadful storm,* she thought, as she began to worry about her father piloting his way through it.

Donald Brillinger—handsome and professional, dressed in slacks, an open V-neck sweater and loafers, paced about the room in mild frustration, his eyes blinking tensely. He spun toward the couch to recapture Jennifer's attention, demanding, "But, you love me don't you?"

She quickly turned, angered. "Yes, Donald!" she exclaimed sternly. "Dammit! Once more, yes!"

He closed his eyes and turned away.

Seeing his wounded reaction, she sighed, rose and walked over to him. He looked lovingly at her as she nuzzled her chin between his neck and shoulder while rubbing his back. "You know I love you, we talk about it enough," she soothed. "Now please don't be insecure around me; you know I can't stand that."

Feeling more at ease, he gently pushed her away, saying, "Then I don't understand why you're worried about moving to California with me."

"You know I don't want to lose you," she replied, her voice filled with the stress from his questions and a growing concern for her dad. She leaned her head back on his shoulder, adding, "But everything is moving so quickly. When did they decide that you should relocate to California, anyway?"

"They hit me with it late Friday afternoon," he answered, putting his arms around her. "I knew they were planning a satellite office in Newport Beach, but had no idea I'd be selected to head up the venture. I guess when the Japanese investors flew in from Tokyo with the overall plan, they brought an American consultant from California who must've thought I'd make a good choice. Although I never met him."

"Donald, I just got settled in with the FAA district office here. What would I tell them?" she asked, looking over his shoulder to see out the window. She cringed as she watched the flashing of lightning strikes split the blackened skies with a ruthless concussion. *Dad, please be close to home, please,* she pleaded inwardly.

Donald embraced her tighter. "Jennifer, this is our future that we're talking about. It's my major opportunity to advance with the corporation."

"I know, darling," she agreed.

He gently lifted her chin until their eyes met, saying, "You know with your aviation background and your father's influence, you could probably transfer to one of the district offices out there; like L.A."

She relented, replying, "All right, Donald, let me do some more thinking. You're going out to Newport Beach tomorrow to scout it out, right?"

He grimaced. "Yes, my flight leaves at noon," he answered frustrated. "I tried to delay it to give us more time, but they said no. Let's face it, the investors are running the show."

She nodded. "I know there's nothing you can do about it. Anyway, in the meantime I want to talk to my parents about things. You understand, don't you?"

"Of course, sweetheart. I know how close you are to them," he answered, relieved over her apparent change of heart.

"Okay," she said, leading him toward the door. "Now I need to freshen up before I pick them up at the airport. And you have to pack. Tell you what, I'll meet you at your apartment in the morning to see you off in style." She winked as he broke into a wide smile.

They kissed good-bye as he left. Then she hurried into the bathroom.

Jennifer, standing rigid before the window, stared out on the rain-swept view. The storm had intensified. Turbulent sheets of rain saturated the Florida inland, showing no sign of letting up. Short, intermittent buffets of hail brutally thumped against the roof, worsening her anxiety. Again, she checked her watch: seven forty-five. *Why haven't I heard from dad,* she thought. *He said he'd be in by six*. He always called when he was going to be late. Maybe he had to hold over somewhere. *No, he'd flown the jet*. He'd fly in any weather with the jet; able to master the worst of the elements. Besides, if he'd held over somewhere he would've called her, knowing she'd be worried.

She glanced at the phone. *No, it's useless to call Inspector Connors again.* He promised to keep a watch out for dad and would call with any news. *Can't bother him again.* He and the other tower personnel would have their hands full right now. The Sunday-night air traffic was bad enough under normal conditions, much worse in this weather.

Maybe dad's lost. Oh God, if he's lost over the gulf, wing icing would be definite. *No way to avoid it!* Frowning, her stomach began to knot.

Relax, she told herself while repeatedly glancing at her watch. *He's not lost; he's flown in plenty of storms.* No one maneuvered around storms better than he did. *But he's so far away!* Why did they have to go to Mexico City with his Air Force friends for his retirement celebration? Why not Miami Beach, or the Bahamas? The Bahamas, that's where mother really wanted to go. *Damn!*

She fidgeted with her watch: eight o'clock. Call Donald and talk to him. No, he's packing. Packing for California! *Dammit.* What more shit did she need to confuse herself with right now? *Dad, please call!* Growing frantic, she buried her head in her hands, massaging her throbbing temples.

Suddenly the phone rang. She turned and quickly rushed to it, hesitating for a moment before answering it. Intuitively, she knew that something was terribly wrong. She just knew it.

Slowly lifting the receiver, she answered shakily, "Hello, oh yes Mr. Connors, this is Jennifer. Thank God you called, I…" Her voice trailed off as the grim news reached her ears. "What?" she managed. She blanched in shock as she listened intently to the FAA inspector's condolences.

"Oh no! Oh my God! No!" she screamed. Dropping the telephone, she fell backward and collapsed in the chair. She clutched at the wrenching churn in her stomach as she began to sob, grasping for breath while paramedics, summoned from the airport tower, battled the pounding onslaught of the merciless storm as they raced to her aid.

Jennifer lifted a tissue from the desktop dispenser to dab her moist eyes as she recalled the bizarre circumstances surrounding the crash. Mysteriously, the plane wasn't even near the storm when it went down. On route over Mexico, Major Harlan Jaynes had learned about the unusual ferocity of the threatening gulf storm and radioed the Mexican air control, requesting to land in Cancun and wait it out. Calm and in control, he'd even talked to the Cancun tower explaining who he was and how to contact the Pensacola airport in case they ended up stranded somewhere.

Then, strangely, only nine miles out of Cancun, proceeding cautiously with tower guidance, the plane suddenly lost communication and plummeted downward, almost as though it had been guided to its fiery demise.

The Mexican aviation authorities were never able to find evidence of a mechanical failure and, consequently, were compelled to blame the crash on pilot error. However, Jennifer knew pilot error couldn't have been the reason. She was sure the plane had gone down with the help of that third person traveling with her parents in the plane. That unknown man, whose voice was captured on the black box cockpit recorder they recovered from the crash site.

She was puzzled as to who it was. She was positive her parents had planned to travel alone. So, who and how had he done it? More oddly, Mexico City reviewed the flight plan the Major had filed before he departed. Only two passengers were listed—her parents.

And even though the remains of that third victim were never found, the existence of a third person in the plane had been real. The recorder clearly contained the voices of three people, although the dialogue was muddled and incoherent. Unfortunately, just like the reason for the crash, the contents of that final terrifying cockpit conversation would forever remain a puzzle.

Jennifer retrieved her purse from the drawer and stood, deciding that she was glad she'd had Donald's companionship during that horrible period following the tragedy. Yes, she was in love with Donald and confident she'd made the right decision about relocating to Newport Beach with him. She paused. Then why was she so stunned when she'd met Fletcher? Why did she feel so strange around him? So plugged into him? Why can't she forget him? She shook her head as she fumbled for her car keys and walked out the door.

By the time Jennifer entered the heavy freeway traffic she'd convinced herself that any attraction she felt toward Fletcher McKeane, regardless of how unusual it seemed, was purely physical. "Enough!" she scolded herself aloud. Mr. McKeane was just another good-looking man and no threat to her upcoming marriage. Anyway she didn't need any more complications in her life. And, dammit, she'd easily get through the test with him on Friday and be done with this whole thing.

CHAPTER 10

Thursday Night, Balboa Beach

Lainey Ann Cole frowned, reading eleven-thirty on the small stove-clock as she shut and locked her apartment door. Why did she have to close the lounge on the eve of such an important day, she wondered. Hungry but physically drained, she drank a glass of warm milk before heading into the bathroom to prepare for bed.

Standing in front of the small medicine-chest mirror, she stared at her tired and drawn face. She noticed that her normally clear brown eyes were dull and drooping and her long blonde hair was matted from the humidity. She was glad she had made her hair appointment for tomorrow morning. At least she didn't have to worry about that. She liberally applied cleansing lotion and skin refiner to wash off the twelve-hour coat of makeup, then added extra night cream to combat the unusual heat.

Refreshed, she walked to the bedroom thinking about the major decision she and Fletcher would have to make tomorrow night. She knew what her decision was and that it was right, yet she feared that something was wrong. Even though she knew that Fletcher loved her, there were signs that he wasn't ready for a commitment. He hadn't even called her in the last two days, another sign of his reluctance to face the issue. Regardless, the time had come. Tomorrow he would have to make a decision. No more stalling.

She opened the window and started the small fan sitting on the windowsill. Then she turned on the bedside lamp and pulled the comforter down to the foot of the small sofa-bed and folded it. It was too hot for any covering tonight. Reaching into the cramped closet, she pulled out one of Fletcher's extra-large T-shirts, undressed and slipped into it. It was comfortable, hanging loosely to just above her knees. She crawled into bed and picked up a book, hoping to relax. But she only rested it in her lap and laid her head back on the pillow.

Closing her eyes, she was soon in deep thought about how she and Fletcher had become so attached over the last year. How they'd talk every day and wonder where each other was. The silly insignificant phone calls they'd make, just to connect. When he'd go off on assignment, then return so excited knowing she'd be waiting for him at his townhouse—as beautiful and desirable as possible. And how he'd moan and writhe passionately when she'd give herself completely to him. Those special occasions when they'd reach orgasm at the same time, feeling a sense of emerging as one being.

Sighing, Lainey then recalled that late afternoon last month when everything in their relationship seemed to change. That June day when she reported for work at the lounge and saw the well-dressed man sitting with Fletcher at his favorite table ...

Lainey sauntered happily over to Fletcher's table on his signal. Appearing pleased, Fletcher stood up and kissed her then turned toward the stranger who had also stood. "Lainey, honey, I want you to meet Tom Berkshire. He's the managing editor of Geographic Unlimited. You know, the publisher I've been freelancing for." He turned to Berkshire. "Tom, this is Lainey Cole, the lady I've been telling you about."

Lainey offered her hand. "Very nice to meet you Mr. Berkshire. Fletcher speaks very highly of your magazine."

Berkshire shook her hand, responding with kindness, "And Fletcher speaks very highly of you. It's my pleasure, Ms. Cole."

Fletcher, beaming, eagerly reached for Lainey's hand as they sat down. "I just signed a one-year contract, beginning on the Monday after I get my pilot's license. Should be in about three weeks."

Lainey, surprised that she had known nothing of this major change, tried to hide her disappointment over not having been told. She forced herself to smile while Berkshire collected the paperwork from the table and stuffed it into his briefcase.

"Listen, I have to leave," Berkshire said. "I know you two have a lot to talk about and I have a long trip back to San Diego. Miss Cole, nice to have met you." He turned to leave, saying to Fletcher, "Now Fletcher, remember, please give me a week or so notice so we can arrange for the movers."

Lainey shot a stunned glance toward Fletcher as he answered Berkshire. "Right. Yes sir, I will."

Fletcher sat back down and noticed Lainey's dejected look. "What's wrong?"

She looked up at him with worried eyes. "You didn't tell me anything about this," she answered sadly.

"It just came up about a week ago. They really pushed it. I couldn't resist the offer. They've promised me a great assignment in South America ...Colombia."

"And you have to move?" she interrupted. "You didn't tell me that either."

He reached for her hand. "Lainey," he appealed. "Moving there is just part of the contract. Please, let's not worry about that right now. Nothing's over between us or anything like that. Everything will work out. I just haven't put all the plans together yet."

She lowered her eyes and rose to leave. "Yes, I'm sure," she whispered.

Fletcher rubbed his suddenly strained forehead as she abruptly turned and walked away.

Recalling that day in June only added to the stress Lainey was now feeling. She turned off the light and, weeping softly, buried her head in the pillow. She dozed fitfully to the rhythmic pulse of the oscillating fan that labored diligently to draw in what little air was available.

Lainey's eyes instantly opened wide to the unusual noises coming from the living room. She turned to focus on the illuminated clock-radio: four a.m. Still sleepy, she forgot the sounds for a moment and realized the room had become very cold. She reached for the folded comforter and drew it up tightly around her. She then noticed a potent stench. Was it an odor from the beach, sucked into her room by the fan?

Whatever, she knew the noises weren't coming from the beach. She didn't move, afraid to alarm whoever or whatever was making the rustling noises. It couldn't be the wind coming through the windows. She always closed them before going to bed, knowing the beach boardwalk was often crowded with transients and unsavory characters. Still, it felt cold and threatening. The kitchen window or the patio door must be open. She again thought how careful she was about locking up at night. However, she'd been so preoccupied with thoughts of Fletcher before going to bed. She probably did lock up...*but then again*...

Then the noises abruptly stopped. Cautiously, she waited some time before reaching up to turn on the light. After more agonizing minutes of silence, she noisily got up and went into the bathroom, shut the door and stood for a few moments with the water running. She decided this was all the warning she could give.

As she left the bathroom, she noticed the cold air had also strangely disappeared and the outside heat had returned. Hesitating, she realized the stench had also gone, and the noises had definitely ended. Boldly, she made her way to the kitchen, turned on the light and immediately looked straight across the room at the patio door. It was open about two feet. *What a fool I am*, she thought. How had she forgotten to shut it? Disgusted with herself she hurried over and slammed it tight, pulling the locking lever down. She tugged on the handle, testing the lock's sturdiness, turned out the light and returned to bed wondering if even on the second floor, she really was safe from a tenacious intruder.

After rerunning her thoughts about the mysterious noises, stench and quick bitter cold, she finally fell into a deep sleep.

Lainey bolted upright at the ringing of the phone. She blinked her eyes to focus on the clock. *Darn, who'd be calling at seven in the morning?* And when she was finally sleeping soundly after last night's ordeal.

As she crawled out of bed she became annoyed with herself for not just letting the answering machine get it. Why had she shut it off? And why couldn't the landlord have put a phone jack in the bedroom when they converted this place into an apartment, she grumbled inwardly, hurrying to the kitchen to answer the phone.

"Hello," Lainey answered groggily. "Yes, this is Lainey Ann. Oh, hi Mom. Yes, but it's okay, I've had enough sleep," she lied. "No, I wasn't sleeping in. But, you always forget that in Chicago it's two hours later. It's only seven here …No, you won't catch me this afternoon, I have a long day planned. I'm getting my hair done and have to be at work early to prepare for Fletcher's party." Lainey was becoming annoyed, knowing where the conversation was headed. "How's Jack? Did he get the promotion?" Lainey quickly asked, trying to change the subject to her stepfather.

She wanted to get on with the day's activities and avoid talking about what she knew her mother always wanted to discuss. "Good, I'm happy for him. Please give him my congratulations. Mother, I really have to go …what? Yes, I'm fine and safe," she said, sighing. "No, I haven't seen him since Monday. He's been busy studying for his pilot license and planning for his move to San Diego…Mother, I don't know!" she snapped. "I think were going to talk about it tonight!" Feeling guilty over her outburst, Lainey relented.

"Mother, I'm sorry I yelled at you. It's just that I'm so busy lately, and it'll be a big decision for us…Of course, I love him. More than anything in this world. But we just have to figure out what's best for our relationship right now," Lainey continued, conceding to her mother's relentless questioning. "What?…No, I won't move to Chicago if Fletcher and …No, I won't move back to Utah. Mother, please. We talk about this every time you call. My life in Utah is finished. I live here now. I never want to leave California or the ocean. Please accept that," Lainey begged, as she turned toward the refrigerator for some juice.

She reached for the handle then stopped short as what she had just seen registered. She slowly turned back toward the living room and gaped. Fixing her eyes on the patio door, she blinked in shock. It was open!

She recalled the noises of last night and how only hours ago she'd made sure everything was closed and locked up tight. Glancing around nervously, she had almost forgotten that her mother was on the line.

"What? Yes, Mother, I'm here. No, I just got caught up with thinking about the time," she lied, concealing any fear in her voice. "Mom, please let me go. I promise to call you first thing tomorrow, okay? Yes, first thing, I promise. Thanks, Mom …bye."

Lainey hung up the phone, thinking at the same time of the quickest exit from the apartment. She eyed her only way out—the door leading from the kitchen to the back stairs and down into the backyard of the two-story building. *Run!* she thought. *No! Dial 9-1-1! No, she might look foolish.* If there was someone inside why would he have waited this long to act?

She decided to investigate on her own and noisily grabbed a butcher knife from the silverware drawer. She wasn't sure she could use it on anyone, but it made her feel safer, and the noise might spur the intruder into flight. After all, it was daylight.

Passing the counter, she paused and removed the rosary from her purse. The one her mother had given to her on the day she'd left Ogden to have in times of worry. Clutching the crucifix, she looked around, becoming uneasier about wearing only a T-shirt. But knowing that she had no choice, she dismissed her concern and began to search the apartment.

She had a clear view of the patio from the small living area. No one could hide there. In the breakfast nook there was only a small well-worn wooden table and two chairs. The living room furniture consisted of a long couch, one end table and a large leather recliner. No one there either.

That left the bathroom and bedroom. She decided to check the bathroom first, not wanting to take a chance on being surprised from behind while checking the bedroom.

She hung the rosary around her neck and walked to the bathroom, tightly gripping the butcher knife. Her nerves were beginning to steady as the full morning sun streamed through the windows, and people had begun settling on the beach below.

She stepped into the narrow bathroom and pulled the shower curtain back to reveal an empty tub. The double-paned window was only cracked, not enough room for anyone to fit through.

Her fear was subsiding as she entered the bedroom, the last potential hiding place. No one could possibly be under the sofa-bed as it was almost flush with the floor. She carefully opened up the closet door, ready to jump back. It was empty except for her clothes, shoes and a small chest of personal treasures she had been accumulating throughout her life.

She inhaled deeply and, for reassurance, calmly retraced her footsteps throughout the apartment. Satisfied, she removed the rosary from her neck, put it back in her purse and returned the knife to the drawer.

With a strong cup of freshly brewed herb tea in her hand, she sat back in the recliner. She needed to review last night's unsettling events, to try and figure out how the patio door had been re-opened.

As a shiver raced up her spine, she recalled the evening last week when she stood at the bathroom sink and had the strong sense that she was being watched. There had been noises in the kitchen then, but not as loud as the noises of last night. Not enough to frighten her. And wasn't there a stench that night too? She strained to remember, but decided it was probably her nerves catching up with her. She stretched to look out the patio window to see what the weather was doing. Yielding to its radiant appeal, she stood and stepped out on the patio, peering down at the boardwalk separating her from the expansive beach. It was teeming with people carrying coolers and beach chairs.

She felt lucky to be renting so close to the ocean and figured that even if the rent was excessive and the apartment old and a bit run down, the struggle was worth it. Whenever she became frustrated that there was so little money leftover from her paycheck and tips, she would just look out the window at the ocean.

With the flaming bright sun relaxing her, she decided to spend some time on the beach before going to her midday hair and manicure appointment.

After soaking her tea dishes in the sink she walked to the bedroom, her thoughts turning to her uncompromising love for Fletcher and wondered what tonight's meeting with him would bring.

Lainey slipped into her two-piece swimsuit in front of the full-length mirror attached to the back of the closet door. Her petite slender frame felt out-of-shape. She'd been eating poorly and hardly worked out anymore. Even her light-blonde hair was getting dry and stringy.

Her busy work schedule and stress from thinking about Fletcher was beginning to take its toll. A sound night's sleep was something of the past. A few weary tears dropped from her bloodshot eyes as she picked up the curling iron to do something with her hair. But she set the iron back down, deciding to just brush it straight back and push on a headband. She applied sunscreen to her face and paused, wondering how smooth her features would be at forty-five or even thirty-five.

She added eye shadow to give her eyes some life but balked over putting on any more makeup. That was enough for now. Later she would concentrate on making herself beautiful for Fletcher. It didn't matter who saw her on the sand this morning. She put on her beach robe, then reached down to strap on her thick-soled sandals and went to the kitchen to leave an outgoing message on her answering machine.

"Hello, this is Lainey, I've gone to the beach," she recorded distinctly. "Please leave a message and I'll get back to you as soon as I can. Fletcher, if this is you, good luck with your testing today. Love you most."

She put on her sunglasses and took another hard look at the patio door before walking down the stairs to the outside storage bin to retrieve her large straw sun-hat and beach towel. She then made her way across the boardwalk toward the seashore.

Out on the sand she found her favorite spot close to the breakwater and spread out her towel. While thinking back on the conversation she'd had with her mother this morning, she shed her robe, sandals and hat. She laid down facing the sun, still surprised her mother had even brought up Utah. *Never going back there*, she thought, as she focused on that eventful April evening, two years before in Ogden. The night when she had impetuously decided to move to Southern California…

Lainey was lying in bed after taking a long soapy bath when her mother knocked on the partially opened door. "Lainey Ann, dear, can I talk to you?"

"Sure, Mom, come in," Lainey answered, propping herself up against the headboard with two pillows while her mother walked in and sat on the edge of the bed.

"Lainey, Jack and I are going to be married," she said with a broad smile.

Lainey bent forward to embrace her mother. "Oh, Mom, I'm so happy for both of you. I know you've been thinking about this for a long time."

"Yes, I thought I'd never marry again after your father left us. It's taken time to get over the pain."

"I know Mom, I know."

"There's more news," her mother said. "Jack's eligible for an important job at his company, but we must move to Chicago very soon. Of course you can come with us. We'd love to have you along."

"No, Mother, I knew this was coming. In fact, I've saved some money from my job at the store. I'm leaving Utah, but I'm not going to Chicago."

"But where are you going?" her mother asked worriedly.

"Mother, I'm twenty-six. I need to start a new life somewhere else."

"But, where?" her mother asked again.

"California, Mom, Southern California," Lainey replied enthusiastically. "I've always wanted to see the ocean. Last month I opened the road atlas and the area just popped right out at me. There was never a second choice. It's odd, but it's like something's drawing me there. I can't explain it." Lainey's eyes opened wide as she smiled confidently. "I'll get a job. I'm not worried about that."

"When are you going?" her mother asked, knowing it was useless to attempt to dissuade her.

"In a few weeks, as soon as I can find out more about the city. I called the Newport Beach Chamber of Commerce. They're sending me information and the local newspapers."

Lainey reached over to retrieve her small travel clock from her robe pocket and set the alarm for ten thirty. The warm sun and lapping surf against the beach boulders began to make her feel drowsy. She'd enjoy a short nap so that she'd be rested up for a special evening of celebrating with Fletcher at the MoonGlade Lounge. Surely Frank would give her some time off.

CHAPTER 11

Jennifer's Apartment, Los Angeles

Jennifer Jaynes stepped from the ceramic Jacuzzi bathtub, pulling the fluffy large terry cloth towel from the rack. Refreshed from her long luxurious bath, she slowly dried herself, savoring the lingering fragrance of the rose-petal bath oil saturating her skin. Although her body had been pampered and soothed, her mind was totally occupied with troubling thoughts of today's appointment with Fletcher.

She finished drying herself and spread the damp towel over the shower curtain rod. Removing her long white velour robe from the door hook, she slipped it on and knotted the wrap belt loosely as she strolled to the bedroom's wide bay window.

She pulled open the drapes and stretched lazily. The glorious morning sun had burst into the azure blue sky, creating a hazy outline of the skyscrapers in east Los Angeles. Elated with her apartment in Hollywood Hills, she took in the panoramic view of the bustling downtown streets and sidewalks, extending to the tree-shrouded Hollywood Bowl.

Turning, she suddenly frowned, recalling the recent letter she'd received from the property management notifying her that next year the apartments in her building would be converted to condominiums and put up for sale. It irritated her that she couldn't qualify to buy one, even with her sizable middle-income. But maybe by then she and Donald would be married and would combine incomes to afford whatever suited them.

Her thoughts changed to the unusual heat and mugginess from the hurricane off Baja that was forcing the tropical air northward. Despite that development, it would still be a fine day for flying. There was nothing more exhilarating than piloting an aircraft on a clear warm day. Seventeen years later she still remembered that day her father let her pilot solo. No other accomplishment in her life had been so rewarding and satisfied her for so long. That clear warm Florida day…

With the morning mist dissipating, the glistening Florida sun created a steamy vapor around the general aviation terminal of the North Jacksonville airport.

Major Harlan Albert Jaynes turned proudly and looked out the window at the spindly teenager leaning against the fuselage of the small single-engine airplane. Her long ponytail, loosely tied with a rubber band, swayed in the breeze as she devoured a ripe Bartlett pear. She stared at the far end of the long runway, mesmerized by the gigantic airliners lifting off while bright pink flamingos were gracefully free-flying high above the salt marshes of the nearby coastal lagoons.

The smiling officer turned back to the reservation attendant. "Well, Joe, I think it's time to let Jenny go up alone."

"You mean you're going to solo her this morning, Major?" the reservation attendant asked, surprised, looking up from behind the counter. "It's a frickin' beehive up there."

"It doesn't matter," the proud father answered, shrugging. "She's ready. Hell, right now it's a single-engine prop, but soon it'll be a jet. I can't hold her back."

"How old is she, Major?"

"Fifteen."

"Does she know you're going to solo her this morning?"

"Nope. But she knows she's ready," he answered, watching Jenny as she methodically checked the fuel level in the wing tanks. "See ya later," he added with a chuckle. "I'd better get out there before she takes off on her own anyway."

"Okay, good luck," Joe said, watching the major walk through the door to join his daughter who was standing by the wing of the sleek Piper Tomahawk.

When Jenny saw her stout, graying father approaching, her eyes filled with anticipation.

"Hi, daddy. I've completed my pre-flight check. Do you want me to go over it with you?" she asked impatiently.

"Nah, I know you did a good job," he answered, looking into her eyes. "How do you feel today, Jenny?"

"Great, daddy. I'm ready for our lesson."

"Good," he said crisply. "Go ahead, get in."

Jenny excitedly climbed onto the wing and squeezed through the cabin door, strapping herself into the left seat. She immediately began checking the various control knobs and tuned the radio frequency to the airport's ground control. She then turned to her father who was kneeling on the wing observing her. She expected him to crawl into the right seat.

Instead, he reached in and lifted the microphone from the cradle and switched it from ground to the tower frequency.

Knowing something far different was happening today, she watched closely, saying, "Daddy, we have to get ground clearance to the runway before we talk to the tower. Are you testing me?" Her eyes gaped at him while he ignored her and clicked the microphone on.

"Good morning, Jacksonville tower," he spoke in a clipped tone. "This is instructor Harlan Jaynes, aircraft ID-NC1877, at general aviation terminal two."

After what seemed like a small eternity to Jenny, the radio finally answered, breaking the tense silence in the small cockpit, "1877, good morning, Major. Sorry for the delay, it's busy up here. What can I do for you?"

"I'm soloing my student this morning," he answered, still avoiding any eye contact with the silent wide-eyed teenager. "I'll be monitoring the flight on the unicom frequency, over."

"Roger, 1877. Any special instructions?"

"Yes. Three landings. Two touch-and-go. Anything else requires my okay."

"Affirmative, 1877. Have your student proceed."

"1877, over." Hanging up the microphone, he paused and looked at Jenny.

She wanted to reach over and hug him and tell him what he meant to her. But she knew it was now more important to listen to him carefully.

"Jenny, you know the rules. Follow the tower's instructions. If you need to talk to me, request permission before changing to unicom frequency." He moved within inches of her. "But sweetheart, remember," he said softly, "In an emergency forget everything and everybody. Just fly the airplane to safety." He reached over and squeezed her hand. "Good luck, honey. See you in a little while."

He backed out, closed the cabin door and shinnied down off the wing, assured of his decision.

She reached over and pulled the cabin door shut, smiling at her father now standing on the ground well away from the plane. He waved.

She tightened the seat belt, started the engine, and radioed ground control for taxi permission to the runway. Receiving clearance, she taxied to the pre-takeoff area and positively executed the engine safety test. Fidgety but ready, she approached the runway threshold and tuned in the tower requesting takeoff instructions. Waiting to be acknowledged, she fully realized that in a few minutes she would be alone up there. No one to bring her down ... *but herself.*

Her thoughts were interrupted as the radio abruptly answered, "1877, enter onto runway twenty-three left and prepare. When cleared, take off and remain in the pattern for three landings. The first two, stop-and-go. Announce your pattern intentions as you proceed."

Acknowledging the instructions, she pulled out onto the runway. She nervously peered down the long cement track to the clump of miniature-looking trees at the far end. The ones her father had taught her to use as a target when practicing landings. *Why should anything be different today?* she asked herself as the radio crisply announced her clearance for takeoff.

She smoothly applied full power as the plane slowly picked up speed and bounded down the runway. Pulling the control wheel back, she eased the plane off the ground to begin its upward soar. Her tenseness was quickly replaced by joy as she flawlessly guided the plane straight out and up.

When she reached the proper elevation she manipulated the turns of the runway pattern and brought the plane in for a perfect landing. With the plane in a controlled roll, she jammed it into full throttle, taking off again and completing the first touch-and-go without incident.

She carefully repeated the procedure for a second time, feeling completely at ease, caught up in the excitement of flight and wanting to just keep going.

Major Jaynes, sitting on the roof of the terminal, gripped the microphone proudly. He was thrilled as he watched his daughter masterfully handle the airplane.

The young pilot picked up her microphone as she entered the downwind leg of the pattern for her third and final landing. "Tower, 1877," she said clearly, "request to tune into unicom frequency to speak to my instructor. Please monitor the discussion."

"1877, request approved," the tower answered. "Please be brief."

She promptly tuned to the unicom frequency. "Aviation terminal two, instructor Major Jaynes, 1877," she addressed confidently.

"1877, instructor Major Jaynes, over," her father replied, somewhat surprised.

"Instructor Jaynes, 1877, request permission to leave the runway pattern to practice extended turns and engine stalls over the ocean."

Her father thought quickly, but never really doubted the decision.

"Honey…err…1877, request approved. Avoid main traffic and stay away from other airports. Be back in one hour. Announce your intentions to the tower and with their permission exit the pattern then…" he paused. "Just fly the airplane …Miss Jennifer Lee Jaynes, fly the airplane!"

He watched happily as the small plane dipped its wings before darting from the runway pattern to head for the ocean.

Turning away from the window, Jennifer again focused on today's plans. She loosened the large robe from around her shoulders and sat down in front of the vanity-mirror. Slowly she brushed and teased the long, flowing black locks that framed the almost perfect features of her stunning face. She chose a full flip style with thin ringlet strands and a top bun. After blotting on beige foundation, she accented her eyelids with a light coat of sea-green eye shadow to complement her oval, emerald-green eyes. Suddenly conscious of her excessive preparation, she paused, feeling uneasy, but again told herself it had nothing to do with her afternoon appointment with Fletcher McKeane. Continuing, she highlighted her eyelashes and meticulously added lip liner after gloss. The final touch was rose-pink lipstick. Satisfied, she got up and stepped to the free-standing full-length mirror.

Shedding the robe, she examined her slender body, pleased that it was still shapely; but smiled at knowing she now had to work for it. She reached into the dresser drawer, selected her bra and slipped it on before pulling blue nylons over her long slim legs and buttocks.

She removed a white cotton blouse from the hanger as she walked over to the big Victorian rocking chair to retrieve a dark blue suit hanging on the back rail. Then she hesitated and sat down. She was disturbed, remembering last night and how she'd had an extremely difficult time pleasing Donald during their lovemaking. She had struggled with distracting thoughts about Fletcher. And when Donald finally left this morning for his long business trip back to Atlanta, she was relieved. She needed the time to help her sort through things, especially the weekend when she could be entirely alone. She hadn't deceived Donald. She did feel that she loved him and undoubtedly would have come to California with him, regardless of what had happened on that horrible spring day in Pensacola last year when her parents died.

So then, what was this unusual attraction for Fletcher and why was it still unsettling her, she wondered. No, she told herself again, it wasn't his good looks. She'd always lived and worked around handsome men. She was used to dealing with the ordinary male-to-female attraction. No, it didn't really seem romantic. She almost wished it did so the explanation for it would be simpler.

She abruptly sat back in astonishment, suddenly realizing that she hardly knew Fletcher but already felt some inexplicable bond with him. It was also apparent that since meeting him she'd been confused about something different in her character that she didn't understand. Something that she didn't feel comfortable with. It was almost like a mystical seventh sense that she had no control over, drawing her into an abnormal state of distraction.

As she stood to finish dressing, she decided that until she understood where this mysterious gravitation toward Fletcher was coming from, she'd avoid him. She would even find a replacement FAA representative to test him today.

Lainey opened her eyes to a noisy flock of sea gulls flying overhead, and the loud buzzing of the alarm going off in her ear. Surprised that two hours had passed by so quickly, she sprang up, slipped on her sandals while grabbing her towel, and hurried home. Eager to get on with the day, she would start with the hairdresser and manicurist then pick up her new dress.

As always, the time at the beach had rested her. She was beginning to feel energetic again. When she got home she found a short message from Fletcher, letting her know he was off for his flight test and would see her at the lounge later that evening. Excited over hearing from him, she immediately called him back but was disappointed when he wasn't home. And, as usual, she was irritated because he still hadn't fixed his broken answering machine.

Maybe she could help him replace it tomorrow when they had the weekend to themselves, she thought as she walked to the bathroom.

Showered and dressed, Lainey, with her usual effervescence restored, cheerfully bustled from her apartment into the noontime sunshine to move forward with the rest of her life.

CHAPTER 12

Friday Afternoon, Shelanary Aviation

It was pleasantly cool and bustling inside Shelanary Aviation as Fletcher, somewhat uptight, pushed open the glass doors. He knew he was ready for his test but still realized the flying was going to be trying. Even at an altitude of five thousand feet, the muggy heat would prove uncomfortable in a plane with no air conditioning. He'd also noticed there weren't any clouds; therefore, no shadows to duck into to escape the intense windshield glare of the early afternoon sun.

Walking toward the FAA office, he was anxious at the thought of meeting with Jennifer Jaynes again. Although he was pleased to be tested by someone of her caliber, there was something about her familiarity that bothered him. He couldn't pinpoint what it was.

Approaching her office, he saw her sitting behind the desk. "Hello again, Ms. Jaynes," he said confidently, "I believe we have an appointment today."

Jennifer looked up from her paperwork and managed a smile. "Oh, yes, Mr. McKeane, please come in."

While she reached into her top drawer for his approval papers, Fletcher entered and sat down, eyeing her wall full of FAA licenses and various aircraft rating documents. He thought of what Chapman had told him about her qualifications.

She looked over, saying, "I reviewed your approval papers that Bob Chapman left with me. Everything seems to be in order. Steve Butler will be here shortly to test you."

"Oh, I thought you'd be testing me," he replied, surprised.

"Yes, I was planning on it, but unfortunately I'm coming down with something," she lied carefully, not wanting to reveal how nervous she felt this close to him. "Probably just a summer cold but I shouldn't fly. That wouldn't be fair to either of us." She smiled, deciding to quickly change the subject. "So tell me, are you ready to earn your license?"

"Sure as hell am. I worked for it. I'm eager to fly into the jungles."

"Jungles?"

"Yeah, I do wildlife photography. Mostly in the jungles."

"Really," she replied, pretending not to know. "Do you hunt the wildlife too?"

"No, not much anymore unless they're threatening or carrying a bounty."

She looked down at his paperwork, replying, "Interesting."

Fletcher began to feel awkward as he caught himself staring at her while she filled out the initial paperwork. *She's so beautiful and classy*. His thoughts were interrupted by a man walking into her office.

Jennifer looked up and quickly rose, extending her hand. "Steve, thanks for coming down on such short notice."

Butler shrugged. "No problem, Jennifer. I had a light day planned anyway."

"How was the traffic?"

"Miserable as always," he replied dryly. "Hell'uva accident on the freeway."

She grimaced with understanding and turned toward Fletcher. "Steve, this is Fletcher McKeane, the man I'd like you to test."

Butler shifted his eyes squarely to Fletcher as they shook hands. "Nice to meet ya McKeane, you ready?"

"As ready as I'll ever be," Fletcher answered, smiling with confidence.

"Okay, then let's go. We'll start with some chart and radio frequency questions, then move on to some FAA regulations. If you get past that we'll fly."

Fletcher nodded in agreement but inside he was disappointed that he wouldn't be testing with Ms. Jaynes. He was even more disappointed that he wouldn't have a chance to know her better. Maybe she'd come to the MoonGlade for his celebration party tonight and let him find out more about her.

Jennifer wished Fletcher the best of luck as the two men turned and left the office. Sitting down, she thought over the way she dodged testing Fletcher. It had worked. She told herself he certainly wouldn't have any reason to approach her again. Everything from here on out could be handled by Butler.

Jennifer was still in her office when she heard the minor commotion outside. Looking out she saw a jubilant Fletcher having his picture taken by Jan, one of the young receptionists. Watching Fletcher boisterously embrace her in a major bear hug caused Jennifer a quick pang over being left out. But she quickly dismissed her feelings and remembered how excited she had been on the day she turned sixteen and earned her first pilot's license. Smiling, she recalled her achievements since then, right up to her airline pilot rating at twenty-five, followed by being selected a FAA Operations Inspector at thirty. Yes, she fully understood the thrill of earning the right to pilot a plane. She remained silent, gazing out at the sky.

Her meditation was soon shattered by Fletcher as he burst into her office. "I did it!" he exclaimed. "Butler says I'm now a licensed pilot. I fu…err, I mean messed up the short-field landing but I completed it."

Jennifer couldn't help laughing as she watched Fletcher ramble, wiping a heavy sweat from his brow with his shirt sleeve.

"Congratulations, Mr. McKeane. I'm sure you'll be a safe pilot," she answered, hiding her mixed feelings over how he had barged into her office. "Did you get some pictures? Your friends will want to see them."

"Yeah, Jan took 'em for me."

Unable to resist a further question, she smiled, saying, "And I'm sure you have a special lady. Did you get a few good ones for her?"

"Yes, I got some good ones for Lainey…" Fletcher hesitated.

Jennifer sensing his regret as he spoke her name, grew more curious. "Lainey. What a lovely name," she said, pretending she hadn't heard it before. "I'll bet she's beautiful."

"Yes, she's pretty, but..." he answered in a whisper, lowering his eyes.

"But what?"

"I'm moving to San Diego and I'm not sure what'll happen after that," Fletcher replied, surprising himself by being so open about something so personal.

"Oh, I see. I'm sorry, I didn't mean to pry."

"It's okay. Nothing's definite yet anyway," Fletcher answered quietly, letting the subject slip away. He then brightened thinking about the celebration party. "Hey!" he blurted. "Why don't you come to the MoonGlade Lounge tonight and celebrate with us? It's close by in Newport Beach. I'm sure Bob Chapman will be there too."

Jennifer was momentarily mesmerized by the little-boy excitement that filled Fletcher's strong face. *Nothing like a pilot's license to bring out the best in someone,* she thought.

"Thank you, Mr. McKeane, but I don't think I can. I mentioned earlier I wasn't feeling well." She began shuffling some papers, appearing indifferent, adding, "Although Bob has mentioned that they probably serve the best food in the area."

Fletcher sensed her growing interest and continued, "Yeah, they do. But getting in there is almost impossible without a personal invitation. I'm a good friend of Frank Conklin, the owner. I have a reserved table anytime I need it. Well, how about it?" he urged. "Stop in and mention my name and you'll get right in. Oh, please call me Fletcher, will you?"

A red light went off in Jennifer's head. *Slow down,* she thought, remembering the pact she'd made with herself to avoid him.

"By the way," he continued, without thinking, "I'd really like to know how someone as young and pretty as you made it into such an influential position so early in life? You must've known someone. I mean…umm."

Jennifer looked up and shot him a furious stare, as he quickly realized his last remark had been a big mistake.

"Mr. McKeane, my professional credentials are on the wall!" she hissed through clenched jaws, pointing a quivering index finger. "I think they clearly prove my aviation accomplishments! Now! If you're implying that …"

He raised his hands, halting her, saying, "Wait, wait, I apologize. Really, I mean it. I don't know why I said what I did. I'm really very aware of your capabilities." Embarrassed, he sheepishly began backing out the doorway.

Realizing that he hadn't meant to offend her, she relaxed her glare, replying, "Look, I'm busy, now and tonight."

"I understand, and I am truly sorry," Fletcher said, feeling extremely deflated as he turned to leave.

"Bye, Fletcher, and again, congratulations," she pardoned, no longer angry.

He turned back to her somewhat relieved, saying, "Thanks, I appreciate that."

She smiled and looked down at her paperwork as he left her office and headed for the front doors.

Bob Chapman saw him leaving and caught up with him in the terminal foyer, exclaiming, "Fletcher! Congratulations! Heard you made it!" They shook hands vigorously. "I'm really pleased for you."

"Thanks. It all went pretty smoothly. Hotter than hell up there, though," Fletcher answered soberly, still humbled from Jennifer's tirade. "The only letdown was that Jennifer Jaynes got some examiner from LAX to administer my test." He wrinkled his face. "I wanted to get to know her a little better."

Chapman shook his head. "Fletcher, if you're interested in her personally, forget it. She has it all; looks, class, brains and, as I understand it, she's in love with some guy named Don that she came with from the East Coast. Anyway, I'm sure she's not interested in you, except professionally. Besides, you've got Lainey. What more could you ask for, or want, for Christ sake? If you're not careful you're going to fuck it up good with her."

"Hey, wait a minute," Fletcher replied, raising his hands. "I'm not sure why I want to know Jaynes better. I just do." He hesitated. "But you're right, Bob," he said, muttering to himself, "I'm just so damned confused right now."

"Okay," Chapman said. "It's just that I like both you and Lainey. I don't want to see anything happen to your relationship. I know how sorry you'd be."

Fletcher looked up and again shook Bob's hand, saying, "Thanks, I appreciate your concern. So will I see you at the MoonGlade tonight? I guess we've some celebrating to do, don't we? You especially, for getting me through all this flying shit." Fletcher grinned widely.

"You bet, Fletcher, I'll be there, but not until later. I have to pick up Joyce and then we're having dinner with some of her friends. I'll see ya after that," Chapman confirmed as he headed for his office.

"Sounds good," Fletcher yelled after him.

Fletcher pushed through the main doors and walked to his jeep. As he climbed in he thought about what Chapman had said, *What more did he want than Lainey?* He started the ignition. *And would he fuck up their relationship with her?* He quickly drove out of the parking lot, confused as usual, especially lately.

The late afternoon sun was still brilliant as the administration employees at Shelanary began to wind down their day's activities. Jennifer sat in her office fidgeting with Fletcher's license paperwork that had been dropped off by Butler for her to finalize and mail off to the FAA bureau in Washington. She thought about today's encounter with Fletcher and how she had learned a little more about him. Yet she still didn't understand what was happening. However, she had learned enough to know that her relationship with him was not over, regardless of how hard she'd wanted to end it. More importantly, she now believed it probably wasn't her choice, or his.

CHAPTER 13

The Celebration, MoonGlade Lounge

The MoonGlade Lounge was jumping. It was prime dinner hour on Friday night and many of the crowd had begun arriving in mid-afternoon. MoonGlade's customers habitually began the weekend early. Most of the clientele would moor their yachts in the Newport Beach Harbor, party all weekend on the boat, but come into the lounge for dinner.

The premises were jammed, except for the beachfront patio where the air was still muggy and a bit uncomfortable for sitting. With air conditioning inside, the dining room and bar were overflowing and buzzing with excitement.

In the late forties Jimmy Conklin had converted the small and rotting eight-bedroom motel into a dinner lounge. He had been persuaded to come west to Newport Beach by a few Hollywood celebrities who had a particular liking for his discreet manner and talents as a restaurateur. He had proved himself worthy in New York City during prohibition.

As the lounge grew in popularity, one had to know an "insider" to squeeze in a reservation. Once inside, celebrities and friends mostly kept to themselves. The penalty for invading someone else's privacy was swift ejection, though this rarely happened.

After Jimmy's death, Frank Conklin, Jimmy's son and only known living relative, assumed ownership. He had managed the lounge for about ten years.

The parking lot was only big enough for thirty cars and it was never full. Most of the guests arrived by limousine or cab. Old George Lazereth, a bit actor from the sixties, did the parking. Hard-bitten, tall and thin, he had aged early from too much whiskey and his failure to make it big in Hollywood.

In 1970 Jimmy let George have a small corner of the back lot in return for light maintenance work. Frank let him stay on, even though he couldn't depend on him to do much other than stay clean shaven and park cars. George's tips kept him supplied with drink.

There was one entrance from the parking lot, a thick walnut door that opened off a raised wooden porch. Past the door, a fifteen-foot foyer led to a hand-carved redwood maitre d' stand. It was old by Hollywood standards, almost fifty years, and had been donated by an RKO movie studio executive. Photographs of visiting celebrities posing with Jimmy, along with a stunning layout of the lounge's interior that Fletcher had created a few years back, adorned the foyer wall.

The inside air was usually fresh from the ocean breeze and the strict no-smoking policy. If you were determined to smoke, you went to the ventilated smoking-room by the front door. It was a quick addition that Frank had built after Jimmy died. Jimmy had detested smoking because he felt it spoiled the aroma of his fine cuisine.

The main dining room could seat sixty people comfortably at fifteen tables, seventy-five with the bar. The patio held thirty-five to fifty.

The decor was rustic and filled with art that had been donated over the years by appreciative clientele. Each of the black cherry Biedermeier tables was draped with a spotless floor-length challis tablecloth. The mahogany Windsor-style chairs at each table had been the gift of a German composer. The musician had visited the lounge in 1975 and offered the chairs in return for a standing reservation.

George's chief maintenance duty was to keep a sharp eye on the condition of the tables and chairs. He was always shuffling one set in or out of his trailer for refinishing.

The music was most often harmonic blues and jazz; the melodies that had been the signature of films from the forties and fifties. There weren't many young people who visited the lounge so there was little call for a live band. By special request Frank would bring in an improvisational jazz band for private parties, or on holidays.

The beachfront patio was set between two gigantic cliff rocks. Entry was from the dining room only. Shrouded by foliage, benches were strategically placed for ocean viewing and romance. Each bench had an electric button to buzz the bar if a cocktail or appetizer was desired.

The menu, featuring some of the best seafood and beef entrees on the coast was created by Jimmy in 1950 and hadn't changed much since then. And Frank worked persistently to make sure that MoonGlade remained one of the most intriguing restaurant-lounges in Southern California.

Fletcher had arrived about half-past four with mixed emotions. Although excited about his license and his move south, he was dispirited and uncomfortable about the upcoming conversation with Lainey. They both knew he would have to tell her of his decision.

He had received a note explaining that Lainey would be back by six. She had gone home to freshen up after working at the restaurant most of the afternoon preparing for his celebration party.

He sat at his favorite table, the best one in the restaurant. It had a breathtaking view of the beach and ocean. It was also located directly under an ungainly but fascinating wild boar's head. He had bagged the beast, a warthog, with his Kodiak bow while in Africa about fifteen months ago, just after he'd met Lainey. He was proud of his archery talents and the mounted beast reminded him of it. But tonight it offered no consolation.

Nursing a Scotch and soda, he graciously accepted congratulations as people sporadically approached him after hearing the good news about his license. He was happy for the attention, but mostly preoccupied with thoughts about tonight's meeting with Lainey.

He was idly chatting with Frank when Lainey arrived. When the two men saw her they froze in awe. She looked exquisite in her baby-blue summer gown. It was trimmed at the bodice and supported by spaghetti straps. The dress fell to just below her knees, showing off her smooth and bare sun-tanned legs. Her hair was teased into a bouffant with kiss curl bangs that covered her entire forehead. Her makeup was applied perfectly and accented her large brown eyes, that began to sparkle the moment she spotted Fletcher.

She and Fletcher embraced in the middle of the dining room. As they walked back to his table, Lainey gave him her congratulations and Fletcher admired her from head to foot.

"Lainey, I don't think I've ever seen you look so beautiful. That's a new dress, isn't it?"

"Yes," she answered cheerfully. "It's not exactly your standard hostess attire, but since the special occasion is you, Frank let me choose what I wanted to wear. He's also filling in for me at the stand."

"That's good of him," Fletcher said. "Hey, let's order dinner."

"Sure. Sounds wonderful, love," Lainey answered.

They toasted each other with a glass of California Brut champagne before enjoying their special Bouillabaisse dinner for two with a bottle of French Bergerac wine. All through dinner she let him talk about his flight test, admiring his enthusiasm for life. But not once did he mention any plans that included her. He was obviously ignoring that part of the conversation. So inside she knew, sadly, what the outcome of the night was going to be.

After the table was cleared Lainey, her eyes downcast, began fidgeting with her napkin. Fletcher, seeing her discomfort, silently braced himself. He knew the time had come to tell her of his solitary plans.

She looked up at him and swallowed hard. "Congratulations, Fletcher," she began. "I know how badly you wanted this. You should feel proud of your achievement. Now you can fly in South America…by yourself."

"Lainey," he whispered, drawing blanks instead of his wordy plea that he had prepared. "Lainey…I…I just…"

"Fletcher, I understand." Tears began to roll down her strained face.

"I need time," he said in a frustrated tone, looking away. "I don't want us to break up. I'll be close in San Diego. I'm asking you to please understand. Please, I love you. I just need some more time."

"Yeah," she said faintly as she got up to leave.

"Lainey, where you going? Please don't go. Let's talk some more," Fletcher appealed, standing with her.

"No," she answered firmly, staring at him. "I think we're through talking. Don't follow me. Just remember the things we held close…God damn you! All I ask is that you don't share them with anyone else. God damn you! God damn you!"

Blinded by tears, Lainey turned and rushed to the kitchen. Fletcher started to follow her, but stopped and sat back down. His mood turned dark and he was about to leave when Bob Chapman approached the table and sat down.

"Jesus, Fletcher, what is it?" Chapman asked. "It's Lainey, isn't it. I saw her on the way in. She's really down. What the hell happened?"

Despondent, Fletcher finally looked up, replying, "She knows I'm going to San Diego without her."

"Oh, shit! You thinking of other women?" Chapman asked slowly. "Like maybe Jennifer Jaynes?"

"What?" Fletcher snapped, his eyes narrowing. "Jaynes nor anyone else has anything to do with this! Drop that whole fucking thing, will you?"

"Okay, sorry, I know you're just confused right now," Chapman apologized, believing Fletcher. "Look, Lainey could have any man, but she wants you. And I know you love her."

"I know we're in love," Fletcher said, grimacing. "It's just that all my life I've seemed to lose what's truly important to me. I just can't take her with me right now." He lowered his head and rubbed his temples. "Shit, I don't know. Sometimes I think I'm going crazy; like something beyond my control is destroying me…"

"Maybe, but I know you well," Chapman challenged. "You won't be any good without her either, and you know it. Now rethink your decision for crissake, before both of you are really destroyed."

Fletcher looked up at Chapman, digesting his statement when he noticed Lainey slowly walking to the bar. She ordered a drink then headed back toward the kitchen. She wouldn't even look Fletcher's way.

Fletcher, growing more confused, pushed his drink aside and abruptly stood up. "Bob," he said, "you're probably right, but I just don't know right now. I'll see ya later." He bolted for the door.

As Lainey watched him leave from the kitchen, she braced herself against the doorway while sipping a rum and coke, her eyes still rimmed with tears. "Good bye, Fletcher James McKeane," she whispered, "I'll never forget you."

Fletcher bounded off the lounge porch and hurried to George who stood at the edge of the parking lot, looking out at the ocean. "George, my keys please."

George turned, startled. "Fletcher, you leavin' already?"

"Yeah," Fletcher answered quietly, repeating, "key's please. I'll get my own car."

"Sure, Fletcher, sure." George lumbered to the valet shanty and reached in, picking Fletcher's keys off the key-rack. "Here ya go. See ya soon, huh?"

"Right," Fletcher answered quickly, taking the keys from George as he handed him his tip.

Fletcher walked to his jeep, opened the door then hesitated as he thought again about what Chapman had said about he and Lainey being destroyed if they parted ways. He turned, shut the door and headed back for the lounge. Then he stopped, deciding Lainey was too upset to discuss the situation further. It might ruin any chance of a reunion. He'd think about it and call her later, after things had calmed down. He returned to his jeep.

As he left the lot he felt more alone than ever before. He missed Lainey already. Driving further away from the lounge, he began to realize that he had probably made a major mistake. He decided he would stop for a drink on the way home to make a final decision, though he already knew what it would be.

Jennifer was apprehensive as she read the sign, a vintage of the 50s, lit up in soft salmon-red over the wooden entranceway.

MoonGlade Lounge

Pulling her car into the lot, she gave in to her compelling desire to learn more about McKeane. She needed to better understand her unusual attraction to him. With Donald away she had the time. She stopped her car next to the small shanty, noticing the old man lower his flask and hobble off the backless stool.

George approached the car window and, not recognizing Jennifer, politely explained to her it was a private party. After she made it clear she had been invited, George apologetically told her that Fletcher had left only minutes before, but that she could go in anyway. Now more curious than ever she got out of the car, handing her keys to George.

Stepping upon the porch, she pulled on the large door handle and entered the foyer, pausing to look over the various photos hanging on the wall. She then turned and was instantly struck by the extraordinary beauty of the woman at the maitre d' stand watching her enter. Jennifer saw the name *Lainey* on the ornamental plaque hanging on the stand and immediately tied the name to the conversation she'd had with Fletcher earlier that day.

Jennifer approached the stand carefully, realizing that something was very wrong. She saw the drying tears staining Lainey's delicate face. She hesitated, sorting out her feelings for Lainey. Jennifer was astonished at the immediate empathy she felt toward her. It was almost like the familiarity she felt toward Fletcher, but not as strong. Looking at Lainey, she asked for the McKeane party.

Jennifer cringed inside when Lainey's eyes watered slightly and closed.

"He's not here but go in if you want," Lainey said in a soft voice.

"Oh, he's gone?" Jennifer asked, acting surprised that Fletcher wasn't there. She was determined to find out what was going on.

Lainey looked up at Jennifer strangely. "Have we met before?"

"No, I don't think so. I'm Jennifer Jaynes from the Federal Aviation Administration. Fletcher and I became friends during his flight training. You must be Lainey."

Lainey nodded and wiped her eyes.

Fletcher and her must have already had their talk, Jennifer thought. She hurt for Lainey and wanted her to know. "Lainey, it's none of my business, but Fletcher has talked about you. I have a feeling I know why you're sad. Give him time, he's only being a man," Jennifer said gently.

Lainey managed a smile as she looked deeply into Jennifer's eyes, feeling a strong need to confide in her. "Thank you, Ms. Jaynes."

Jennifer sensed the same immediate bond and held out her hand to Lainey. *I know more than you know*, Jennifer thought.

Lainey shook her hand, saying, "Nice to meet you, Ms. Jaynes."

"Oh, please, make that Jennifer," she said, pulling a business card from her purse. She handed it to Lainey. "And please call me if you ever want to talk."

Although Lainey smiled, Jennifer's words couldn't soothe the hurt. She nodded slowly, then abruptly turned and ran to the kitchen, struggling to contain her sobs. The breakup with Fletcher was still too much for her to hold inside.

Jennifer sadly watched her leave and entered the dining room looking for Bob Chapman.

He was sitting at the bar and jumped up dumbfounded when he saw her coming. "Jennifer!

What a surprise," he stammered. "Fletcher is gone. Did you come here to see him? Of course you did, but..."

Jennifer interrupted him, saying, "Bob, please slow down." She smiled, sitting down at the bar. He sat back down next to her, perplexed and silent.

Jennifer rubbed her forehead as she began to feel trapped by the whole situation. Although she was beginning to sense what was going on, she wasn't sure why.

"I don't know why I came," she said, breaking the silence. "I don't even have an answer for myself." She blinked as she noticed her reflection in the unusually short bar mirror. She maneuvered to gaze at herself, noting her own confused expression.

Bob looked at her, replying, "Well, I don't really understand what you mean, Jennifer. But you wanna talk about it over a drink?"

She hesitated a moment before shaking her head. "No thanks, I have a long drive ahead of me." But she wasn't finished yet. "Bob, how long have you known Fletcher?" she asked, still sizing up the stunted mirror.

Chapman shrugged. "Oh, I dunno, two or three years I guess. Frank Conklin introduced me to Fletcher after Frank had hired him to do a freelance photo layout of the MoonGlade for some Orange County magazine."

Jennifer remembered the photos on the foyer wall when she had arrived. She then recalled Fletcher's mention of Frank's name at the terminal. "Oh, yes, Fletcher talked about him today. He told me they were good friends."

Chapman nodded. "Right, we all are. Why?"

"Just wondering, Bob," she said, rising quickly. "I have to go. I'll see you next week. Have a good weekend." She turned and hurried for the foyer leaving Bob sitting there stunned.

As she approached the maitre d' stand, Jennifer saw the slightly graying, chisel-featured man standing there appearing professional. *Right out of central casting,* she thought, deciding to question him. But the closer she got, the more she felt a mysterious lure, like an insect approaching a spider web.

She suddenly felt chilled, but shrugged it off as she came up to him. "Excuse me, do you know where Lainey is?" Jennifer asked.

"She just left," he answered slowly, looking solemn. "I saw you talking with her earlier. Are you here for Fletcher's celebration?"

"Yes," she answered, barely acknowledging him, wanting to leave.

"So, you must know them both."

"Yes," she confirmed impatiently, turning toward the door. "Do you know where she went?"

"No, not exactly," he answered coolly, shrugging. "She grabbed a bottle of rum and ran out in tears. I tried to stop her in the parking lot, but she just mumbled something about a moon-glade. She then jumped into her car and drove off toward Laguna Beach. I understand she and Fletcher broke up tonight. I suppose he just can't be tied down."

Abruptly frustrated by his coldness, her lips pursed as she turned back toward him. "Dammit!" she snapped. "I just asked where she was, that's all."

"Okay, lady," he replied defensively. "I'm sorry, I don't know exactly. Like I said, she headed for Laguna."

"Thanks," Jennifer answered curtly, turning for the door.

"Maybe she'll be back. Would you like to wait?" he asked politely.

"No, I don't think so," she declined, walking through the foyer.

"By the way, I'm Frank Conklin. You're welcome anytime," he called loudly.

Without turning around she nodded and kept walking, picking up her pace.

Driving the freeway to Los Angeles, Jennifer was growing alarmed over what had happened. Why were these people affecting her the way they were? First it was Fletcher, then Lainey. And now Frank Conklin!

Slowly her keen intuition and heightened sixth sense began telling her what she had suspected. But the question that bothered her the most was, *why*? Where was it all coming from? She hardly noticed the long drive home as she tried to piece together the strange events that had suddenly changed her life.

Frank bid George good night and locked the front door behind him. As he walked toward the dining room to turn out the lights he heard the phone ring. Approaching the maitre d' stand, he picked up the receiver. "MoonGlade Lounge, Frank Conklin... Fletcher! Where are you? It's late," Frank said, looking at his watch. "Where? Oh, at home? What...No, Lainey's not here. She took off outta here earlier, very upset." ...Frank hesitated before slowly answering Fletcher's next question. "Ah...no, I have no idea where she headed. I never saw her leave. Have you tried her at home?...You did, well, I'm sure she's all right wherever she is. What's up, anyway?...Oh, I see. I knew you'd come to your senses and change your mind." Frank paused a moment. "Fletcher, get some sleep. Don't worry, I'm sure she'll be waiting for your call tomorrow ...good, see ya."

Frank hung up the phone and leaned against the wall, his eyes narrowing as he pondered their conversation.

Lainey set the bottle of rum down on the wooden planks and leaned against a lamppost, shifting to remove her shoes. Barefoot, carrying her shoes and the bottle, she stepped off the walkway and gingerly walked through the gravelly sand, making her way toward the moonlit edge of the towering sea cliff.

Noticing the bluff area was deserted, a slight shudder went up her spine. She quickly shrugged it off, glancing back over her shoulder at the patio of the Mexican restaurant, located at the far end of the walkway. Though the last of the patrons were leaving, she felt safe, knowing that the waiters would be there cleaning up before closing down for the night. Turning back, she carefully approached the edge of the steep cliff face. Testing her footing, she moved closer to the rim and peered out to sea.

Far below, the boiling surf was unforgiving, smashing violently against a rocky shoreline peppered with sharp serrated outcroppings that edged a thin thread of beach.

Lainey stood transfixed, staring toward the horizon where a wide swath of shimmering silver split the dark ocean down the middle. The immense pathway of moonlight began just beyond the whitecaps, and continued narrowing until it seemed to meet the bottom of the brimming moon. Tears fell from her eyes as she remembered the many nights Fletcher and she had come up here to catch a moon-glade. *Would he know and come here tonight,* she wondered and hoped.

Sighing, she turned and walked away from the rugged edge. Reaching her favorite boulder, she set her shoes down and began fidgeting with the cap of the rum bottle. Her hands began to shake. As a devastating ache of hopelessness enveloped her, she let the bottle drop to the sand.

Leaning against the craggy boulder, she burst into tears, pleading inwardly, *Oh, please, Fletcher. Come and get me...don't do this to me...please don't.*

Taking deep breaths, she quickly regained control, knowing that carrying on this way was useless. He didn't care anymore and was probably home packing for San Diego. It was over with Fletcher. Pulling one of the lounge napkins from her pocket to wipe her tears, she looked at it and realized that she could never go back there to work. She needed to think about her immediate future. She dried her eyes, pulled her hair back with a barrette and hiked her dress up past her knees. Clumsily, she climbed to the top of the boulder and sat, her legs dangling, gazing at the moon-glade. She tried to clear her head and forget the terrible misery she felt over Fletcher.

She couldn't return to Utah. That was impossible. Maybe she'd go to Chicago to see what opportunities were available there. Yes, Chicago, she decided, a small smile spreading at the thought of beginning a new life. She'd call her mother in the morning and...

Her thoughts were interrupted by an abrupt icy chill. Wishing that she'd brought a sweater, she folded her arms across her chest to ward off the cold. She looked around, unable to understand where the chill was coming from. Only a moment before it had been so warm. Noticing a strong foul odor, she looked to the ocean. The breeze must be picking up the stench of dead fish from the shoreline below. Glancing up at the branches of a giant palm tree, she was alarmed to see they hung limply. *There is no breeze!* she thought.

Beginning to feel uneasy, she sensed that something strange was happening. She anxiously looked back toward the Mexican restaurant, noticing that most of the patio lights were now dimmed. Only the bright insect-burning lamps were still on.

She was slightly relieved when she saw a waiter sweeping off the patio but decided she should leave before he too was gone and she was left all alone.

Scrambling down off the boulder, she was startled by a distant shriek growing in the air. Emergency sirens she told herself, though puzzled because the sound had a tone she'd never heard before.

Reaching for her shoes, she decided to get out of there fast. Tense, she balanced herself against the boulder and took time to slip on her shoes, deciding she could trudge through the rocks and sand faster if she wasn't barefoot.

Now oblivious to the putrid smell and chilling air, she still hesitated, trying to figure out the shriek as its shrill pitch increased in volume. About to pick up her purse to run, she froze in her steps when a dark man-like figure slowly emerged from the back shadows of the boulder.

"Who is it?" she asked nervously, squinting into the darkness.

She quickly glanced over at the restaurant patio and knew that the waiter was too far away to help her. She turned back toward the boulder.

"Please, who is it? Fletcher is it you?" she asked again. Her eyes darted nervously, filled with fear. She reached into her purse, pulling out her rosary and praying that it was Fletcher.

"It's me, my love. You do not remember?" the figure murmured softly, as it moved toward her into the faint glint of the moonlight, one hand toying with the sheath of an ivory-handled dagger.

When the head of the gruesome figure became visible, Lainey was consumed with terror. Speechless, she clutched the rosary tightly and began backing up as the figure advanced menacingly.

Dazed, with her escape blocked, she folded her arms across her chest and looked up toward the stars. *No, please. Oh no, God. Someone help,* she mouthed in near-hysteria.

As she stumbled backward, approaching the crumbling cliff edge and a watery grave, the eerie piercing screech drowned out the alarmed cries coming from the patio of the Mexican restaurant at the far end of the walkway.

CHAPTER 14

Saturday, Fletcher's Town House

Leaning heavily against the kitchen counter, Fletcher started in on his second pot of coffee. Aching and feeling disoriented from a lack of sleep, he dreaded the long day of preparing for the movers who were due to arrive early Monday morning.

The stress of yesterday's events, especially the unhappy encounter with Lainey, had taken its toll. But everything would be okay after he talked to her this morning. He looked up at the wall clock: eight-fifteen. Too early yet, he'd call her later. After talking to Frank last night, he knew she must've gotten in late. He'd also call Chapman later and thank him for not allowing him to make the mistake of losing Lainey. Chapman had been right. The only thing Fletcher was running from was fear itself. And if there was any fear about being close to Lainey, he would face it.

But, regardless of his fatigue, he still had to start packing for Monday's move to San Diego. He reluctantly stood up, thinking about where he should begin. He decided to start with the tools of his trade.

Although he didn't have to worry about the photographic equipment that was already packed and shipped to his new office, his weapons were still here.

He walked to the tall red cedar weapon-hutch in the far corner of the living room, taking in the cedar's spicy aroma. It was his constant reminder of the faraway, untamed country. It pleased him that his new job of photographing in the wilds would also allow him to go on adventurous safaris and experience his excellent marksmanship and hunting skills.

Staring into the hutch, he opened the glass doors and reached for his favorite firearm, a special edition Colt Python .357 magnum. The six-inch barrel was finished in royal blue and its ivory handle bore unique paladin etchings. Fletcher was proud to own what was considered the Rolls Royce of Colt revolvers. He had it with him most of the time, as he had a special permit to carry it. When he gripped the handle and cocked the hammer he knew there was no equal. With his accurate aim and the true front sight, his targets—mainly poisonous snakes—rarely escaped. He wrapped the cartridge belt around the holster and set it in a box.

He then lifted out the rifle. A Colt-Sharps single shot, 30-06 magnum, tucked inside an aluminum and brown-leather case. As far as he was concerned it was the last word on sporting rifles. If necessary, it could bring anything down, though he wasn't happy about killing game unless it posed a danger or was authorized by the authorities. The rifle always reminded him of what he had learned in Vietnam. When you aim at an enemy, disregard the heart. Even if you hit the mark, it still allows a few seconds for an enemy to react, maybe even get a return shot off. Instead, one should aim for the smile. A gullet-shot snaps the nervous system, instantly demobilizing the victim. He would collapse, cross-legged dead. Fletcher, unfortunately, had had to prove this fundamental principle many times over there.

He laid the rifle next to the box containing the pistol and lifted out the Remington 870 twelve-gauge shotgun. A semi-automatic that held eight shells in the magazine, it had been tooled to seventeen inches for increased velocity. During the war, the modification also made the gun easier to hang from his uniform fatigue belt.

He couldn't use it much now, except when he was in the wilds, as the barrel size was illegal. However, for one reason alone he would never part with this keepsake. It had come in handy once to eliminate two Viet Cong about to carve up his Cajun partner, Leblanc, who had been tied to a tree. He packed it in its leather case and set it with the others.

He reached up and removed the bow, mounted on the top keystone. Archery was one of his main recreations in life. He felt it was the only real sporting method of hunting. The bow was a sixty-five-pound pull made of yew wood. It possessed enough power to bring a croc dead out of the water. He knew that because he had done it. The Port-Orford cedar arrows with a triple-barbed head were tailor-fit for a quick release from a full pull. It did the job quickly. The prey never suffered long, he thought as he laid the bow in a long cardboard box that would fit in the back seat of his Jeep. He removed the quiver and arm-guard from the hutch's bottom drawer and laid them in the box.

He paused and sat down, leaning against the wall recalling the last time he had used the bow in Africa, right after he had met Lainey. And he remembered how much he had missed her while he was on that trip…

The blazing late-afternoon sun baked the arid soil around the makeshift tent camp, located on the outskirts of Botro, a small town on the grassy plains just east of the dense rain forest of Ivory Coast. The African summer was coming to an end, as was the three-week trip Fletcher and the Cunningham family had been enjoying.

Marsha Cunningham was sunning herself in a hammock, admiring the glistening mountains to the south. Although the beauty of the African wilds excited her, she had not been comfortable in this part of the world and was eager to leave.

Loosening her halter-top, she bared most of her large bosom to the sun before closing her eyes to catch a nap. As she rested, her thoughts turned to Fletcher and their lovemaking of the night before. How he had sneaked into her tent carrying a bunch of African lilies. How corny, she thought, smiling. But then, he always did get his way.

She could never resist his little-boy charm even though she knew all along what he really wanted. She lingered at the memory of how after they'd made love he'd held her so tenderly and of how they had talked for hours. Oh, but how he had slipped, mentioning the new waitress, Lainey, from the MoonGlade Lounge. Marsha quickly realized that's probably where his mind had been for most of the trip.

Regardless, Marsha knew it was useless to think he'd truly ever loved her. With Fletcher a relationship was only a matter of convenience. You went along for the ride, if you wanted. If not, well, that was your choice. He was straightforward about it. He never lied about his intentions or of his desire to be free from the hurts and demands of a commitment. The past losses in his life had proved too devastating. But she enjoyed being with him and knew she even needed him. Unfortunately, she also knew that the ride had been worth the fall she'd be taking very soon.

She turned and balanced her tall, slender body sideways on the hammock. Before dozing off, she wondered where Fletcher and her father might be. She remembered how excited Fletcher had been this morning when they left to go hunting inside the rain forest.

The two men, their hair matted with sweat, swatted at the giant mosquitoes and pesky flies as they floundered down the side of the stony foothill. They finally reached bottom and ambled toward the high scrub grass that surrounded the pond some fifty yards away.

They had decided to leave the heavy-duty jeep at the top, not wanting to risk the noise or tolerate the uncomfortable ride down the steep incline.

Fletcher, with constant thoughts of Lainey flooding his mind, wanted to go home. But he was disappointed by the possibility of leaving Africa without a trophy. Time was running out. They had to be out of the forest and back on the grassy plains well before dark.

When they reached the tall straw-like grass, they knelt and quietly separated it, not wanting to spook any game. Fletcher focused his powerful low-light binoculars on the distant pond and was stunned by what he saw.

"My God, Arthur, look at that! It's a warthog! See the large humps just above the honers?" Fletcher exclaimed in a near-whisper, motioning for Arthur to stay still. "It has to be the one they were talking about back at the village. It's a male, no sow could have honer-tusks that big."

Arthur Cunningham squinted through his compact field glasses. "He's as big as a cow," he replied quietly, paralyzed with awe. "Damn! Those bottom jaw rippers are razor thin. He could gore your guts out with one swipe."

They began to cautiously crawl through the heavy grass, all the while watching the hulking beast drinking on the far side of the pond. Fletcher stopped and slowly reached around his back for the quiver that carried the cluster of barbed-nosed arrows.

"He's old. His guard hairs are almost pure gray," Fletcher said, not taking his eyes off the grotesque, spade-shaped head. "His sense of smell must be failing him or he'd damn well know we were here by now."

"Fletcher, he's ferocious," Arthur said worriedly. "Why don't you take him out with the rifle? Why take the chance?"

"I need to take him with the bow," Fletcher answered, dismissing Arthur's request. His voice quickened with excitement. "I'll have to drop him on the first shot or I may lose him behind that row of thorn bush behind him."

Fletcher handed Cunningham the rifle, along with a couple of cartridges from his ammunition belt, saying, "Here, you might need these."

Cunningham reluctantly accepted the rifle and cartridges knowing Fletcher's mind was made up.

Fletcher carefully manipulated the quiver down over his arm, hardly wasting a move, saying, "Keep a close eye on the pond. I'm sure the rest of the drift is around somewhere. Male warthogs travel with the sows most of the time." He scanned the surrounding area. "Yeah, look Art. There they are! About forty yards to his right, behind the thorn bush."

Cunningham remained motionless, following Fletcher's point.

"Jesus! Even the piglets are big!" Fletcher exclaimed "I'm sure they have a burrow somewhere close. If he's able to reach it, I'll never get him. I can't take on that sow and piglets. They're too damn intelligent. They'd scatter like they were spooked until I was close, then fan out and surround me. I'd be no match for their attack."

Arthur nodded nervously, tightening his grip on the rifle.

"Now listen carefully," Fletcher said, barely mouthing the words. "We'll have time for two shots. I hope we won't need yours. I can get an arrow off in three seconds. If I miss him and he heads my way, don't shoot. I'll take him for sure on the second try. But if he starts back for the thorn bush, he may go out of my range. Then shoot. But if you have to shoot, don't aim for the head. Shoot to maim him until I can finish him off. I want his head in tact for the trophy."

Fletcher unstrapped the stunted shotgun from his belt, but kept the pistol and bayonet strapped to his waist, adding, "Remember, if he ends up anywhere near me don't shoot at all, I'll take him somehow." He quietly placed the shotgun on the ground.

Cunningham looked at the shotgun, then Fletcher, his face filled with concern.

"Too bulky and messy," Fletcher said, smiling. "I want him intact for MoonGlade's wall." He looked back at the pond. "Damn!" he whispered, frowning. "He's lying down to sun himself. It'll be tough to get a good shot off."

Fletcher paused and scanned the area while Cunningham waited for instructions. Fletcher pointed. "I'm going over there about thirty yards to the left. Keep an eye on me. When I've got the arrow ready, cock the rifle bolt handle once or twice. The timing must be perfect. I'm depending on his hearing."

Fletcher took his boots off and grabbed the bow and two arrows from the quiver. He began moving swiftly but noiselessly to the left. Cunningham raised the rifle and peered through the scope. His hand trembled a little as he leveled the cross-hairs between the front shoulders of the snorting brute, rooting a hole in the mud with its snout. Cunningham then moved his left eye to capture Fletcher in his peripheral vision, waiting for his cue.

Fletcher slowly stood, cutting a striking figure against the shadowy sunlit horizon as he positioned himself. Excited but confident, he methodically set the arrow at the nocking point of the bow. Firmly gripping the handle, he powerfully drew the bowstring back to its limit and aimed the arrow about twelve inches above the shoulder, taking into account that the animal would vault upright at the sound of his most feared enemy, the rifle bolt.

Now, Cunningham, Fletcher urged. *Dammit! Now!*

Suddenly, the sound of the metal bolt clicked twice, immediately sending the swine upward. The string snapped and the arrow flew, producing a twanging sound and a soft thud as the arrow was buried half way up the shaft, into the animal's left shank near its heart. The blood spurted from the wound as the dazed animal reeled and looked for its predator. Falling forward on its forelegs, the beast shook his head, snorting and squealing wildly while the rest of the drift looked on.

"Cunningham, shoot toward the sow!" Fletcher screamed. "But don't hit it. Just get it the hell outta here." He readied and released the second arrow, burying it deep into the crazed, collapsing animal's belly.

Fletcher heard the crack of the rifle as he dropped the bow to the ground and pulled his army bayonet from its sheath. He ran through the grass, splashing across the pond toward the twitching animal that lay flat, appearing near death.

"Fletcher, the drift is running away. I'll stay here and watch for them!" Cunningham yelled as he ejected the spent cartridge and reloaded. He fired the rifle once more at the fleeing animals. Then he realized Fletcher hadn't heard him. *Not now,* he thought. *Not when Fletcher McKeane was operating in his element.*

Fletcher reached the pond edge and stood over the animal. He reached down to steer its head to the left so he could cut its throat. As he grabbed the leathery ear, the head whirled and squealed. Fletcher instantly recoiled. But he wasn't quick enough as the spiked honer caught the top of his hand and sliced his knuckles to the bone.

"You fucking bastard!" Fletcher screamed in frenzy. He repeatedly plunged the bayonet deep into the barreled body until the immense head slumped to the ground. Fletcher, still filled with rage, yanked out his Colt pistol and wedged it between the rippers of the snout, arched the head backward with all his strength and pulled the trigger twice. He wanted to make sure there were no further surprises. He also was careful to ensure that the bullets went into the body and not out the back of its head. *It must be kept intact for MoonGlade's wall*, he reminded himself, regaining his calm.

The sun was dipping below the horizon as Fletcher sat on a log next to the gutted beast. He was holding his bloodied hand, wrapped tightly in a handkerchief, and thinking about how Frank and Lainey would be proud when they saw what he'd bagged for the lounge. He smiled when Cunningham pulled up close with the Jeep to take them, and Fletcher's trophy, back to camp, some twenty-five miles to the east.

Fletcher thought proudly of that day as he stood and opened up the remaining drawers of the hutch, emptying the ammunition, various hunting knives and the bayonet. He packed them in the box with the pistol.

After taping the boxes shut, he reached up to the hook on the side of the hutch and removed the leather hunting vest; the one Lainey had given him the night she declared for the first time that she loved him. He laid it neatly across the box containing the pistol and bow and stared at it. He was somewhat relaxed now that the weapons were stowed for traveling. He'd let the movers dismantle the hutch.

Sitting down at the table, he put his feet up and poured another cup of coffee, thinking about his departure the next day. The drive to San Diego would be easy. The sun was always sparkling off the beach shoreline and the weather would be clear after the morning clouds burned away. Lainey's smiling face next to him would be the final addition to the pleasant trip, he thought.

He then realized how much he and Lainey loved each other. How could I have been so stupid, he thought. It's not a question of wanting Lainey. I need her! All of his foolish fears, be damned, he decided, reaching for the phone. He couldn't wait any longer and called Lainey's apartment. But his eager excitement turned to anxious irritation when the machine answered with Lainey's usual bubbly voice.

"Hello, this is Laincy. I'm sorry I'm not here to take your call. I'm at work. Please leave a message after the beep and I'll get back to you as soon as possible. Fletcher, if this is you, I'll see you at your celebration tonight, love you most."

Damn! Why had she left yesterday's message on the machine? The same one he'd heard late last night when he'd called. He knew she was faithful about keeping her machine updated. She must still be upset. Sure, that's it. She must be there sleeping. It was too early for her to be anywhere else.

Fletcher breathed deeply and spoke very clearly, "Lainey, baby, Lainey Ann. Please pick up the phone. I need you. Please talk to me. I was wrong last night, please talk to me." After a long silence, he shook his head in confusion and hung up.

It's okay, he told himself. She's probably at the beach or something. He glanced at the clock. No, too early. Okay, whatever, he would catch her later and explain to her how much she meant to him. She would understand. It wasn't too late. It was only last night that they'd fought.

He thought about the movers as he quickly showered. They might have to postpone the move if he wasn't ready, he decided. He made plans: First to the jeweler, then he'd propose to Lainey. Both of them could then go to San Diego to begin their new life.

As he dashed out the door, he worried again about not being able to reach Lainey by phone.

When Fletcher returned to his town house that afternoon with a ring, he was more positive than ever of what Lainey meant to him—love, companionship and soon, inner peace. Why couldn't he have seen it before? Why? He would propose to her tonight at the lounge, on the patio at their favorite bench.

He again tried calling her, getting the same aged answer. Frustrated, he looked at his watch, now showing three-fifteen. She must be at work. Sure. She always goes in early on Saturdays. She'd probably tried to call him back when he was gone. Damn! Why hadn't he ever gotten his answering machine fixed, as she had constantly asked him to? He decided to call the lounge.

He dialed impatiently, cursing the endless rings.

"MoonGlade Lounge," the somber voice answered, "Frank Con…"

"Frank, this is Fletcher," he said, cutting Frank off. "Is Lainey there?"

Fletcher heard a deep gasp, then, "Where've you been, Fletcher? I've been trying to reach you."

"Frank, I want to talk to Lainey. Is she there? Please tell me!"

Fletcher waited a moment. Frank remained silent.

"Dammit Frank, put her on, I need her," Fletcher demanded.

"Fletcher, I'm sorry…she's dead." Silence filled the line. Frank continued, "They found her at the bottom of a sixty-foot Laguna Beach seaside cliff lying among the outcroppings. The police suspect suicide." He paused. "You know she didn't have anyone here besides us. The police didn't know who to reach until late this morning after we opened. They traced her back here through one of our napkins she had in her pocket…Fletcher, you still there?"

"Yeah," Fletcher's hoarse whisper barely sounded through the phone.

"When we couldn't find you," Frank said, "I went to the morgue to identify her. I just got back. I had hoped it wouldn't be her. I'm really sorry, Fletcher. The body…it was her."

Frank heard Fletcher's loud groan on the other end of the line.

"Fletcher, I'll call you soon. We're not opening tonight and right now there are some real bad feelings here. I know we're friends, but I need time to think this through. Like I said, I'll call you."

The telephone's buzz echoed throughout the room after Frank hung up. Fletcher slumped to the floor and ripped the phone from the wall.

He reached up and dragged the framed picture of Lainey off the snack bar. Lying against the wall shocked and sickened, he stared at the picture as he pulled the diamond ring from his pocket. He realized that he was now cruelly alone again, with only his memories and his strength to help him keep his sanity. His tortured thoughts screamed over and over through his head. *God, why did you do this? Only one day before I knew what I had! Why, God? Why didn't you take my life instead? Why hers? Why, God?*

CHAPTER 15

Tuesday, Geographic Unlimited, San Diego

Clifford Grahme II, the president of Geographic Unlimited, rose from his plush highback leather chair and walked to the long conference table. The elderly but fit man sat at the far end to observe the large stuffed polar bear, appearing mighty on its hind legs in front of the fireplace. Grahme would often sit and admire the magnificent gift that was given to him in 1982 by the Russian premier in return for Geographic Unlimited's magazine spread on the Kremlin.

He started in on his late morning snack of coffee and Danish as he heard a soft knock on his office door.

"Come in. It's open," he said boisterously.

A solemn, professional looking man walked in.

"Thomas, how are you? Was your long weekend good?" Clifford stood and shook hands with Tom Berkshire, the managing editor and Fletcher's boss.

Tom smiled, joining Clifford at the table. "Yeah, I used the extra day to putter around the house. Then yesterday I took the wife and kids to Sea World again.

"I'm sure that I know every porpoise, whale and snake in that place, we're there so much."

Clifford laughed, then pointed to the tray. "Danish and coffee, Tom?"

"No thanks. I hope I didn't interrupt your day."

"Nope, I've been concerned ever since you called this morning. What's going on, Tom?"

Tom sat back with a worried look. "Well, sir, I'm sure you know of Fletcher McKeane. He was supposed to come down here and sign a new contract with us. All the preliminaries had been completed and we were planning to meet today, here in my office."

Clifford nodded, answering, "Sure, I remember you briefing me during your contract negotiations with him. According to you, he's one of the best damn roving wildlife photojournalists in the business. What's the matter, didn't we snag him?"

"I don't know," he replied as he got up and began pacing. "Last night when I got home there was an incoherent message from him on my machine. He sounded drunk or exhausted…my guess is drunk. He said he'd be down when he could, but wouldn't be here today. That was the extent of the message. I tried calling him back both last night and again this morning. He didn't answer, and he doesn't seem to have an answering machine…"

"I wouldn't worry yet," Grahme interrupted with a wave of his hand. "He was probably hung up somewhere. I'm sure he'll call sometime today."

Tom stopped pacing and turned toward Grahme, shaking his head. "No, something's wrong. He had planned to begin moving down here yesterday. When I found out that he hadn't, I called the moving company we hired for him. I can't believe what they told me really happened. It just sounded too crazy."

Tom paused, sitting down as Clifford furrowed his brow with interest.

"They arrived at his town house early yesterday morning and banged on the door," Tom continued. "When they didn't get any answer, they assumed he was on his way here and had the rental office manager let them in. But Fletcher was there, in shambles, slumped in a living room chair and dressed only in his undershorts. He hadn't shaved, didn't recognize anyone and was sitting there with a whiskey bottle in his hand." Tom stopped talking and sat back, bewildered by his own report.

"Tom, please go on," Clifford said, moving closer.

"Well then, as I understand it, Fletcher kept mumbling that he wasn't leaving, and to get out. When they tried to reason with him, he stood up, launched a tirade of obscenities and raised a pistol. When he cocked it, they got out of there fast and nobody's heard from him since. The rental manager thought about calling the police, but decided Fletcher hadn't really done anything wrong. They had intruded upon him and lawfully can't approach him because his rent has been paid through the end of the month."

He paused and threw his hands up. "Clifford, I just don't understand it. Fletcher called me last Thursday afternoon. He sounded positive and excited about getting his pilot's license and talked about how he would be able to fly himself in the jungle bush. I just don't get it..." Tom slowly shook his head.

"Hey, relax Tom," Clifford said, smiling. "The guy probably found some woman and can't leave her right now. She was probably passed out in the bedroom when the movers got there yesterday. Maybe they were partying over the weekend and it got away from them."

"No. I don't think so," Tom said, unyielding. "I've worked with him a lot over the years. I know him well. He likes the good life, but it doesn't get away from him. Besides, he knows he's up for one of the most exciting assignments we've ever had. You know, the layout shoot in Colombia. He craves adventure. We'd probably have to keep him off the drug cartels' farms. This assignment is how we hooked him into a new contract in the first place. He was planning to freelance for the industry. No sir, I feel I know this man. He wouldn't pass this up for a fling with some woman."

Tom reached over to pour himself a cup of coffee.

Clifford sat back. "Hmm…okay Tom, you've got my interest. What else do you know about him?"

"Well, let's see," Tom reflected. "He's about forty or so, maybe a little older. He came to America from Ireland with his father, I think soon after his mother died. I understand they lived in Portland, Oregon with some relation for about five years before his dad committed suicide."

"Really," Grahme interrupted, "killed himself?"

"Right. Fletcher told me that one winter night he jumped off the bridge into the icy river that runs through town."

"Why?"

Tom shrugged. "Fletcher said it was strange, because the old man had never showed any signs of being suicidal. But they just assumed he couldn't handle being alone any longer and probably never got over losing his wife, who was Fletcher's mother."

"Interesting," Grahme said, reaching for his coffee cup to empty it.

"Yeah, kinda," Tom agreed, continuing, "Anyway, Fletcher joined the army right after that. He did a tour in Vietnam as the war was wrapping up. I think he had to get special permission to join, because of age or citizenship, though I'm not sure which. But anyway he was determined and got in. Vietnam is where he acquired his love for the jungles. After the war he moved to California for the job opportunities and the beach life. We discovered him through a freelance photo spread he had done for the Southern Beach Reporter magazine…"

"Tom," Grahme interrupted, "maybe he's shell-shocked from the war. You know, the reality finally hits home after thinking about the dangerous cartels in the Colombian jungles or…or…" He fell silent as he saw Tom's doubtful look.

"No, that doesn't figure either," Tom disagreed. "With Fletcher's help, I obtained access to his service record. There was a report in it from his commanding officer. McKeane didn't show any signs of stress or even care if the war ended. He performed his duties well, in fact, usually beyond what was asked. He was teamed with a New Orleans Cajun and a bloodthirsty pit bull terrier. They were deadly together. They used the Cajun's cunningness in the swamps and jungles and McKeane's intelligence and innate ability with weapons. The dog would smell out what the two men couldn't. McKeane hardly ever missed his target. He was certainly a gifted shot. I guess his squad nicknamed him 'The Emerald Guillotine.' The three would go on patrol anytime they wanted and come back whenever they wanted. And almost always with some Viet Cong souvenirs." Tom exhaled loudly. "That's about all I know. It was hell getting his record during our background check but, like I said, McKeane helped."

Grahme pushed his empty coffee cup away, saying, "Maybe the Cajun knows something about McKeane. Can we reach him somehow?"

"Nope, he's dead."

Grahme grimaced and said nothing.

Tom continued, "McKeane mentioned once that he and the Cajun remained in close contact after the war ended; almost like brothers, I guess. But the Cajun couldn't cut it on the outside. He got caught up in a Baton Rouge police confrontation during a robbery. Drug-related, I think. Rumor is that he could have had two cops but he let them take him out with a forty-five. He must have been strung out, because I understand the last thing he yelled was for McKeane to get them from the rear. It was rather sad, of course, because McKeane was nowhere around. He was in California at the time. It really hit him hard when he heard of the Cajun's death. He told me when he went to the funeral in New Orleans he was the only one there, and even had to pay for everything."

"I see," Grahme replied, comprehending the value Tom had placed on Fletcher. "Tell me, what's the salary we agreed to pay McKeane?"

"We settled on $125,000 annually, plus expenses," Tom answered. "Although he could probably earn a lot more working freelance. I know he's been offered many lucrative opportunities, including mercenary work, but he likes our organization. He was especially happy about the list of upcoming assignments he was assured of getting with us."

Grahme paused, pondering Tom's report, then said, "Tell you what, Tom. Give it a few days to a week. Postpone the Colombia shoot. I just want to make sure this isn't some contract ploy to hold us up for more money or something. If nothing changes do what you think is right."

"Sure," Tom answered, his face brightening. "Thank you, sir. Oh, also, I think I'll call his attorney, a Mr. Arthur Cunningham from Newport Beach. He helped Fletcher with the contract negotiations and may know something." Tom stood up to leave. "In fact," he added, "I may do some personal nosing around up in Newport Beach. I remember we did our final negotiating in a fancy restaurant that's located there. I forget the name, but I'll dig it up from my day planner. There was a lady who worked at the restaurant and sat with us for awhile. She and McKeane seemed pretty close. I remember her name was Lainey because it was different, and she was extremely attractive. Maybe if she's still there, I'll chat with her before I try Fletcher again. Next week though, as you said."

"Right, I agree," Grahme replied. "Let's do everything we can to keep McKeane."

"Believe me Clifford, this guy was born with exceptional talents," Tom replied. "If we can keep him, it'll do a number on our competition."

Clifford nodded as Tom left, gesturing with a wave.

Berkshire left the building for a long walk in the bright San Diego sunshine. He knew that Fletcher McKeane wasn't undependable or greedy, and definitely not the type to be lured away from Geographic Unlimited by the competition. He was determined to find out what was going on.

Chapter 16

Wednesday, Rancho Arroyo Apartments

The afternoon sunshine fell brightly through the tree-lined entrance of Rancho Arroyo Apartments as Jennifer parked her car in the rental office lot. She anxiously stepped out and marveled at the sky. Why this cold mission on such a beautiful California day, she thought, sighing.

Entering through the large glass doors of the office, she quickly walked to the wall where a large map of the complex hung. Scanning it, she located Fletcher's town house address, the one she'd acquired from his pilot license application.

A young leasing agent, who was filing some paperwork, spotted her by the map. "Hello, can I help you?" she asked pleasantly.

Jennifer smiled and took a deep breath, straining to maintain eye contact. "Yes, I'm Jennifer Jaynes, here to see Mr. McKeane who lives in unit 201. I'm a relative from Los Angeles. He's expecting me but didn't know when I was arriving," Jennifer lied. "I called, but he doesn't seem to be at home. I thought if I show you my identification, perhaps you might let me have a key so I could wait for him in his apartment."

"Sure, I'll just check the key release roster," the young agent answered as she walked to the front counter and picked up a clipboard. "I'm sure he must have signed it for you."

She glanced up and down the sheet while Jennifer frowned, knowing the agent wouldn't find Fletcher's approval.

"Oh, I'm sorry Ms. Jaynes, I guess he didn't fill it out. Unfortunately we have a strict policy against handing out keys without the tenant's permission. Maybe he's at home now. Would you like to use our phone to call again?"

"I just tried about fifteen minutes ago from my car. He didn't answer. I really need to wait for him," Jennifer replied.

"I am sorry but we just can't let you in without his permission," the agent answered, becoming concerned.

"Miss, may I help you?" An older woman asked from the doorway of the manager's office.

Jennifer turned around and forced a smile. "Yes, hopefully. I've come down from L.A. to see a relative of mine, Fletcher McKeane, but he's not home. I was hoping I could get a key to let myself in and wait for him?"

Jennifer pulled out her official FAA identification card and displayed it.

The matronly-looking lady glanced at the card and pondered a minute.

"Well, usually we wouldn't do it Ms. Jaynes. However, after the episode we had with him on Monday I'll let you have a key. I just hope you two are friends and maybe you can find out what's going on."

Jennifer, still smiling, gave her an affirmative nod.

"And please ask him to stop down and let us know what his plans are for the town house. I'd appreciate it," the manager said while pulling a key from the drawer. "Incidentally, he was in terrible shape on Monday. If you want me to go with you, I will."

Thinking quickly, she concealed her concern and replied, "No, it's okay. That's why I've come to see him. I know he's been through a rough time lately."

The woman nodded and handed her the key.

Jennifer thanked her and left, heading toward the cluster of buildings pointed out by the manager.

Walking along the winding, shrub-lined sidewalk she wondered what the manager had meant about the 'episode' she'd had with Fletcher. Maybe she'd find out from Fletcher himself, she hoped as she came upon his building. She stopped abruptly in front of the attached half-garage, recognizing the open-air Jeep she'd seen at the airport. *It's Fletcher's! He was there! She knew it!*

She quickly approached the building then stopped. From the outside his town house looked spacious. And being located in such a posh ocean locale meant a high rent, she thought as she stepped onto the slightly raised porch of number 201. She noticed a stack of old newspapers and a heavy layer of dust that hadn't been disturbed. The dry Santa Ana winds had been blowing since Monday afternoon. Apparently no one had left or entered since then.

Without warning, she came face-to-snout with a huge grayish-blue palm tree rat. It scampered from out of the corner across her feet. Startled, she fell backward, grabbing the railing. "Damn!" she huffed aloud. She hesitated and thought, Jennifer, you can leave now. Who knows what you may find? She turned back toward the steps, but then stopped. *No! I'll do what I was told,* she decided and walked to the door.

She took a deep breath and rang the doorbell. When no one answered, she threw off her fears, placed the key in the lock and slowly opened the door. "Fletcher," she called. "Fletcher, it's Jennifer Jaynes. Are you here?" When there was still no answer, she boldly stepped inside.

The doorway opened into the kitchen. There was a large dining and living room leading to a patio just beyond. She quickly saw that the rooms were empty and that the windows and drapes had been shut tight. The trapped air was dry, hot and musty. The kitchen was fairly clean except for an aged mess of dirty breakfast dishes piled in the sink. Rancid coffee had been left in the pot. A few empty beer bottles lined the counter.

She couldn't help noticing and reading the formal lease papers sitting next to the wine rack on the snack bar. Hmm, a town house in Mission Bay, San Diego. *Impressive,* she thought, as she put the papers down and began looking around the dining room. The dining table and chairs were dusty but in place. One chair had been pulled out and the telephone book open to the jewelry store section. She suddenly froze, seeing the disconnected phone, the diamond ring and the picture of Lainey, lying on the floor. Jennifer read the heartfelt message written across the bottom of the photo:

'To Fletcher, My Everything for Always, Love, Lainey'

Good God! What suffering he must be going through, she thought, trying to compose herself. She picked up the picture, ring and phone and laid them on the table before sliding open the dining room drapes and window. The gentle breeze flowed in and began to air the room.

She stood and glanced at the painting equipment set up by the patio door. The easel was empty. The sketch box and paintbrushes were clean except for one that was stuck to the dried-up paint on the palette. Two half-finished, amateurish seascape sketches were loosely stuffed in a large cardboard box. *Painting is obviously not one of his talents*. She chuckled.

The living room was Southwestern style, well decorated with masculine, rustic furniture. The rectangular rust-finished iron and glass sofa table, covered with wildlife adventure magazines, was centered on a pastel-colored braided throw rug. It accented the jade-green leather couch. The adjoining deep-back chair had a decorative Indian wool blanket draped over the armrest. Two small western-style solid oak tables were placed on either side of the couch and decked with one of a matching pair of lamps made from Indian vases.

Then she saw the weapons sitting in front of the weapons hutch, all neatly packed, except for the pistol holster lying on the floor. It was empty! *Oh, no, please no!* She feared the worst but tried to stay calm as she continued her search, determined to find him.

Hurrying toward the patio, she drew back the draperies and pulled on the door lever. As the door slid open, the onrushing ocean air blew the drapes wide as Jennifer stepped between them and out onto the deck. She found nothing except a lounge chair and a charcoal grill, both covered in dust. No one had been out there lately, she figured, leaving the door and drapes open.

She eyed the hallway off the dining room. It led to the guest bedroom and a connecting bathroom. Beyond stood a staircase leading to the master bedroom level. She entered the guest bedroom first and saw it had no furniture, but was full of boxes containing mementos and pictures of hunting expeditions. Hanging on the wall was a large colorful poster of a fierce Bengal tiger surrounded by beautiful, scantily-clad African women.

She stopped as she spotted a selection of women's clothing hanging in the closet. Must have been Lainey's. He sure as hell wouldn't wear them, she mused. She turned and looked past an open door into the guest lavatory. It was sparkling clean and stocked for a woman, with feminine soap, towels and perfumes. It appeared that it hadn't been used for a while.

Okay, quit stalling, she decided as she went to the stairs leading to the master bedroom. She looked up the staircase knowing her answers must be up there.

As she stepped up the thick carpeted steps she could hear strong chords of choral hymn music coming from the bedroom. She reached the door and slowly pushed it open. The king-size bed was unmade, the sheets and blankets lying on the floor. An empty whiskey bottle lay on top of them. The clock radio on the bedside table was tuned to a FM religious station.

Cautiously entering the bedroom, she detected a putrid stench coming from the adjoining master bathroom. The door was slightly ajar and the light was on.

She inched her way to the door, struggling against the thought of what she might witness. Even though she was fully trained for the investigation of aircraft accidents and had witnessed the worst of their aftermath, she'd never become used to the carnage. She nudged open the door and swiftly looked inside.

She gasped, but stood firm. Her stomach turned as the reek and repulsive sight hit her full force. But she remained staring at Fletcher while grasping for her next move.

She spun and immediately ran for the phone, dialing Southside Medical. "I need Dr. Colletti!" she cried into the phone. "Please page him. I know he's in the building! Please hurry!"

She waited impatiently for the doctor to answer his page. Finally she heard his acknowledgment.

"Dr. Colletti, I was right. He's here. Please hurry. I think he's alive, but I'm not sure. If he is, I know only barely. He must be dehydrated and needs fluids…what? Cold water? Yes, I'll try. For God's sake, he's already in the bathtub. He's unconscious, but I'll attempt to force some water into him. Rancho Arroyo Apartments, 1602 San Romeo Drive. It's number 201…No, no paramedics! Please, I want to keep this quiet. I'll explain later, please rush!"

Hanging up the phone, she raced back into the bathroom. She kicked the tequila bottles out of the way and reached into the bathtub for Fletcher.

His pulse was slight and his skin dry. She raised his eyelids, seeing his sunken eyes confirmed severe dehydration. She immediately recalled her FAA medical training and realized there was very little she could do without intravenous equipment.

She nervously looked around the room, frustrated, and screamed, "Damn it! What is happening? Damn it! Damn it!" She looked down at him. "Fletcher, talk to me! Please talk to me!" She turned the shower on to wash him off and maybe get cold water into him somehow.

Sure, Fletcher! she exclaimed inwardly. Crawl in the bathtub to make it easier to clean up after you. That's typical of you damn proud Irish to do something like that. Well, you should have filled the tub and drowned yourself with water instead of booze. You aren't dead yet. Too bad you couldn't find the pistol to finish the job. Well, I know where it is and you won't find it. She turned and kicked the Colt away from the edge of the tub before turning back to him. This shower will clean you up. Damn it Fletcher! Talk to me!

The tears were streaming down her face as she continued in a frenzy to wash him off. "Fletcher," she wailed again. "One is already gone, I can't handle another. Waaakke up! Let me tell you about the great Fletcher McKeane, nude in the bathtub, lying in his own vomit and waste…C'mon!"

Jennifer was still frantic and nearly exhausted, desperately trying to get cold water into Fletcher when she heard the loud knock at the door. She stumbled downstairs and into the kitchen, unlocking the door when she saw that it was Dr. Colletti. Barging in with his black leather bag, he rushed past her as she pointed toward the stairs.

She slid down the side of the counter and sat in the corner, breathless and terrified, reliving the day's horrid events. Her sixth sense was now at its peak as she thought about all the events that had occurred lately, especially at Lainey's funeral. And now this! She gripped her forehead and massaged the throbbing as she began to grasp what was happening around her. She knew it now. *Oh God, help us!* she screamed silently. *Please help us!*

Thursday evening was clear and windy as darkness fell upon Fletcher, lying unconscious in his freshly made-up king size bed. His arm was extended out flat with an intravenous needle pumping the remainder of the life-sustaining Ringer's Lactose into his veins.

Jennifer, curled up in the padded lounge chair across the room, began dozing off. She was fatigued from yesterday's ordeal and now caring for Fletcher according to Dr. Colletti's instructions.

Sluggish, she forced herself from the chair and walked to the bed, trying to concentrate on Donald, whom she hadn't talked to since yesterday morning. She was deciding what to tell him while unhooking the intravenous needle from Fletcher's arm, when she heard him moan softly. She glanced at him, stunned. These were the first sounds Fletcher had made since she'd found him. She bent down close to his face.

"Fletcher, Fletcher," she said softly, not wanting to risk the danger of shocking him awake.

She reached for his hand and gently squeezed it, feeling a faint pressure in return.

"Where am I?…Is it you, Lainey Ann?" Fletcher asked weakly. His eyes fluttering as though in a trance.

Jennifer paused, realizing he'd called her Lainey Ann. She bent down closer. "Fletcher, this is Jennifer Jaynes. Lainey is close. Now sleep for a few more hours. I'll be here when you wake up."

He turned his head sideways on the pillow without acknowledging her.

Jennifer waited until he was asleep again before reaching around him for the phone on the night stand. Unable to reach Donald in his room, she left a message for him on the room's voice mail: "Donald, I'm okay. Sorry I haven't been able to reach you, but I've been nursing a sick friend. Please be patient, I'll call you tomorrow. Thanks. Love you, Jennifer."

She hung up the phone and rubbed her weary, burning eyes, managing a slight smile over the trite but true message she'd left Donald.

She glanced at Fletcher as she stood up, satisfied he was sleeping soundly. Making her way downstairs, she collapsed on the living room couch and immediately fell into a deep sleep.

Jennifer woke up with a jolt as the sunrise streamed brightly through the window. Her thoughts raced. *Damn...morning. I left him alone too long!* She jumped up and rushed upstairs to Fletcher's bedroom only to stop in the doorway, stunned by the sight of Fletcher propped up on two pillows—quietly gazing out the window.

"Fletcher, you're awake!" she exclaimed.

He slowly turned and looked at her. "Jennifer Jaynes! What? Why are you here?" he sputtered, surprised.

Jennifer felt chills and shook her head as she ran over and hugged him, shedding tears of relief.

Fletcher, confused, gently pushed her away and looked into her eyes. "I don't understand," he asked again, puzzled. "What are you doing here?"

"I'll explain later when you're stronger. You hungry?"

"Pretty much starved."

"I would think so," she answered, laughing. "But I hope you're hungry for breakfast because that's all there is."

Seeing his quickening nod, she backed off the bed and headed for the kitchen.

Fletcher rested comfortably after finishing off six scrambled eggs, bacon, toast with orange marmalade and close to a quart of orange juice. He suddenly became more aware of his surroundings and looked under the covers. "Hey! I'm hardly dressed. Have you been taking care of me?"

"If you're embarrassed about that, you should have seen how I found you." Jennifer answered, chuckling. "Nude in the bathtub with a bathroom full of booze bottles. Just like you Irish. Too damn worried about having someone go to a little work to clean up after you. Well, fortunately, we didn't have to do that and you're here to stay. Dr. Colletti thinks you were in there for three or four days. He treated you for dehydration and malnutrition. It took four sessions of intravenous feeds to bring you around. He also thought it would be a little more humanizing if you were in bed instead of in the tub during your rehabilitation. All right?"

"Yes, all right," Fletcher replied, smiling.

"Oh, also, don't worry," she quickly added. "No one knows what happened. Dr. Colletti is a friend of mine from the FAA. He handles all of the pilots' physicals. He won't say anything."

"Okay, Jennifer. I realize when I'm well taken care of. But why did you come? How'd you know I was in trouble? Nobody knew anything. How did you?"

"Fletcher, I do want to discuss that," she answered carefully. "But I have to be at the airport for an early afternoon appointment. I've been here almost two days. I need to go home and freshen up. I also need to talk to Donald, the man I'm committed to. I wonder what I'll tell him? Maybe the truth," she said, answering her own question. "I know. Let's talk about things tonight, over dinner, something simple like pizza. In the meantime, try and get some rest."

"Sounds good to me," he agreed. "By the way, I assume you have a key to the place."

"Yes. Oh, that reminds me. Yesterday I walked down to the rental office and told them you've been sick. I also told them you'd be down in a few days to straighten things out. They're expecting you. See you later."

He nodded as he heard the front door shut and lock. He then turned over and immediately dozed off, thinking about Lainey and still groping for answers.

Jennifer walked to her car, stretching in the bright mid-morning sun. She felt rested but tremulous inside. She needed to regroup her thoughts and plan on how to tell Fletcher what she believed was happening. She would have to move slowly, especially with the part about Lainey's funeral. He was recovering, both mentally and physically, but still weak from his ordeal. She'd have to be careful not to put him over the edge again.

Would he believe her? No. Did she really believe all of this herself? She would know more after talking with Fletcher tonight, she decided, as she slowly opened the car door. Driving away, she again wondered how everyone fit into the growing puzzle? And, again, from where had it come?

CHAPTER 17

The Funeral, Chapel of Beloved Memories

Fletcher lifted his feet onto a chair across from him at the dining table as he watched Jennifer clean up what was left of the cheese, onion, and mushroom pizza. Finished, she opened two bottles of Pilsner dark and sat down.

"You're looking stronger by the minute," she said, handing him a beer.

"Thanks, I feel stronger by the minute," he answered, sipping from the bottle as he leaned back. "By the way, did you talk to Donald?"

"Yes, I told him I was helping out a new friend who's been sick." They matched grins. "Well, it's the truth, isn't it?"

"Yes, Jennifer, I think we're getting to be friends. I already owe you a lot."

Jennifer decided this was the right time to begin talking. "Fletcher, I think we're already good friends," she said soberly, gaining Fletcher's attention. "And it may not have been our choice alone."

"What do you mean by that?"

She took a deep breath. "Hold onto your chair, because I need to share this."

Fletcher leaned forward, cocking his head quizzically.

"Well, I ended up at the MoonGlade Lounge last Thursday right after you left," she began. "I'm not even sure why I went. I just did. When I got there I met Lainey in the foyer. We seemed to connect, even though she was extremely upset." She paused for emphasis, then continued, "It was very strange, but I seemed to sense enough about her to empathize with her sorrow. And the last thing I told her was that I'd be around if she ever wanted to talk."

Seeing that she had Fletcher's complete attention, she decided it was time.

"Fletcher, I think she took me up on that offer…on Tuesday night."

Setting his beer down, Fletcher slowly contemplated what she'd said. His mouth abruptly gaped, sputtering, "Wait…Tuesday…How…She was dead…I mean…how could she?" He fell mute under Jennifer's firm stare.

"Be patient," she said softly, "I'll explain everything."

He nodded, hanging onto her every word.

"On Monday afternoon Frank Conklin called Bob Chapman at the airport, looking for you. He was finalizing Lainey's funeral services and no one had seen you since her death. Frank and Bob decided you were probably in San Diego avoiding the whole situation like a coward. I decided that issue didn't concern me."

"Damn, if they only knew," Fletcher interjected tensely, shaking his head. "So Frank took care of all the arrangements, huh?"

"Yes," she replied. "He saw to the details while Lainey's mother was making plans to get here. He'd found her in Chicago through Lainey's employment record. Her mother decided to have Lainey buried here because of how much she loved the area." Jennifer stopped talking as Fletcher's eyes lowered.

Fletcher looked up. "Please keep going," he said, massaging his clenched fist.

"Are you up to hearing more about the funeral?" she asked delicately.

"Yes, I need to know."

Jennifer took a swallow of her Pilsner. "All right," she continued. "The ceremony was held on Tuesday afternoon. I was hesitant about going but for some reason I felt obligated to see Lainey once more…"

Jennifer and Bob Chapman were somber as Bob pulled their car into the parking lot of the placid-looking funeral home, modeled after an ancient Spanish mission. As the car moved past the front entrance and into an angled parking space, they both read the name, carved in the overhead granite:

The Chapel of Beloved Memories

In solemn lock-step, they made their way up the winding sidewalk and through the carved wooden doors. Entering the carpeted foyer, bedecked with ornamental Persian rugs, they saw an attentive looking man who was dressed professionally, standing by the hallway entrance. He was politely assisting another couple with information. Jennifer stayed slightly behind Chapman as they waited to be noticed.

After the couple moved on, the thin man turned to Chapman and smiled. "Good morning, sir. My name is Andrew Dunmore, the funeral director. May I be of help to you?" he asked kindly.

"The Lainey Cole room, please," Chapman answered.

"Oh, yes," he replied cordially as he turned and motioned toward the end of the lengthy corridor, past several other viewing rooms. "Down that way. Ms. Cole rests in the far slumber chamber on the left. Mr. Conklin will greet you there."

"Thank you," Chapman said, starting for the room. Jennifer followed, mildly amused by the staid demeanor of the director. *'Slumber chamber'...how morbid sounding*, she thought.

Walking down the long dimly-lit hallway, Jennifer felt mournful and pensive. Reflecting on the bizarre events of the past week made her want to turn around and leave. But she needed to see this through. It was as if she was bound by some mysterious allegiance to pay her last respects to Lainey.

Reaching the chamber's entrance, they paused. The French doors with tinted beveled-glass panes were open. Elegant floor-length sheer curtains veiled the arched doorway. Directly above, a colorfully decorated windowed tympanum was embossed with a sculpture of Mary, the mother of Jesus.

Peering curiously through the fabric, Jennifer inhaled apprehensively, seeing silhouettes gathered around the raised oblong outline resting at the far end of the room. *What am I doing here?* she asked herself. Then, following Chapman's gentle prod, Jennifer turned toward a gold-edged plaque that was attached to the wall. Beneath it, a brightly polished Victorian-style table supported a cluster of small flickering devotional candles that illuminated the plaque's bold black script:

In Beloved Memory
Of
Lainey Ann Cole
1969-1997

Next to the candles sat a neat stack of wallet-sized parchment pamphlets. The cover pictured a miniature seascape just above Lainey's name. Jennifer picked up two and handed one to Bob. Unfolding hers, she silently read the inscription of the twenty-third Psalm and the details of Lainey's funeral rites.

Jennifer looked at Bob and took a deep breath as they pushed through the curtains. Just inside the doorway a large guest book lay open on a wooden desk. After Jennifer signed it, she handed the pen to Chapman and turned, taking in the full view of the room.

She blinked as she scanned the breathtaking spectacle. The decor was in soft colors, set off perfectly by the precise brightness level of the recessed lighting. Thick wall-to-wall carpeting had been newly laid. Exquisite Regency tables, the finest style of the early 19th century British, and matching velvet tufted chairs adorned the room. A vast assortment of stunning floral tributes consisting of pots, planters and bouquets were perfectly arranged throughout. Hardly a gap in the room had been missed.

She slowly focused on the far center of the chamber. A richly burnished all bronze casket with natural-grained mahogany handles and pure gold hardware sat atop a solid marble casket table, partially covered with scarlet silk. Large standing wreaths bordered a red plush pathway leading to a padded kneeling-rail at the side of the casket. Flowered garlands, heavily scented and garnished with greenery, were laid all around the casket table. Just above, the sun poured through large gothic windows—stained blue, amber and ruby-red—casting a diffused shroud of glorious light upon the majestic scene.

Jennifer sighed to herself, thinking, *Damn, this is scary. Frank hasn't memorialized Lainey, he's enshrined her!*

As Chapman joined Jennifer they made their way past the neatly arranged rows of guest chairs and into the center of the room. Lainey's mother and a few misty-eyed friends quietly mingled as sorrowful hymns chimed in the background with a resonant pitch.

Jennifer braced herself when she saw Frank, impeccably dressed and groomed, emerge from a small throng of people in the opposite corner. He spotted them and smiled as he walked over to greet them.

"Hi, Bob. Good to see you here," Frank whispered, shaking Chapman's hand.

"Thanks, Frank. Good to see you too," Chapman replied.

Frank then turned to Jennifer. "Hello, Ms. Jaynes." He extended his hand. "It's also a pleasure to see you again."

Jennifer swallowed and accepted his hand. She cringed inwardly at Frank's cold, clammy clasp. "Mr. Conklin," she acknowledged, forcing a smile. She quickly withdrew her hand, adding, "You did a marvelous job with the arrangements."

"Thank you," Frank responded, turning toward the casket. "Lainey deserves it all. I only wish I could've provided more for her."

Provided more? How could he have provided any more, Jennifer wondered, puzzled. But she only nodded as she noticed the casket kneeling-rail was clear. "Please excuse me," she said, leaving them.

Slowly approaching the casket, Jennifer was struck by Lainey's rigid, yet still radiant appearance. Her face showed no ashen or graying pallor. Her long blonde hair glistened softly and had been spread out over the baby blue pillow. Her milk-white skin, lightly touched up with pink rouge, almost glowed next to her bright yellow sundress. Seemingly at final peace, she lay on a lavish white-satin quilted mattress, matched flawlessly with a plush shirred drop and overlay. Her rosary had been hung around her neck and the crucifix placed delicately in her folded hands, resting gently across her breast.

Awed, Jennifer knelt down and gazed at Lainey's still body, thinking that even in this state she seemed lovely and serene, her demeanor silken and smooth. Jennifer was saddened that such a beautiful young life had ended so tragically. She closed her eyes and said a short prayer for Lainey's soul. She comforted herself in knowing Lainey was surely resting close to God.

Then, as Jennifer opened her eyes to rise, she hesitated. She sensed something strange, some kind of stirring connection to Lainey. Jennifer closed her eyes, as the feeling only grew stronger. *What's happening,* Jennifer wondered, astonished. Lainey's trying to communicate! *No, it can't be!* Feeling uneasy, Jennifer again tried to rise but found she couldn't. An inner intensity compelled her to turn back toward Lainey.

It was then she felt a premonition concerning Fletcher, a keen perception of him in danger. She bowed her head to concentrate, thinking, *Fletcher's not in San Diego, and he's in trouble!* More thoughts of Fletcher began to flood her mind. Desperately, she tried to sort it all out. Suddenly she felt a firm tap on her shoulder, immediately clearing away her thoughts. Surprised, she abruptly turned her head and looked squarely into Frank's hard stare. He slowly signaled toward the small lectern in the corner.

Looking over, Jennifer saw the chaplain preparing for the eulogy. She turned, noticing Chapman was standing in the seating area waiting for her. Tremulous, she rose and brushed past Frank to join Chapman, now sitting down with the rest of the mourners.

Throughout the lengthy eulogy, Jennifer replayed the mysterious experience she'd had as she knelt next to Lainey. She thought over the startling premonition that Fletcher was in danger. But finally, she decided to ignore it, as nothing more than a figment of her imagination. *What other real choice was there,* she asked herself as they all filed out of the funeral chapel.

Fletcher remained still as Jennifer rose from the table and began preparing a pot of raspberry almond coffee. She pressed the 'brew' toggle-switch on and sat down, saying, "So after we left the funeral I dismissed the premonition."

Amazed, Fletcher shook his head, replying, "There has to be more to it."

Jennifer nodded, answering, "Yes, things got more strange after the ceremony."

Fletcher straightened, transfixed on Jennifer as she continued, "The burial was held at Laguna Harbor

Memorial. Frank, of course, had provided to have Lainey's remains placed in their finest mausoleum overlooking the ocean." Jennifer paused and looked questioningly at Fletcher. "The weather was very unusual. Throughout the internment it rained, inland as well as up and down the coast. It was a light rain, with the sun still shining. But then it stopped. Never once did it rain on the funeral proceedings."

"Wait," Fletcher blurted. "No rain on the funeral? I heard once that's a bad sign."

"Folklore claims it is," she answered shrugging. "That's what I meant about another strange thing. Anyway, after the ritual it cleared up nicely." She looked upward to gather her thoughts. "Frank really did an outstanding job." She couldn't help thinking, *maybe too outstanding.*

"Sounds like he did," Fletcher remarked.

"Yes," she went on. "Chapman told me that he even footed the bills. It was generosity at its finest." She hesitated. "But, Fletcher, I think you should know that for some reason I'm really left cold by Frank."

Fletcher's face wrinkled in surprise. "Really, why?"

"I don't know. Just a gut feeling. Still, I think he's a very discerning man. He even hired a small dance combo and staged an elaborate feast at the MoonGlade after the burial." Jennifer furrowed her brow, appearing pensive before continuing, "Although the festivities were exceptional, I left early. I just wasn't comfortable around Frank, and the experience with Lainey at the funeral home was still bothering me. After I got home I tried calling you to see if you were all right. But when I couldn't reach you I again let it go. I guess I just decided that you couldn't be in any trouble."

"Okay then, please tell me what made you come here to find me," Fletcher pressed.

Jennifer inhaled deeply and looked him in the eyes, seeing he was prepared for her answer.

"Lainey told me to," she answered slowly.

Fletcher shot backward. "For God's sake, tell me what you're talking about!"

"It happened that night of the funeral, when I was at home falling asleep."

Fletcher slowly moved forward as Jennifer explained…

Jennifer opened the medicine chest and put her toothbrush away, preoccupied with thoughts of Lainey's funeral. She washed her face, slipped on her nightgown and crawled into bed, deciding to read. Realizing that her attention span would be limited, she passed on the novel she'd been reading, and picked up a magazine from the nightstand.

Feeling exhausted, but restless, she soon chucked the magazine to the floor, grabbed the remote and switched on the TV to catch the late news. Again, she quickly lost interest and shut the TV off.

Rising, she walked to the bathroom and downed some aspirin, hoping to relieve her stress. After returning to bed, she tuned the clock-radio into an easy-listening FM station, and set the auto-shutoff for forty-five minutes. As she reached to turn out the light she convinced herself she would soon be asleep and wake up in the morning refreshed, finished with all of this confusion. She prodded the pillow, laid her head down and closed her eyes, deciding Lainey was put to rest and Fletcher had moved away. *It was over, dammit, over!*

Tossing and turning, Jennifer finally began to drift off, lulled to sleep from the gentle music and the mild drone of the sparse late-night traffic. Her body became heavy and her senses dulled. She was detaching herself from the day's events, though remnants remained entrenched in her mind. As the bedroom began to brighten, she lay still on the bed. She felt as though heavy weights had been placed on her chest. She sensed that the brightness was increasing but she was unable to focus clearly. Gradually Jennifer began to perceive strange voices along with making out faceless forms gathering around and above her. One image emerged more clearly before her—the beautiful golden-haired Lainey!

Jennifer's terrified thoughts began to swirl wildly within her subconscious. *I'm having a nightmare*, she thought. She tried to wake herself up but failed, still unable to focus clearly or even move. Inwardly she screamed, *No more! No more of this! No more!*

Then Jennifer heard it, Lainey's repeated cry, "Go to Fletcher. Find Fletcher." Over and over again the same alarming appeal rang from Lainey's lucid image, still hovering at the foot of the bed: "Go to Fletcher."

Finally Jennifer managed the strength to wrench her head off the pillow. The brightness began to subside, the voices and the images fade. Gasping for breath, she sprung up and switched on the light. The room was empty. *The voices must have been from the radio,* she thought, shooting a glance toward the nightstand. Stunned, she realized the radio was off and had been for hours.

She rubbed her taut forehead, then returned to bed. The rest of the night she lay there desperately trying to dismiss the ghostly experience as a bad dream. But by the morning sun she knew it hadn't been a dream. She now knew for certain that none of what had been occurring lately had anything to do with a dream.

Jennifer set her empty beer bottle down and looked at Fletcher, concluding, "That's what happened. The next day I decided to come looking for you."

"Christ! Unbelievable!" Fletcher blurted. "But, why were you so sure it wasn't a dream?"

Jennifer remained rigid as she replied, "The intuitive impression of Lainey being there was too clear; the appeal in her voice too strong. Her cries to find you became more intense as she repeated them. So, the next morning I contacted the receptionist at Geographic Unlimited and simply asked for you. They told me you had never reported for work. That convinced me there was a problem and I should come here looking for you—like Lainey told me to."

"Incredible," Fletcher said, stunned, "incredible."

"Fletcher," she asked. "Do we really know all the answers about life and death?"

Fletcher shook his head, answering, "After listening to you, I'm not sure of anything anymore. Ya know, I also had a weird dream. At least I thought it was a dream."

Jennifer's eyes widened. "What? A dream? Tell me."

"Yeah," he replied. "Remember when you found me this morning? I was trying to understand something that happened to me while I was unconscious."

"Please tell me," she urged.

"Well, at different times I'd fall into this dream-like state. I felt separated, detached; like I was floating. But the space around me was bright and warm. At first it seemed peaceful and then it would become dark and cold and Lainey would appear. Her beauty was bright against that dismal darkness. I could see her face and her smile clearly. When I called out 'Lainey Ann,' she tried to come closer to me, but somehow she couldn't. I couldn't move either. Then this grim, shadowy shape appeared and whisked her away…"

"Did Lainey say anything?" Jennifer interrupted excitedly.

"No," he answered, while thinking it through. "That's all that ever happened. But I do vaguely remember the time when I came around and saw you as I was calling to her. That was just before I regained complete consciousness." He paused. "Damn, it seemed so real. This is all so crazy." Fletcher sat back. "So what do you think now?" he asked, still feeling troubled.

Jennifer hesitated to gather her thoughts before she spoke. She didn't want to tell him everything just yet. Not only did she want him to digest what he'd heard so far tonight, but also she needed to find out more before she revealed everything she knew.

"I think we need to piece all of this together," she answered. "However, before we can do that, I need to understand more about Lainey."

Jennifer slowly got up from the table and grabbed the pot of freshly brewed coffee, saying, "C'mon, let's go make ourselves comfortable."

Fletcher bewildered by all they had spoken of, nodded and rose to follow her.

CHAPTER 18

Fletcher and Lainey

Fletcher and Jennifer made their way to the comfort of the living room. Setting the coffee on the sofa table, she settled herself into the deep-backed chair and raised her feet onto the matching ottoman. She pulled the wool Indian blanket over her to ward off the ocean chill, seeping through the slightly opened patio door.

Fletcher chose the couch and supported himself with a pillow, leaning against the armrest and dangling his legs off the middle cushion.

Jennifer smiled warmly at him, asking, "Relaxed?"

"Yeah, as much as I can be," he answered, returning the smile.

"Good," she replied. "Let's start with how you met Lainey, okay?"

"Sure." He poured himself a cup of coffee and reflected, "I'd met her about a year and a half ago. It was my birthday, so Marsha Cunningham and I decided to have dinner at the MoonGlade…"

"Marsha Cunningham?" Jennifer interrupted.

"Yes, my attorney's daughter. I was dating her."

She nodded. "Oh, I see. Please go on."

Fletcher began reminiscing about the night he'd met Lainey and how they'd talked out on the patio while admiring the picturesque moon-glade.

Fletcher reached over for more coffee. "That's about it," he finished. "After that first night I saw Lainey only once or twice over the next week or so. We hardly even communicated. Although I was attracted to her, I didn't push it. I suppose I was just sensitive about her powerful effect on me. Anyway, I thought I'd wait to see how I felt after the African trip..."

"African trip?"

"Right. I took the Cunningham family to Africa on vacation while I did a freelance layout of the wilds."

"Oh, I'd love to hear about it.

"Okay," he agreed, gathering his thoughts.

Fletcher told her of how he and the Cunninghams had first visited a large game preserve in Kenya, then traveled west to hunt near the territory of Ivory Coast. Jennifer listened intently as Fletcher sipped on his coffee, and proudly recounted his thrilling encounter with the savage warthog.

Jennifer was leaning forward in her chair when he finished and sat back. "That sounded so exciting," she said, realizing there was a side to Fletcher she hadn't seen before. She was learning quickly that Fletcher was a good man but apparently capable of sudden ferocity. She wondered what the trigger was but kept the question to herself.

She smiled and sat back, saying, "Obviously, you didn't forget about Lainey while you were in Africa."

"Not by a long shot. No pun intended," he replied, chuckling. "Hell, I thought about her constantly. I came to realize that I'd fallen in love with her on that first night, though it was hard for me to accept. I'd never believed in love at first sight because it didn't seem logical, even though deep inside I probably knew better. It was as though my head had just met her but my heart had known her forever…and …" Fletcher paused to control his emotions.

Jennifer leaned forward and put her hand on his, nodding agreeably. She knew he was becoming upset but she needed him to continue talking about Lainey. "When did you two become close?" Jennifer asked, withdrawing her hand and readjusting herself in the big chair for comfort.

Collected again, he replied, "Right after we got back from Africa I realized I couldn't forget about Lainey. So Marsha and I broke off our romantic attachment—although we did remain good friends. Feeling free I went back to the lounge and was more impressed when I found out that Lainey had been promoted to hostess. She smiled proudly when I congratulated her. But again, we didn't say much to each other."

"Lainey must have been promoted right after she started working for Frank," Jennifer interjected.

"Right," Fletcher confirmed. "Frank told me that he'd promoted her because she was a quick learner and would charm everyone she met. Personally, while I'm sure she deserved it, I think the move had a lot to do with him being in love with her. He always did act crazy around her. And she once told me that she felt a strange attraction toward Frank, but couldn't explain what it was. Although she knew it wasn't love."

Jennifer was concerned about the attraction statement, yet she only nodded.

He continued, "Then Frank told me Lainey had been asking about me when I was in Africa so I decided to talk to her. That night we agreed to meet after she finished work. We took the best bench on the patio for viewing the ocean and called it ours. We talked for hours. I felt really happy and realized I'd found something that had been missing from my life. She seemed to feel the same way..." He paused, turning away to deal with the torment of his reminiscence.

Jennifer remained still.

He went on, "After that we saw more and more of each other until we became lovers. Many times after our lovemaking she'd talk about how we'd become one being. And how she'd never felt that complete with anyone else." His eyes moistened. "She was so beautiful. It was like making love with an angel."

Jennifer looked down, slightly embarrassed by what he had said.

"We never moved in with each other," he said. "I wouldn't ask because of my respect for her, but she wouldn't have anyway, though she would stay with me on most weekends. She knew that if we were ever meant to be married it would happen. She'd always tell me that only I could decide what she meant to me. And the truest path to love was through the heart, the center of one's being where all the passions lie...she said that often..." His voiced lowered. "She would openly admit her total need for me. But I never could. Something just wouldn't let me until it was too late."

Fletcher grimaced, obviously emotionally distressed.

"Fletcher, where was she from and why did she come here?" Jennifer asked, attempting to burst the air of sadness.

"She'd been living in Ogden, Utah with her mother. Her dad had left them both when Lainey was a baby. About two years ago her mother decided to get married again and move to Chicago. Lainey wouldn't go. She chose Newport Beach instead, even though she hadn't ever been to California and didn't know anyone here."

"What?" Jennifer interrupted. "Then why did she move here?"

"Well, I remember she mentioned many times that she'd felt really strange about the strong urge to move to this area. She told me that she didn't know why she'd picked Newport Beach, and even more odd, why she went to the MoonGlade Lounge to look for work. I understand she'd never really doubted either choice."

Fletcher paused and exchanged a moment of silence with Jennifer.

"Maybe it had something to do with her past before Utah," Jennifer suggested.

"I don't think so. She'd have told me," Fletcher answered, now openly disturbed by the discussion of Lainey.

Jennifer sat silently while he recovered from his moment of distress.

Fletcher shook his head, concluding, "I guess that brings us to the lounge, last Thursday night. I'd gotten there in the late afternoon. She'd been there earlier to decorate my table, excited and happy for me. But we both knew the night was going to be bittersweet. We always minimized the impact of my moving to San Diego, deciding that I'd still be close to Newport

Beach. But we knew all along that we'd been lying to ourselves about the distance issue. It wasn't that; the issue was whether we were going to stay together."

Jennifer slowly nodded in agreement.

Fletcher attempted to keep his composure. "Well, I just couldn't go through with the commitment!" He blurted haltingly. "Damn! Jennifer, when I met her it felt as if God had put His hand on my shoulder, telling me how important she was. Why couldn't I see what was offered me before it was too late? Why?"

Jennifer couldn't find the words to console his hurt. But she knew she must let him vent before she could tell him any more.

Fletcher pounded his fist in his hand out of frustration as he stood and walked to the window. He breathed deeply, trying to relieve his mounting anguish.

Jennifer hesitated, then rose and walked over to Fletcher. She slowly turned him around and embraced him as tears rolled down his face.

Fletcher was calmer now and whispered in her ear, "It's so strange the way things happened. Why would God do something like this? We were both good people. Why did he punish us? Why did it end this cruelly?"

Jennifer slowly pulled back and looked up at him, deciding that he was now strong enough to know more.

"Fletcher, I don't think God was responsible for this," she said in a low tone as Fletcher's eyes widened. "I'm afraid it gets crueler and stranger still."

As a tense silence enveloped the room, she gently took his hand. "We'd better sit down," she said, "I have something more to tell you."

CHAPTER 19

Lainey's Cryptic End

Jennifer led Fletcher back to the couch and sat down beside him. She wanted to be close when she told him. Continuing to hold his hand, she took a deep breath and struggled for the words she wasn't even sure she could say aloud.

"Fletcher," she began gently, "I don't believe Lainey committed suicide or fell to her death accidentally. I think she was coerced into death."

Fletcher jumped up in angered anticipation. "What do you mean!?" he shouted. "She was murdered?"

Jennifer stood, grabbed his shoulders and looked him straight in the eyes. "Calm down," she said firmly. "Sit down. Please listen to me."

Fletcher went blank and sat back down.

"Fletcher, this is hard enough on both of us. Now please listen. I think she was coerced into death…but…not murdered," she said slowly, allowing Fletcher to begin comprehending.

He sat subdued while she continued, “Dr. Colletti pulled some strings for me. I was able to see the full police and coroner’s report of Lainey’s death.”

Jennifer paused again, testing Fletcher’s mental strength. She went on after his reassuring nod, “They didn’t find the body of a depressed suicidal woman at the bottom of the sea cliff. They found the body of a terrified woman. She was clutching a rosary and her eyes were wide open, facing the sky. Her expression showed she was paralyzed with fear just before she died.”

“But what caused her death?” Fletcher asked, stunned. “Was it the fall?”

“Apparently, yes. The only unusual marks they found on her body were her own nail marks that she herself had dug into her upper arms. She’d had her arms crossed, backing away from whatever it was she couldn’t fend off.”

“She must’ve been drinking,” he interrupted.

“No, the coroner took a blood sample at the scene and the preliminary toxicology tests from the lab indicated she wasn’t intoxicated. Her blood alcohol level was negligible. In fact, they found the rum bottle that she’d taken from the lounge. It was at the top of the cliff, unopened.”

“Well then, why and hell did she…” Fletcher interrupted.

Jennifer squeezed his hand, halting him. “Wait, there’s more,” she said. “I talked to the Orange County deputy coroner, John Komarek, who performed the autopsy. It was difficult squeezing the information out of him. According to Dr. Colletti, Komarek is very experienced, usually rather clinical and impersonal. But he was visibly shaken by this case. He didn’t want to talk about it, but he did. He told me he would have liked to assign the post-mortem to another anatomical pathologist but couldn't because she'd died under such suspicious circumstances."

"Why was Komarek so upset about this?" Fletcher asked.

"I asked him that too. He said that even though she was dead she still radiated a life-like beauty. He felt as though there was still a strong presence about her. So much of a presence that it didn't feel right to him, eerie even, as though he was violating her during the examination."

"What's that mean?"

"I don't know," she shrugged, sighing. "Anyway, they couldn't find anything internally or externally to pinpoint foul play. No homicide. Therefore, the investigation was closed unless something turns up."

Jennifer suddenly embraced Fletcher, beginning to feel the effects of the weeklong pangs of anxiety. "Oh, Fletcher, this is so hard. I feel so sorry for her because of what she must have gone through." She rested her head on his shoulder.

Fletcher, emotionally drained, put his arm around her and stared straight ahead. "She always carried a rosary with her," he said, reflecting. "Her mother had given it to her to have in time of danger."

Fletcher lifted Jennifer's face to wipe her tears as she said, "Fletcher, if only she'd not gone up to Scenic Point alone. It wouldn't have happened."

He thought a moment before his face stiffened. "Oh no, Jennifer! Did you say Scenic Point?"

"Yes, why?"

Struggling for words he whispered hoarsely, "That was one of our favorite spots. She was up there looking for a part of us. She told me once that she'd never be alone as long as there was a moon-glade to remind her of me. Damn, if I'd only known she was up there."

"Right," Jennifer said, sighing. "I was aware she'd headed for Laguna but I had no idea she…"

"How'd you know?" Fletcher interrupted, surprised.

"Frank told me she'd headed that way when she left the lounge."

Fletcher appeared more surprised. "That's strange. Frank told me when I called the lounge that night that he didn't know where she went and hadn't seen her leave. I specifically remember that because I told him I wanted to go looking for her."

Jennifer shot him a blank stare as he gently pushed her away. He shook his head and stood, silently walking to the patio to scan the ocean. He suddenly turned, asking tensely, "Is there any chance that this whole thing isn't right? I mean, it all seems so bizarre."

"No, it's accurate. And it grows more bizarre," she answered, now composed. She stood and walked over to him, saying, "The police have a complete and signed eyewitness report. I read it. His name is Fernando Vasquez. He works at the restaurant near the point."

"Yeah, I'm familiar with the place," Fletcher interjected.

Jennifer continued, "Anyway, Vasquez says it was closing time and he was cleaning the patio when it happened. He'd seen Lainey there earlier while he was serving customers. The whole area is floodlit, which made it possible for him to see her very clearly. He says she sat on a large rock, about twenty-five yards from the cliff edge, staring at the ocean. Then, curiously, after she climbed off the rock and put on her shoes, she began to back up toward the cliff edge. He shouted to her, but she didn't stop. She didn't even look his way. She never screamed. She just kept backing up, clutching her rosary and her upper arms, looking straight up and then straight ahead," Jennifer's eyes widened, her voice quickened as she stared at Fletcher. "Vasquez said there was also a sudden smoky putrid stink in the air, like rotting flowers, or spoiled fruit. It was so powerful, he could hardly stand it and…"

"Wait, slow down," Fletcher interrupted. "Who was after her for God's sake?"

Jennifer took a deep breath. "No one," she answered.

"What!?"

"His sworn testimony stated that there wasn't anyone in front of her," she answered. "In fact, it was so late, no one was around except his boss who was in the restaurant kitchen. Vasquez did report he heard a faint but shrill cry in the air. But he couldn't say where it was coming from."

Jennifer paused while Fletcher leaned against the patio door, transfixed, shocked at what she was saying.

"Fletcher, listen to this," she went on. "Vasquez dropped everything and attempted to run after her but couldn't. He described it as something out-of-body, like when you're dreaming and you begin free falling or are trying to escape from something bad, but you're helpless and winded." She hesitated, reaching for more of her thoughts. "Fletcher, do you remember how hot and muggy it was that day? You know, the day you tested for your pilot license."

Fletcher nodded vacantly.

"Well, Vasquez reported that during the few minutes that this was all happening the air became icy-cold. When he finally recovered his strength and rushed down the cliff steps to reach her, she was already gone and very cold to the touch."

Jennifer stopped at Fletcher's sudden glance of skepticism.

"The reporters must have gotten wind of this," he said wearily. "Why wasn't all of this in the papers?"

"I asked about that too," she answered quickly. "Komarek explained that they get all kinds of weird witness reports every day."

"How do they know it wasn't just Vasquez?" he asked. "His imagination, or maybe he was on drugs or something."

"No. His boss swore by affidavit that he had heard Vasquez hollering and ran to the patio just in time to see Lainey back off the edge and Vasquez running toward the steps," she countered. "So Komarek's position is that when the police found her all the physical evidence pointed to it being either a suicide or an accidental death from a fall. The autopsy can't prove otherwise. So, at this time, they have to report it as exactly that—an accident or a suicide. The media agreed and put only a small blurb in the paper."

Fletcher conceded, walking back to the couch. "Okay, I want to talk to this guy, Vasquez."

"Can't," she answered. "He's not around."

"What?" he shot back, sitting down.

"He lived in a boarding house in Laguna," she answered, sitting down on the edge of the chair facing him with a riveting stare. "When I went there to talk with him, the housekeeper told me that he's just disappeared, left his clothes, everything. No sign of foul play, however."

"Hooh, booy," Fletcher said, rolling his eyes.

Ignoring his sneer, she remained rigid, adding, "The housekeeper told me it was hell cleaning his room after he'd left. There was a strange stench and small spots of greenish slime scattered all over the floor."

Fletcher furrowed his brow and continued to give her a skeptical look.

"Okay, think what you want, Fletcher," she continued, "but I believe his story, regardless of his disappearance. I don't think he was delusional. At first, I tried to write off this whole incident as crazy, but my intuition wouldn't let me."

Jennifer hesitated and sat back, appearing nervous.

Fletcher noticed, asking, "What is it now, for God's sake?"

"Fletcher," she said, "when I was studying for my masters in aerospace engineering, I was required to take numerous social science courses. They were necessary because of the various world cultures that I would come in contact with during my career with the FAA. Most were theologically based because religious ethics and principles are very important to the infrastructure of any country's culture," she rambled, staring downward. "And some of principles included paranormal beliefs…supernatural experiences…"

"Jennifer, what are you driving at?" Fletcher snapped, his patience spent. "Jesus, get to the point!"

"Please, Fletcher, it's difficult for me to go against the grain of my rational nature," she replied, wincing, before looking up. "Okay, I'm convinced that Lainey didn't die from an accident or suicide. But I also don't believe it was a homicide. I think she was coerced into death by an apparition...an apparition of horror."

"An apparition? An apparition of horror? What horror?"

"I don't know!" she replied. "But I'm sure something wicked has enveloped our lives; mine, yours and Lainey's...maybe more."

They locked stares.

"I don't believe it's over," she added. "I believe Lainey is near, along with the merciless terror she encountered on the cliff that night."

"Lainey, near? How? This sounds insane."

"Listen, I'm not sure of what it all means right now," she hedged, looking away. "But I've thought a lot about it while you've been recovering. It may have something to do with an alternate reality."

"Alternate reality? Jennifer, I have no reason to argue with what you're saying. But this can't be right. She's dead! That's all there is to it!" he exclaimed, bewildered. "Why can't we just leave it alone and get on with things?"

"No!" Jennifer protested, looking back at him sharply. "I've tried to forget it all, but I can't any more. The signs that something mysterious is happening are too powerful. Think about all the events that have occurred lately. What about the incidents surrounding Lainey's funeral? And what about that incident in my bedroom? Dammit! I didn't fabricate these things."

Fletcher eased up at seeing her deep frustration, trying to take in what she was saying.

She moved forward, asking, "Do you remember that strange dream you were having before you regained consciousness? That was a near-death-experience that many people have encountered while coming out of a life-threatening crisis. I stopped by the library this afternoon and did some reading on it. Probably what you saw and felt was real. I think you willed yourself into an alternate state of consciousness to what they call the 'astral plane.' You were then close to Lainey's soul…and also close to the demonic entity that is now shielding her from you."

"Demonic entity," he repeated.

"Yes, I feel that something spectral and fiendish took her from you. We need to understand what. And if I'm right, she's stranded in another realm, but within some kind of reach." She stood. "If so, you have to find out. And I'm convinced that I need to help in any way I can without even knowing why yet."

She picked up the coffee pot and cups and walked into the kitchen.

"It still sounds crazy," Fletcher said, drained, shaking his head. He stood and followed her. "Look, I'm not a religious man. I believe in God and an afterlife of some kind. But I haven't dealt much with supernatural beliefs…" he hesitated. "Oh, shit, I dunno. Right now I'm so tired and confused from all that's happened. I'm not sure I understand any of it." Frustrated, he threw his hands up. "Anyway just what are you suggesting we do now?"

Jennifer set the dishes in the sink and turned to him looking perplexed but confident. "I don't know yet. But I'm sure whatever we do is gonna take time. I only hope Donald will understand. I'll talk to him tomorrow afternoon when he gets in from his business trip." She sighed, adding, "On Monday I'll contact the FAA district office in Los Angeles to ask for a leave-of-absence. I certainly can't perform my job under these crazy conditions." She leaned back against the counter and looked at Fletcher.

He picked up his queue. "I think that first I should go to the MoonGlade and talk to Frank," he said quietly. "I owe him an explanation. I'll go and see him on Sunday during brunch. I'm just going to lie around here tomorrow and get some sleep."

"Fletcher, I think you're right, but please remember that Frank doesn't know the full extent of what's happened. I think it's best to leave it that way until we know more. Do you agree?"

"Oh yeah, sure," he replied, "I'd like to know what the hell I'm talking about before I discuss this situation with anyone, especially Frank. Which reminds me, I also need to talk to Tom Berkshire next week. But I'm not really sure what to tell him. Any ideas?"

"Unfortunately, not at this point," she answered. "But don't worry, you'll have time to plan for that. Right now we both need some rest. I'm going home."

"It's a long drive. You can stay here," he offered. "I'll sleep on the couch."

"Uh, no, I have to be home in case Donald comes in early or calls," she said as she picked up her purse from the dining table and walked to the door. "Bye," she said, waving, as she stepped off the porch. "I'll try and call you on Sunday night."

He returned her farewell with a nod, closed the door and slowly walked to the patio. Sitting down on the chaise lounge, he leaned back and stared out at the ocean, wondering desperately what had taken over his life and where he was headed.

It was only fitting that tonight the moon was pale and it was cloudy. There would be no moon-glade.

Jennifer drove only a few blocks before turning into a motel on Pacific Coast Highway. Her head was splitting from a throbbing tension headache.

She was confused and had been forced to make up that excuse about Donald coming in early in order to leave Fletcher. She couldn't tell him any more tonight. He had heard enough. If she had stayed, she knew she would have told him everything. He wasn't ready for that yet. She was also perplexed over her growing relationship with him. She was feeling closer toward him. A different closeness than she'd ever known with any man, but couldn't explain what that all meant.

After checking in, she collapsed into bed. As she fell asleep, she reran her last thoughts over and over in her head. *If the pattern of losing people close to him is true, why am I not in danger? Or am I?*

CHAPTER 20

Sunday, Newport Beach

Fletcher was feeling vigorous as he backed out of his carport, well rested and finally sleeping without the aid of medication. Yesterday's relaxing picnic on the beach with the Cunninghams was what he needed. He was glad they had all remained friends and that Marsha understood what he'd lost when Lainey died. She knew how much he loved Lainey and couldn't be with another woman romantically right now—maybe somewhere down the road, but definitely not now. Yet, Fletcher was pleased they had agreed to remain friends and would occasionally get together when their schedules allowed.

Even though it was cloudy and chilly, the ocean air felt good pressing against his skin as he began the cruise down the coast highway toward the MoonGlade Lounge. He considered himself lucky just to be enjoying the sensation again.

Newport Beach was hushed. Sunday-quiet. He appreciated the mid-morning hours before the crush of people began to congregate, crowding the beach. He was sometimes uncomfortable around the crowds, but addicted to the action and excitement of Southern California. There was always something new to experience and photograph. He also enjoyed painting the seascapes, dabbling in his relaxing recreation when times were less demanding.

His thoughts turned to Jennifer and the events of the last week, especially the mystical experiences that she had described on Friday night. Could she be right? Was something going on around them that they didn't understand yet? And if he was somehow able to reach Lainey again, could he handle it? *Would he really want to?* What alternative world might they discover? World? Would it be a world? Would it be diabolical, satanic? Damn!

But then, what if they pursued Jennifer's mysterious perceptions and she was wrong. He would have to re-live the whole nightmare of Lainey's death for nothing. He then wondered if Jennifer had told Donald yet that she had to take time off to investigate this puzzle. Fletcher would find out tonight when she called him—that is, if she was still serious about all of this and *would* call him.

His chain of thought shattered as he maneuvered into the small parking lot of the MoonGlade Lounge. Pulling the jeep up close to the valet-shack, he saw George sitting on a large rock facing the ocean, and sipping on a beer. Fletcher smiled and shook his head. It's never too early for George to fight last night's hangover with more drink.

"Hey, George," Fletcher yelled.

George turned, did a double take and dragged himself down off the rock.

"Fletcher," he rasped, lumbering toward him. The deeply tanned furrows etched in his forehead wrinkled with his smile. "Haven't seen ya in a while. Where ya been?"

"George, it's a long story," he said as they shook hands. "One that I'd like to forget for right now, if you don't mind."

"You betcha," George replied lethargically, "I understand. I've had a few falls myself."

"Thanks, George. Is Frank inside?"

"Yeah, they're getting ready for the champagne brunch crowd. They're a bit slow in there this morning. Big party here last night. A bunch of 'Hollywooders' showed up. About three yachts full. I'm sure they'll be back shortly. They pretty much reserved the place again this morning."

"Good," Fletcher said cheerfully, flipping George his keys. "I could use some company today. See ya later."

George slowly nodded and watched him walk to the door, unable to tell him what he would find inside...unable to tell him about the *new* crowd.

Fletcher walked in and felt an immediate rush of dejection as he looked down the foyer at the maitre d' stand. He hesitated, reading the new placard attached to the stand. It now read ***Janice*** instead of ***Lainey.*** *Shit, how could Frank replace Lainey already,* he wondered, proceeding toward the stand.

The tall brunette in a flowered sundress looked up at him. "Yes Sir, may I help you? Do you have a reservation?" she asked, flashing a wide smile.

Fletcher, momentarily stunned, stammered, "Ah, yes...I mean, no."

"I'm sorry Sir, but the champagne brunch is reserved this morning. We're full up."

Fletcher, speechless, abruptly felt empty. He remembered Lainey's loving greeting and the embrace she would give him every time he'd come in. He now realized that part of his life was over and would not return.

"It's okay, Janice," the voice from the bar bellowed, bursting the uneasy stillness. "Let him in."

Fletcher looked over at Frank, who was sitting at the bar with a Bloody Mary.

Fletcher walked over to him offering his hand, saying, "Hello, Frank."

"Morning, Fletcher," Frank greeted coolly, returning a limp shake. "How are you feeling?"

Fletcher sat down next to Frank, motioning for the bartender to bring him the same drink as Frank's. "I thought okay," Fletcher replied cautiously. "But maybe not, after seeing the new hostess up front. I'm surprised you hired one so soon."

"Sorry, Fletcher, the world changes quickly and so do I," Frank responded blankly. "Janice is a friend of Kent Fitzroy, the producer from Beverly Hills. He bought the place. I completed the deal a few days ago."

Fletcher looked at him in surprise. "You sold out? How come?"

Frank remained unemotional, answering, "I decided it's time. I'd been thinking about it for a long time."

"I never knew that," Fletcher said.

"I know," Frank replied. "I didn't talk about it much. I suppose Lainey's death helped me finalize the decision. Things won't ever be the same around here again. My work here is finished, so to speak."

"I see. But we can still stay in touch, right?" Fletcher asked, testing Frank's feelings.

Frank hesitated, then answered, "Listen Fletcher, I'm sure you had a good reason for what you did to Lainey. But like I said, things won't be the same again. Lainey meant a lot to me, and to everyone else here."

"Frank, I'm sorry," Fletcher replied directly, "I just couldn't meet her commitment that night. You know I tried to reach her later to tell her I'd changed my mind and wanted her to go to San Diego with me, but it was too late. I couldn't find her."

Fletcher paused, not revealing Jennifer's perception of what really might have happened on the cliff that night. He wanted to tell him, but knew it wouldn't do any good. Frank's mind was made up that he was responsible for Lainey's death.

Frank remained silent and only stared straight ahead, offering no compassion for Fletcher's appeal.

Fletcher was suddenly disgusted by Frank's impassive attitude. "Dammit, Frank!" Fletcher blurted out. "I thought we were friends, good friends! If you'll please give me a chance, over time I can make it right! You'll have to believe I lost a lot with Lainey as well as you. But there's nothing I can do to bring her back!"

Frank finally managed a slight smile. "Sure, Fletcher," he relented, "we all need time. I'll be around. I'm checking on a lounge that's for sale on Catalina Island tomorrow morning. I asked Chapman to fly me over. He might even let me sit in the left seat and fly a little. But he'll have to land it on that cliff. I wouldn't attempt that one."

Fletcher looked up, relieved that the tension in the air had finally broken. "I know," he agreed. "It's one hell'uva landing."

"Yeah," Frank replied. "Anyway, if the property doesn't look good I'll probably head for New York. There are plenty of new opportunities there. However, we can keep in touch. What are you going to do from here?"

"I'll probably move to San Diego, as planned. I'm driving down there tomorrow to meet with Tom Berkshire. I talked to him at home yesterday afternoon."

"Oh yeah, Berkshire called here Thursday or maybe it was Friday," Frank recalled. "I told him what had happened. About Lainey, I mean. He told me he understood your situation and would wait for you to contact him."

Fletcher nodded, replying, "Right, he mentioned your conversation. Thanks for the support."

Frank stood up, saying, "Sure. Well, I have to prepare for Fitzroy's brunch crowd. You're welcome to stay if you want. I'm sure we can find room for you here at the bar. I'm sorry your table has been taken over by Fitzroy. It's the best one in the place, ya know."

Fletcher looked down at hearing of another disappointment. "I understand," he said, then looked up at Frank. "I think I'll pass on brunch. Thanks anyway. I'm going to take a long walk on the beach and grab a bite by the pier or something."

"Okay, but take your time finishing your drink," Frank said obligingly. "I'll see you in a day or two, after I get back from Catalina."

"Thanks again," Fletcher replied, watching Frank walk away.

He stood and began to slowly scan the room, recollecting the past. He realized there wouldn't be any more good times here as he walked over and stood next to his favorite table, the table that wasn't his anymore. He looked up at his prized African trophy, deciding he wouldn't take it with him. It really did belong to the lounge. He remembered the night of his birthday, the night he had promised the trophy to Frank…the same night he had met Lainey. The nostalgic pain pierced him cruelly as he lowered his gaze to the window and peered out at the beachfront. He stared at the bench he and Lainey had shared on those evenings when they would look for the moon-glade, recalling how they would laugh and love and discuss everything that mattered at the time.

He closed his eyes and tipped his drink, finishing it, vowing that life would go on. He would wait for Frank to settle somewhere else before contacting him again. A new environment would help both of them. Best he just leave quickly. He turned, seeing Frank wasn't anywhere in sight. He set his empty glass on the table and hurried toward the front door.

Janice bid him a pleasant good-bye as he brushed past the people starting to file in through the foyer. They were all jovial, laughing and joking. The new crowd had arrived—Kent Fitzroy's crowd. It was fitting that no one recognized Fletcher, or even noticed him leaving.

Outside, Fletcher retrieved his keys from George, shook his hand heartily and wished him the best of luck with the new management. Then he climbed into his jeep and pulled out of the lot, heading for the Newport Beach pier. He didn't look back. He would never again look back, he decided.

Jennifer walked to the door at hearing the ring of the doorbell. Peeking through the peephole, she saw that it was Donald. She was surprised that he hadn't just knocked lightly and walked in as usual. *Maybe he knew something had changed,* she thought as she stepped back and hesitated. He'd probably suspected something was far different when she stayed with him for only a short time after she brought him home from the airport yesterday; begging off from a certain long night of conversation and lovemaking by telling him she needed sleep. She just wasn't ready to face him yet. She had needed more time to think about how she would tell him what had been going on—and at a time when they both weren't so tired. But tonight she was ready, having decided to tell him the truth. Maybe all of the truth, maybe not. It would depend on how the night progressed. Whatever, she was convinced she was prepared as she took a deep breath and slowly opened the door.

"Hi, baby," he said, immediately reaching down to draw her into his arms.

"Hello, darling," she answered, returning his embrace, but not demonstrating any excitement, her way of beginning the confession. "How are you feeling tonight?"

"Great," he replied buoyantly. "I think you were right about us needing sleep last night."

"I know," she replied with a grin, gently pulling away from him. "We both needed it. And I'm sure we wouldn't have gotten much rest if we'd stayed together." She forced a wink, then asked, "You hungry for dinner? I picked up a couple of steaks, though I forgot the wine."

"Yeah, I'm hungry, but truthfully I sort of had something else in mind first," he answered with a gleam in his eye, testing her.

"Oh, darling," she replied, "let's have dinner first. It's always so much better after a little food and wine."

She then drew him close and squeezed him. Looking out past his shoulder, she thought of how it was going to be a long night for them. He tightened his grip, seemingly knowing what was about to happen.

She tightened her embrace, deciding she could do one more night for him. She must give herself to him one more night; for memories if nothing else. And maybe she'd even come back to him one day, come back mentally from wherever she had gone so suddenly.

"Okay," he said, smiling, as he separated from her. "Steaks and Merlot sounds great. I'll head to the store for the wine. You start the salads. Deal?"

"Deal," she agreed, returning the smile.

He turned and left, giving them a chance to regroup. Temporarily relieved, she inhaled and walked to the kitchen.

They sat quietly at the dining table finishing their dessert of orange sherbet. It had been a pleasant dinner. She had listened to him talk about the business trip, and how he might run the new satellite office here in Los Angeles. This allowed her enough time to gather her courage. Finally, she pushed her small bowl aside and began to finger the stem of her wineglass. Noticing, he stood and began clearing the dishes, forcing her hand.

"Darling," she said slowly, looking up, "let's forget the dishes for a while and go into the living room and talk."

"Sure," he agreed, noticing the tears in her eyes.

He gently took her hand and they walked to the sofa and sat down. He lifted her chin, saying softly, "Baby, don't torture yourself. I knew by the messages you sent last week and the strange way you've been acting lately that something has seriously changed between us. Is it another man?"

She paused to carefully choose her words. "Yes," she admitted, looking away, not wanting to face his anguish. "But not necessarily in the way you think," she quickly added to relieve some of the hurt. "His name is Fletcher McKeane. I met him at Shelanary's. It was odd that I felt so close to him, so quickly, without even knowing him. I'm not even sure why I feel so attracted to him."

She stopped there, deciding not to tell him everything. She hadn't lied, just withheld some things that wouldn't make any difference to their lives. It would only confuse things more than they were already.

"Are you...are you...?" he sputtered, unable to finish the question of his greatest fear.

"In love with Fletcher?" she said, looking straight at him. "I don't know what you'd call it. I don't think I could make love with him. Isn't that the true test?"

He nodded, appearing somewhat relieved.

"However," she continued, "I do realize that he and his situation have become a priority in my life."

"His situation?"

"I mean, he was sick," she said, catching herself. "He's doing better now. His girlfriend was killed in a tragic accident. It hit him quite hard." She paused and shook her head. "Oh Donald, you must think I'm crazy. I've changed so much, so quickly, the last week most dramatically. I need time to sort things out. I don't understand everything myself. Can we please just leave it at this point for right now?" she pleaded, her eyes brimming with tears. "We'd never be happy under these conditions. I'm sorry. Please understand."

He looked away, groping for words, and then looked back up at her. "Is this good-bye forever?" he asked quietly, the disappointment flowing from his eyes.

"I don't know. I can't lie to you about this, darling," she answered faithfully. "But I do believe that I'm not doing this because I'm in love with another man. It's just that something has changed and I'm not emotionally attached to our relationship right now."

They sat awkwardly for a few minutes before he reached for her hand. "Jennifer, I've always prepared myself for something like this," he said confidently. "I'll be close if you need me again. Can we make love once more before I leave? I suppose I need to take something with me."

She hesitated and thought. "Of course, I still want to and need to," she lied, seeing no use in hurting him any further. She was not in the mood for lovemaking but it was the least she could do until she found out for sure what their relationship meant anymore. After all, she wasn't sure this was the end.

She stood and reached up, putting her arms around him. Pressing close together, they kissed before walking to the bedroom to carry out their fervent good-bye.

CHAPTER 21

Monday, North of San Diego

Fletcher slammed hard on the brake pedal! The wheels locked, pulling the jeep wildly onto the asphalt shoulder of the Interstate. It came to a screeching halt, only inches from the steel guard rail.

He grimaced as he looked across the vast sprawl of barren hills and grassy valleys bordering the ocean. *Shit! Nothing around but the Marine base! The nearest public phone is in Oceanside, twenty miles away!* Why didn't these bad thoughts about Chapman's flight to Catalina happen before he'd left this morning? Why all of a sudden, in the middle of nowhere? *Dammit!*

He glanced at his watch. It's only nine. Maybe they hadn't left yet. Determined to quickly find a phone and get a message to Chapman, he crushed his foot on the accelerator and squealed back onto the freeway. He decided to take his chances with the Highway Patrol and was soon topping ninety, easily passing the moderate Monday morning traffic.

Bob Chapman swung his leg back and kicked the bulky wooden chock out from behind the nose wheel of the sleek single-engine plane. "I think we're all set to go, Frank."

Leaning quietly against the wing, Frank Conklin watched Chapman step back for a final look at the entire plane.

Satisfied, Chapman looked up at the brightening sky and let out a slight whistle as the emerging sun warmed his face. "It's gonna be a hell'uva good day for flying. Shouldn't take us long to get to Catalina."

Frank, with a reserved tone, replied, "Good, Bob, I'll be glad to get my hands on the controls again."

"No problem, Frank," Chapman answered, reaching up to retrieve his logbook from the briefcase sitting on the floor of the cockpit. "Once we're up I'll let you take her over for a bit. In fact, you can assume the pilot's seat today."

"Thanks," Frank replied.

Bob, noticing Frank's casual manner, frowned and turned toward him. "Frank, you feeling okay? You haven't said much since you got here."

"Sure, just tired that's all," Frank replied impatiently. "You know, dealing with all the upheaval that's happened lately."

"Yeah, I understand," Chapman answered, breaking into a grin. "Oh, that reminds me. I heard Fletcher stopped by the lounge yesterday."

"Yes, how'd you know?"

"Joyce told me," Chapman answered. "He'd called the house last night but I was here late with a student and didn't get a chance to call him back. I tried this morning but he was gone. Joyce said he was heading for San Diego this morning."

"Right," Frank agreed. "That's what he mentioned to me at the lounge."

"Incidentally," Bob said, "I understand Fletcher was really disappointed you'd sold the MoonGlade."

"But I also told him it couldn't be helped," Frank replied coldly.

"I know, I understand," Chapman said, surprised at Frank's lack of emotion over disappointing his good friend. But he shrugged it off, adding, "I'll give him a call when he gets back from San Diego."

"Sounds good, Bob."

"All right, I think we're ready," Chapman said, turning toward the terminal. "I'll be right back. I'm gonna check in with Catalina airport just to make sure everything is okay over there."

Frank nodded nonchalantly.

Chapman, whistling to himself, turned and walked into the terminal while Frank watched him with narrowing eyes.

Fletcher pulled into the Oceanside gas station, jumped out of his Jeep and raced to the phone booth. He dialed, heard the answer and exclaimed, "Jan, this is McKeane! Is Chapman there?...Dammit! What time did they leave?...A few minutes ago? Could they possibly still be in the tiedown area? Please do me a favor and check for sure somehow. Thanks, I'll wait," he said anxiously, his voice filled with worry.

Fletcher waited nervously, fiddling with the change return cup. ..."Yes, I'm still here, Jan....Shit!" He hesitated, thinking. "Huh?...No, never mind, forget the unicom frequency. Oh, by the way, have you seen

Jennifer Jaynes there by any chance?...Okay. No, no message. Thanks, Jan, see ya soon." He hung up the phone, grimaced, and stepped out of the booth, slamming the door shut behind him.

He got back in his Jeep and thought over his worry of not catching Chapman. The startling premonition he'd received about his friend's trip was probably foolish anyway. It must have grown out of the strange events of the past week. His mind was beginning to play tricks on him. He would only have made a fool of himself if he'd found Chapman or tried sending him a radio message on the unicom, asking him to turn back. Chapman would have laughed and kept going anyway. No one flew that route better than he did.

Fletcher pulled back on the Interstate, heading south to San Diego. He began thinking about today's afternoon lunch plans he'd set up with Berkshire to discuss his new work schedule and when he'd move to San Diego. If he did begin his new job right away, he would stay at the Alpine Towers in Mission Bay and only return to Newport Beach to move his belongings.

His thoughts turned to Jennifer and how she hadn't called him as she said she would. She must have decided that the whole scenario she'd told him about was crazy. She probably went back to her usual life with her boyfriend and her FAA job. He'd miss her, though. She'd quickly become a strong force in his life. He would write and thank her. After all, she did save his life.

He leaned his head back against the headrest and looked at his watch. He relaxed, deciding he would detour to Del Mar and have some coffee by the ocean. He had plenty of time.

Bob Chapman, sitting in the right seat, eased the plane off the short runway, soaring northwest toward the bright horizon. Reaching the desired altitude, he guided the plane around the giant cotton-like clouds that dotted the clear blue sky. Having had a good night's sleep and no other appointments to crimp his day of leisure, Chapman felt good. Moreover, his good friend Fletcher seemed to be coming out of his depression over Lainey's death. He smiled faintly as he thought about meeting Fletcher for a few beers at the MoonGlade before he made his final move to San Diego.

Frank sat quietly in the pilot's seat staring out at the ocean and, out of the corner of his eye, watching Chapman.

"Hey!" Chapman exclaimed, looking over at him as he pointed toward the mountainous outline on the horizon. "There's Catalina. We're only about fifteen minutes away. Wanna take it over?"

"Sure," Frank answered. "But how about if I fly around a little before we land?"

"Hell yeah, why not? If you're not in a hurry, I'm not. Why don't you head down toward San Clemente or something. It shouldn't be busy there. Then we'll zip back up to Catalina. Go ahead take it over."

Chapman leaned back as Frank took the controls and smoothly banked the left wing, easing the plane southeast. Chapman felt pleased about Frank's calm command of the aircraft. Relaxed, Chapman daydreamed and looked down at the miniature yachts and schooners gliding along the California coast. Frank easily leveled out the plane, cruising southward.

Chapman then looked up and out the windshield, seeing the horizon begin to whiten. He blinked as the skyline suddenly blurred. *Sea fog? No,* he decided. *Sea fog is quick but not that quick.*

Frank appeared unconcerned, remaining in cruise mode as the sun's sharp outline began to dim.

Chapman quickly glanced down and watched the boats and the aqua-blue ocean slowly vanishing beneath a thickening layer of gray. Now worried, he said, "Frank, better let me take the plane. I don't understand this, I wanna get us back to Catalina."

Frank looked over at Chapman. "Whatever," he agreed, shrugging. He leaned back and released the control yoke.

Reaching forward to take control from his side, Chapman thought Frank's calmness odd, but said nothing. He was more concerned about the troubling flight conditions. His eyes were frozen on the altimeter and gyroscope as he banked the plane steeply, abruptly turning to the right. As he leveled the plane, a blanket of ashen gray quickly shrouded the windshield.

Grabbing the microphone, Chapman tuned in the Catalina unicom frequency and spoke rapidly, "Good Morning, Catalina, Piper NC1465."

The radio replied immediately, "Catalina, here. Go ahead, 1465."

"1465, here," Chapman responded tensely. "I'm suddenly mired up in some heavy sea fog or something. The worst I've ever seen. What's the weather like there?"

"What? It's perfect weather here, 1465. Where are you?"

"About ten minutes south of you, I figure," Chapman replied urgently as the billowing gray swirl began seeping through the aircraft vents, clouding the instrument panel.

Frank, now only a fuzzy outline remained still, staring at Chapman.

Straining to focus on the rapidly fading instrument panel, Chapman, now panicked, blurted into the microphone. "Damn, I can hardly see anything in front of me! I'm even losing my exterior bearings! I'm now declaring this flight an emergency!"

"1465! We don't understand!" the radio cried. "I have my glasses on you! We can even see an outline of your passenger. You've entered the bay! You're not in any fog, it's clear! Are you drunk or something!? 1465! You're too low! Pull up! You're heading for the cliff! Pull up! 1465, please respond!"

But Chapman couldn't hear the emergency appeals. A high-pitched shrill had drowned out the radio while a foul stench filled the cockpit.

Chapman, frozen with dread, knew the plane was out of control and doomed. Managing to depress the microphone, he prepared his final words for his beloved wife, Joyce. But he stopped as he heard a voice saying, "Mr. Doherty I shall take over now."

Chapman turned to his left as the figure slowly began to appear. In stark horror, Chapman screamed into the microphone as the plane swiftly veered toward the unyielding rocky face of the sheer Catalina cliff.

Fletcher slowed his Jeep to a crawl, pulling up in front of the new fifteen-story, glass office building. Located a short distance off the Interstate overlooking the San Diego Zoo, the building had large white lettering printed on the front:

GEOGRAPHIC UNLIMITED PUBLICATIONS

He drove up to the security gate, showed his ID badge and was admitted. After parking his Jeep, he got out, no longer feeling nervous. He had decided that his premonition about Chapman had been exaggerated.

Wearing a broad smile in the noontime sunshine, he pushed open the tinted glass doors of the main entrance. He felt refreshed thinking about how his life would be taking a turn for the better. He walked through the plush lobby and winked as he showed his badge to the perky young lobby receptionist. "I'm here to see Mr. Tom Berkshire, please."

She smiled and read the badge then quickly looked up. "Oh, Mr. McKeane, you have an urgent message. You're to call a Ms. Jaynes in L.A. at her office. She left the number…Mr. McKeane, are you all right?"

"Yeah," he whispered, turning ashen. "Please give me the message."

"It's just that you are to call her immediately upon your arrival. Here's the number." She handed him a piece of paper.

He grabbed it and anxiously hurried to the lobby phone and dialed the number.

"Hello, this is Fletcher McKeane. I'm trying to reach Jennifer Jaynes." He waited, becoming agitated at knowing it was more bad news. *What fucking other kind of news has she ever given him?* he lamented inwardly. The time dragged until she picked up the phone.

"Yes, Jennifer it's me, Fletcher. What is it?…Oh Christ, no! Damn! When, how?…Jennifer, I knew it, I knew it!" he said, pounding his fist against the booth. "Never mind, I'll explain later…Yes, I would like you to come down. I'll postpone my meeting with Berkshire until after you get here…Good, I'll pick you up at the airport…Right, I understand. Montgomery Field at the general aviation terminal…Okay, see you there…Bye." Fletcher, dispirited, hung up the phone and returned to the receptionist desk.

"Miss, I was supposed to have lunch with Tom Berkshire today. Please tell him I'm in town, but an emergency has come up. I'll get back to him this afternoon and explain." Fletcher bolted away without hearing her reply: "Yes, Mr. McKeane, I'll tell him."

Fletcher felt traumatized as he waited for Jennifer. Watching from the terminal window at Montgomery Field, he finally saw the small FAA jet roll up to the personnel gate and stop. Fletcher hurried through the door as Jennifer climbed out of the pilot seat, jumped down from the cockpit and quickly walked toward him.

She was dressed casually in jeans, a white blouse tucked under a sweatshirt and flats. Her hair was pulled back and her face was only lightly made up.

They embraced on the tarmac.

"I was in the office requesting a leave-of-absence when the call came in from Catalina this morning," she said softly. "I'll tell you what I know, although I don't have any details yet. Steve Butler flew to Catalina about noon to formally investigate the accident."

"Has either of them survived?" he asked as they separated.

Her silence confirmed his fears. She then took his hand, saying, "Fletcher, we don't know for sure why, but we do know the plane went into the side of the cliff." She shook her head. "I don't know how it would be possible for either of them to have survived." She hesitated, noticing his blank stare. "Fletcher, what is going on? What?" she asked nervously.

"I don't know, but now I'm starting to recognize and feel the same bad vibes as you," he answered, exasperated, grabbing onto her elbow. "C'mon, let's get some coffee." They turned and walked inside the terminal.

As they sat sipping on black coffee, Jennifer broke the solemn silence. "Fletcher, I'm sorry I didn't get a chance to talk to you yesterday. But after telling Donald that I needed to be alone for right now, it turned out to be an extremely long night."

"Sure, I understand," he answered.

"Anyway, what did you decide to tell Berkshire?"

"Well, I had just decided that I was going to go back to work. Now, I don't know," he replied, looking at her with increased intensity.

"What's the matter?"

He clutched her arm, replying, "Listen, I felt they were going to crash. I had a strong premonition on the way down here, a bad one. I even stopped and tried to phone Chapman to keep him from going. But when I called, I found out I was too late. Just like with Lain…" His words trailed off as they stared at each other, both immediately thinking the same thing: *Each time, just a little too late.* But neither would voice it aloud.

"Fletcher, I'm going to call the office to see if Steve has left a message on my machine. He knows I'm anxiously waiting for his report. I'll be right back."

She hurried to the phone booth. Fletcher watched her as she spent a few minutes listening on the phone. She must have gotten a message, he thought.

She slowly stepped from the booth and walked to Fletcher with her eyes cast downward.

He looked up at her and exhaled deeply. "Tell me," he said.

She sat down and put a hand on his wrist, saying gently, "It's the worst. They were able to reach the wreckage. It was embedded in the side of the cliff, near the bottom. They found Bob's remains near the top, settled on a rocky plateau."

Fletcher jerked back and grimaced. "What? How'd he end up there?"

"Somehow he apparently opened the cabin door when the plane was in the air and fell off the wing. I suppose he wanted to try and make the water. Either he got caught on the plane or the force of the air took him into the mountain."

"Oh, Jesus!" Fletcher exclaimed. "What about Frank?"

"We don't know. They can't find him."

"Huh? They can't find him? He must've gotten out before Bob then."

"Don't know. A witness supposedly saw it all from the tower," she replied. "He saw only one man jump. It must've been Bob, but who knows right now? It's only preliminary information. We'll try to get the full details tomorrow. Maybe there's a recorded radio conversation of some kind on one of the unicom stations or in the tower or something. Oh, I don't know! Damn!"

Fletcher put his arm around her shoulder, saying, "Don't worry, we'll find out." He sat back and thought for a moment. "Well, I guess that's about everybody."

"What?" she asked, looking up at him.

"That's everyone that I was close to. They're now all gone."

"Fletcher, I'm scared."

They both looked away. Again, neither would say aloud what they were thinking. His friends weren't all gone. There was one person left who had just become close. A new friend—*her*.

He reached over, grabbed her by the shoulders and looked her in the eyes. "Jennifer," he pleaded, "Whatever is happening must revolve around me. Get out now. Go. Just leave L.A. Get married or go back to Pensacola. Please. You don't deserve this mess. I can handle it."

"Maybe you're right," she said. "This whole thing could be fate instead of just coincidence. Then again, maybe there's nothing to it at all. All I know is that my whole life is screwed up. I even left Donald last night. And I'm not even sure why." She began to weep.

He tightened his arm around her to console her. "Tell you what," he said softly. "Fly home to Donald today. Go back to him. I'm staying to meet with Tom Berkshire tomorrow. I've made reservations at the Alpine Towers hotel in Mission Bay. After my meeting with Tom, I'm going back to Newport Beach to deal with the accident. I'll call you from there. One day we'll laugh over this fated stuff. Please think about it while I call Berkshire to let him know what's going on."

She nodded. "Okay, make your call. I'll wait.

Her tears had dried by the time he returned.

He sat down and took her hand in his. "How about it?" he asked. "Are you all right to fly?"

"Yes, I'm all right to fly. I think I'll take your advice if you really don't mind."

"Nah, I don't mind," he answered. "Look, we conjured up a bunch of bullshit between us, that's all. We scared the hell out of ourselves. Let's say we just forget it and get back to our lives as best we can. I made an appointment with Berkshire for tomorrow. I told him I was ready to come back to work."

"Okay," she replied, sighing, as they stood up.

They embraced and faintly smiled at each other as they walked outside to the parking lot.

"I'll call you soon, see ya," he said. Turning quickly to walk to his jeep, he already felt the loss of her. But as he had told her, she didn't deserve this mess. He climbed into his jeep and didn't turn around. He couldn't let her see his pain from yet another loss.

As the jeep faded into the traffic, she waved, then slowly walked back to the plane to prepare it for the short flight home. She thought about contacting Donald as soon as she arrived back in LA. Why not try and get back to her old life? Fletcher was probably right, she thought, *they were only scaring each other with all this conjured up bullshit.*

Fletcher felt miserably alone. He was oblivious to the buzz of the dinner crowd as he sat fidgeting with his dinner receipt in the Alpine Towers restaurant. He wanted desperately to figure things out. Could he forget the lingering horror of Lainey's death and today's plane crash that had taken the lives of his friends? And maybe the worst of all, Jennifer was now gone too, and possibly in danger. Could he just forget everything and go back to work, business as usual?

Yielding to his inner turmoil, he dropped the receipt and cradled his head in his hands.

Suddenly he heard from behind him, "The only bullshit, Mr. McKeane, came from you this afternoon."

He spun around to face a smiling Jennifer.

"Now stand up and hold me," she said. "We'll remain together until we know for sure what in hell is going on. No pun intended."

Relieved, he quickly leapt up and embraced her. "Thank you," he whispered in her ear, unable to hide his happiness at seeing her. "Thank you."

"Sure, anytime," she responded warmly, gently nudging him. "Now if you're through with dinner let's go to the front desk so I can get a room for tonight."

The other dinner guests smiled and exchanged knowing looks as they watched Fletcher and Jennifer walk out, arm-in-arm.

CHAPTER 22

The Alpine Towers, Mission Bay

Fletcher and Jennifer, lost in the bright moonlight and undulating surf of the calm sea, leisurely strolled along the hotel beachfront. Deciding to stop and rest on a grassy knoll, they sat down and stretched out flat, looking up at the sky that was clear and full of stars.

"What made you come back?" he asked.

"I never really wanted to leave. I don't know how to run away from anything. I'll admit, though, you were pretty persuasive this afternoon. Typical Irish blarney." She chuckled. "But it was Steve's last report on the plane crash that really convinced me to come back. I decided to talk to him before I left the airport. Afterward I needed to think, so I..." She paused. "Promise you won't laugh."

"Laugh?" he questioned, turning toward her. "No, I won't laugh. What?"

"You sure?"

He nodded and she continued, "Okay, I rented a car and drove to Escondido and toured the Wild

Animal Park. I went to see the world you love. As I walked around, I realized that I wanted you to be able to enjoy that world again. I also decided that I need to help you do that, because you don't deserve this mess either."

"You're wonderful, thanks," he whispered, riveted to her words.

She smiled and returned her gaze to the sky. He did the same.

"Fletcher, I found out that Catalina has a radio conversation of the crash on tape. It's kinda weird."

"Nothing surprises me anymore," he said, unmoved. "Let's have it."

"The FAA is positive they were both definitely in the plane. Gary Shelanary saw them leave the terminal this morning and a controller in the Catalina tower swears he'd seen two figures in the plane when it entered Avalon Bay."

"Okay, what about the radio conversation?"

"They told me that there's only one voice on the tape. They know that it's Bob's. Shelanary listened to it and confirmed it." She paused. "I understand there were multiple distress exchanges between Bob and the tower, and the last thing that Bob screamed was, 'Oh no, oh my God, no' just before the crash. It's bloodcurdling. The tower had no idea what was happening. They didn't know if there was a mechanical problem or the landing was botched or what. They kept asking him and he just kept repeating, 'Oh my God'…"

"Nobody flew that Catalina run better than Bob," Fletcher interrupted. "I don't know what could've gone wrong, but if it was mechanical Bob would've brought the plane down on the beach, or in the shallow surf. And it couldn't have been a botched landing. Bob was too damn good of a pilot for that."

Jennifer sat up and looked at Fletcher, saying, "It's also strange that the tower never heard any background pleas from Frank, not one. Maybe he wasn't even in the plane at the time. The tower doesn't know because at that point they couldn't see the cockpit clearly, the plane had plunged into a downward attitude. Maybe Frank had already jumped out through the cabin door somehow."

"That's what must've happened," Fletcher replied, continuing to look upward. "Frank was probably in the right seat and got out first. He must be in the ocean somewhere or washed up on some beach by now."

"I suppose you're right," she agreed. "Although some people on shore claim they saw everything and swear they saw only one man jump. Anyway, until they find him we won't know."

Fletcher inhaled. "Jesus, how crazy all this is."

"Sure is," she continued, lying back down. "Regardless, if they're right and Frank didn't jump earlier, he must somehow have been thrown clear on impact. But it's odd they can't find any indication of that. They're going to keep looking." She hesitated then asked, "Incidentally, was Frank really a good friend of yours?"

"I think so, why?" Fletcher answered impatiently, growing weary.

"Never mind, it's not important," she replied, quickly realizing that Fletcher was more upset than he'd first appeared. For right now she would leave the whole issue of Frank alone. She would wait for a more appropriate time to ask her questions.

The balmy breeze was soft and caressing as they both became quiet, exhausted from the long day. He reached over and touched her hand. She turned toward him. They looked into each other's eyes but neither said anything.

She felt the beginning of a new attachment between them. The sensation of him becoming closer, more than a friend, spread a new warmth throughout her body. Although she felt it, she couldn't admit it, not yet.

"Fletcher, let's go before we become more confused about things. I need sleep." She gently pulled her hand away as she stood up.

He said nothing as he stood, realizing that she was becoming uncomfortable.

"I'm glad you want me to go with you to the meeting with Berkshire tomorrow," she said as they headed for the hotel. "Let's meet in the restaurant for breakfast to talk about it. How about seven thirty?"

"Sounds good to me," he agreed as they entered the hotel lobby.

They embraced, said goodnight and headed to their rooms.

Lying in bed, Jennifer slept lightly. She couldn't help comparing today's horrific incidents surrounding Chapman's plane crash with her parent's tragedy, especially the fact that both crashes had a missing body.

❖ ❖ ❖ ❖ ❖

The corridors of Geographic Unlimited were abuzz. Employees, rushing to meet the deadline for next month's publication, scurried busily around Fletcher and Jennifer as they walked through the front lobby.

The receptionist looked up smiling as they approached her desk. "Good morning, Mr. McKeane. How are you today?"

"I'm fine, thanks. Would you please tell Mr. Berkshire that I'm here."

"Of course," she replied, picking up the telephone.

Jennifer looked at Fletcher, asking, "You ready for this? You'll have to tell them. No hedging."

"I know, I know," he answered nervously. "I'm just not sure how they'll take it. If only I'd been able to somehow warn Berkshire. They're both going to think I'm crazy."

Jennifer laughed. "It's not your fault he wasn't in when you called back this morning."

"I know, maybe I can tell him before we meet with Grah…never mind, here comes Tom," Fletcher said.

Tom Berkshire moved briskly through the lobby in their direction. Fletcher and Jennifer turned and headed his way to greet him.

"Fletcher! Good to see you," Berkshire greeted, vigorously shaking Fletcher's hand.

"Thanks, Tom, it's good to be here. This is a friend and new colleague of mine, Jennifer Jaynes. Jennifer, this is Tom Berkshire, the managing editor of Geographic Unlimited."

"Nice to meet you, Ms. Jaynes," Berkshire said, extending his hand. "Fletcher mentioned yesterday your strong support of him."

"Nice to meet you too, Mr. Berkshire. Please call me Jennifer." She shook his hand. "And Fletcher has told me many good things about you and your organization."

"Well, my thanks to you both. I see we're all starting off on the right foot this morning," he said with a broad smile.

They all laughed.

"Seriously," Berkshire continued, "I appreciate you waiting until now for our meeting, Fletcher. Mr. Grahme wasn't available until right now."

"No problem, Tom. It gave Jennifer and me a chance to relax over coffee this morning. We both had a pretty rough day yesterday."

Berkshire's expression turned serious. "Yes, I understand. I'm sure it's still shocking to you," he said looking at Fletcher. "I'm sorry about everything that has happened to you recently. Incidentally, did they find out what caused the crash?"

"Not yet," Jennifer interjected. "I work for the Federal Aviation Administration and just received the latest report. They're still searching for one of the men. Of course, we're all hoping to find him alive."

"I'm very sorry," Berkshire repeated, glancing at his watch. "Well, shall we go and meet with Mr. Grahme? I know his time is limited this morning. He has an important luncheon he needs to attend."

Fletcher nodded, knowing he wouldn't be able to adequately warn Berkshire about his new plans. He'd have to tell him, along with Grahme, about his latest decision of not coming back to work.

"Tom, Jennifer is going to join us, if you don't mind," Fletcher said.

"No, not at all. Come this way, please." Berkshire led them down the carpeted hall toward the line of plush corporate offices. They approached the large secretarial station in front of a pair of tall mahogany doors. The bespectacled middle-aged woman saw them, smiled and greeted, "Good Morning, Tom. Mr. Grahme is expecting you."

"Thank you, Cheryl," Berkshire said, as he walked over and knocked on the door.

"Come in," a voice boomed from inside the office.

As the three filed in, Clifford Grahme rose from his desk and walked over to greet them.

"Mr. Grahme," Berkshire said, "this is Fletcher McKeane and his colleague Jennifer Jaynes. Fletcher, Jennifer, this is Clifford Grahme, the president of Geographic Unlimited."

After exchanging the obligatory greetings, Grahme led them to the large conference table where they sat down.

As Fletcher looked around the room at the wildlife photographs, he began to feel more nervous about the upcoming conversation.

"Mr. Grahme," Berkshire began, "As you know, Fletcher is with us this morning to finalize the plans for his coming back to work for us. I knew you'd want to hear the details first hand, especially after last week's turn of events."

They all remained silent as Grahme nodded. "Right, Tom," Grahme agreed, turning to Fletcher. "Fletcher, we were definitely worried about you last week. We didn't want to lose someone of your caliber."

Fletcher smiled faintly, thinking of how long it would take to get this conversation finished so he could leave. "Thank you, Mr. Grahme," he said politely.

"Unfortunately, Clifford," Berkshire continued, "Fletcher has experienced another tragic accident. Two of his friends were involved in a fatal airplane crash on

Catalina Island yesterday. His move to San Diego will be delayed again and..."

"That Goddamned airport should be closed down," Grahme interrupted loudly, before catching himself. "Sorry, but I lost a close business associate there some years back," he added, looking toward Fletcher.

"Yes, sir, I understand," Fletcher said.

"Anyway, Fletcher," Grahme said, calming. "I'm sorry to hear about your loss. And we can handle the delay. So, when do you expect to be back down here to begin working for us? We're really eager to have you do the Colombia shoot."

Fletcher swallowed hard, answering slowly, "Ah, I'm sorry, gentlemen, but now I'm not sure. It could be quite a while before I'm able to come back."

Silence enveloped the room as Berkshire and Clifford locked stares, stunned.

Jennifer looked at Fletcher and slightly rubbed his arm for support.

Fletcher looked up at Berkshire. "Tom, I am sorry. I wanted to prepare you for this before the meeting, but I wasn't able to reach you this morning."

"I don't understand," Berkshire answered, puzzled. "I know you've been through a bad time recently, but yesterday afternoon you said that you were ready to come back to work."

"I know, but a lot has happened since then," Fletcher said as he stood up. "You may think I'm crazy, but I'll tell you the truth." He paced, turning his back on everyone as they sat silent.

He suddenly whirled, brimming with confidence. "Okay, here goes. I can't come back to work right now because Jennifer and I don't believe that the recent tragedies in my life were accidents."

Fletcher looked at Grahme, who scratched his head in bewilderment, then Berkshire, who slowly sat back and frowned.

Fletcher continued, "All of the circumstances surrounding the deaths are too extraordinary to be normal. There's too many unanswered questions."

"What do you mean?" Berkshire asked.

"Well, I don't know exactly. Jennifer and I only know that we've both experienced what we feel are paranormal events over the last couple of weeks."

Berkshire appealed, "Fletcher, this is a shock to us. Can you give us anything more direct to go on? We've been more than fair with you. Please give us reason to continue with that fairness."

"Yes, Tom, you're right. Frankly, I'm surprised you haven't just gotten rid of me by now. I appreciate your patience because I do want to work for you and I know I can do a good job for you…but…" He hesitated, looking at Jennifer for support.

"Go ahead, Fletcher," Jennifer said, "tell them about Lainey."

Fletcher nodded. "Gentlemen," Fletcher said slowly, "we think that my girlfriend Lainey was coerced off the sea cliff by a fiendish apparition. An evil spirit of some kind or…"

"Preposterous!" Grahme exploded, unable to contain himself. "Bullshit! What kind of damn game are you playing, McKeane? If this is a contract ploy…"

Everyone turned toward Grahme who quickly realized that he was being too harsh and only aggravating the situation.

"Ah, look, I'm sorry," Grahme said, embarrassed. "That language was uncalled for. But, Fletcher what do you expect from me with outlandish logic like that?"

"Mr. Grahme, I don't blame you for your reaction," Fletcher replied. "Let us give you some more information."

Grahme and Berkshire listened patiently as Fletcher sat down and he and Jennifer began to explain all the unusual events surrounding the deaths of his friends.

Fletcher shrugged and said, "Well, gentlemen, that's about all we know. Unfortunately, neither one of us can do a competent job for anyone right now. I guess I'm just asking for time. However, if you can't wait for me, I understand." Fletcher glanced at Jennifer. "I suppose we'd better be going."

"Wait," Berkshire said. "Where are you going? What are you two going to do?"

"I don't know," Fletcher answered. "I suppose just head back to Newport Beach and somehow sort things out. Regardless, Tom, you and your organization don't deserve this."

Berkshire thought a minute. "Fletcher, maybe our organization does deserve this."

Grahme quickly turned toward Berkshire, but held his tongue out of respect for his key successor. Fletcher and Jennifer appeared perplexed.

"Clifford, may I have a few words with you in private?" Berkshire asked

"Ah, yeah, sure, Tom," he agreed.

"Fletcher," Berkshire said, "would you and Jennifer wait outside, please? I'd appreciate your patience. This could take a few minutes."

"Sure," Fletcher said as he and Jennifer left, closing the door behind them.

About forty-five minutes had passed before the phone rang on Cheryl's desk. She picked it up and listened. "Yes, sure Tom," she said, hanging up. She turned to the curious couple sitting on the couch. "You two can go back in now."

Rising, Fletcher and Jennifer walked back into Grahme's office as he was returning to his desk.

Berkshire, still sitting at the conference table, gestured for them to sit down.

"Fletcher," Berkshire said, "you're very adamant about leaving our organization to look for your answers, aren't you?"

"Yes," Fletcher said. "We don't have a choice."

"Okay then, here's our offer," Berkshire replied. "We'll postpone the Colombia shoot. You can go on assignment and search for your answers at our expense. Although we wouldn't be bound to pay your salary. We'll treat it as freelance."

"I'm not sure I understand," Fletcher responded.

"It's very simple," Berkshire explained. "First and foremost, we believe you're sincere and we don't want to lose you. Secondly, we want you to photograph and chronicle your experience. Then, if our executive board finds the story worthy, you'll give us exclusive publishing rights for only the salary you would have earned if you'd been on another assignment for us."

Fletcher cocked his head, replying, "You believe in us that much?"

Berkshire hesitated, demurring. "Look, I'll be honest with you. We can't really say that we rely on this being legitimate, but then again, how can we pass up the opportunity? It's intriguing that one of our star wildlife photojournalists may be involved in a ghastly chronicle with supernatural overtones." He hesitated, then asked, "Well, what do you think about our offer?"

Fletcher rubbed his forehead, answering, "I'm not sure. I mean, I don't mind giving Unlimited the story if there is one. But I may not want it sensationalized."

"Oh, please understand," Berkshire promptly replied, "we respect you and accept what you're going through. We wouldn't sensationalize anything. You know we're not in the business of producing supermarket tabloid journalism. But who knows what we might discover from your search? We owe it to ourselves and to our readers to publish the facts if they exist. If nothing else maybe we could convert the story into a general chronicle of life's mysterious side."

Fletcher glanced at Jennifer, who sat silent, signaling it was Fletcher's decision to make.

Berkshire continued, cautioning, "However, on the other hand, Fletcher, if you didn't gather anything worthwhile you'd be out the salary. Of course, then we'd discuss a new contract for your services based on future assignments more pertinent to our publication."

Fletcher nodded and sat back thinking. He then shrugged and replied, "Why not? What have I got to lose? I was leaving without any work anyway."

"Wait, it's a gamble for everyone," Berkshire disagreed. "You could be giving up millions. It may be an incredible story that you couldn't sell to the highest bidder because it would belong to us. Yet, we could be out a hefty expense tab for nothing, not to mention delaying the important Colombian shoot. But it's a gamble we're prepared to take."

Fletcher looked at Jennifer's smile, realizing the decision was made. "Agreed!"

"Good," Berkshire answered, standing. "Let's work out the details over lunch."

Fletcher and Jennifer bid good-bye to Grahme, before leaving his office with Berkshire. Just outside Grahme's office, Fletcher stopped them. "Tom, please give me a few minutes with Jennifer."

"Sure, I'll be in my new office, straight down the hall on your right. You can't miss it. See you shortly." Berkshire left for his office after bidding Jennifer good-bye.

Walking to the front lobby, Fletcher and Jennifer stopped at the front door. "Well, I guess we have a job," Fletcher said. "I'm staying to work out the details with Berkshire and drive back either tonight or tomorrow. I know you have to get back to L.A. Can you catch a cab back to the airport?"

"Sure," she said. "We'll talk when you get back to Newport Beach. Call me at home and leave a message if I'm not there. By the way, would you be upset if I don't make Bob's funeral service?"

"No," he answered. "I know you've a lot to do."

"Thanks," she said as they embraced.

"Jennifer," he whispered in her ear. "If you suspect anything odd on the way back, especially at the airport, please don't go."

"I won't," she reassured him. "Don't worry, I'll be on alert the whole time. And I'll leave a message at the Alpine Towers when I land in L.A."

They separated and smiled at each other. She left through the front door concerned about him as he turned and walked back toward Berkshire's office, concerned about her.

CHAPTER 23

Days Later, Newport Beach Harbor

The early morning fog had lifted but the air was still misty as the slender schooner rocked gently amid the slight ocean swells. When the boat came to a slow, almost halting pace, Joyce Chapman walked to the stern carrying a small, hooded pewter vase. She kissed it, removed the top and leaned over the railing, scattering the ashes into the water. Joyce's head was lowered, her tears flowing down as the ashes were swept away by the mild wake created by the idling engine. She turned and walked back to the throng of mourners who, led by a priest, had bowed their heads in prayer.

With the service over, Joyce began to bravely mingle with Bob's friends, extending her appreciation for their show of respect. Fletcher stood with moist eyes when she approached him.

She reached for his hand. "He loved to complain about you the most," she said with a slight smile. "He must have cared about you a great deal. I know he was worried you'd never get your pilot's license. He was really happy when you finally did."

Fletcher cupped her hand with both of his. "I'll bet he was. He deserved to be proud with all the work he put into my training. He was a good man and will always be with me when I fly, keeping me company and reminding me to be safe."

"Mr. McKeane, you're very kind. Will I see you at my home for the luncheon?" she asked as she turned to move down the line.

"No, I'm sorry, Mrs. Chapman, I can't. My life is really hectic at the moment. I'm preparing to leave for San Diego this weekend."

"I understand, thank you for coming this morning."

"Of course," Fletcher answered, "Bob was a good friend."

The people aboard were subdued as the schooner skimmed into Newport Harbor and docked among the immense three-mast galleons and frigates that had arrived for the annual ancient ships' festival. Appearing majestic, their sails were furled and the cannons protruded ominously through the bulwark.

Fletcher was wondering where Jennifer might be. He hadn't heard from her since she'd left the message at his hotel in San Diego, letting him know she'd made it back to L.A. all right. But why hadn't she returned his calls he'd been leaving on her answering machine? He was concerned about her. It was also annoying that he'd had to call the MoonGlade Lounge and get the latest news about Frank from Fitzroy's girlfriend, Janice. He would attend tomorrow's memorial service for Frank, though he'd thought they'd given up the search for him much too quickly.

He then thought about the drive he'd be making to San Diego on Sunday. The relocation would be for real this time. He was ready, pleased that the movers had already packed everything and would move him into the town house on Monday. Although uncomfortable about staying at a hotel until then, he was thankful that Berkshire had arranged for the transition to be immediate. He was also looking forward to meeting the employees at the office party Berkshire had set up for him next week, though it would be difficult keeping his new assignment concealed from them.

Again he thought of Jennifer as he lined up with the people disembarking the schooner. He was still worrying about her as he stepped across the gangplank and onto the dock.

He made his way along the beach sidewalk, dodging the scores of people hustling about the harbor preparing for the weekend festival. Spotting a phone booth by the pier, he stopped and dialed Jennifer's number. The answering machine gave him the same message as before: "Hello, this is Jennifer. I'm unable to answer your call at the moment. Please leave your name and number and I'll call you back. Thank you."

"Jennifer," he spoke into the phone. "This is Fletcher again. It's Friday morning about eleven thirty. I'll be at the Seascape Inn in Newport Beach. Dammit, lady, I'm worried. Please call me as soon as you can. Thanks." Frustrated, he hung up and promptly called her FAA office.

"Steve Butler, please. Tell him it's Fletcher McKeane...Yes, I can wait." He turned and leaned against the side of the booth, becoming captivated by the panoramic view of the early 19th-century vessels. They were all lined up in a neat row with a large mass of chirping sea gulls circling over the tall masts.

He was wondering what it would be like to have lived in that era when suddenly he saw a brilliant halo of light on one of the ships. It lit up the complete stern by the aft mast. He looked up and was startled by the realization that there was no direct sunlight. The sky was still drab and dark from the cloudy marine layer that hadn't burned off yet.

Dazed, he looked down and saw two female figures emerging from inside the halo. In the foreground he thought he saw Lainey in an old-fashioned white dress. She was looking at him and smiling. A woman with long dark hair stood just behind her shoulder. But he couldn't make out her face. Fletcher started to open the door and run toward the ship when he heard Steve's voice on the phone. He glanced at the phone and turned quickly back toward the figures—they had disappeared!

Still dazed, but regaining his composure, he spoke into the receiver, "Steve, Fletcher. Yeah, I'm here. I was just lost in thought, that's all." Fletcher began to shake off his vision as an illusion. "Sorry to bother you, but I haven't heard from Jennifer and I'm interested in the status of Frank Conklin," he lied, not wanting to overly express his worry about Jennifer, knowing Steve wouldn't understand…."Oh, you've called off the search? Uh huh, I see, he's presumed lost at sea," Fletcher answered, pretending ignorance. "Oh, Steve, by the way, have you heard from Jennifer since she arrived back from San Diego on Tuesday?…Yes, I know she was planning on taking a leave-of-absence. But I thought maybe she might've checked back in...No, I'm not worried about her," he lied again. "Yes, I'll try her at home. But, if you do hear from her, please have her call me at the Seascape Inn in Newport Beach, or in San Diego at Geographic Unlimited after tomorrow. Thanks for your time, Steve, see ya."

Fletcher depressed the plunger before slamming the phone in its cradle, realizing he now cared more about Jennifer than he did Frank.

Jesus! How much more would he be able to take, he thought, slapping at the phone. He abruptly left the booth and headed for the tall galleon where he thought he had spotted Lainey. He stopped in front of the ship and looked up. It appeared dark and lifeless. He shook his head, turned and walked to his jeep.

I need to get good and drunk and forget this crock of shit! Fuck it! Forget everything! And that includes Jennifer, he thought, as he began driving to his hotel. "I'll park the jeep and let it all go tonight," he said aloud, "Fuck it!"

Fletcher sat in the Captain's Lounge of the Seascape Inn. It was dim and uncrowded. The piano player played soft blues music as Fletcher toyed with his Scotch and soda, not doing a very good job of forgetting Jennifer, or even getting drunk. He realized he didn't want to face a hangover tomorrow anyway. It was going to be a long day. He again thought of seeing Lainey's figure on the galleon while he was in the phone booth, but again, he quickly shrugged it off as a delusion.

Fletcher was now desperately worried about Jennifer and wondered what his real feelings were toward her. Love? *No,* he reasoned, she was strong and close when he needed her most, that's all. And she'd saved his life. But he loved Lainey, even though all he had left was her memory. Still, he knew that Jennifer was now firmly entrenched in his life and he was very concerned she was in danger. Tense, he wrinkled his napkin into a ball. Maybe the figure of Lainey on the ship was really her soul and the figure with the long black hair next to her was...*No!* He wouldn't think that! *He couldn't!* But then where could Jennifer be? She'd made it safely back to L.A. from San Diego, then just vanished. She wouldn't have gone back to Pensacola without telling him. Maybe she went back to Donald. *No*, she would've told him that too.

Emotionally drained, he finished his drink and motioned for the bartender, who approached him cautiously. Fletcher had been curt and edgy with him earlier. The bartender had dismissed the attitude; however, knowing there was probably a woman involved. He was well aware of the symptoms.

"Another one, sir?"

"No!" Fletcher snapped. "Just the bill."

"Of course, sir. Sorry to have bothered you."

Fletcher felt embarrassed by his testy outburst, but said nothing and signed the bill as he showed his key to the bartender. He looked at his watch. Damn, only eight fifteen. It's going to be a long night. Might as well take a walk on the beach, he decided as he walked to the front desk to check once more for messages.

"Excuse me, are there any messages for Fletcher McKeane, room 314?" he asked the attendant.

She went to the row of boxes. "Why yes, Mr. McKeane," she said, pulling the folded paper out of the box. "It's from Jennifer Jaynes. It came in about six forty this evening."

"Let me have it," he said excitedly, grabbing the note from the startled lady's hand. He jerked it open:

'Fletcher, I'll meet you at your hotel tonight. Please wait for me. Jennifer.

He crumpled it up and instinctively looked around, spotting Jennifer draped comfortably on a large cushioned chair by the door. She was wearing a broad smile, amused at his abrupt actions. He stood motionless, not knowing how to react. He was relieved but embarrassed by his demonstration over her note.

Her eyes glittered, saying, "You're going to hurt someone reading messages like that."

He put his hands on his hips. "Do you make it a point of sneaking up on me in hotels? Is this some dark side hidden in your personality, or what? Nice of you to show up. Where in hell have you been?" he asked, appearing angry.

His facade failed. Jennifer knew he was happy to see her. She kept smiling, stood up and walked to him.

He'd never seen her look so beautiful and carefree. Her hair was loose and flowing, her face fresh, rested and carefully made up. She wore an all-white shorts and tank top outfit, with tennis shoes and no socks. A red sweater was draped over her shoulders. Fletcher was mesmerized.

She put her arms around his shoulders. "I missed you," she said quietly.

"Dammit! I don't hear from you for days and the first thing you tell me is that you miss me."

"Yes. It's what I feel. I can't help it."

"Well, I…I…" he stammered.

"Shhh," she whispered, putting her finger on his lips. "You need to relax. I'll help you. Let's go into the lounge and have some champagne and I'll tell you where I've been."

He was still stunned but took her by the hand as they walked back into the lounge. They ordered a bottle of champagne and walked over to a table by the piano. The bartender smiled as he approached their table to serve them. He now knew that Fletcher was content, and it *was* because of a woman.

"Really, where've you been?" Fletcher asked as he pulled the bottle of Brut from the ice-filled urn and worked to uncork it.

"Westwood," she answered. "I'm sorry I worried you, but I had to be alone without any distractions. I needed to sort out my feelings. I didn't even pick up my telephone messages until tonight. I stayed at a hotel and spent two days at the UCLA library. I learned a lot."

"Well," Fletcher said as he began to fill the two flutes, "you're okay and you brought me good news tonight. Until now, every time I've seen you it's been all bad."

"Fletcher," she said slowly, looking at him with a serious gaze.

"What? Oh no. What?" he asked with a sudden worried look.

"It's early yet."

He froze, spilling the champagne from the over-filled flute while she burst into a hearty laugh. He then did the same, shaking his index finger at her wildly.

They never made it past the door of his darkened hotel room. He shut it and immediately turned her around. Jennifer flushed, swallowed hard and leaned back, staring vulnerably at him through half-closed eyes. She was filled with excitement and the champagne was creating a mellow glow.

"I can't stop myself," Fletcher gushed through an intense whisper, stroking her hair falling loosely across her shoulders. "You're so beautiful. I can't stop myself...please forgive me, for Lainey's sake. I need you so much..."

She nodded *yes* to his pleading stare. She would have consented with or without the champagne. She had decided during her time alone that she wanted him, all of him. As he began to caress her back, she was now sure. It didn't matter what was right or wrong, or how quickly things had happened between them.

She had put Lainey out of her mind. She had no choice. She needed him to go crazy with her. To explode inside her. There wasn't anything she wouldn't respond to. They needed to take this another step further.

She arched her back as he gently slipped his hand under her tank top and undid her brassiere hook. He delicately fondled her breasts. She pressed up against him and began to breathe heavily. Her nipples hardened. She ground her loins into his firm manliness while he slid her tank top and bra completely off. They searched for each other's lips and kissed with a fervent sense of urgency.

"Please, let me have you...Let me have you," Fletcher whispered feverishly as he got down on his knees and began to unbuckle the belt of her shorts.

She leaned her back against the wall while he fumbled with uncontrolled excitement, but was successful. He slid her shorts and panties down her legs and over her feet. He stared up at her for a moment before grasping her arm and gently pulling her toward the floor. She didn't resist. She couldn't, because she needed him. She let him know that she was his. He was free to do anything he desired.

"I love you," she whispered hoarsely while maneuvering downward to him. "So much, Fletcher James McKeane. Oh, so much."

CHAPTER 24

Morning, Seascape Inn

Jennifer pressed the pillow up around her head, trying to block out the irritating late-morning sunshine streaming in through the patio door. With a foggy head, she blinked her eyes to slowly wake up.

Naked and covered by only a sheet, she felt uneasy at first. Then she became fully conscious of where she was and what had happened. Contented, she opened her eyes wide and turned over with a smile, expecting to find Fletcher. Instead, she found only a note lying on his pillow. She propped herself up and read it:

Morning. I didn't want to wake you. Off to Frank's memorial service. I'll see you back here later. Fletcher.

Jennifer's mood quickly turned gloomy as she folded up the note and heaved it into the wastebasket. Pulling back the sheet, she slipped out of bed deciding that Frank Conklin might be a good place to start when she talked to Fletcher later today. She grabbed her cosmetic case and headed into the bathroom.

Fletcher arrived back at the hotel after Frank's memorial service confused and weary. Hearing again about Lainey's death and the aftermath of all the recent tragic events were taking their toll. And what did last night's lovemaking with Jennifer mean? Where were they headed? Frustrated, he needed to talk about his feelings with Jennifer but didn't find her in the room. He was disappointed until he spotted the big note on the mirror: POOL.

Relieved, he quickly put on his swimming trunks, a hotel terry-cloth robe and grabbed a towel from the bathroom.

When he reached the pool deck he saw Jennifer's flowing black hair hanging off the end of the chaise lounge. She had leveled the lounge before lazily sprawling on it to soak up the sun.

Approaching her, he noticed that she was asleep. He sat down gently on the edge of the lounge and paused to gaze at her. He began to loosen up and set aside his personal anguish to admire her natural beauty. Her face looked clean and refreshed. He could tell by her dry suit that she hadn't made it into the water. Her sandals and white V-neck cotton T-shirt lay under the chair. A nearly full glass of iced tea, now warm, sat on a small round table next to her.

He reached over to nudge her awake but pulled back. He was puzzled when he noticed the gold chain attached to a crucifix hanging around her neck. He hadn't seen her wear religious jewelry before. Reaching over, he lightly tugged on her arm. She slowly opened her eyes, focusing in on him with a gradual smile.

"Hi, how ya doing?" she asked sleepily, gracefully maneuvering to sit up.

"I'm okay," he answered gently, helping her position the lounge back upright. "How are you?"

She stretched and leaned back. "Hmmm," she purred. "I must've fallen asleep. I had a long night."

He put his hand on her arm. "Jennifer," he said tenderly. "Last night, I mean it was fantastic, but I just don't understand what happened. I mean it was more than just sex, whatever the hell that means…I mean…"

"Hey," she interrupted softly. "You don't owe me, or us, any explanation. Even though I don't fully understand everything yet either, I don't regret it. Damn, Fletcher, we're adults! We're human beings with emotions and needs. We both expressed how we felt. I have no guilt about anything that happened, nor should you."

"Yeah, but what about Lainey, and you and Donald?…Oh shit! If it ain't one thing screwing me up, it's another."

"Fletcher, please!" she exclaimed, becoming tense at hearing Donald's name. "Let's drop it. Dammit! I know things have developed quickly between us, but it wasn't like you picked me up and laid me on the first night or something…" She paused, then said, "I'm sorry, but please, we can't take on another burden with everything else that's going on."

He reached for her hand. "Okay, okay, I'm sorry," he said, transfixed by her words and her beauty. "You know what? You sure are something."

She smiled, relieved. "Thanks, so are you." She looked toward his wrist. "What time is it?"

He snapped out of his trance and glanced at his watch. "Twelve forty-five."

"Have you had lunch?"

"No. I just left Frank's memorial service," he answered, beginning to feel agitated again. "I didn't want to stay for the lunch. Hell, I could eat for the rest of my life at my friend's wakes."

She remained silent, but squeezed his hand.

"I'm sorry," he said curtly. "Bad joke."

"It's okay," she responded affectionately, knowing he needed to vent.

He abruptly looked away. "Aw fuck it!" he huffed. "The service for Frank was bullshit! All my friends are gone. I felt alone and out of place. I hardly knew anyone there. Everyone seemed like strangers. Kent Fitzroy handled everything! There wasn't even a fucking coffin or a body, for Christ's sake! To me it didn't even seem like Frank ever existed!"

Jennifer thought about his last statement, but said nothing.

"I kept thinking about how they all died," he continued, bewildered. "Chapman, Frank, and Lainey…especially Lainey…" He paused and looked at Jennifer. "Christ, I had to hear it again today. I understand from the MoonGlade crowd that the police positively ruled it a suicide."

"Oh, I forgot to tell you," she lied. She hadn't forgotten. She was only waiting for a more appropriate time to tell him. She just couldn't bring herself to do it last night. Now she had no choice. "Yes, that's true," she said carefully. "I called Komarek at the coroner's office on Thursday. They've closed the investigation on Lainey. They had no choice but to rule it a suicide because they didn't really have anything substantial to conclude otherwise."

"What about that witness, Vasquez?" Fletcher asked skeptically. "Did they ever find our vanishing friend?"

"Nope, he's still missing. They assume he went back to Mexico."

"Figures," he said, growing angrier. He yanked his hand away, snapping, "That fucking Vasquez must have been a real loser. That jerk probably made up that whole story just to gain attention."

"I'm still not convinced of that," she said, realizing too late that this was a wrong thing to say.

He pulled away, sprang up and stared hard at her while pounding his fist in his other hand. "Oh, no. Are you going to start with that horseshit about demons and monsters again?" he shot back harshly. "Can't we forget this shit and just get on with our lives?"

She retreated, answering cautiously, "Yes, if that's what you want."

"Yes! Goddammit, that's what I want!" he rasped through clenched teeth.

"Fletcher, I'm sorry, I know it's been a traumatic time for you lately," she said quietly, still trying to calm him. "But, please try to relax and sit down."

"Don't fucking patronize me, dammit! I need a drink!" he barked, storming off toward the hotel lounge, leaving Jennifer sitting there stunned.

Entering the lounge distraught, he sat down hard at the bar and ordered a beer noticing it was the same bartender who had served them the night before.

"Christ," Fletcher growled, "do you work here twenty-four hours a day?"

"No sir, just twelve hours a day this week," he responded carefully, remembering Fletcher from the night before.

Fletcher shrugged as he turned and watched Jennifer through the window. She appeared troubled as she stood, slipped into her T-shirt, picked up the rest of her belongings and headed for the room. Fletcher shook his head in confusion as the bartender set the beer down in front of him.

"Friend, excuse me. I know I'm chancing a busted head," the bartender said, looking at him. "But I think you'd better go after her. From what I see, losing her would be a big mistake."

"What the hell you butting in for?" Fletcher retorted, glaring up at him. He then caught himself, realizing that the bartender was on his side. He looked out the window at Jennifer's empty lounge chair, realizing he'd been wrong. She hadn't deserved his foul tantrum.

Fletcher began to calm. "Thanks, you're right. See ya later," he said quietly as he flipped a five-dollar bill on the bar and pushed the barstool back.

When he walked into the room Jennifer was standing by the bed pulling her shorts out of the small suitcase. She laid them on the bed and closed the case.

He walked over and stood beside her, placing his hand gently on her shoulder. "I'm sorry," he said. "Where are you going?"

She didn't look up. "Maybe it's better if you're alone for a while," she answered quietly. "I can't tiptoe around worrying about how you're going to feel and react to everything I say. I know you've been through a lot lately, but so have I." She took a deep breath.

"Maybe…maybe we should be alone to sort out our feelings," she finished.

He gently lifted her chin and turned her head toward his. "I made a mistake. I know you want only the best for me. Sometimes I think I'm losing it. Please don't leave," he appealed, "I need you."

She looked at him and closed her eyes, signaling in her expression she wasn't going anywhere.

He reached over and picked up her suitcase, setting it down on the floor. He then drew her into his arms as she began to cry, releasing all the frustration, worry and confusion that had built up inside her.

"We can't fight this alone, Fletcher. We can't," she muttered through her streaming tears, her head buried into his shoulder. "It'll destroy us if we're apart. We need each other."

He nodded and began drying her wet cheeks with the sleeve of his robe. She nuzzled up to him. He tenderly raised her head and kissed her.

Relieved, she reached up and began to rub his chest. "Let's lie down," she whispered, loosening the belt of his robe. "Just hold me and caress me…and dammit, say nothing. No matter what happens. No apologies. Please, nothing at all."

Undressing, they slowly collapsed onto the bed.

CHAPTER 25

Tall-Ships Festival, Newport Beach Harbor

It was close to 6 p.m. when he awoke cradled in her arms on the bed. He opened his eyes and met her gaze. She had been awake but hadn't moved, only held him.

She smiled, saying, "I'm famished. Let's go eat."

"Okay," he agreed groggily. "I think I need a good meal and few drinks."

"Probably," she replied, breaking into a grin as she separated from him. "Probably so."

Showered and dressed, they sat on the edge of the bed as Jennifer put on her gold chain and crucifix.

"That's new," Fletcher said as he reached over, fingering the chain. "It's very pretty. Is there a special reason you bought it?"

"For safety sake, I guess. Actually, I bought two."

"Two?"

"Yes. And I had them blessed at St. Patrick's Cathedral in L.A. One is for you." She reached into her purse, pulling out the silver chain and crucifix, urging, "Come closer."

He moved and bent his head as she carefully placed it around his neck.

"Thanks," he said, looking down at the cross resting in the middle of his chest.

"Now we're spiritually bonded as well as love-bonded," she said, pecking him lightly on the cheek.

He then remembered Lainey and the telephone booth incident. His mood turned solemn. "Jennifer, let's go up to the Newport Beach harbor. They're hosting the ancient mariner tall-ships festival. We can get some great seafood there."

"Sounds good to me," she agreed. "Isn't that the festival where all those historic English and American naval war ships come in for the week? I understand they put on a pretty good show."

"Right," he said. "I haven't gone before, but I heard it's fun."

Rising, they walked out the door, cheerful and refreshed from their afternoon rest.

Fletcher and Jennifer wove through the heavy crowd, feeling comfortably stuffed after sampling the food and wine at several seafood and pasta booths.

Reaching the seaside, they sat down on a bench facing the long column of ships. Leisurely, they took in the salty sea breeze and watched the shows being performed on the decks of the ships by actors in period costumes. The clothes reminded Fletcher of Lainey.

He gripped Jennifer's hand and turned to her. "You still think something abnormal is going on around us, don't you?"

She exhaled. "Not think. I know," she answered, continuing to look straight out at the ships. "I've done a lot of paranormal research lately."

"Tell me about it."

"That's not easy. The information we have is all so vague." She paused. "I do know that if we continue to investigate it, we should prepare ourselves for anything, which means that when 'it'—whatever 'it' is—materializes, the whole thing could be unearthly and shocking." She turned to him. "Keep in mind how they found Lainey, and how Chapman had jumped from the plane."

Momentarily stunned over her statement, he interrupted, "Before we go any further, can we agree that we'll always know where the other one is, until we find out for sure what's happening?"

"Agreed," she answered. "And from now on we mustn't let our emotions unravel us. We don't need any more sessions like the one at the pool. Right?"

"Right," he replied, turning back toward the ships.

Inspired at knowing she had Fletcher's interest back, she couldn't quit now. It was time. She drew a deep breath, asking, "Fletcher, can we talk about Frank?"

He shrugged. "Sure."

"I'm sorry, but I never liked him," she began. "It's strange. I didn't even know him. I'd never even talked to him before that night at the lounge, yet I was immediately put off by him. The moment I saw him in the foyer I just wanted to leave. He seemed an enigma. He had no expression or emotion, especially when he talked about you and Lainey." She hesitated, surprised, realizing that she was losing control.

Fletcher remained silent while Jennifer regained her composure.

She continued, asking, "How'd you meet Frank, anyway?"

He thought as he answered, "About three years ago he contacted me through the Southern Beach

Reporter magazine when I was freelancing for them. He saw one of my layouts in the magazine, so he hired me to do a promotional shoot of the MoonGlade."

"I think I saw the photos," she interrupted. "Weren't some of them hanging in the foyer?"

"Yeah, the ones by the maitre d' stand."

"How'd you get the wide-angle shot of the bar? The one where it looks tilted and expansive."

"With mirrors." He laughed at the cliché. "Really though, that's how it was done. I strategically placed them in the dining room to get the reflected angles."

"Mirrors, huh? Interesting," she commented. "Was Frank in any of the pictures? I don't remember seeing him in any."

"No," he answered. "The day I did the layout he left for a business meeting in San Francisco. He said he wouldn't pose for any of the photos anyway because he was camera shy. Said he didn't want to take any glory from the lounge, since his dad had made it what it was."

"Fletcher, have you ever seen a photograph of Frank?"

He was surprised at her question, but thought before answering, "No, I guess I haven't, why?"

"You were good friends, weren't you?"

"Yeah, he used to say the best of friends."

"And you never had any pictures taken with him?"

"No, why?" he asked again.

"It just seems odd, that's all, but it doesn't matter, I suppose. Incidentally, did Frank remodel the lounge at all?"

"Yes," he answered quickly. "I asked him about that for background information on the shoot. He said he'd painted and refinished the bar when he took over after Jimmy died. He also had the liquor shelf changed so the lighting and reflection was just right. He said he'd arranged the recessed lighting to make it look really sleek."

"Right," she replied. "I noticed it that night when I was in the bar sitting with Bob. Frank must also be the one who shortened the bar mirrors."

"Yeah, he took down all the large mirrors in the place. He said it added to the ambiance of privacy. With no mirrors, you couldn't see the other patrons. He thought that fact would make for interesting commentary in the magazine article."

"I see," she said, deciding that she'd better hold off any more discussion about Frank for the time being. "Fletcher, let's lay off Frank. I don't have any substantial reason to single him out for anything."

"Okay," he agreed. "But I don't mind talking about him."

They fell silent, turning their attention back to the ships. Fletcher eyed the ship where he thought he'd seen Lainey yesterday. He was unable to keep his experience to himself any longer.

He clutched Jennifer's forearm, saying, "Now I have something to tell you."

She looked at him with widening eyes. The tone of his voice told her something was up.

"C'mon, let's take a walk," he said excitedly. He took her by the hand and pulled her to her feet. They picked up their pace as they walked toward the narrow cement pier while Fletcher described what he'd thought he'd seen from the phone booth.

The tall-timbered ships appeared colossal, towering over Fletcher and Jennifer as they approached the special galleon docked in the middle of the line.

Jennifer stared upward, intently scanning the wide-angled bow, asking, "Why didn't you tell me about this earlier?"

"Because at first I didn't believe it," he replied, following her scan. "Everything happened so fast. The vision hardly lasted a minute. I assumed Lainey had appeared because I wanted to see her and I had willed it unconsciously, so I shrugged it off. But after our conversation tonight, I've decided to tell you."

"Where exactly did you see them?"

"Up there, at the bottom of the aft mast," he answered, pointing at the tall wooden column with the broad crossbar that supported the bundled sails and rigging. "At first I thought the ship was on fire, it was so bright. But then the figures emerged. The glow surrounding them was shaped like a horseshoe."

"Did it get cold or did you notice any unusual sounds or smells?"

"I didn't notice any. But remember, I was in a phone booth and I was also wearing a windbreaker." He began to appear uncertain. "Now I don't know. Maybe I didn't see anything."

"Maybe or maybe not," she replied quickly. "But let's not forget about it. Do you remember how they were dressed?"

"They were wearing old-fashioned clothes," he answered. "I couldn't tell you the exact time period but they were similar to the ones in the show." He hesitated and then threw his hands up. "Ohhh, right, that's it! The women must have been in costume, taking part in the festival ceremony!"

"You mean there was a show yesterday afternoon?"

"No, I don't think so. But they must've been rehearsing...Sure! The brightness I saw must have been caused by some type of stage lighting."

Jennifer thought a moment. "Well, there's one way to find out. Let's go aboard the ship and ask."

"Okay, why not?"

They quickly made their way to the steep planked gangway leading up to the bulwark of the second deck. Seeing that the entrance was open, they grabbed onto the rope railing attached to each side of the gangway and stepped upward.

Reaching the top of the gangway they came face-to-face with a short stocky man wearing a black eye patch and dressed in a fluffy red-striped shirt and scarf. His baggy trousers, held up by a wide-buckle black belt, were stuffed into old pirate boots.

He bowed, swinging his wide tricorne hat across his chest. "Aye, mates," he bellowed through a bush of shaggy whiskers. "Welcome aboard Her Majesty's Ship, Trafalgar. The men of pirate Jack's crew has just commandeered it, we have indeed."

Fletcher and Jennifer looked at each other and laughed as they gestured a hello, then turned and hurried to the stern.

"The time period is early 19th century," she said quietly to Fletcher. "The great naval battle of Trafalgar was fought during the Napoleonic wars."

"Know-it-all," he quipped as they pushed through the amused crowd watching the pirates tying up the ship's crew. When they reached the aft mast they studied the spot where Fletcher thought he'd seen Lainey, but they found nothing unusual. Shrugging at each other, they began to look around when they noticed loud laughter coming from the large enclosed cabin across the deck. A large sign was hanging above the entrance:

THE GALLEY LOUNGE

They entered through the open saloon doors and even though the room was jammed with people, they were able to squeeze into a spot at the end of the bar.

The burly bartender, also dressed in pirate garb, noticed them and asked, "What'll it be there, mates?"

"Why, a couple of navy grogs, of course," Fletcher cracked.

"Aye, navy grogs coming up," the bartender replied.

The bartender soon returned and set the drinks down. "There ya be," he said boisterously, laying the tab down and turning to walk away.

"Excuse me," Fletcher said, stopping him. "We're wondering how much preparation and rehearsal goes on to put on this show. I say every day. My friend here, disagrees."

The bartender looked around, not wanting to get caught letting his pirate facade down. He bent down close to Jennifer. "Lady, you really think we could all do this British stuff off-the-cuff?" he whispered.

"You aren't British?" she asked.

"Nope. Us local people have to reap some of the profits of the saloons and restaurants, ya know. Oh there are a few British blokes aboard and they rehearse all the time." He turned to leave.

Fletcher looked at Jennifer. "I knew it had to be rehearsals I saw yesterday."

"Oh no," the bartender interrupted, turning back toward them. "Not yesterday. Yesterday was festival set-up day. They didn't rehearse at all."

"What?" Fletcher exclaimed, whirling back to face the bartender. "But I swore I saw two women on board yesterday afternoon dressed in 19th-century clothes, right outside this lounge."

"Nope, couldn't have been," the bartender answered stubbornly. "I'd have seen 'em. I was here all day working in the lounge. Besides, there aren't any women in the show on this ship. All males. Pirates and soldiers. Maybe they were on another ship you saw."

"No, this was the ship," Fletcher said quietly.

Jennifer looked up questioningly at the bartender. "So you were here all afternoon yesterday?"

"Yup. Stocking the bar. Never took a break."

"Do you remember if it suddenly got cold, or did anything unusual grab your attention?"

He thought for a moment. "Yeah, lady. As a matter of fact it did get damn cold for a few minutes!" he exclaimed. "I remember thinking I should've brought a coat. But then it went away."

"Thanks a lot," Jennifer said, handing him cash for the drinks.

"Aye. See ya later mates," he said loudly, walking away.

Fletcher slowly looked at Jennifer who had raised her eyes upward in an I-told-you-so expression.

"Okay, what are you thinking?"

"Plenty," she replied, "C'mon, let's get out of here and go where we can think. It's too crowded in here."

Leaving their drinks, they left the ship and picked up a steaming cappuccino from the nearest food booth and walked back to the pier in deep thought.

CHAPTER 26

The Unfolding, Newport Beach Harbor

Fletcher and Jennifer sat down on the seaside bench and peered out at the ships. Fletcher took a swallow of his milk-frothed coffee and turned to her. "So, now tell me what you're thinking."

Toying with her cup handle in serious thought, she replied, "Oh, I have no doubt that what you saw was an apparition of Lainey along with some other soul."

"Soul!" he repeated, surprised. "That's the first time you've used that word."

"I know, but it's the first time I've been totally convinced."

"Okay," he replied, "I'm not arguing anymore because I sure as hell don't have any other explanations for what I saw up there. And Lainey definitely looked real."

"Oh, yes, even though spirits appear and disappear very quickly they can be as real as life itself," she agreed, still looking out at the ships. "They're not always ghostly and transparent." She turned back to Fletcher with a puzzled expression. "By the way, where's your camera?" she asked, mildly irritated. "You should always have it with you."

"All I have with me is a small 35 mm. It's in the jeep. The rest of my professional equipment is in San Diego," Fletcher replied bluntly. "Remember, I have an office there. I've been trying to get down there for a couple of weeks!"

Jennifer smiled sheepishly. "Back to Lainey."

He smiled, then became intense. "Okay, if it was Lainey that I saw, why do you think she was dressed in those old-fashioned clothes?"

"I agree it's confusing," she answered, perplexed. "When I was at UCLA last week, I did a great deal of research on spiritual apparitions. They usually manifest themselves dressed in the period during which they've lived. But Lainey lived now, not in the 1800s. She must be trying to communicate something different."

Fletcher, stimulated over Jennifer's revelation, interrupted, "But why do you think she just can't communicate with us?"

Jennifer thought a moment. "Well, think back to your dream of seeing Lainey when you were sick. Remember how she was whisked away by a dark spectral figure just before you could reach her?" She paused before continuing at his nod, "She's probably being shielded by something evil."

"Then what about the other female figure that appeared with Lainey?"

Jennifer sighed and looked away, unsure. "I don't know since you didn't recognize her. Maybe it was someone who was close to her when she was in Utah, or maybe a guardian angel. Oh, I dunno right now. Let's not confuse things."

Fletcher remained silent as Jennifer's face grew more serious. "Fletcher, I just remembered. When I was at UCLA I chatted with a professional theologian, a professor of diversified theology. I told her everything that was happening…"

He squinted and cocked his head. "And…"

"She theorized that we've all lived together before, during another lifetime."

"All?"

"At least you, Lainey and me," she replied.

"Lived before? Do you mean we could be reincarnated from another lifetime?"

"Yes, Fletcher," she answered enthusiastically, becoming more convinced after hearing it aloud. "At first I decided that notion was impractical, but now I think maybe she's right!"

"You mean we might've all came back at the same time?" he asked

"Yes, there must be a special connection…a bond that exists between us! Think about it! The unusual attraction I felt for both you and Lainey was almost unworldly. And don't forget, Lainey has also communicated with me!" Jennifer paused, then suddenly turned to Fletcher. "Sure, that's it! Lainey is trying to communicate something far removed from today! The clothes she's wearing—she's trying to communicate a different time period to us!"

Fletcher wasn't convinced, not yet. "Oh, I agree that I was damn attracted to you Jennifer. Although I just assumed it was because of your beauty and intelligence."

She shrugged. "What else would you think, based on your lifelong masculine beliefs?"

"Yeah, you're right. What else would I think?" He smiled. "So, if maybe we were together before, do you think we were past lovers or something?"

"It's possible I could have been your lover," she answered. "I could also have been somehow attached to Lainey. Maybe a friend, or a brother."

"Huh? Did you say brother?" he interrupted. "You could've been a man?"

"Yes, the theologian told me that incarnated souls aren't necessarily embodied in their past gender..." She paused, noticing his stunned look. She then laughed, realizing what he was thinking. "Fletcher, I hardly think your attraction to me is in jeopardy if my soul existed before in the body of a man."

He laughed with her. "It just threw me for a moment, that's all. Okay, I'm not doubting anything any more. What else do you think?"

"Well, if the theologian is right I suspect that we were all brought together again for a special reason," she continued, now appearing troubled. "And based on what has happened, it must be for a diabolical reason."

He stopped laughing and leaned toward her. "Keep talking."

Her delivery slowed. "I think that you and I are caught up in a realm of another consciousness that includes a sphere of mystical evil, a dangerous mystical evil. And I think Lainey's soul is trying to communicate that to us, from wherever this realm is. That's why she can't rest."

Fletcher sat back, inhaling deeply. "Yeah, I've felt all along that we were in some kind of unusual trouble. I just haven't wanted to admit it."

She nodded. "Yes, probably we are. And we have to find out what that trouble is and how to escape it. If we don't, neither of us may ever be safe, or sane, again."

"Jennifer, I assume from your earlier questions that you think Frank was connected with all of this, don't you?"

She turned her full gaze on him. "Yes, although I don't know how or why yet. But I sense there's something very bad about him...and maybe still *is.*"

"Jesus! Still is?" Fletcher exclaimed. "Still! With Frank? Do you realize what you're saying?"

"Yes, I fully realize what I'm saying," she answered, reaching inside her blouse to pull out the chain hanging around her neck. She fingered the cross. "Unfortunately, very much so."

"Frank is dead," Fletcher replied incredulously. "And he sure as hell didn't act or look evil when he was alive. He was intelligent, groomed, and professional. I even remember you saying good things about him."

"Yes, I know, but on the surface that doesn't really mean anything. It's like he had an underlying viciousness just waiting to pounce free. He enjoyed being cold." She hesitated, growing strained. "Oh, damn, I don't know. I just can't explain it!"

"It's okay," Fletcher conceded. "But how'd you come to this conclusion about him?"

"Well, of course, I'm going mainly on my intuition." She thought, then added, "I think it was a celestial presence that warned me about him the night I met him at the lounge."

Fletcher furrowed. "But Frank was Jimmy Conklin's son. I mean...we all knew him."

"Do we really know who he was for sure?" she challenged. "Is there a way we could check on Frank's background? By the way, where did he live?"

"In Balboa, a small apartment on the beach," Fletcher answered. "It was right down the street from

Lainey's. She'd told me that he's the one who found the apartment for her. I stopped there once or twice on my way to see her."

"What was his place like?"

Fletcher thought a moment. "Now that I recall, it did seem dark and dreary inside—pretty much empty. He hardly had any furniture or wall decorations. I noticed he kept the drapes closed."

"Figures," Jennifer replied, frowning. "I'd sure like to see the apartment but I know we couldn't get in legally. I'm sure the police would be watching it."

"Yeah, you're right," he agreed. "In fact, Kent Fitzroy asked me at Frank's memorial service if I knew of any relatives or anyone legally connected to him. I guess they tried but couldn't trace anyone down. I couldn't help them either."

"Where's he from originally?"

"New York. He talked about it all the time."

She grimaced. "Hell, it would be almost impossible to check that out." She suddenly lit up. "Hey! Wait a minute! Maybe old George from the lounge could shed some light…on…" She paused abruptly, noticing his growing expression of gloom. "What's wrong?"

"George," he answered through a solemn tone.

"George? What about him?"

"I forgot to tell you because of all the confusion today. When I was at the memorial service, Janice told me that they found George's body behind the MoonGlade, floating in the surf. The police don't know everything yet. They figure it was a heart attack, or maybe even suicide."

She sighed. "Oh, Fletcher! How sad."

"Yeah, I understand Fitzroy fired him last Thursday. He'd told George they couldn't use him after the end of the month. Worse yet, they told him they needed the space in the back of the building and he was going to have to move out."

"Damn! And he appeared to be the last potential link to Frank," she said in disappointment. "But now he's gone."

"Right, the last probable link to Frank is gone," he repeated, slowly.

"Okay, since we don't have George," she said, "let's get back to Frank's apartment. Try and remember. Did you notice anything strange there?"

Fletcher lifted his head in thought. "Yes!" he exclaimed. "There was no mirror in the bathroom. And I don't remember seeing any photographs either. And now that I think about it, there were none in his office at the lounge either." He paused, then continued, "I can understand why he'd had no photographs taken; he was a very private person. But what do you think the missing mirrors have to do with anything?"

"I don't know what the connection is yet, but there is one, I'm sure." She shrugged and sighed, leaning forward resting her chin in her hands. "Fletcher, the theologian at UCLA suggested we get some help from spiritually-gifted people."

"You mean like a psychic or something?"

"Yes, but I don't really know where to go from here," she replied, sounding discouraged. "Even though things are becoming clearer, I'm stymied. We need a break."

"Yeah," he agreed, looking out at the ocean. "You're right, where do we go from here?"

"Well," she answered, "let's go over all of the events that have occurred, again."

Fletcher gently clutched Jennifer's arm. "Wait, maybe it's nothing, but, look." He pointed to the hull of the ship he'd seen Lainey on and the bright white letters: **H.M.S. TRAFALGAR.**

She looked up, following his point toward the ship.

"It's British," he said. "Maybe we should concentrate on something British."

She turned to Fletcher, her eyes opening wide as she thought about his statement. "Oh, Fletcher!" she exclaimed. "You sighted Lainey on a British ship! Yes, that could be it, and..."

"And what?" he interrupted, slowing her pace.

"Her period dress! Maybe she was telling us something about the 19th century...Wait! Maybe it really wasn't just Lainey you saw, but a soul of someone else. Oh, Fletcher!" she rasped in excitement, "Maybe Lainey is not the answer, but her soul is!"

He remained silent so as not to interrupt her speculation.

She then remembered the 19th century British furniture that Frank had provided for decoration at Lainey's funeral. *No. It can't be related! Or can it?* She sprang up, grabbing Fletcher's hand to pull him along.

He balked. "Whoa, where we going?"

"England!" she answered excitedly. "We may be wrong, but why does it really matter where we work from? And there must be spiritual help there."

"Yeah, but I don't know if I can just..."

"C'mon," she interrupted. "Let's check you out of the hotel. Then we can drive me home to get my clothes and..."

"Wait a minute," he said, tugging on her arm. "I'm moving to San Diego on Monday. And Berkshire is expecting me to be at Geographic Unlimited on Wednesday."

"Hey, aren't you officially on assignment?" she asked through pursed lips, upset over his lack of urgency. "Don't you agree that we should concentrate on England?"

"Sure, but I just can't leave now. Just up and go."

"Okay," she replied calmly, raising her eyebrows toward the ships. "I'll go back home to L.A. When you're ready, call me and we'll fly out from there."

He grimaced. "Wait a minute. Didn't we agree we'd stay together?"

"No. We agreed that we'd always know where the other one was. So, trust that I'll be waiting for you in L.A."

"That isn't what we meant and you know it," he retorted. "Don't do this to me!"

"Sorry, but I'm not going to San Diego," she replied insistently. "And you know very well that we should go to England as soon as possible. Remember, Britain was your idea in the first place."

"But what'll I do about my furniture and new town house?" he argued weakly.

"The moving company will store the furniture. Just tell them you've been delayed. And your new town house is secure. You've paid your first month's rent."

"Yeah, but…" he stammered, realizing she was right. "Aw shit! How will I tell Berkshire that I won't be coming down to San Diego next week?"

"Don't worry," she replied, smiling. "He'll understand. Doesn't he always?"

"Aw, shit!" he huffed again, standing up defeated.

"Oh," she said excitedly as they hurried down the pier to the jeep. "Do you think Berkshire would mind if you flew to London on the Concorde? I know I can fly free, I did some work for British Airways last year.

"It leaves out of New York and I can get us there on a complimentary flight."

"Nah, I don't think he'd mind," he answered nonchalantly as they settled themselves in the jeep. "Berkshire said he'd pay my expenses. Any idea how much the flight is?"

"Oh, just a couple thousand." She quickly turned her head to look out the side window. "Each way."

"Huh? Oh shit," he murmured as he pulled out of the parking space.

As they hurried back to Fletcher's motel, Jennifer grew a little suspicious thinking about how the events had fallen into place so easily: Fletcher being at the harbor when the British ships were there. And then him sighting Lainey on a British ship. *Damn, could it be a cleverly laid trap? Are they really being lured to England for some fiendish reason?* However, she quickly put the thought of an evil entity entrapping them out of her mind. If anything, she'd rather believe it was celestial guidance bringing them closer to solving their macabre dilemma.

Arriving back at the Seascape Inn, Fletcher grabbed his clothes and checked out. They returned to the freeway just after midnight, heading for Jennifer's apartment in Los Angeles to pack her clothes and make the reservations for London. *Berkshire would just have to understand about his delay,* Fletcher decided as he easily speeded down the barren freeway. *Jennifer was right,* he thought, *they needed to pursue this immediately*.

CHAPTER 27

High Above the New York Skyline

The long slender nose of the thundering supersonic began to dip, then leveled off as it soared high above the Atlantic Ocean. Fletcher looked up at the speaker, noisily clicking on over the plush front row:

"Good evening ladies and gentlemen. This is Captain Rhinehart on the flight deck. We have just leveled off at fifty-five thousand feet. We'll cruise over the Atlantic for approximately an hour before we begin our decent into Heathrow Airport, arriving in London on Wednesday about 1 a.m. local time. Well folks, the Big Smoke is living up to its name. It's damp and foggy there, but we don't expect any delays. So please sit back and enjoy the rest of your short flight, halfway around the world at faster than the speed of sound."

Jennifer busily thumbed through the thick, black-covered book, oblivious to the announcement.

Turning to her, Fletcher put his hand on top of the page, causing her to look up at him.

"Hey," he said quietly. "This plane moves."

Looking up at the cabin machmeter, she saw it approaching mach-2, twice the speed of sound. "Yeah," she said, then cocked her head, chiding, "Incidentally, how'd you break it to Berkshire? I mean about flying the Concorde?"

"Ahh…I didn't," he hedged. "I tried calling him when you were packing yesterday. He wasn't home so I left a message on his answering machine explaining I wouldn't be making it down to San Diego this week. I left it at that."

"Good move," she replied with a slight grin.

Setting the 'Spiritual and Paranormal Encyclopedia' on the floor, she reclined her seat to lie back and rest her eyes.

Following suit, Fletcher pressed his seat back and turned to look out the window. "Jennifer?"

"What?" she responded lazily.

"Could you fly this plane if you had to?"

"I suppose I could," she answered through a sluggish yawn. "I went through the cockpit simulator in Toulouse, France, once. But, I'd probably need ground assistance from British Airways. Why?"

"Oh, I dunno, I just got to thinking," he replied slowly. "We're in a hell'uva position up here."

She turned, joining him in a pensive stare through the window. Transfixed by the pitch-black shroud, she pondered his statement, then replied lightly, "No, I don't think we're in trouble up here. You're never a target of any tragedy, except for the suffering afterward. I think that as long as you're up here, we're probably all safe." She turned her gaze on him.

He reached for her hand and squeezed gently, saying, "I guess you're right, Jennifer. So let's stay close together until we find out what's happening. You're in this too deep now. Both with me and with…'it.' He squeezed her hand harder. "I really care about you. If I lost you…I…"

"Shhh," she shushed. "I know. You don't have to tell me. And I agree, we should stay close together."

He smiled, nodded and let go of her hand.

She then turned a frown, saying, "I've been thinking. If Frank was wicked and mixed up in this, maybe he's finished. I mean, maybe if he was somehow responsible for the deaths of Lainey, Chapman and George, he feels it's enough and has disappeared."

"I thought about that too, but we don't know for sure," he replied. "You know we can't go on wondering if it's really over."

"Of course, you're right," she quickly agreed. "We must find out if we're able to."

He looked around the cabin, then asked, "I know this sounds stupid but do you suppose if you're right about that other spiritual realm we're actually being seen and heard right now?"

She looked back at him and nodded, answering, "I don't know, but, I don't think anything sounds stupid anymore."

They lay back against their headrest and closed their eyes, both deciding to pass on the meal. Dozing, she thought about her last statement, realizing that she had felt very strongly they were being *watched* lately. Yes, she'd felt it more than she wanted to admit to him…*or even to herself.*

Fletcher and Jennifer jolted forward as the speaker announced: "Ladies and gentlemen, this is Captain Rhinehart. We have just begun our descent into Heathrow and should be arriving at the gate in about forty minutes."

Shaking off their short nap, they adjusted themselves forward in their seat as the plane's throttles cut back, smoothly pitching the herculean airliner downward on its final swoop for home.

Jennifer sluggishly picked up her book. "I'm ready for a hotel room," she said. "I'm beat."

"Me too," he replied. "I'll sleep well tonight. Tomorrow I want to check in with the American Embassy. If we can somehow establish another contact for our associates back home, it'll be better for everyone."

"Good idea," she agreed. "And I've been reading about the Association for Mystical & Paranormal Research, located in London. I'd like to get the embassy's opinion on the organization."

"What's the book say about them?"

She flipped open the encyclopedia and paged to the segment. Reading, she replied, "They've been in existence a long time; since the late 1800s. The society is made up of a lot of scholarly people but they openly welcome anyone who wants to participate in their work. There are no requirements for joining." She paused, skipping through the article. "It says they look at all areas of paranormal activity and try to apply a natural scientific understanding to it."

"Interesting," he remarked.

"Yes," she answered, looking up at him. "It also says that one of their main goals is to uncover the phenomena of whether we actually survive bodily death, primarily in the area of reincarnation."

"Sounds good," he said. "Any idea on what they'll do to directly help us?"

"Nothing concrete yet," she answered, appearing unsure. "But I'm hoping to make significant contact there with someone who's spiritually gifted. I also understand the organization has quite a library. Maybe we can find information about other cases like ours. Other than that, I don't really know."

Fletcher and Jennifer were relieved when the elevated nose-wheel touched the wet runway, and the pressure of the reverse thrust killed the speed.

They looked at each other and smiled as the plane turned off the runway and began the slow taxi toward the immense airport complex.

Trekking through the lengthy passenger hub, Jennifer sensed an unnatural aura slowly surrounding her. She felt as though a 'presence' of some kind was close behind her. She cringed as an icy chill whisked across the nape of her neck. After pulling her trench coat collar up, she nervously gripped Fletcher's arm as they entered the main terminal. He turned and smiled. She said nothing, assuming the sensation she felt was simply a bite from the London chill.

After verifying their accommodations with the London hotel reservation desk, they gathered their baggage, hurried through the customs tunnel and exited the terminal to wait in line at the taxi stand.

Dodging the curbside puddles, they slipped into the back seat of the black, boxy cab that had pulled up.

"Good evening," Fletcher said to the husky driver, bundled up in a heavy woolen sweater.

The cabby thumbed his frayed fedora up past his eyes and looked at Fletcher, greeting, "Evenin', yank. Where shall I get ya to?"

"Mayfair, please," Fletcher answered. "The Hilton on Park Lane."

The cabby nodded and pulled away from the curb as the rain began to come down in heavy sheets. Fletcher squinted at the heavy airport traffic through the rain-swept windshield and clutched Jennifer's hand. She remained silent, realizing Fletcher's grip felt strangely distant. Yet the cold, unnatural sensation she'd experienced in the terminal had left her. Now she felt intensely warm inside. *What a weird combination*, she thought.

Reaching the hotel, they checked in and immediately climbed into bed, knowing tomorrow would be a long day. While Fletcher quickly fell into a deep sleep, Jennifer lay awake, deep in thought. Although the mysterious aura from the terminal had completely disappeared, her keen intuition was at work again. Maybe things *were* falling into place too easily after all. Maybe something was drawing them to an evil force in London, something beyond their control. She slept fitfully.

❖ ❖ ❖ ❖ ❖

The taxicab darted skillfully through the brisk mid-morning traffic as the steel-gray skyline loomed thickly over Mayfair's stylish neighborhood. Slowing, it pulled up in front of a six-story, U-shaped building.

"You're here, ol' chap," the cabby said. "One Grosvenor Square and the American Embassy. That'll be four pounds."

"Thanks," Fletcher said, muddled from a difficult morning of trying to get over the eight-hour time change. He handed the cabby a five-pound note, waving off the change.

Jennifer exited the cab, still troubled over the strange feeling she'd experienced upon arrival in London. Confused about whether it was only her imagination, she decided to say nothing so as not to worry Fletcher.

Fletcher followed her from the cab as they stood looking up at the giant gilded American eagle sitting on top of the building face. They smiled at each other, feeling more comfortable.

Jennifer looked around the corner, saying, “Damn, it’s a city-block square. We could be in there all day.”

“Yeah, the place is big, all right,” he replied as he pulled out a piece of paper and glanced at it. “The hotel concierge told me that our best chance for help is with the consular services branch.”

“Okay, but let’s test the waters before we tell them anything.”

He nodded as he took her hand and led her up the steps to the large glass doors. They entered the vestibule and walked single-file over the marble floor, and through a large scanner. The security guard let them pass when it showed they carried no weapons. When they reached the broad reception lobby, Fletcher questioned the information clerk and was pointed in the right direction with a cordial smile.

Approaching the consular services counter, they spotted a youthful looking man with a brushed-back mop of mussed blond hair. He looked up and flashed a broad toothy grin.

“Hello,” he greeted them cheerfully. “My name is Harvey Donovan from Boston. How can I help you?”

Oh, boy! Jennifer thought, immediately sensing that Donovan wouldn’t be the right one to help them. *We don’t need this*, she decided.

Fletcher wavered, also feeling uneasy. “Well, we just flew in from the States and were hoping maybe you could help us,” Fletcher answered the attentive young man. “But we have a rather unusual request.”

This caught the attention of a man sitting about ten feet away in a paneled office. He put his pen down and peered over his reading glasses at the couple standing at the counter.

"Sure, what is it?" Donovan asked, still smiling.

"We're going to be in London for a few weeks and may be doing some unexpected traveling," Fletcher replied. "And we're wondering if we could establish a contact here in the embassy for our associates back in California, in case we're unavailable and they need to reach us."

"Oh," Donovan said, looking apologetic. "I don't think we offer that kind of service."

The man at the desk leaned back, loosened his tie, and rubbed his graying temples as he listened to the conversation.

"I see. Okay, I understand," Fletcher said, turning to Jennifer.

Jennifer asked, "Mr. Donovan, can you tell me anything about the Association for Mystical & Paranormal Research?"

"Ah, yes," he paused. "I think so. Isn't that a temple of some sort?"

"Thanks, Mr. Donovan," Jennifer said, no longer tolerant of the obliging but ineffectual representative. She looked at Fletcher and rolled her eyes upward. "C'mon, let's go," she said as they turned to walk away.

"Please wait," a deep throaty voice said from the paneled office.

They all turned to see a tall, wiry man stand and walk over to the counter. He looked at Donovan, saying quietly, "Thanks, Harvey, I'll talk to these folks."

"Sure, Mr. Beaucamp," Donovan agreed, walking away.

The man turned to Fletcher and Jennifer. "Please go to that door on your left, and I'll let you in."

Now feeling optimistic, Fletcher and Jennifer walked over to the opening door. They entered, following the man into his office and sat down across from him.

"My name is Peter Beaucamp. I'm the senior foreign service officer in this department," he said, extending his hand. "Please excuse Mr. Donovan, he's new, but really very good with people."

Fletcher nodded as he firmly shook Beaucamp's hand replying, "My name is Fletcher McKeane, and this is my colleague Jennifer Jaynes."

Jennifer felt instantly at ease with Beaucamp. She shook his hand.

"Now then," Beaucamp said courteously, leaning back in his chair. "Why don't one of you please tell me what you're doing in London."

Fletcher looked at Jennifer, who signaled her consent. "We're here on a search," Fletcher said slowly, testing the reaction of Beaucamp.

"Okay," Beaucamp responded encouragingly. "What kind of search?"

"An unusual search … maybe even dangerous," Fletcher replied more confidently. "It might involve the supernatural."

Beaucamp nodded patiently. "I'm listening. Please go on."

Fletcher now relaxed, answered, "We feel that we're caught up in a paranormal realm that involves some sort of evil element, but we're not sure yet."

Jennifer interrupted, "We think that Fletcher is fatally involved with something evil, maybe satanic."

"I see," Beaucamp said, looking toward Jennifer. "And this element of evil has pursued you all the way to London?"

"No," Fletcher answered sharply, drawing the older man's attention. "We've come to London to pursue *it*."

Jennifer looked over at Beaucamp, saying, "We've both seen, and have been involved in actual communications with spirits."

"Okay. What led you to London?"

She continued, "We feel that everything that's happening is a result of a past life that we were both involved in...and the spirits have brought us here...Oh hell, Mr. Beaucamp," she stammered, turning away. "You must think we're nuts."

He hesitated and calmly pursed his lips. "Ms. Jaynes, I heard you ask about the association for paranormal research," he replied directly. "If I'd thought you were crazy I wouldn't have asked you into my office. I also wouldn't represent the embassy very well if I made personal judgments on what people believed in, especially two people who appear as professional as yourselves."

Jennifer sighed a breath of relief, saying, "Thank you."

Beaucamp nodded. "Now what do you want from the embassy?" he asked.

Fletcher answered, "We're prepared for whatever happens, but we're confused and scared as hell. For starters we'd feel more comfortable if we had a contact at the embassy."

"And what exactly would be required of that contact?"

"Just someone here we can trust, a person who might always know where we were, for our safety," Fletcher answered. "He or she would act as an intermediary to our associates back in the States also. They do know why we're here."

Fletcher then explained how he was under contract to Geographic Unlimited to create a photographic chronicle of their search. And that the story would possibly be published. Beaucamp, familiar with the prestigious publication, was impressed and listened intently until he finished.

"I understand," Beaucamp replied. He looked upward to gather his thoughts while Fletcher and Jennifer remained silent. "Now I know why you asked about the paranormal research association."

"Good," Jennifer responded. "Are you familiar with them?"

"Somewhat," Beaucamp answered. "I've been in London for about eight years and the association has occasionally come up in different conversations. I do know they're very well respected."

"Excellent!" Jennifer exclaimed.

"Tell you what, maybe we can find out a little more about them," Beaucamp said. He stood up, motioning for them to follow. "Let's start at our commercial library. It's on the ground floor."

Fletcher and Beaucamp walked ahead as Jennifer leisurely lagged behind, observing the impressive works of art hanging in the hallways. She was enjoying herself until she detected a sharp draft of icy-cold air and a faint scent of burnt ash. Suddenly, feeling as though she was in a crowded elevator or room, she whirled around. But no one was near her. Oddly, she didn't feel frightened. She almost felt at ease as the icy air dissipated and pleasurable warmth welled up inside her. She sensed a close presence that was tantalizing and exciting. But when it passed she was frightened, catching her breath.

She hurried to join the men who, busily talking, had hardly noticed that she hadn't kept up with them.

Now walking with the men, she had lingering feelings of rapt passion. Yet, unable to understand why or explain it to Fletcher, she managed to disregard it.

When they reached the library entrance, they saw the administrator sitting at the desk in front of a computer.

"Hi, Millie," Beaucamp said to the older lady.

"Morning, Peter," she greeted back.

Beaucamp introduced Fletcher and Jennifer then glanced at the computer asking, "Got anything on the Association for Mystical & Paranormal Research?"

"Let me check," she answered, punching on her keyboard while staring at the monitor. "Yes, we do. Check section 103, to your right, Peter. It looks like we have some pamphlets, possibly even a booklet."

"Thanks," he replied as they headed for the area she had pointed to.

Beaucamp picked up a small yellow three-page pamphlet, browsed through it and handed it to Jennifer.

"It looks as though they have an office in South Kensington," Beaucamp said. "You might try calling them."

"I will!" Jennifer exclaimed, bubbling with enthusiasm as she read through the pamphlet. "I'm sure we can get some answers there."

Fletcher and Beaucamp smiled at her excitement as they left the library for his office. This time Jennifer stayed close, walking abreast of them.

Inside Beaucamp's office, Fletcher and Jennifer sat anxiously as they waited for Beaucamp's decision on the embassy contact issue.

Finally, he looked at them, saying, "We don't normally provide any type of intermediary service for visitors. But I've grown really curious about your situation so I'll personally be your contact. That is on one condition."

"Of course, Mr. Beaucamp," Fletcher replied agreeably. "What is it?"

"Well," he answered. "Since I will have this responsibility, you must take the time to leave messages letting me know where you are. Please don't think anything is insignificant. Oh, and please call me Peter."

"Sure, thanks," Fletcher said.

Beaucamp pulled out two business cards, wrote his home number on them and handed one to each. "My phone at home and the one here, both have voice-mail. I check them frequently, even on weekends. Drives the wife crazy but I feel it's part of my job." He shrugged. "Please call me anytime. I also live close by in Marylebone. I could meet you here quickly if necessary."

"Great," Fletcher said. "This'll help."

"Good," Beaucamp answered. "Glad to be of service. Also, I must be honest. Some good press about us in your magazine wouldn't hurt. Maybe a few pictures of me." He smiled and winked. "I mean, after all, I'm only human. I'm looking to get promoted one of these days."

They all laughed.

"By the way," Beaucamp said, "where are you staying?"

"Close by," Jennifer answered as she pulled out one of her business cards and wrote the hotel information on it.

Fletcher also pulled out his card and handed it to Beaucamp. Standing, they all shook hands while Fletcher explained that after they visited the association for paranormal research he would call Beaucamp and advise him of their plans.

Relieved, Fletcher and Jennifer left the embassy into the gray, chilly day and flagged down a taxi for the trip back to their hotel.

Arriving back at the hotel, they stopped in the coffee shop and ordered the customary afternoon snack of cream tea and scones. While they sat enjoying the light treat, they chuckled over, 'When in Rome, do as the Romans do.'

"Let's call our offices and tell them about Beaucamp," Jennifer said excitedly. "I'd like to fill Steve Butler in on what's going on. I think it's time."

"Good idea," Fletcher replied, standing. "You use the phone on the table here. I'll call from the lobby."

Jennifer reached for his arm. "Okay, but don't be gone for too long," she said, smiling. "Remember our pact."

He bent down and kissed her. "Yes, I remember our pact. How could I forget it?" he said, winking with a roguish gleam.

She slapped at him playfully as he scooted away.

When he was out of sight, she stopped smiling, as she thought about her experience in the Heathrow terminal and then again at the embassy. She didn't know how to explain them to Fletcher and, for some reason she didn't really want to. She felt baffled as she picked up the telephone.

Fletcher came back to the table where Jennifer sat, not noticing that she looked disturbed.

"You first," she said blankly as he sat down.

"Well, as luck would have it," Fletcher answered, chuckling, "Berkshire wasn't in yet. I left a message and gave him our hotel information and told him how to reach Beaucamp in case of an emergen…" Fletcher noticed Jennifer's mood had changed. "Hey, what's up?"

She stared at him. "I talked to Butler at my office…" She paused.

"Okay. What is it?" Fletcher pressed.

"They found Frank."

"What? Where?"

"The body, or what was left of it that is, washed up on the beach at Catalina. The identity was questionable, it was burned, bloated and decomposing, almost beyond recognition." She wrinkled her face.

"Jesus," Fletcher remarked, shaking his head.

"It gets worse," she continued. "It appears that the sharks had gotten to him, though I asked Steve to spare me those details. Anyway, they're quite sure it was him because of the facial features and the height and bone structure were about the same as Frank's. Also Kent Fitzroy identified a ring that he had given Frank last Christmas."

Fletcher sat back, questioning, "Can't they positively identify him from dental records or something like that?"

Jennifer's eyes opened wider. "First thing I asked. Steve told me there aren't any. There's no evidence of Frank ever visiting a dentist, or doctor for that matter. So I suppose DNA testing is out too. At least it appears that way right now."

"How weird," Fletcher said, rubbing his forehead.

"Yeah, it sure is," she agreed. "Anyway, they're still convinced it's him, or they want to be." She grimaced. "Regardless, they're going to entomb the remains, or to be more precise, *what* remains, as soon as they can complete the paperwork."

Fletcher nodded. “Well Jennifer, I guess this pretty much shoots holes in your theory about Frank being a fiend of some sort, right?”

“I don’t know. My intuition hasn’t been wrong yet, but this does cause me some doubts. I’ll admit that,” she said, frustrated. “Damn!”

“C’mon,” he said, taking her hand. “Let’s get some rest and go out tonight. We’ll do dinner and the theater. Tomorrow we can rent a car and start again when we’re fresh.”

“Damn!” she exclaimed as they rose and left the restaurant. She shook her head. “Damn! Damn! Damn!”

CHAPTER 28

Association for Mystical and Paranormal Research

The early afternoon sun barely eked through the heavy cloud layer as Fletcher hugged the left lane of the grassy traffic circle, tensely maneuvering the Land Rover onto Collingham Road in South Kensington.

Jennifer, peering out the windshield at the addresses on the weathered buildings, exclaimed excitedly, "There's 1651! It was in that row of suites you just passed on the right."

"Figures," Fletcher responded as he looked up ahead for a place to turn around. "This driving on the left side of the road is bullshit."

Jennifer turned to him. "I've driven in England before. Would you like me to drive?" she asked carefully, not wanting to bruise his male ego.

"No. Just stick to your airplanes. I can handle this, thank you," he answered gruffly, cranking hard on the steering wheel to complete a sweeping U-turn.

As he clumsily brought the car to a stop in front of the building, the tires bounced off the curb, causing a jolt. He mumbled a couple of obscenities while

Jennifer looked down and loaded some film into the camera. She smiled but said nothing as they got out of the car.

Walking up the sidewalk toward the narrow porch, Jennifer snapped some pictures of the outside of the building. She pointed up toward the archway where a small sign was bolted under the stained-glass window.

Association for Mystical and Paranormal Research

Stepping onto the porch, Jennifer banged the brass door knocker, set in the center of the broad dark-hickory door. After a few minutes and another bang of the weighty knocker, a diminutive elderly lady slowly opened the door.

She stood a bit over five feet, including the thick bun of pure gray hair piled on top of her head. Her aged, but still lively eyes crinkled through her round plastic-rimmed glasses as she smiled pleasantly at Fletcher and Jennifer.

"Might I help you?" she asked in a distinct but pleasant tone, clutching her heavy knit shawl to ward off the biting breeze.

"Yes, thank you," Jennifer answered. "My name is Jennifer Jaynes and this is Fletcher McKeane."

"How do ya do?" The old lady replied. "I'm Catherine O'Grady, the attendant member for the association. Nice to make your acquaintance Jennifer, and yours Fletcher."

"It's good to meet you, too, Ms. O'Grady," Fletcher answered hesitantly, feeling somewhat pensive.

Jennifer immediately perceived a special warmth about the woman. Feeling at ease, she said, "I called earlier this morning. We feel we have an important matter to discuss with the association."

"Yes, I recall our brief chat this morning," she replied, opening the door and moving aside. "Please step in out of the chill. 'Tis a fright out there."

Jennifer turned to Fletcher. "I suggest you go back to the hotel and prepare your report for Berkshire," she said with a smile. "You should be prepared when he calls. His message sounded very aggressive. I didn't know he used language like that." She winked.

Fletcher looked over her shoulder and past the little old lady inside. Uneasy, he turned back to Jennifer. "Are you sure you want to do this alone?"

"Yes, now go," she answered firmly, pushing on his shoulders. "You don't want to disappoint Berkshire by not being there when he calls." She glanced at her watch, analyzing the zone time difference. "You'll have just enough time to prepare before he gets to his office."

"Okay. But I'll only be gone a couple of hours. Please don't go anywhere until I come back for you."

"I promise," she said, reaching up to give him a reassuring kiss.

Although apprehensive, he turned and made his way to the car.

Jennifer quickly stepped inside as the old woman closed and bolted the door behind her. Removing her trench coat, Jennifer handed it to the attentive lady who hung it up in the large walk-in hall closet.

Jennifer followed Ms. O'Grady's quick gait down a long carpeted hallway, its walls adorned with oil portraits of the eminent-looking founders of the association. Jennifer paused in front of two open double doors and peered into a dimly-lit spacious room that appeared to be a library.

"Oh," Jennifer said, stopping O'Grady. "Is this your library?"

O'Grady turned abruptly, entered the room and snapped on the overhead lights. "Yes. You might have a look if ya fancy."

Jennifer stepped in and gazed around the room. The walls were solid with shelves of books that reached from the floor to the ceiling. There were wooden study-tables with cushioned-back chairs spaced around the room.

"Thank you," she said to the patient old woman.

"Surely," O'Grady replied. She turned out the light as they left the room and continued down the hallway into a formal reception room.

It looked regal, but comfortable and roomy, with large throw rugs placed uniformly on the heavily lacquered wooden floor. A large four-cushioned couch and soft leather chairs formed a semi-circle in front of a high-arched, red-brick fireplace that gave off a modest blaze. Next to the fireplace stood a tall mahogany grandfather clock. The golden pendulum was polished brightly and glittered as it swung gracefully behind crystal-clear glass.

A wide dining table with matching chairs was set in the middle of the room. On the table, covered with a clean white starched tablecloth, sat a teapot full of freshly brewed tea. A tray of flowered china saucers and cups and a plate of blueberry tarts, still steaming from the oven, were sitting next to the tea.

"Please sit down," O'Grady said, pulling two chairs away from the table.

"A spot 'o tea and tart for you?" O'Grady asked while they both sat down at the table.

"Just tea for me please. I'm still stuffed from our late breakfast."

"Now then, dear child," the old woman said as she poured them both some strong green tea. "Perhaps you're interested in becoming a member of the association, or is it maybe ya just want to pitch an article into the quarterly journal?"

Jennifer thought for a moment, trying to figure out where to begin. "Well, possibly both," she answered awkwardly. "Fletcher and I have come to London seeking spiritual support. I understand you allow public access to the members of the association, and the information they provide, don't you?"

"Oh, surely. Our studies and publications of the paranormal are indeed meant for the community, 'tis." O'Grady smiled as she sipped on her tea, adding, "The library here is open from two to five in the afternoon, three days a week. But 'tis really open anytime you need if I'm here."

Smiling appreciatively, Jennifer answered, "Thank you Ms. O'Grady, but we may need more help than that. Tell me, are you spiritually gifted?"

The old lady became solemn, rose slowly and walked over to the fireplace. "I must tend the fire a moment," she said, drawing the black mesh fire screen out of the way. She reached into the rack of honed fire irons and pulled out the poker. Prodding methodically, she stoked the glowing ashes into a small pile before carefully exchanging the poker for a double-pronged log fork. With all her strength she skillfully speared a log and added it to the fire.

She turned around, pushed the screen back across the outer hearth and broke the silence. "I fancy a fire. I always ensure that one's aflame, I do." Walking slowly, she sat back down at the table and looked at Jennifer. "My dear Ms. Jaynes, do you ask if I possess the powers to see and reach beyond?"

Jennifer slowly nodded, remaining mute.

"Perhaps, my dear, my greatest gift is possessing the patience and prudence to believe in the abnormal with only a snippet of evidence. Perhaps my gift is not looking upon the paranormal as mere tripe because I cannot explain it..." She hesitated as Jennifer leaned forward, listening closely to the old woman's words.

"Oh, yes," O'Grady continued, "I have been blessed with a gift of faith, but not the power to aid people in distress. It wouldn't be fair to them. It wouldn't at all."

"I understand," Jennifer answered, somewhat disappointed.

The old woman placed her hand on Jennifer's. "For sure," she said softly, "it wouldn't be fair where the devil is involved, as I feel is the case in your situation. Please tell me what it is you need. Perhaps there is some way I can help." She slowly withdrew her hand and refilled their cups with tea.

"Yes, I'm sure you can help," Jennifer replied, sitting back. "Fletcher and I have been strangely drawn into something vile. We don't understand it yet, but we're very sure it's from the paranormal..."

"Drawn together, dear?" O'Grady interrupted as she carefully pulled a warm tart apart with her fingers.

"Yes," Jennifer said. "We think by an unnatural being. An evil entity of some sort that is close, but in another realm. Both Fletcher and I need to communicate with that realm."

"Oh, quite," O'Grady said, daintily wiping her shiny, aged fingers with a white cloth napkin. "Most all members of the association do agree that there is another domain, where chosen souls—good and evil—do prowl at whim." She slowly looked up. "Please go on, my dear."

"Many of Fletcher's close friends have been killed in terrible ways," Jennifer continued. "We've come to believe it must be acts of revenge."

O'Grady suddenly sat back scowling. "Oh, be assured young lady, the damned are gradual and wreak their wretched revenge in ghastly ways. The evil knows well that suffering lingers greatest under those terms."

Jennifer looked at her nervously, growing anxious, saying, "We think it's because of a past life we were involved in and that the answers may be here in England. That's why we need help from the spiritually gifted. Someone who can unlock what had maybe transpired during that other lifetime."

"Oh, quite surely," O'Grady agreed. "You shall never draw a peaceful breath until you know." She paused for a moment. "My dear, I think I can speak for the association and tell ya that we shall support you and your man. Now, mind you, you must take the lead and we surely can't promise the best of findings."

Jennifer looked at her and reached for her hand. For the first time since this all started she felt trust toward someone besides Fletcher. "I understand," Jennifer whispered, her eyes moist with tears. "Thank you."

"Ah, splendid!" The old woman exclaimed, strongly gripping Jennifer's hand in return. Her wrinkling cheeks and large smile emphasized the immediate harmony between them.

"Now then, my dear," O'Grady said enthusiastically, "There is someone in London who may be able to help you. She is a favorite of the association because of her proven mystical powers. She's an unusual one, mind you, but well educated and very successful in past life findings. Her name is

Madame Lena Von Bruen. She's from Salzburg, Austria, but she stays in London because of the weather and to be close to the association."

Jennifer was puzzled by the comment about the weather but let it pass, asking excitedly, "How do we reach her?"

"Oh, I shall ring her up today, actually," O'Grady answered. "I will arrange an appointment for you and Mr. McKeane to meet with her at her flat in Chelsea."

"Thank you!" Jennifer exclaimed as she wrote down the hotel information on her business card and placed it in the old woman's outstretched hand.

"Yes, quite surely," O'Grady replied, smiling.

When Jennifer looked into the woman's concerned eyes, she realized that she'd truly gained a new friend.

"Ms. O'Grady, may I come back and visit you for tea some day soon?"

"Yes, anytime you like," the old lady replied. "I'm here every day, except Sunday, when I'm visiting with the Lord Almighty..." She paused, looking into Jennifer's troubled eyes. "You are very frightened, Ms. Jaynes. More than I thought. 'Tis indeed quite a clash you must be caught up in, 'tis."

Jennifer paled, replying, "Yes, I'm frightened like never before. May I confide in you? There's something I haven't told anyone, including Fletcher."

"Yes, of course," O'Grady said gently, again reaching for Jennifer's hand. "Come, let's set next to the fire where 'tis warmer."

They rose and walked to the couch. As Jennifer sat down, O'Grady stoked the fire before carefully placing the fire tool back in the rack.

"Must be mindful of those sharp stokers, ya must," she said as she sat down next to Jennifer, offering her complete attention.

Jennifer told her everything, including the abnormal experiences that she'd been having since she'd arrived in London. And how she couldn't tell Fletcher because she felt some strange attraction toward the presence that left her scared and confused.

The old woman listened with empathy and told Jennifer that she would help by being there whenever Jennifer needed her. She also suggested that if Jennifer truly trusted Fletcher she would have to tell him everything, and have faith that he would understand.

The repeated clanking of the door knocker shattered the lively conversation of the two women as they browsed through some books in the library. They both walked to the door to welcome an anxious Fletcher, who was very worried about Jennifer. He was relieved when he saw her smiling face.

As they all stood at the front door, O'Grady promised to call Jennifer as soon as she had arranged a meeting with Madame Von Bruen.

"Cheerio," the old woman hailed as she began to close the door.

"And cheerio to you Catherine. I'll see you soon," Jennifer responded.

She and Fletcher stepped off the front porch and into the ash-gray late afternoon. The breeze had turned into a slight icy bluster with unseasonable snow flurries stinging their skin.

Reaching the street, Jennifer cheerfully entered the passenger side of the car and Fletcher got in behind the wheel on the driver's side.

Hesitating, he turned to Jennifer. "You look happy. Your visit must've gone okay."

She broke into a broad smile and put her hand on his arm. "Yes. Not only do we have help; I've made a new friend. I feel safe around her and plan to visit her often while we're here."

"Good!" he exclaimed, relieved by her good spirits. "I'm really glad."

She sat back. "How'd it go with Berkshire?"

"Well," he answered slowly. "I settled everything. He wasn't real happy that we left for London so fast, but he realizes that we're on an assignment and they're only responsible for our expenses. He said if he needs anything he'll call us or Beaucamp at the embassy."

Fletcher started the car, but paused when he saw the heavy traffic on Cromwell Road. Gripping the steering wheel, he frowned as he slowly put the car into gear and pulled away, scraping the tires against the curb.

He repeated his usual obscenities as Jennifer turned away and grinned, mildly amused by his frustrated efforts to drive in London.

Chapter 29

The Seduction, Mayfair

Fletcher turned and faced Jennifer with a concerned look as he stepped into the hotel lobby. He put his hand on the door to block the closing. "I really wish you'd come along," he urged. "I'd feel a lot better."

Cocking her head, she returned an oh-no-not-again glance and pushed his hand away. "For the last time, no," she argued, smiling.

He backed away, frowning.

She slowly began to close the door, saying, "Quit worrying about me. Go out and enjoy a drink with Peter and let him know what's going on. I'll be fine."

"All right," he relented, "but I won't be out late."

"Okay, come back whenever you want. I'm going to take a long refreshing bubble bath and read myself to sleep. Now go. Don't keep Peter waiting."

Nodding reluctantly, he turned and made his way down the hall toward the elevator.

Shutting the door tightly, she locked it, hearing the dead bolt snap into place. She wiggled and pulled on the knob to confirm its security.

Walking toward the bathroom, she began unbuttoning her blouse when the phone rang. She turned to the bedside table and picked up the receiver.

"Hello? Oh, hi, Catherine," Jennifer said, greeting her warmly. "No, you didn't disturb me. Fletcher just left to meet with Mr. Beaucamp from the embassy…Of course I've got time to talk. Really, I'm glad you called. I was just going to soak in a hot bubble bath."

Jennifer sat down on the edge of the bed…."Yes, we received your message about meeting with Ms. Von Bruen tomorrow morning. We were at dinner when you called. I really apprecia…" Jennifer paused when she heard sudden noises in the bathroom. Her eyes slowly scanned the room…"What? Yes, Catherine, I'm still here…Oh, nothing. I just thought I heard something in the bathroom. It's probably coming from the room above us…Okay, hang on and I'll go see. Be right back."

Laying the receiver down, Jennifer calmly walked to the bathroom, convincing herself that the noises had come from another hotel room. Entering, she felt a sharp chill and detected a strange smell of burnt ash. Now growing alarmed, she froze. *Oh no, not again!* Tense, she looked around but saw nothing unusual. Nor did she feel or sense anything mysterious. Then, seeing the window was open, she relaxed, assuming the annoying elements were coming from outside. *Probably somebody's fireplace.* Yet she was puzzled that the odor was so strong. Shrugging, she closed the window and returned to the phone.

"Catherine, it wasn't anything," Jennifer said, sitting back down on the bed. "It must have been noises from next door and my active imagination." She chuckled…."Oh yes, sure, I'll mention it to Fletcher when he gets home, but not to worry. Anyway, as I was saying, I really appreciate your setting up the meeting for us. We're eager to meet Ms. Von Bruen...What? Sure, tomorrow afternoon for tea, it is. Thank you. I know we'll want to tell you about our meeting with Ms. Von Bruen. See you then...Yes, you have a nice evening also. Cheerio, Catherine."

Delighted over Catherine's call, Jennifer hung up the phone and sprung off the bed thinking about tomorrow's meeting with Von Bruen. She undressed, put on her long bathrobe and entered the bathroom.

Finding that it was still cold and foul-smelling, she became nervous and stood still in the doorway. But within moments, her feeling of worry had turned to one of tranquillity. She relaxed as a warm tingling sensation enveloped her body, ending the chill. The rank odor had become spicy-sweet and inviting. Filled with a rush of erotic desire, she untied her robe and let it fall open to expose her naked body. Bending down over the tub, she adjusted the faucets to full-force. An intense flow of hot water cascaded into the tub with a hammering thump.

Although sensing that someone was behind her, she remained calmly enchanted and only casually turned around to look. Seeing no one, she turned back toward the tub, the warmth in her body increasing. Electrified with waves of mounting desire, she became flushed and her nipples hardened. The steady stream of scalding water created a misty vapor that caressed her body, adding to her state of intense rapture. Aroused to a heightened level of sexual awareness, she moved to lean back against the tub, sensually stroking at her long moistened hair. Her loins began to quiver with lust as she gently massaged her parted thighs.

Fully enthralled in sexual abandon, her eyes darkened with passion and her mouth parted as she leaned forward, slipping the robe off her shoulders and down her back. As her breathing increased, she uttered shallow moans from the back of her throat. She lowered herself to the floor, writhing vulnerably. Reaching up, she searched hungrily through the steamy shroud for the source of her ecstasy.

Yanking hard on the nylon cord, Jennifer separated the thick drapes, allowing the brilliant morning sunshine to stream in. Dressed only in her bathrobe, she leaned against the sill, lost in thought. She cupped her chin in her hand and gazed out the wide hotel window and across Park Lane at Hyde Park. Crowds of people were bustling in and out of the new Queen's Gate entrance.

The sparkling air and gentle wind rippled the Serpentine Lake and powered the few small sailing boats enjoying the warm weather. She remained still as Fletcher emerged from the bathroom fully dressed.

"Christ, this weather changes every day," he remarked, walking toward her and putting his hands on her shoulders. "Think I'll need my windbreaker today?" he asked, peering out the window past her loosely bound ponytail.

When she didn't answer or show any reaction, he slowly turned her around. "Hey," he said softly. "Where are you today? What's wrong? You haven't said more than two words all morning. And you're not even ready. Didn't you say we had to meet with Von Bruen this morning?"

"Yes," she answered, looking downward.

"Why the sudden change in disposition?" he asked. "After the visit with Catherine O'Grady yesterday, you were extremely optimistic. What now?"

She looked up at him. "I know," she answered with a glum expression. "I'm very troubled this morning and we need to talk. Catherine convinced me I shouldn't hold anything back from you."

Fletcher sensed she was shaken and afraid. Concerned, he embraced her tightly. "No, Jennifer. Never hold anything back," he appealed. "We must trust each other. C'mon let's sit down."

She lowered her eyes in remorse, but was determined to tell him everything.

As they sat down, he took her hand. "Please. What is it?" he asked tenderly. "Take your time."

She looked at him sadly. "I think…um…" she stammered, "I think something bad is happening to me."

"What do you mean?" he asked, inhaling.

"I mean something vile might be overtaking me. Ever since we landed in London I've felt drawn to a strange presence." She hesitated, flustered. "I can't explain the feeling, but I know it's unnatural."

"Could it somehow be Lainey?" he asked, dazed.

"No," she answered, "Lainey is good. This presence feels evil."

"For God's sake," he replied, growing upset. "Why haven't you told me?"

"Because…" she mumbled, "because it doesn't frighten me while it's happening…I…I even feel secretly contented by it."

He stared at her, puzzled. "I don't understand."

"Damn! I don't either!" she exclaimed, now visibly strained and rubbing her forehead. "That's what's so confusing." She looked up at him. "I'm never scared until afterward, when I realize what has happened."

"When was the last time something happened?"

She looked away, answering, "Last night, right after you left to have a drink with Beaucamp."

"Please tell me about it," he said calmly. "Describe what happened. Everything."

She whispered, a pleading look filling her eyes, "Promise me you'll be understanding until we know everything. Please, tell me you'll understand."

"Yes, I promise," he replied impatiently. "Yes."

"All right," she began slowly, "after you left for the pub, I was on the phone with Catherine when I heard something in the bathroom. I checked it out but didn't find anything. So I disregarded it." Jennifer looked away nervously.

"Please keep going," he said calmly. "Obviously there's more."

She continued, again whispering, "Later when I was preparing my bath, everything suddenly became warm and passionate. I started relaxing, and…" She hesitated.

"Sweetheart, go on," he said tenderly, holding her hand.

"Soon it was dreamlike. I saw an image, a masculine image. I can't tell you exactly who or what the image was. I don't even know if it was a human image. I felt helplessly drawn to it, excited…sexually stimulated. I lost consciousness of reality when it came closer. I couldn't move. I was helpless." She paused, looking up at him with tears in her eyes.

He squeezed her hand tightly to reassure her of his understanding.

"Then I didn't want to fight it. I…I…let it happen."

"Let what happen?"

She closed her eyes. "I don't know exactly, but it felt like I was making love…wildly…uncontrollably."

"Do you mean you actually made love with something, or someone?"

"I don't know for God's sake!" She gasped, turning away, spent from frustration. "But I know that I had multiple orgasms and I don't think it was from self-stimulation. I wouldn't be this upset over the need to simply masturbate."

"Jesus!" Fletcher exclaimed, shaking his head.

She looked back up at him. "When it was over and the presence was gone, I was terribly scared. I cried, took my bath and went to bed. I heard you come in, but pretended I was asleep. I was so confused." She began to weep.

He gently lifted her head. "Were you thinking of me when…I mean…"

She looked at him with reddening eyes. "That's just it darling. No. You're the only one who's ever aroused me that strongly, but it wasn't you last night." She turned away.

Again, he gently turned her head back toward his. "Were you physically harmed at all? I mean was there evidence that you…"

"I don't know," she interrupted. "I just jumped in the bath immediately after it happened and scrubbed myself. I was so confused. Oh, please I don't want to talk about it anymore," she pleaded.

He drew her in tightly, whispering in her ear, "Sweetheart, it's okay…It's okay." Then he slowly pushed them apart. "Jennifer! What is it we're up against? What?"

"I don't know," she answered angrily, wiping her tears. "I just don't know!"

Frustrated, he abruptly stood up. "That's it!" he huffed as he began to pace the room. "We're getting the hell outta here. Let's go home."

"You know we can't," she disagreed. "Not yet."

He walked to the window, paused, then replied, "I know, I know. Shit!"

Jennifer slowly stood up and began walking to the bathroom. "I'm going to get dressed," she said. "I want to meet with Von Bruen."

"Okay," he said sternly, stopping her. "But if anything more happens like last night we're going home. There'll be no argument."

She nodded and turned toward the bathroom.

He continued to stare through the window, shaking his head.

Jennifer came out looking fresh and relieved, glad she had told Fletcher about last night. As he watched her walk up to him, she put her arms around his waist and looked up at him appreciatively.

He smiled, bending down to kiss her. "C'mon we'd better get moving."

Walking to the bureau, he picked up the keys to the car, but then hesitated. He glanced discouragingly out the window, seeing the heavy traffic on Park Lane.

Jennifer knew what he was thinking, but appeared nonchalant.

"Aw fuck it," he said with a wide grin, throwing her the keys. "You drive."

They were still laughing over Fletcher's surrender of the car as Jennifer smoothly shifted into third gear, pulling the Land Rover onto Knightsbridge Street to head for Chelsea and Madame Lena Von Bruen's flat.

Fletcher was enjoying the ride. Folding up the London street map, he picked up his camera and snapped a few pictures of the Wellington Monument through the rear window.

"Fletcher?" Jennifer said questioningly.

"What?" he answered, loading new film in the camera.

"Did you update Beaucamp about everything last night?"

"I think so," he replied, recalling last night's conversation in the pub. "Why do you ask?"

She quickly glanced at him. "Does Peter fully understand that everyone you get close to seems to be endangered?"

"We talked about it. He said if he notices anything crazy going on with him or his family he'd tell us. But right now he wants to remain in the loop."

"He's a brave man," she said as she turned onto Brompton Road.

"Yeah, he is," he said. "But what about your new friend, O'Grady?"

Jennifer slapped at the wheel. "Damn!" she exclaimed. "I never thought about that. I enjoy her company so much."

"I'm sorry I brought it up."

"It's okay," she said, sighing. "I told her we'd stop by for tea this afternoon after the meeting with Von Bruen. I'll tell her that I'm concerned about her possibly endangering herself by helping us."

"Good," he said as he snapped the camera shut and listened to the film automatically advance. He checked the frame counter to make sure it loaded properly and wiped off the lens. He looked through the viewfinder at Jennifer and made a loud smooching noise like a kiss to get her attention.

She looked over, smiling broadly as he snapped a picture. But inside she was not smiling. Her mind couldn't stop recalling the strange pleasure of last night's bathroom incident.

Fletcher glanced again at the address on the piece of paper as Jennifer drove slowly along Chelsea Embankment, bordering the River Thames.

"There it is," he said, pointing up ahead toward a two-story house that had been converted into flats. "That's the address you wrote down, 3201. It looks like there's room to park on the street."

She pulled up next to the curb in front of the house, which looked drab and was badly in need of repair and paint.

The car parked, Fletcher snapped a few pictures of the meandering river. Except for a flock of frolicking birds and a few children playing on the riverbank, the area was quiet.

As they walked up the steps of the wooden porch, Fletcher looked at the paper again and then at the two mailboxes loosely attached to the side of the wall. He looked into the bare window on the ground floor. "Von Bruen must live in the flat upstairs. The one downstairs looks empty and there's no name on the mailbox."

"Black drapes!" Jennifer exclaimed in a puzzled tone as she arched her head upward. "Who would put black drapes on their windows? And they're closed, on such a gorgeous day."

Fletcher shaded his eyes from the bright sunlight and followed her gaze. "Who knows?" he said, chuckling. "Seems fitting though, doesn't it?"

She laughed. "And Catherine says Von Bruen loves the London weather."

"Really?" he said, rolling his eyes upward. "Well, let's find out why."

They approached the entrance and peered through a smudged sidelight window. Seeing a stairway leading to an upstairs flat, Fletcher opened the door. Entering the hallway Jennifer nervously gripped Fletcher's hand as they carefully began to ascend the dingy, darkened stairway. When they reached the top Fletcher knocked on the door.

After a few moments a small peephole opened up. "Yes?" a low, husky tone trickled through.

Jennifer gripped Fletcher's hand tighter. He stepped closer to the hole. "My name is Fletcher McKeane and I'm with Jennifer Jaynes," he said. "We were told to meet here with a Madame Lena Von Bruen. Can you help us?"

"Yes," the voice said. "One moment, please."

There was a clicking of several locks being removed before the door finally opened.

A tall woman dressed in black, with a heavy shawl draped around her shoulders, stood in the shadows of the doorway. A large knitted scarf was wrapped tightly around her head. Fletcher and Jennifer could not see her face. She was silhouetted by candles placed throughout the room.

"I am Lena Von Bruen," she said as she backed away from the door. "You are welcome to come in."

Fletcher released Jennifer's hand as she followed him into the room. All the windows were draped shut, eliminating all natural light. Von Bruen shut the door and walked into the kitchen, brightly lit by multiple candelabras sitting on the kitchen table.

Looking at each other, Fletcher and Jennifer followed her, not knowing what to expect. They still hadn't seen her face.

Von Bruen moved the candelabras to the far edge of the table and pulled out three chairs. She turned back toward Fletcher and Jennifer, slowly removing the scarf from around her head, revealing stark, almost colorless features. Her long milk-white hair was combed back. The pupils of her eyes were more red than black and her chalky eyebrows provided little contrast to her pale pink skin.

Albino! Jennifer thought. No wonder she avoids the sunlight.

"Please come in," Von Bruen offered, "and join me at the table."

Though stunned by her bleak, haggard appearance, Fletcher and Jennifer managed to conceal their surprise. They sat down at the table, hopeful that the next few hours would give them some insight into the source of their torment.

CHAPTER 30

Madame Lena Von Bruen

Madame Lena Von Bruen reached across the table to the candelabra and replaced two burnt stubs of tallow with fresh candles, saying, "I hope you don't mind. I prefer a flame over artificial light. It feels more natural."

"No, of course we don't mind," Jennifer answered politely. "We're in your home, seeking your help."

Fletcher nodded in agreement, then asked anxiously, "Madame, do you think you can help us?"

"Perhaps," Von Bruen answered, looking over at him. "After talking to Catherine O'Grady yesterday I have thought about it a great deal." She paused. "Had you told Catherine everything? You haven't forgotten anything?" she questioned again, turning toward Jennifer who glanced downward.

Sensing remorse in Jennifer, Von Bruen said, "Miss Jaynes, if I am to assist you, you will have to tell me all that has transpired. I am sorry if it will be uncomfortable, but you must trust in me."

"Yes," Jennifer conceded, slowly looking up at her, "I'll tell you everything that's happened."

Jennifer appeared subdued after describing the hotel-room incident, when she was sexually drawn to the strange presence. As Fletcher held her hand tightly, she kept her eyes fixed on the flickering candles.

Madame Von Bruen sat silently, contemplating every detail of their baneful experiences. Shattering the fragile stillness, she pulled her lanky body away from the table and walked to the miniature dormer window over the sink. Pulling the coal-black vinyl shade back, she peeked out through the crack. "It's getting cloudy and chilly," she mumbled. "Maybe before dark I can go outside for a walk by the river."

Fletcher and Jennifer remained still as Von Bruen returned to the table.

Turning to face Fletcher and Jennifer, she said slowly, "Yes, as you do, I also suspect that you're afflicted by fiendish spiritual encounters."

"Then it must be spirits from Hell," Fletcher interjected.

"Perhaps," Von Bruen agreed. "But from what you describe, I don't think so. There is another plateau of spiritual authority."

"Another plateau?" Jennifer repeated, excited by hearing what she'd suspected for so long.

"Yes," Von Bruen replied. "We believe it's an aura of turbulent darkness that exists just beyond the earthly senses."

"And it's not Heaven or Hell?" Fletcher asked.

"Not in that sense," Von Bruen answered. "We think this domain exists between the abode of the Almighty and the abyss of the damned."

"And we're being affected by an evil spirit from there?" Jennifer asked.

Von Bruen confirmed, "I am most sure of it."

Jennifer glanced at Fletcher, then directly back at Von Bruen, asking, "Madame, what else do you think?"

"I'm not able to understand everything yet. It is still very awkward," Von Bruen answered, her brow creasing with thought. "Yet I am most convinced that you, Fletcher and the other people you spoke of must have somehow been entangled in a past life…along with the evil soul."

Fletcher and Jennifer stirred nervously in their chairs.

"But what brought us all together now?" Fletcher asked.

Von Bruen pondered his question before responding, "It is not unusual for souls from the same past era to draw toward each other in a new lifetime. Souls of companions willingly and commonly search for each other…"

"As well as the souls of enemies," Fletcher interrupted, shaken.

He received a grim nod from Von Bruen as she gathered her thoughts and continued, "However, it is unusual that many souls from past shared lifetimes would come together at once. Therefore, the gravitation to this place you speak of in California must have been aided by a spiritual force, most likely a satanic force."

"You mean we were unknowingly brought together there?" Jennifer asked.

"Most probably," Von Bruen confirmed. "Your place in California is situated near the ocean and water is the main element used to induce mystical energy—good or evil."

Jennifer recalled Catherine's high value of Von Bruen's mystical powers. "Is that the reason you live near the river?"

Von Bruen seemed saddened by the question, surprising Jennifer. "Yes," she whispered in a tone signaling that she didn't wish to discuss it further.

Although curious, Jennifer tactfully changed the subject. She returned to the incident in the hotel bathroom. "Madame, why do you think I'm attracted to a soul that seems so evil?"

Von Bruen answered gently, "I am not certain. Possibly you harbor some inner feelings of attachment to it."

"But, why so suddenly?" Jennifer pushed, becoming frustrated.

Von Bruen leaned back. "Again, I am unsure at this time. Perhaps it has to do with whatever guided you to England. I do think you may be correct in presuming this is where the past lives occurred. Possibly you're close to the answers and have now become the object of *its* revenge."

"Damn!" Jennifer huffed, losing control. "Why in that manner, for God's sake? Why not like the others…" Jennifer's voice trailed off.

"To seek a greater revenge on Herr McKeane, of course."

"What do you mean?" Jennifer blurted again.

Fletcher silently reached for Jennifer's hand.

Jennifer returned the squeeze, but her eye's remained fixed on Von Bruen.

Von Bruen remained calm, responding, "To befoul you Miss Jaynes. Your body is most beautiful and I am sure your soul is just as beautiful. It is known that evil despoils the virtues of beauty. Wouldn't that be the evil's gravest punishment to inflict upon you and Herr McKeane at this time?" Von Bruen hesitated, then added, "Yet, I must caution you. There is never a set pattern of punishment."

Fletcher dropped his head in his hands.

Jennifer looked bewildered as she asked, "But how is this getting to me?"

"From what you describe, I would think through your subconscious mind."

Jennifer, startled, jerked backward. "My mind?"

"Yes." Von Bruen's eyes began widening as she continued her clarification of a subject that she understood well. "The thoughts from that past lifetime are locked away in your brain. The evil one must be exploiting those memories, causing intense feelings to re-emerge."

"Jesus!" Fletcher exclaimed. "Are you saying that all thoughts of our past lifetimes are locked away in our brains?"

"Undoubtedly," Von Bruen replied, turning toward him. "And it is possible to retrieve those thoughts. We call it cryptomnesia."

"Cryptomnesia?" Fletcher repeated.

Jennifer, still thinking about the hotel bathroom incident and Von Bruen's dire warning of probable future punishment, swallowed hard and then asked, "Madame, could this evil spirit make actual contact with humans?"

Von Bruen lifted her head in thought. "Yes, it has been said they can make physical contact. We have studied a great number of such cases through the association."

Jennifer, speaking slowly, asked, "Do you think that…that somehow on that night in the hotel bathroom...I...I..." Jennifer hung her head. Fletcher put his hand on her shoulder.

"Actually copulated with the spirit?" Von Bruen interrupted, anticipating her question. "That has always remained a mystery among cases such as this. Of course, your intruder would have had to take a bodily form of some kind. Unfortunately, I regret to tell you that we have no way of knowing for sure." She hesitated. "Although there is a good possibility you were only mentally seduced."

Jennifer appeared somewhat relieved.

"But, again, I must warn you, Miss Jaynes," Von Bruen quickly added, "your anguish is warranted. The subliminal seduction attempts may reoccur. And it is very possible that a bodily form could materialize."

Fletcher and Jennifer stiffened.

Von Bruen continued, "I also must tell you that your feelings of eroticism might overcome any denial, rendering you helpless against its assault."

Jennifer inhaled deeply as Fletcher put his arm around her. "Could it," he asked haltingly. "Could it physically hurt us...Or even kill us?"

"Unfortunately there is evidence that these souls have rendered physical harm."

"How could that be done?" Fletcher pressed, astonished at the idea.

Von Bruen answered slowly, "It has been reported that innocent humans have become possessed by the evil soul, causing them to commit violent acts."

Jennifer thought about Frank and Lainey's death, asking, "Then it's possible that the soul seeking revenge could have taken over the soul of someone on earth? Maybe the one we talked about named Frank?"

"Yes, it is possible," Von Bruen answered, arching her thin chalky eyebrows. "Though I cannot determine this for sure."

"But if we are correct about Frank," Jennifer continued, "and he was possessed by the vengeful spirit, could he have somehow coerced Lainey to back off the cliff?"

Von Bruen's eyes hardened, replying, "It may be that this Frank was possessed, or was chosen to possess the powers of the damned and appeared as something ghastly while in the presence of Lainey."

"But I knew Frank well," Fletcher said, "Why wouldn't I have suspected?"

Von Bruen turned to him with a cold stare, answering, "Who really knows and understands the cloaking powers that Satan bestows on his minions."

Jennifer inhaled worriedly, pulling her metal crucifix out from under her blouse. "Will this help to protect us?" she asked, feeling insecure. "I mean, I know it's only a common cross, but it was blessed by a priest."

Looking at the humble symbol, Von Bruen emitted a rare soothing smile. "Ms. Jaynes," she answered gently, reassuring Jennifer, "regardless how trite the amulet, it is the celestial faith conveyed from within that grants it protective power. Yes, with you two it should help to fend off any evil."

Fletcher quickly felt for his cross through his sweatshirt. At Jennifer's questioning glance, he nodded to confirm it was there.

Von Bruen quickly regained their attention, waving her bony index finger. "However," she said through a strong tone, "we are taught that the best defense is to rid oneself of the vile soul."

Fletcher quickly looked at Von Bruen. "How?"

"There are many ways, Herr McKeane. In your situation the best way would be to locate the grave of the vengeful spirit, then exhume and incinerate the bones. Finally soak the ashes with holy water. That deed, I would hope, would end *its* siege."

"Hope?" Jennifer asked.

"Ms. Jaynes," Von Bruen answered stoically, "nothing is ever certain with the disembodied."

Fletcher abruptly stood up and began pacing the small room. He turned and leaned against the rust-stained sink, asking intensely, "But how do I find the grave? Maybe it doesn't even exist."

Jennifer, suddenly excited, exclaimed, "The grave must be here! Somewhere in England! Maybe Lainey could somehow lead us to it!"

Fletcher and Jennifer quickly looked toward Von Bruen for confirmation.

Von Bruen rubbed her pointy, ashen chin, asking skeptically, "Have either of you had any contacts with her soul since you arrived in London?"

Fletcher and Jennifer both shook their heads.

"And I am doubtful that you will. I suspect the evil one will block any attempt she makes to communicate with you."

"Well then, Goddammit," Fletcher interjected, pounding his fist on the chipped counter-top, "how in hell can I get to her? We're all convinced that she's close. And I saw her once when I was almost dead! Goddammit!"

Jennifer stood up and put her arm around his shoulders. "C'mon, sit down," she said calmly. "Let's not lose control, okay?"

He inhaled and exhaled deeply. "Yeah, okay," he agreed, returning with her to the table. "You're right, it doesn't help." He sat back in his chair and folded his arms across his chest. "I'm sorry," he said, stifling his frustration. "I just need to put an end to this shit."

Jennifer turned to Von Bruen who had remained collected throughout Fletcher's outburst. "Madame, what do you think now?"

"Herr McKeane is correct," Von Bruen said. "Lainey is close, most probably within that guarded realm." She paused. "However, it is believed that if mortals are to somehow penetrate that realm, the soul must depart the body and the ultimate price might have to be paid."

Fletcher looked up at her, fear filling his face. "Do you mean die?"

"Very possible," she answered solemnly. "You may have to confront the unknown forces of death if you press forward with this pursuit. It is most unpredictable for one who doesn't possess celestial protection."

Jennifer wondered what she meant by *celestial protection*, but lost her train of thought when Fletcher abruptly asked Von Bruen, "Then, if we can't reach Lainey in that realm, what can we do?"

Von Bruen placed her hand on his arm. "I may be able to assist you in discovering the answers from your past life. That, in turn, may lead you to the grave of the vengeful spirit."

"Discover the answers from my past life?" he asked eagerly. "How?"

"By interrogation of your hypnotized mind," she answered, deep in thought. "However it may be very difficult as we would have to find out which past life is affecting you. You may have lived many."

"We need to try," he urged.

She frowned toward Fletcher. "But I must warn you that it could be dangerous to you if we overstep the boundaries. If we press too hard and too deep you could be lost from reality forever."

Fletcher shook his head, saying, "It doesn't matter how dangerous it is. We'll never be right until we're somehow able to get away from this mess."

"Madame, please," Jennifer appealed to Von Bruen. "Catherine is convinced you're the best help available in London."

Fletcher added with new urgency, "Yes, Madame, please help us."

Von Bruen reached over and put her hand on top of their clasped hands. "Of course," she said softly, for the first time showing some emotion. "I will help."

Madame Von Bruen buttoned her long woolen coat and pulled her heavy scarf down over her forehead. She tied it tightly around her chin, exposing only a small part of her face. "Come, I will walk out with you," she said, opening the front door. "With the weather as it is, I can now go for a walk by the river."

They moved carefully down the narrow stairway and into the graying chilled air of late afternoon. At the bottom of the porch steps, they stopped to part.

Von Bruen turned to Fletcher. "Remember, we must meet here tomorrow and begin to explore your past."

"As we planned," he said. "I'm ready to get started."

"Good. And for now, I shall keep this." She held out the gold pinkie-ring Fletcher had given her. "I will need it to pick up vibrations as I begin our search in the Akashic archives."

"As we agreed," he replied crisply.

"Most satisfactory," Von Bruen responded, turning to Jennifer. "My dear Jennifer," she said, smiling, grasping Jennifer's hand. "We shall meet again. Stay close to Herr McKeane and you will be safe."

"Thank you," Jennifer said, grateful for Von Bruen's concern.

Turning, Von Bruen pulled on the scarf ends to tighten the knot. Walking toward the river, she slipped her hands into her coat pockets and bent her head to deflect the intermittent blasts of the cold river wind.

Jennifer watched the woman, her body slouched over, stride down the walk. She felt sad about the pitiful life Von Bruen must lead. She turned to Fletcher, disturbed, wishing they could show the lonely woman more affection.

Fletcher tugged at Jennifer's sleeve, understanding her feelings. "Hey, she's okay," he said gently, as he put his arms loosely around her waist. "Leave her be."

"No," Jennifer resisted, pulling away. "I want to invite her to come back with us for tea."

Fletcher watched as Jennifer raced toward Von Bruen, calling out her name.

The woman turned slightly toward Jennifer, but seemed to only increase her pace. Catching up with Von Bruen, Jennifer gently turned her around. When she saw the tears running down the old lady's pale cheeks, she stepped back, stunned.

Jennifer instinctively reached down to grip her hand, causing Von Bruen to drop a small square object she had been holding. Picking it up, Jennifer saw that it was a wallet-size picture of a man, laminated in plastic and framed in worn leather. He had the same stark albino features as Von Bruen.

Handing the photo back to the saddened woman, Jennifer realized that she was now infringing on Von Bruen's very personal life. "Umm...Madame,"

Jennifer stammered. "I just wanted to invite you to come back and have tea with us and Catherine."

"Miss Jaynes," Von Bruen said tearfully, looking toward the river, "thank you, but do not worry yourself about me. Now I must go. He is waiting impatiently for me."

Jennifer backed up as Von Bruen again ducked her head and hurried toward the river. Slowly, Jennifer turned and returned to Fletcher who was calmly waiting for her.

"Come on," he said tenderly, taking her hand, "let's go see Catherine."

"Okay," she agreed quietly, shaking her head as they headed for the car.

Once in the car, Fletcher began fidgeting with the camera. He paused and looked up. "What do you think Von Bruen meant about the Akashic archives?"

"I don't know," she answered, putting the car into gear. "I'll ask Catherine."

Fletcher nodded and snapped a few pictures of Von Bruen's house.

As she pulled away from the curb, Jennifer decided that she would also ask Catherine about Von Bruen's albino man.

CHAPTER 31

Kensington, Catherine O'Grady

Catherine O'Grady reached up to embrace Jennifer warmly, then closed the door behind her and Fletcher. "Well dear, how was the chat with Madame Von Bruen today?" Catherine asked with a sprightly smile as she stepped back. "You surely look brightened, you do."

"Surely I am," Jennifer answered with a slight laugh, mimicking Catherine's favorite word. "Surely I am."

Catherine turned toward Fletcher. "And you, young man? Are you as pleased as Jennifer?"

"Yes, Ms. O'Grady," he answered, grinning, secretly amused at the old lady's directness. "I think that Madame Von Bruen can help us."

Catherine stood back and faced them both. "Bloody well, then! Come along, come along and tell me all about it," she said as she turned and shuffled toward the reception room. "I've stoked a flame and brewed a fresh pot o' tea."

Fletcher and Jennifer followed her down the hallway. After seating themselves at the dining table,

Catherine poured the piping hot tea into the three cups as she and Jennifer immediately became engaged in enthusiastic conversation.

Fletcher, unable to get a word in edgewise, sat patiently. He was glad that Jennifer felt so comfortable around Catherine and he was supportive of their friendship. When he noticed that the fire was dying, he got up and walked to the fireplace catching Catherine's watchful eye. After stoking the ashes, he threw a pine log on the fire, replaced the fire screen and carelessly laid the poker against the outside of the fire-tool rack. Turning toward the table, he froze, knowing he had made a big mistake. The hardened silence that abruptly gripped the room was only surpassed by Catherine's shocked expression.

"Oh my! My dear fellow!" Catherine scolded. She hopped up and scurried over to the hearth, saying, "You can't be frivolous with such a perilous tool." She cautiously picked up the poker and set it into the rack, the flanged-spiked point facing downward. Shamed, Fletcher stood still.

Jennifer turned away with the grin of a Cheshire cat as Catherine scooted Fletcher back to the table before sitting back down.

Catherine calmly looked at Jennifer. "Now then, my dear, do catch me up. Where were we?" she asked pleasantly as she removed her glasses and held them up to the overhead light. She reached for a tissue and wiped away the smudges after puffing on each of the small round lens.

Fletcher suddenly arose from his chair, interrupting, "Ms. O'Grady, could I visit your library while you two talk?" He was still uncomfortable after Catherine's stern reprimand.

"Yes, very well, Fletcher," Catherine replied kindly, looking up at him.

"Thanks," he said, hurrying from the room.

"Well," Jennifer said, grinning, still amused by Fletcher's embarrassment, "before we were interrupted, I was mentioning how it was an eventful day. Madame Von Bruen appears to be a very remarkable woman."

"Quite remarkable," Catherine agreed, sipping on her steaming tea with care. "Surely she can be of a help to ya."

"Yes," Jennifer said, becoming solemn, "Madame is going to work with Fletcher alone. She thinks he is the main target of a vengeful spirit and, even though I'm somehow involved, I would probably only confuse things right now."

"Indeed," Catherine affirmed while adding a splash of heavy cream to her tea. "I'm sure if she needs to, she'll fetch you straightaway."

Jennifer sipped on her tea, looking quizzical. "Catherine?" she began, "Madame said it is likely that our souls have lived more than one mortal life and that she will begin searching the Akashic archives for the life that we are involved with. What does that mean?"

"Ah yes, the Akashic archives," Catherine answered, pausing to gather her thoughts. "It is believed that all records of the activity of the Universe are pitched into the archives, yes indeed."

"Really?" Jennifer asked. "Since creation?"

"Oh yes, surely," Catherine answered, "including all thoughts and emotion. Madame will use her powers to dip deeply into the records for the vibrations of Fletcher's soul."

"How can she pinpoint the past vibrations of his soul?"

"Madame will use one of his personal possessions as she probes."

"Oh, right," Jennifer replied, recalling the day's events. "She kept Fletcher's ring."

"I would suppose so, yes. The possession must be an alloy. She will attempt to determine what lifetime has negative or evil spiritual energy attached to it. After that she'll hypnotize Fletcher and probe his unconscious." Looking upward, marveling, Catherine continued, "Yes, indeed, the Akashic archives, they're located in the wide aura of the astral plane. 'Tis where all the great mystics delve to find the answers."

"I see," Jennifer said, pondering Catherine's answer. She glanced at the fire then back at Catherine. "Incidentally, we were very surprised at discovering Madame was an albino."

"Yes, surely," Catherine replied as she nonchalantly reached for the teapot. "One of the purest of albinos, she is. 'Tis simply appalling that she has to be so mindful of the weather. She cannot venture outside often. No coloring to protect her from the sun's blaze, ya know."

Jennifer nodded, replying, "It's sad that she must live a very solitary life, being as isolated as she is..." She paused, remembering the photograph that Von Bruen had dropped by the river. "Although I saw her with a snapshot of a man. He also had the features of an albino."

Catherine quickly turned back to her. "Oh yes, quite right," she stated as Jennifer listened attentively. "'Twas her husband, Fredric. He was indeed an albino." Catherine pursed her lips in thought. "Fredric has since departed us...late last year, it was."

"Sounds very sad," Jennifer responded tenderly. "Madame looked very despondent this afternoon. She must miss him a great deal."

"Quite," Catherine said, smiling. "But she does visit with him often."

"Visits with Fredric?" Jennifer repeated.

"Oh yes, indeed," Catherine replied directly, setting the teapot down while moving closer toward Jennifer. "Although she is of a peculiar sight, the good Lord blessed her with the most masterful of mystical powers. She says she talks to Fredric often. Perhaps through the forces of that other realm we spoke of."

Jennifer sat back taking in Catherine's statement, then asked, "Catherine, when she visits Fredric, do you think he communicates back to her?"

"Oh, my dear," Catherine replied, surprised, "why wouldn't I think so?"

"Yes, of course," Jennifer quickly agreed, sitting back, realizing that had been a dumb question to ask of Catherine. "Where does Madame visit with him?"

"She has a favorite spot at the river's edge," Catherine answered, turning to check the fire.

Looking upward in thought, Jennifer remembered Von Bruen's statement about water being the main mystical drawing element. She remained silent as she began to drift, thinking about how much Von Bruen had known about Lainey's possible domain—in that other realm. And maybe Von Bruen's late husband was even there. *But who really knows for sure*, she thought.

"Jennifer, Jennifer, my dear," Catherine prodded.

Jennifer blinked herself back to reality. "Oh! I'm sorry. I just became lost in thought. Please continue about her and Fredric. What happened to him?"

"Yes, very well," Catherine answered as she poured herself more tea. "Fredric was purblind since he was a slight lad. Could hardly see a thing except blurs, he couldn't. Madame would guide him to the river whenever she could. They'd sit and chat about her mystic powers and she would probe for answers about a clue to their past lives…" Catherine paused and looked downward, saddened. "Even though he held no special powers, they were attached most dearly, they were indeed..." Again her voice trailed off in a hushed tone.

"Please go on," Jennifer said gently, unable to control her curiosity. She reached for Catherine's hand.

"He passed quite dreadfully, actually," she answered slowly, rubbing her chin in thought. "One night, when Madame was lecturing to the Association, Fredric came out of their flat entrance door and tumbled down the steps to his death. He took a terrible bashing to his head, just terrible."

Jennifer gasped. "For God's sake, how awful!"

Catherine suddenly scowled and began shaking her index finger in earnest. "But to this day," she said, her eyes squinting, "Madame knows it was the work of a demented hand, in revenge for Madame's use of her powers against evil and exposing the work of the devil for the association."

Jennifer eyes widened.

"Yes, indeed!" Catherine huffed, with a piercing stare. "Now mind you, there is no proof, but Madame swears she had closed and locked the door before she went out. Fredric wouldn't have opened it. He wouldn't. The steps were very steep and dreadfully dangerous for him." Catherine, calmer now, pushed her chair back and rose, walking over to tend the fire.

"Catherine?" Jennifer asked while the old woman began poking at the flickering embers, "why wouldn't Madame herself be endangered?"

Catherine put the poker in the rack and turned toward Jennifer. "Madame has been granted a divine favor. The gift of 'illumination.'"

"What is that?" Jennifer asked.

"The gift of the glowing white light from a higher source, 'tis," she answered softly, smiling. "A light from above to illuminate and guide her mystic process and protect her from evil. Indeed, 'tis well known that Madame Von Bruen has been gifted with the light."

Jennifer, mystified, looked into Catherine's eyes, asking with concern, "Do you also possess the gift of illumination?"

"Oh no," Catherine answered quickly, "'tis a celestial bequest. One that the Almighty grants wisely and only rarely."

Jennifer, still concerned, said worriedly, "But you've helped us. Aren't you afraid for yourself? How are you protected?"

Catherine remained mute as she lifted the sharply honed log fork from the rack and walked over to the brass wood-basket. She turned toward Jennifer. "My dear, I will be protected as we all are, by the grace and account of the good Lord," she said crisply before turning back toward the basket. "I am not afraid. My fate is up to God, as we are taught," she concluded, drawing the fork back to pierce a log.

Jennifer and Catherine walked to the library where they found Fletcher slumped in a deep, thickly upholstered club chair with an open book spread out on his lap. Catherine chuckled as she watched Jennifer gently shake him. Lightheaded, he emerged from his fragile doze and quickly sat up. Shaking his head, he smiled and rose from the chair to join the ladies as they headed to the front door.

As Jennifer entered the driver's side of the car, she turned and waved at the old woman standing on the porch. She then settled herself in the seat and turned the key to start the ignition. As the car pulled away from the curb, Fletcher maneuvered the camera in the fading daylight, snapping a picture of Catherine who was waving at them and pulling tightly on her heavy woolen shawl.

Jennifer glanced at Fletcher. "It's been a long day. Let's have a quiet dinner and go to bed early."

"Sure, that nap in the library only made me more tired," Fletcher agreed sluggishly, looking over at her. "How'd it go with O'Grady?"

"Very well. She's a wise and wonderful person."

"Did you remember to talk to her about the risks of her helping us?"

"Uh huh, just before we left," Jennifer answered. "It didn't seem to worry her."

"It didn't?"

Jennifer shook her head. "Nope. She's brave and is full of faith in God."

Fletcher shrugged. "You're right, she's a brave woman."

"Very," Jennifer replied. "Incidentally, I'd like to visit her while you're with Von Bruen tomorrow. I'll stay with her until you pick me up."

"Yeah, of course, I like the sound of that much better than your first plan to go shopping," he answered with a reproving scowl.

"Well," she conceded, smiling, "I just felt that downtown London would be busy with people. I certainly wouldn't be alone. But anyway, now it doesn't matter. I'll look forward to visiting with Catherine instead."

"Right," he agreed, leaning his head back against the seat and closing his eyes.

They enjoyed a quiet uneventful dinner and were in bed early as they'd planned. But as they both slept soundly, Jennifer subliminally sensed an oppressive presence gradually entering the room. She pulled away from Fletcher's side, inching toward the far edge of the bed, close to the cold smoky air wafting into the room.

CHAPTER 32

Chelsea, The Search

The nip of the pre-dawn chill lashed sharply at Madame Von Bruen as she sat rigid on a thick tweed blanket facing the riverbank. Leaning back against a tall tree, she sighed heavily and slowly raised her head, peering at the river. The rude drone of a passing fishing-boat and the loud swishing of the trailing wake breaking against the rocky shore had broken her brittle state of meditation.

She was strained and disappointed that after hours of intense transcendency she'd failed to find the precise Akashic records of Fletcher's past life. She'd been able to detect pertinent recollections of his life that had occurred in England, but the overall results were poor. She'd received only tempered vibrations and insignificant details before the vision had vanished. Convinced that this was the correct life she'd been searching for, she knew she must delve further into the records if she was to be effective at Fletcher's first session today.

She shook her head, realizing this case was strangely different. She was aware that something demonically powerful was inhibiting her search, preventing her from finding the answers. Maybe even the archfiend himself. Growing tense, she also realized that if she did find anything decisive, there was a threat of danger. It could be perilous and unpredictable for her. Maybe she'd even fail to recover from her trance. Regardless, she was steadfast in her quest to aid Fletcher and would risk any consequences. This was her purpose in life. But now she needed to ask for help.

Pulling snugly on her shawl, she molded an overlapping hood around her upper torso and looked upward, observing the cracking horizon. Grimacing, she realized she had only a short time before the sun might break through the ashen-gray clouds. If she was then unconscious, entranced within the astral plane, the elements might, or could become extremely hazardous to her.

She drew her lanky legs up against her chest and wrapped her arms around her knees. Fiercely gripping Fletcher's pinkie ring and the weathered keepsake containing Frederic's photo, she extended her hand outward and closed her eyes. She bent her head forward until the crown touched her knees. Motionless, she concentrated totally on Fletcher's ring, reaching into the depths of her mystical subconscious.

She whispered to her former beloved, "Fredric, help me find the answers to the past life of Fletcher McKeane, his wretched life in England."

Gradually descending deeper into her subliminal senses, her body began to slacken. Her spindly arms went limp, falling at her sides as she slumped backward against the tree. Her breathing and circulation decreased and her brain waves drifted to a near halt. With her earthly consciousness rapidly subsiding, the subtle noises of her surrounding environment began to diminish. All earthly distractions were disappearing. Finally, the rush of the mighty river current faded away.

Feeling detached, swirling within an alternate reality, she sensed herself being swept up into another aura by a power of a superior force. Lacking any perception of her physical being, her altered state of spiritual consciousness slowly illuminated. Obscure people-images began to appear in a brilliant shaft of light. Distant voices became perceptible; yet, none were decipherable—only gibberish. Still clutching Fletcher's ring, she focused her gifted power on the drawing strength of the metal alloy and the mystical allure of the river water. Receiving moderate vibrations, she again appealed for Fredric to assist her in her journey. *Oh, Fredric! Help me find the records to aid Herr McKeane. Fredric, help!*

With the pitch of the vibrations increasing, she finally recognized Fredric's cry, "Christopher," the voice rang out. And again, "Christopher." Now upon the vital Akashic records she'd been seeking, her body straightened and shuddered. The records flashed through her subconscious: early London; a man hanging from the gallows; Stratford-on-Avon. And, finally, a graveyard! But what graveyard? What grave? *Fredric, tell me a surname! Fredric!*

The vibrations strengthened to a painful level, spiking at her repeatedly. Undaunted, she knew she'd have to endure the suffering until she had learned all she needed to. Then, abruptly, she heard Fredric's frantic plea to her: "Leave. Escape!" His voice faded as the brightness of this inner world began to wane. As a mysterious, threatening figure emerged on the horizon all images and voices dissipated, like small birds escaping from a menacing hawk.

Sensing the growing danger, Von Bruen struggled inwardly to escape this new state of imposing evil and the intensifying agony of the piercing vibrations. Trembling with physical pain, Von Bruen found the torment almost unbearable. Her body thrashed, bucked and writhed as she fought desperately for earthly consciousness. Then, as a slender ray of ivory-white light slowly enveloped her body, her subconciousness came to rest. Her body lay still at the base of the tree.

The bustling lunch-hour traffic had little effect on Fletcher as he drove effortlessly through downtown London. He was now familiar with the British driving habits and more comfortable with the layout of the city.

Jennifer sat quietly, her head laid back against the headrest.

As Fletcher thought about his upcoming session with Von Bruen, he was apprehensive about being entranced and yielding control of his inner consciousness. But he was intrigued by the idea of her probing his immortal psyche for thoughts that might have laid dormant for generations. He recalled Von Bruen's ominous warning that if they probed too deeply or for too long it could threaten his return to reality. Yet he regarded the risk as minimal. She could explore at her discretion. They all needed to find out what was happening to him. He knew the answers must come from within his mind and his chance of finding those answers lay with her.

He turned to Jennifer. "You're very quiet," he said gently. "I thought you'd be excited over our breakthrough with Von Bruen and especially happy over your visit with Catherine today."

Jennifer lethargically lifted her head and blinked her eyes. "I guess I'm still tired, that's all. I must not have slept very well."

"Huh?" Fletcher replied sarcastically. "Hey, when I woke up this morning I know you were sound asleep. I even heard you snoring. C'mon, I'll bet you didn't move the minute your head hit the pillow last night. I even let you sleep in."

Jennifer cocked her head quizzically, replying, "Oh, I don't remember."

Fletcher shot her a surprised glance. "Really? Well, you should have heard your language when I tried to wake you up before I left this morning." He laughed. "By the way, did you even notice when I left?"

"Umm, no. I must've been in the bathroom," she answered unemotionally. "Where'd you go?"

"Harrods," he replied. "I picked up the tools that I'll need if we locate the grave."

"Oh, the grave. Yes, I see. Good," she answered blankly, closing her eyes and laying her head back against the headrest.

Fletcher shrugged off Jennifer's indifference but wondered what she'd meant about being in the bathroom when he'd left this morning. She'd been sitting on the edge of the bed, he recalled. She'd even said good-bye to him. He looked over at her, surprised at seeing she was dozing off again.

Pulling up in front of the Association suite, Fletcher waved at Catherine who was chatting with some people gathered with her on the porch. Noticing the approaching car, Catherine peered around the group, displayed a wide smile and returned the wave.

Letting the car idle, Fletcher reached over to kiss Jennifer, but was taken aback when she responded with only a silent brush across his lips before abruptly getting out of the car.

He frowned, puzzled over her continuing aloofness. He wondered if her distant behavior this morning was a result of her being worn out by all of the emotional pressure. *She'll come out of it, she's strong,* he decided, while watching her make her way up the walk, past the departing visitors. When Jennifer reached Catherine, who was waiting patiently for her on the porch, Fletcher straightened himself in the seat, put the car into gear and sped away.

Standing in front of Von Bruen's flat, Fletcher felt a bit uneasy without Jennifer's usual support. He glanced up at the sky, noticing dark clouds were beginning to form. Their gloomy appearance only added to the cryptic ambiance of his first day for entering into the unknown of his darkened past. *Suitable,* he mused inwardly.

Without further hesitation, he stepped upon the porch and entered the dank hallway. Making his way up the stairs, his apprehension slowly gave way to excitement as he thought more about the adventurous prospect of discovering a previous life.

Reaching the landing, he knocked boldly on the door. Almost immediately the peephole opened and closed, followed by the usual numerous clicks of the locks. As Fletcher stepped through the opened door he was silently directed toward the kitchen with an extended index finger.

Sitting down at the table he closely observed the gangly woman as she walked into the cramped living room. Maneuvering methodically, she carefully positioned a tall wooden stool directly across from the tattered sofa. Then she turned to the pewter candelabra and lit three fresh Flambeau candles. Shimmering flames reflected in the credenza mirror, their exaggerated silhouettes fluttering wildly on the walls and ceiling of the shadowy room. Finally, she uncovered the two censers sitting next to the candelabra, and struck a match to light the Frankincense joss sticks. A sweet, spicy aroma began to slowly fill the room.

Madame Lena Von Bruen then backed up, stood still and scanned the room to assess the setting. Satisfied, she walked back into the kitchen, sat down at the table and solemnly looked over at Fletcher.

"Welcome Herr McKeane," she said, her eyes filled with a fierce determination. "I think we are prepared. I know where to begin the search into your past."

They stood, and he obediently followed her into the living room.

Catherine set a fresh cup of tea down on the small table next to Jennifer, who was reclining silently on the couch facing the fire. "I'm sorry you're not fit today, dear," Catherine said softly. "Do get some rest."

With her half-closed eyes remaining fixed on the fire, Jennifer only nodded.

Walking to the fireplace Catherine began to gently stoke the burning logs. Her thoughts were only on Jennifer. She was puzzled over Jennifer's cold and unfriendly greeting, almost as though she hadn't recognized her. And she was more puzzled over seeing that Jennifer's once bubbly inquisitive nature was now listless and unresponsive.

She stopped poking at the fire and turned around to see Jennifer breathing heavily, falling into a deep sleep. She reasoned that Jennifer must be ill or exhausted. Perhaps that's why she had appeared so detached, removed from reality. Turning back to the fire she decided it was premature to pass any judgment on Jennifer's unusual behavior today. After all, she'd only met and chatted with Jennifer a few times. *Did she really know Jennifer,* she wondered, stoking at the flame. *Quite surely, time would tell.*

CHAPTER 33

The Following Week, Mayfair

Fletcher paced the length of the hotel room, keeping an anxious watch on the locked bathroom door. Distressed, he paused to peer out the window and massaged the back of his head. The mental strain of the past week's events was getting to him. The intense sessions Von Bruen was putting him through were demanding enough, but now Jennifer had changed. She had become increasingly aloof, alternating between hostility and total detachment. She showed no interest in the outcome of his meetings with Von Bruen. *What's happening to her,* he wondered, glancing at his watch. Turning abruptly, his patience had finally run out. He charged over to the bathroom door and pounded on it, vigorously jiggling the doorknob.

"Jennifer! Jennifer!" he shouted. "We have to get going. I told Beaucamp we'd meet him for lunch. Jennifer! C'mon, please!" He placed an ear to the door, listening for a response.

He backed away as the door slowly opened. Jennifer, wearing only her shower robe, stood scowling in the doorway with dripping-wet hair. "Why are you yelling at me?" she asked, her voice filled with indignation.

"But, Jennifer," he appealed calmly, "you've been in there all morning. The shower ran for over forty minutes. You know that we have to meet Peter for lunch."

She glowered with fierce anger. "Why don't you understand?" she snapped. "When I'm ready, I'm ready! Not until! Now, Goddammit, get off my fucking ass!" She backed up and slammed the door.

Fletcher, exasperated, threw his hands up in the air, walked to the telephone and dialed the embassy.

"Consular services, Peter Beaucamp, please." Fletcher stood nervously, before finally hearing Beaucamp's greeting. "Peter, this is Fletcher. We have a problem with time this morning," he said, attempting an upbeat tone and managing a faked half-laugh. "What?...No, I'm afraid we can't make it, maybe tomorrow...No, I'm okay. It's Jennifer, she isn't well."

He hesitated, realizing that she'd been like this for a week and was getting worse by the day. He drew a deep anxiety-ridden breath and continued, "Oh Peter, shit, there's no reason to lie to you. There is something really wrong with her, but I don't know what yet...Yes, I'd like to talk about it. Can you rearrange your schedule?...Good, thanks. I'll take her to Catherine's and call you just before I leave there...Sure, the same pub as usual. See ya soon. Thanks again." He hung up the phone slowly, deciding that the time had come to confront her.

The bathroom door opened and Jennifer wandered into the main hotel room, still dressed only in her robe. Her matted hair was carelessly combed back.

Fletcher sat down on the couch, appearing perplexed.

Obviously annoyed, she asked curtly, "Well, where and when are we going to lunch?"

"We're not. I canceled our lunch date with Peter. Jennifer…I…I want…"

"What?" she interrupted rudely, sitting down in the desk chair facing him. "What the hell do you want?"

"I want to talk," he answered. "There's something wrong with you."

Jennifer rolled her eyes in mock frustration. "Look, I happen to be in a bad mood today. I'm having my period, that's all."

He looked at her more directly. "No you're not," he challenged. "I know better. Why are you lying to me? What's happening to you?"

Her hostility increased. "Dammit! I don't know why you can't just leave this shit alone. I don't feel good. That's all there is to it!"

He shook his head. "No. It's more than that," he continued, unyielding. "Ever since that day we met with Von Bruen, you've changed. You're constantly complaining and irritable. You're distant and you've shut me out. I assumed it was just the stress all of this has put on you, but I don't think that any more."

"Maybe you're tired of me and the trip!" she yelled. "Maybe we should go home!"

"I don't know," he countered. "If I thought it would make a difference, we would. We'll talk about it after my session with Von Bruen today."

She sneered. "Fine! Goddammit! To hell with it! Just dump me off at O'Grady's! That's where I want to go!"

He hesitated, still looking at her. "That's another thing. I talked to Catherine on the phone this morning.

"She told me that while I've been with Von Bruen, you just sleep on her couch or sit in the library by yourself. She thought you'd been sick."

Jennifer bounded up with a condemning glare and stomped over to the window. She stood with her arms crossed and looked out for a few moments. "This is bullshit!" she blurted defiantly. "Absolute fucking bullshit!"

"Jennifer!" he barked, "I'd appreciate it if you'd talk to me civilly under these circumstances!"

Jennifer sighed and continued to look out the window, tapping her fingernails on the sill. "The hell with you," she replied with a surly rasp.

"Jennifer! If you keep this up, I'll knock that bitchiness out of you."

She whirled around and froze, watching him come toward her with clenched fists.

"You're repulsive!" she growled with piercing eyes. "You wouldn't."

"Try me! Go ahead, try me!" he challenged, holding his ground a foot away from her.

She turned and looked back out the window, saying nothing.

"Now get yourself ready, we're going to Catherine's," he demanded through clenched teeth. "Now!" he shouted as he grabbed the collar of her robe. When he saw her exposed neck, he held her steady.

"My God! Where is your crucifix?" he asked, stunned.

She lowered her head and looked at her bare chest. "I dunno," she mumbled, "I suppose I lost the damn thing."

"God Damn it!" he howled, as he turned to the table and picked up a pitcher full of ice water. He heaved it against the wall, shattering it into a mound of wet jagged glass.

Frenzied, he turned, glaring at her while barely controlling his temper.

She backed away.

"I've never hit a woman," he seethed, trembling with rage, "but I care enough about you that I will. Now get in there and get ready. We're going to Catherine's! Move!"

She turned her eyes downward and quickly walked into the bathroom. Fletcher followed closely behind. When she tried to shut the door, he jammed his foot in the threshold.

"You can shut the door when you need to," he said, calming as he caught his breath. She looked up and gave him her full attention. "But if you ever lock it again, I'll break it down." He pulled his foot away as she closed the door halfway.

Jennifer finally emerged from the bathroom, her face slightly made up and her hair loosely knotted on top of her head. Still silent, she reached into the closet for her blouse.

He put his hand on her waist and gently turned her around. "Look, something is very wrong. We need to figure out what it is," he said softly, removing the crucifix from around his neck. He offered her the chain. "Here, take this."

She recoiled, but relented when he grasped her shoulder and hung the chain around her neck. He embraced her tightly but she remained rigid, resisting his desperate plea for her warmth. As he released her and backed up, she put one hand on the chain and lightly fingered the cross, but said nothing.

Confused and stressed, he turned and walked to the closet. Reaching into his suitcase, he pulled out his Colt pistol and stuffed it between the belt and waistband of his jeans.

Her eyes widened. "I didn't know you'd brought that with you," she finally uttered. "What are you going to do with it?"

"I don't know what's going on anymore," he answered flatly, slipping on his windbreaker. "I may need some added protection."

"But you're not supposed to have a gun over here. If you get caug…"

"Never mind," he interrupted, "let's go. Catherine and Beaucamp are expecting us. I won't keep them waiting any longer."

With her eyes fixed on the pistol bulging through his windbreaker, she followed him out the door.

Catherine O'Grady grasped Fletcher's hand as he stood on the porch of the Association suite. "She'll surely be better, Fletcher," she said, smiling. "I'll tend to her while you're gone. Ya put quite a jolt into her, ya did." She winked.

"Thank you, Ms. O'Grady," he said, relieved. "I'm not sure what I'd do without your help." He handed her a piece of paper. "I'll be at this pub in Westminster for a couple of hours before I meet with Von Bruen. And I'll check my hotel for messages whenever I can."

"Yes, it might be good if Jennifer stays with me tonight," O'Grady offered. "We'll see how she is later. We'll chat before you come back for her."

"Okay," Fletcher agreed. "Oh, if an emergency comes up and you can't reach me, call Peter Beaucamp from the embassy."

"Very well, I will," Catherine obliged with a soothing smile.

"Do you have his numbers?"

"Yes," she answered with a nod. "I noted them when he rang me up the other day looking for you. He's a nice man and most concerned about you both. Now scoot off and meet your friend. Don't worry."

"Thanks," he said as he loped off the porch and hurried toward his car.

Catherine closed and locked the door behind him. Turning for the reception room, she shook her head, perplexed. She now knew that there was something very wrong with Jennifer as she hurried down the hallway. Something much more wrong then she had let on to Fletcher.

Fletcher looked harried as he walked into the pub and scanned the room. Spotting Beaucamp, he took off his windbreaker and slid into the wooden booth across from him. He reached over to shake Beaucamp's hand. "Thanks for changing your schedule, Peter."

"No problem, Fletcher," Beaucamp replied as he motioned for the pub keeper to bring them two pints of beer. He turned to Fletcher. "How's Jennifer doing?"

Fletcher emitted a troubled sigh. "So-so, I guess. I just dropped her off at Catherine O'Grady's. I really don't know what the hell is going to happen next."

"What's it look like to you?" Beaucamp asked as the pub keeper set two dark-brown pints of warm ale on the table.

Fletcher shook his head. "I'm not sure," he replied, still uneasy. "Her mood's ugly and getting worse. It started last week, right after I began the therapy sessions with Von Bruen. She's totally hostile and isn't looking after herself. I've never seen her like this. It's just not her." He paused searching for the right words. "She's becoming dysfunctional."

"I see, damn," Beaucamp empathized, sipping on his beer. "Maybe she's just stressed out. You've both been through quite a bit of turmoil lately."

"Yeah, maybe," Fletcher agreed, "but I finally took all I could this morning and lost my temper with her."

"I'm sure she'll be okay with Ms. O'Grady," Beaucamp replied. "Incidentally, how are your sessions going with Von Bruen? Are you getting anywhere?"

"Somewhat, I guess," Fletcher answered as he changed thought patterns. "We've been through about four meetings so far. She has me responding to the name of 'Christopher.' But nothing definite yet."

"At least you're making progress with a name," Beaucamp said encouragingly.

Fletcher continued, "Yeah, I guess I was an actor or poet in London, maybe a sculptor. Something along those lines, anyway..." He paused, becoming frustrated. "Aw shit, who fucking knows. Von Bruen can't keep me under for too long. She's afraid I might not come out of it."

"I see," Beaucamp responded. "Anything surface about Jennifer yet?"

"No, not really. Although Von Bruen says I talk about another man's wife, like maybe I was in love with her. She thinks this might be the reason for my problems."

"Could the woman from that life be Jennifer?"

"Not sure," Fletcher responded, taking a swallow of his ale. "I see faint images of women in the background, but nothing has been significant." He then brightened. "You know what though…something interesting did come up at the last session."

"What?" Beaucamp asked, eager at Fletcher's sudden upbeat tone.

"Well, during yesterday's session I saw an English pub," he reflected. "It looked old inside and had old worn furniture. I remember a horseshoe-shaped bar. It all seemed very real."

Beaucamp moved forward. "Can you remember anything that you can go on? Any names or faces of significant people? Think man, think!" Beaucamp pressed.

Fletcher squinted hard, immersed in thought. "I saw people, men mostly," he answered slowly. "There was one woman who sat in a small room in the corner. She was dressed elegantly…in old-fashioned clothes."

"That fits, doesn't it?" Beaucamp interrupted impatiently.

"Yeah, I guess," Fletcher answered, continuing his train of thought. "But the whole scene was blurry. When I tried to face her and talk to her it all faded. The next thing I saw were dark drapes closing off the room. That's all I remember. Von Bruen is going to work on it again today." He looked at Beaucamp quizzically. "Do you think there might be a way to locate the pub if I find out more?"

Beaucamp shook his head. "Wow, Fletcher. That's a tough one. There are thousands of pubs and many of them were opened in the 19th century. And do you really know for sure that the place was even located in London?"

"No, dammit, not for sure," Fletcher replied. "It just seemed so real to me."

"If only you could see a name or something more identifiable," Beaucamp replied with a frown. He sat back and paused, thinking. "Tell you what, when I get back to the embassy I'll have Millie check our library for the records they keep on pubs. I can also check with the Licensing Justices at the Home Office. They keep some kind of records. But frankly, I think it's a shot in the dark."

Fletcher grimaced. "I'm sure it is, but what the hell isn't right now?" He gripped his glass of beer tensely. "I think that if today's session with Von Bruen doesn't go any better, I'm going to pack it in. Especially now, with what's happening to Jennifer."

Beaucamp cocked his head and furrowed his brow, asking, "Are you sure that's wise at this point?"

Fletcher looked at him in surprise. "Dammit Peter! I'm not going to jeopardize Jennifer's health and sanity. She was never seriously affected in any way until we arrived here. We don't even know what we're after, for crissake."

Beaucamp held up his hands. "Hey!" he countered firmly. "I'm on your side. Remember?"

Fletcher regained his composure and conceded, "Yeah, sorry."

Beaucamp smiled. "It's okay, I understand."

Fletcher looked up at him curiously. "What were you getting at, anyway? I mean…before I jumped all over you."

Beaucamp carefully selected his words, "Well, if you leave London before you get your answers, you'll never rest. The problems may not stop…and…"

Fletcher's eyes remained firmly on Beaucamp, asking, "And what?"

"What if your theories are right and you unknowingly take something evil back to the States with you?"

"What the hell are you saying?"

Beaucamp continued, "I'm not sure exactly, but what if Jennifer's soul is now evil or something like that? I mean, maybe it isn't *only* Jennifer anymore. Oh, hell, I don't know."

Fletcher pulled his eyes away and thought for a moment. "Shit! Maybe you're right!" He fidgeted nervously in the booth. "I have to talk to her and Catherine, now." Distraught, he looked around for the phone. Spotting one, he slid out of the booth. "I'll be right back."

As Fletcher stood and turned, Beaucamp saw the pistol. "Fletcher!" he said sharply, stopping him. "Come back here and sit down."

Fletcher, disoriented with worry, hesitated but then complied and sat down. "What?"

"What are you doing with that pistol tucked in your belt?"

"Protection," Fletcher answered defiantly. "I have a permit."

"Not here you don't. Not in England," Beaucamp challenged. "And you know it."

Fletcher rubbed his forehead and sighed. "Yes, I know," he conceded lightly.

"Even if it was legal, you're in no shape mentally to carry it," Beaucamp replied directly. "You'll kill the first damn thing or person that looks cross-eyed at you. Then what good will you be, especially to Jennifer? Now give it to me."

"I can't…I…I," Fletcher stammered.

"Now," Beaucamp repeated, uncompromising, extending his open palm across the table. "I'll square it with the authorities and keep it at the embassy. And dammit, I'll be the judge of when you get it back. I will assume that's the only one you have with you."

Fletcher pulled out the pistol and handed it to Beaucamp. "Yeah, it's the only one I have."

Beaucamp exhaled and shook his head as he watched Fletcher hurry away toward the phone. He stuffed the pistol in his briefcase.

After making the call, Fletcher returned to the table appearing a bit more relaxed. Beaucamp remained silent as Fletcher slipped into the booth and looked up at him. "You're right, Peter. I shouldn't have brought the pistol to England. I'm just not myself lately. Thanks."

"Sure," Beaucamp answered calmly. "But you gotta keep your head about you. Now what did you find out about Jennifer?"

"I didn't talk to her. I talked to Catherine. She told me that Jennifer is sleeping and that everything appears under control. She'll probably end up staying with Catherine tonight."

"Good. Now what?"

"I'm heading for Von Bruen's for another session like I planned. However, like I said, if I don't learn anything more and Jennifer seems to be herself again, I'm going to talk to her about leaving London tomorrow. I don't think we really have a choice."

"Yes," Beaucamp replied, "I suppose you're probably right."

Fletcher tipped his head back and drained his glass, indicating he was ready to leave. Beaucamp threw some cash on the table as they both slid out of the booth and walked out the front door.

When they reached the street Beaucamp laid his hand on Fletcher's forearm, halting him. "I managed to get the sulfuric acid you asked for." He pulled the thick chromium canister from his briefcase and handed it to

Fletcher. "After the pistol incident I was leery about giving this to you, but I guess it'll be okay."

Fletcher took the shiny container and fingered the protective shrink-wrap sealed tightly around the metal cap. "Thanks, Peter, I appreciate your help."

"Sure," Beaucamp replied with a concerned look. "But be damn careful with that stuff. I asked the chemist to beef it up. The strength is so corrosive that if you get any of it on you there won't even be time to wash it off. It'll eat away at you immediately. Oh, and its been laced with slight nitric compounds. It's extremely flammable. Anyway, there's about a half liter there. That should be enough for what you'll need it for."

Fletcher grimaced, asking worriedly, "Christ, will this stuff blow up on me?"

"No," Beaucamp answered with a chuckle. "But with a match it'll sure help disintegrate any remains."

"I understand," Fletcher replied, relieved, as he carefully shoved the canister into his coat pocket.

Beaucamp began scanning the block. "Don't worry about me, I'll take a cab back to the embassy," he said, hailing down a passing cab. He climbed into the back seat, hollering at Fletcher before closing the door, "Please keep me informed of your whereabouts until something is settled."

Fletcher nodded and waved at the departing cab as a light rain began to fall. Turning, he zipped up his windbreaker and hurried toward his car to make his way for Chelsea.

CHAPTER 34

Chelsea, Past Life Therapy

Fletcher sat down at the kitchen table facing Madame Lena Von Bruen. Removing his windbreaker, he hung it on the back of the chair and reached down, stuffing his car keys into the pocket. On edge from today's chaotic episode with Jennifer and the intense meeting with Beaucamp, he appealed wearily, "Madame, I'm desperate. I need to know what is happening with my life."

She hesitated, reflecting on his emotional plea. "I sense that your inner emotions have erupted most vigorously today," she responded.

"Yes," he agreed, appearing dispirited. "The whole day has been damn strenuous."

"Did your rush of emotions include anger?"

"Rage," he replied, turning away with guilt.

"Most excellent!"

He looked up in surprise. "What? Why in hell are you glad about that?"

"Because your anger may release some thoughts of the grievous events that you have experienced in your past life." She paused, reaching out her hand. "Today, I will use your metal crucifix for our session. It may bring stronger vibrations as we probe. Perhaps the Almighty will mercifully aid us with more answers."

He slowly lowered his eyes, replying apprehensively, "I don't have it. I gave it to Jennifer. She lost hers this week."

Von Bruen peered at him suspiciously. "Herr McKeane, this is not good. I thought we'd agreed that I must know of everything that occurs if I am to help you."

He drew a nervous breath as she sat patiently. With a troubled voice he answered, "Jennifer hasn't been at all well lately. I thought it was the pressure from our situation so I didn't mention it to you. Now I don't think so...Catherine and I think she's being affected by an evil presence."

"Please explain to me everything that has occurred with her since we met," she insisted.

Nodding, he stood and began pacing, recounting the past week's hectic events surrounding Jennifer's puzzling condition.

Fletcher sat down, feeling spent. "That's all I know, Madame. Right now Jennifer is with Catherine."

"Yes," she responded gravely, looking into Fletcher's distraught eyes. "I suspect that you are correct. A venom has in some way been entrenched into Jennifer's subconscious being."

"Do you mean her mind is possessed?"

"Conceivably," she replied slowly. "Maybe a karmic possession of some type, but I am not sure yet."

"Karmic possession?"

"Yes. A possession where the thoughts of corrupt deeds from a past life exploit her mind, blocking all reality of today. And this state may include violent thoughts, thoughts controlled by the evil one."

"Shit, what next," he mumbled, appearing downcast.

"You said earlier that she is using extremely foul language," Von Bruen said. "Have you heard her speak in a foreign tongue? Or has she proclaimed any type of ecstatic worship towards Satan?"

"No, not that I know of," he answered, recalling Jennifer's dark moods. "Mainly, she just seems cold and distant. And she keeps pushing me away, as though she is unaware of why we're even in London."

She gently laid her hand on his, saying, "Although she seems afflicted by evil, I do not think she is totally possessed."

Fletcher, although still anxious and worried, was somewhat relieved by Von Bruen's statement.

"However, it is critical Jennifer be watched with vigilance," she advised. "If the evil one continues to have a firm grip on her soul, it could lead to suicide."

His eyes widened. "No!" he exclaimed, stunned. "Why suicide?"

"The evil one would then truly possess her," she answered. "He would have her total spiritual being."

Fletcher massaged his throbbing head. "Oh no, not her. She's too strong to do that."

Her face stiffened. "Herr McKeane," she replied firmly, "I must make you understand that she is not acting alone any longer."

Fletcher looked up at her, appealing in a strained whisper, "But Madame, suicide? I couldn't handle that. She's become the most important thing in my life. I need her. I'll always need her."

Von Bruen nodded. "I have perceived that, Herr McKeane," she replied. "And so does the evil one know of that."

Fletcher stared past Von Bruen's shoulder with a look of despair.

Von Bruen added, "You must also guard yourself with care. Jennifer may become dangerous to you as well."

Fletcher abruptly jerked backward. "Dammit!" he huffed, releasing his frustration. "Dammit!" he repeated, pounding his fist into his other hand, looking downward.

Von Bruen stood and walked to the smudged, rotary wall phone and slid the bell-adjuster lever to the 'off' position. She turned to the dormer window and peeked out past the shade to observe the weather. She sighed when she saw the moon was in its waning crescent, shedding only a faint glow in the darkness of the early evening sky.

"Oh Fredric, be cautious," she murmured under her breath, knowing the moon was in the most dreadful cycle for spiritual unrest. Turning, she walked to the table with a glum expression. She paused next to the table when she noticed Fletcher's concerned look.

"What do you think?" he questioned, looking up.

"Presently, I do not know the severity of her siege." She thought, then continued, "However, according to your account, Jennifer has not rejected the crucifix you have given her. The evil one may not yet be powerful enough to have taken her over completely."

"What do you want me to do?" he asked.

"Bring Jennifer to me soon," she answered. "Perhaps I may be able to help her by invoking the Lord's faith into her. That's the trusted way."

He nodded and stood. "I will as soon as I can."

She turned toward the living room. "Come," she said. "We must push forward and again talk about your life…your past life. We must continue our quest to find the grave and destroy the bones of the evil spirit."

Fletcher lay half-reclined on the sofa with his shoulders and neck resting against the raised armrest, his eyes tired and bloodshot with stress. Von Bruen placed the candelabra on the floor in front of him and reached for the silver candle snuffer, smothering all but one of the ornamental candlesticks. Thin wisps of smoke from the quenched wicks threaded upward through the trivial glimmer of the single candle. She moved the high stool across from him as she inhaled deeply, savoring the spicy fragrance of the burning incense filling the room.

Fletcher closed his eyes tightly. "I don't know if I can do this today," he said.

Madame Von Bruen ignored his doubts as she sat down on the stool across from him and pulled the long golden chain from her pocket, his ring dangling from it. She began to rhythmically swing the chain just above his eye level, centering it in the small halo of smoky light. "Turn back to me, Herr McKeane…You must relax," she said softly as he turned his eyes toward her. Tilting his head back, he lifted his gaze upward, focusing on the glittering object.

Von Bruen remained silent, swaying the chain smoothly and evenly, knowing that Fletcher's opposition was subsiding. She began her soothing rhetoric. "You must relax…become free of anxiety to allow the prolonged, suppressed emotions of your past life to surface. Release the vast knowledge that is harbored within…the past knowledge that is attached to your soul…"

She paused to let her words take affect as Fletcher's eyelids started to droop from the upward strain of his focus.

"You must relax and unwind every muscle in your body…become totally motionless," she continued in a low-pitched masculine tone. "Concentrate deeply and respond to my suggestions...respond to me while I explore your deepest thoughts…as we travel backward in time…back to your life in London."

His head slipped slightly forward, falling against the armrest. He began to drift, feeling loose and detached.

"You have cooperated with me and trusted me before," she pressed on with a smooth tempo. "You must trust again today as we probe into your earlier life in London…become free to explore inward…walk and talk with the people you have lived with before in England…They are real…You are real."

"Yes," he complied in a whisper, his eyes closed. "I shall."

"Yes, close your eyes. Find yourself on a winding staircase...stepping down to a deeper level of relaxation and consciousness...one more step down…Take one more step down and we can begin to talk."

"Yes," he responded in a distinct tone. "On the staircase, stepping down to a new level."

Her voice quickened, "Expose your inner senses...the inner senses that have been with you forever…the inner senses that are locked away in your brain. Be 'Christopher' again…be 'Christopher' as you were before...during that infinite span of time in London. Do not let today's world hinder you in any way. Come Christopher...come and bring your friends and enemies to me. We will all talk from your memories...Come Christopher and we will all talk together."

Von Bruen droned on until Fletcher appeared to be in a dreamlike state, entranced. Yet, she needed to be sure that his mind had entered the mesmerized alpha state. She quietly slipped the chain into her pocket.

"Christopher," she said, testing his level of consciousness, "do as you always do when we talk. Raise your arm and keep it raised until I ask you to put it down. You will not tire or feel pain during this time."

"Yes," he obeyed, gradually raising his arm and pointing it outward.

She reached over and felt his wrist. His body temperature was falling and his pulse was slow. Realizing that his blood pressure had lowered, she knew he was fully entranced. She asked patiently, "Christopher, where are you?"

"In London. Downtown, London. There are carriages and people. Hyde Park."

"Horses? Carriages?" she probed. "What year is it Christopher?"

"Sometime in the 1800s. I don't know exactly."

"Will you try and find your companions for me? We will talk."

"As you wish," he answered with a clipped tone, his accent now heavy British.

"Splendid, Christopher. Splendid."

She reached over to the table and flipped the hourglass. As the fine silvery sand began seeping from the top bulb, she picked up her small notebook and pencil.

Catherine O'Grady stood silently in the dimmed reception room with her arms crossed, staring at the fading flare of the dying fire. She diverted her concerned gaze toward the couch. The faint illumination of the glowing embers reflected the outline of Jennifer's gaunt face. She slept restlessly, curled into a fetal position, her mouth uttering indistinguishable words.

Catherine turned and switched on the small table-lamp sitting on the drop-lid of the oakwood secretary. She carefully moved the lamp to the top of the desk, not wanting to chance disturbing Jennifer.

She sat down in the rocking chair and leaned her tired body against the spindled backrest. Rocking gently, she fixed her fearful eyes on Jennifer. The slight squeak of the rockers meeting the hard wooden floor shattered the eerie silence as Catherine began thinking about Fletcher. She had not heard from him since the afternoon when he had called her from the pub. She regretted telling him that Jennifer seemed better when she really hadn't improved. But she understood what he was going through at Von Bruen's and felt he shouldn't be distracted further.

Catherine, growing extremely concerned about Jennifer's unstable condition, decided that she should stay with her that night. She turned to the secretary and picked up the phone, intending to reach Fletcher at his hotel. She knew it was useless to try Von Bruen's. Even if he was there, she couldn't reach him anyway. Von Bruen wouldn't allow that. She dialed his hotel. When she didn't get an answer, she left him a message on the voice mail.

"Mr. McKeane. 'Tis Catherine O'Grady here," she began in a level monotone, "Don't fear for your Jennifer this evening. Her situation is a bit off, but surely safe. Please sleep fit tonight, and fetch her from here in the morning. Cheerio."

She depressed the plunger and pulled a piece of paper from the small letter drawer. Releasing the plunger, she lifted the receiver to her ear and dialed.

"Yes, 'tis Catherine O'Grady here. Is Mr. Beaucamp at home, please?...Thank you." While waiting for him to pick up the phone, she tugged on the extra-long phone cord, enabling her to walk to the fire-tool stand. She grabbed the poker and stoked the stubby charred logs, igniting the last of the available flames. Walking back to the secretary, she replaced the poker back in the stand as Peter Beaucamp greeted her from the other end of the line.

"Oh yes, hello, Mr. Beaucamp," she greeted back. "Just wanted to alert you about Jennifer in the event ya talk to Mr. McKeane before he retrieves my message. Jennifer is staying with me tonight, she is...Yes surely, I will take her to my flat safely...Say again please...Yes, we'll be leaving shortly, Mr. Beaucamp...Yes, I have both numbers...Yes, I will ring ya up if I need. Thank you...Cheerio." She hung up the phone and looked again at Jennifer, who was still babbling incoherently.

Catherine turned and walked down the darkened hallway, deciding that she needed to think over the situation before waking her. Entering the library, she switched on a small bank of dim track lights and walked to the desk containing the card-index of the monthly periodicals. Opening the drawer labeled 'D,' she fingered through the file until she found *Depossession.* Pulling out the card, she read the reference number and turned toward the row of thick black binders.

Suddenly, she was jolted by Jennifer's piercing scream: "No! Annabella! Oh no, Annabella!" A bloodcurdling shriek followed, ringing throughout the building.

"Oh my Lord, my Lord," Catherine cried, as she raced from the library.

Reaching the reception room, Catherine stopped, frozen in the doorway. Jennifer was sitting straight up, shaking. The glow of the fire lit up her terrified appearance. Her hollowed eyes were wide open and encircled with dark rings. Staring vacantly at the fire, she slowly began to pull off the crucifix over her head.

Catherine crossed herself, reciting the Lord's name as she rushed to Jennifer and knelt before her. "No, Jennifer dear, you surely can't do that," she begged, grabbing Jennifer's hand to keep the chain and cross hung around her neck. Catherine crossed herself again with her free hand. "Reach for the Lord's help, my dear. Please reach for the Lord's help to fight this evil. The Lord will help us, reach up from within your heart…" she cried again.

Jennifer remained rigid, showing no emotion.

"The Almighty is close by," Catherine chanted, attempting to jolt Jennifer back to reality with thoughts of the Lord. "He shall surely help and protect against the evil if you will only ask."

Jennifer slowly looked down at Catherine, her eyes filled with an icy glare of contempt.

Catherine looked away to avoid Jennifer's deadly stare. "Our father who is in Heaven, hallowed be Thy name," Catherine began, holding the chain tightly as tears streamed down her cheeks. "Thy kingdom come, Thy will be done as earth as it is in Heaven…Give us this day…"

Fletcher's eyes remained closed, his arm still extended as Madame Von Bruen rested against the back of the stool. She glanced at the hourglass, watching the final grains of sand seep through the waist of the timepiece and into the lower bulb. Bending forward, she felt his wrist to check his pulse. It was sluggish but steady. She sat back, determined to find some meaningful answers today. Deciding to carry on with the session, she reached over and flipped the hourglass once more.

"Christopher, can you still hear me?" she asked as she opened her notebook and began to carefully browse through the pages.

"Yes," he answered, turning slightly toward her voice.

"Christopher, what is your surname?" she asked slowly. "I can write it down. I have paper and pencil...Please tell me your surname, Christopher...I am ready."

"No, I don't know! I told you I can't remember my complete name."

Von Bruen sighed, scanning the page of the notebook. "Are you married?"

"I told you before. No." he answered curtly.

"I am sorry, but I have to ask again. I must know this information," she challenged, undaunted. "You are in love with a married woman, yes?"

"Yes," he conceded.

She looked down at the notebook and checked off that answer. "What is the name of the one you love, Christopher? The one who is elusive. The one who is married to the vicious man."

She wearily began to check off the answer of 'I don't remember her name,' but then hesitated and slowly looked up at him. He remained silent. His face contorted with an expression of pain and anger. She quickly put the notebook down and moved closer toward him.

"Christopher…step down another level into your thoughts," she urged cautiously, employing her hypnotic power of persuasion again. "Step down the staircase…further downward…Behold the one who you love with your inner eyes…Tell me her name…"

He finally mumbled the word: "Annabella."

Von Bruen stiffened at the breakthrough. "Yes…Christopher…that is her given name," she said calmly as though she had already known the name, attempting to encourage him further. "What is the name that she has acquired through her marriage vows?"

His face went blank. "I don't want to talk about it," he said sadly. "She died. Let's talk about my painting of portraits."

Von Bruen quickly looked back over her earlier notes, the ones relating to his words about being an artist. She decided against his request and would press on with more questions about Annabella—as Von Bruen was now certain the answers lay with her. She would chance proceeding against his will, even though he might stop cooperating altogether. She swallowed hard as she glanced at the hourglass, knowing that soon she would have to end the session.

"Christopher," she pushed, "Christopher. How did Annabella die?"

He paused, his face twitched with pain. "He did it?"

"Was it Annabella's husband who killed her?"

"Yes," he answered, his body tense and his face clouded.

Von Bruen decided to gamble. "Christopher…did you, in turn, kill him?" She backed up to give him space and closed her eyes in a silent prayer of hope.

"Yes! Yes, I killed him! He took Annabella from me!" he exclaimed, his face tight with anger. "No! No more! I don't want to talk about it any more." He jerked his head toward the sofa back.

Von Bruen knew she still didn't have enough answers. However, she was worried that this insistent questioning could be counterproductive and plunge him into total depression. This could be dangerous because of his weakened physical state. She decided to ease up and ran through her notebook, keeping a watchful glance on the hourglass. She found the page with the pub notes on it.

"Christopher," she said in a gentle tone, "please relax. We won't talk about Annabella. You may lower your arm. Let's visit your friend at the pub."

"Yes, indeed," he agreed willingly, lowering his arm and turning toward her voice.

"Christopher, what did your friend Daniel look like?"

"A short, fat Irishman."

"Do you remember your friend's surname?"

"No. Only Daniel."

She checked off that same information she had recorded before. Although fast becoming frustrated, she was not yet ready to forfeit the session. She decided again to challenge him further.

"Did Daniel know of Annabella?"

"Yes, why!" he answered abruptly, sounding agitated. "You said we wouldn't speak about Annabella again!"

"I know, I am sorry Christopher," she said, deciding to abandon any further questions about Annabella. "Tell me more about the pub."

"It was large and barren," he answered. "I tossed darts there. I engaged in many contests."

Von Bruen was pleased as she jotted down the new information, but grimaced. She knew she would have to begin bringing him out of his trance. She suddenly thought of a way to attempt one last quest for information.

"Christopher, we're going to start our trip back to the present...We're going to find the staircase and climb up, one step at a time..."

"Yes. Good," he answered.

"Christopher, before we start up the staircase, I want you to go out the front door of the pub...Go now Christopher...But remember, stop at the street in front of the pub...Go now...Walk slowly and tell me when you reach the street."

She sat back and waited a few moments.

"I am there. I am in front of the pub."

"What do you see?" she asked.

"People, children, carriages. The city. The streets are very busy."

"Turn and look around, Christopher. What else can you see? Is it the city of London?"

"Yes...'tis London," he answered, pausing. "I see trees and fields of large gardens, and the palace. I see Buckingham Palace."

Von Bruen contained her growing excitement. "Christopher," she said softly, "we are almost at the staircase to come home...but first turn and face the pub...See it clearly, Christopher. What is the name of the pub? Is there a sign or a name on the outside of the pub?"

He squinted his closed eyes. "Yes, but the sign is small and blurry."

"Look hard, Christopher," she urged carefully. "Move closer toward the sign...Tell me what it says."

"I see part of the name across the top of the sign, but it's fading. One of the words is 'MEN,' and I see a name…'Doherty,' the proprietor's name is 'Doherty.'" He suddenly went silent with a frown. "'Tis gone," he said, discouraged. "All gone. Everything's gone."

She completed recording the information and realized that he was finished. "Come back Christopher…Come back to the present," she said slowly, beginning to bring him out of his trance. "Start up the staircase…one step at a time…Begin counting aloud when you are at step number ten…Count loudly as you ascend the staircase. Come back Christopher…We are waiting."

"Yes," he answered. "I'm at step number ten and climbing. I'm coming back…I am now at number nine…climbing to the top."

"Yes," she agreed with mild satisfaction, "you are coming back. When you reach number one…the top step, you will be at present consciousness, Herr McKeane. Come on back, Herr McKeane…We are waiting."

CHAPTER 35

The Next Morning, Mayfair

Peter Beaucamp glanced up at the morning sunshine falling through the skylight as he walked past the spacious garden atrium and entered the hotel coffee shop. Spotting Fletcher sitting alone at a corner table, he sat down across from him and reached for the coffee pot. Filling his cup, he remained silent, waiting for Fletcher to wolf down the last of his pancake breakfast.

"Morning," Fletcher greeted as he looked up, pushed his empty plate aside and flashed a wide smile of satisfaction. "Damn!" he exclaimed. "That sure hit the spot."

Beaucamp took a swallow of coffee then grinned. "Good morning. It's good to see that you seem relaxed today."

"Well," Fletcher replied, "finally, things seem to be a little brighter this morning."

"Great," Beaucamp responded. "How's Jennifer?"

"Better, I think. I didn't talk to her because I got in too late. But after listening to O'Grady's message I assumed everything was okay."

Beaucamp nodded. "Yeah, O'Grady also called me and told me she was taking care of her. I never heard anything after that." Beaucamp tipped his head back and finished his coffee.

Fletcher leaned back against his chair, crossed his arms and threw Beaucamp a smug look.

"Okay, what's up?" Beaucamp asked, cocking his head. "I knew when you called so early that you had something important to tell me."

Fletcher leaned forward, answering through an excited whisper, "The reason I was so late last night was because Von Bruen really grilled me during our session. We think we've found some answers about the pub."

"Fantastic! That'll sure help," Beaucamp replied, energized, "because yesterday afternoon I contacted The Brewers' Society."

"What's that?" Fletcher asked.

"It's a trade organization that represents England's brewing and pub industry. I talked with a lady named Julia Mitchell, she's employed there as a secretary."

"Did you tell her why we're looking for the pub?"

"Sure," Beaucamp replied, puzzled by the question, "Why not?"

"And she believed you?"

"Of course, why wouldn't she?" he answered, indignantly, "I believed you, didn't I?"

Fletcher shrugged. "Yeah, you're right, sorry. What about the British government? Wouldn't they have formal records of all the pubs?"

Beaucamp appeared discouraged. "I called the Home Office, where the Licensing Justices are located and they weren't very interested in helping. I didn't get very far. I think our best chance of finding it lies with the Mitchell woman."

"How would she find it?"

"She told me they have a computer data base of all the pubs and breweries that belong to the Society. Maybe the pub we're looking for is in there. Anyway, she said she would do her best to find it after she received more information from us."

"Sounds good," Fletcher replied, pulling a folded piece of paper from his shirt breast pocket. "Here's the information."

"Excellent," Beaucamp said, holding out his hand. "I'll call Julia this morning while you pick up Jennifer."

Fletcher handed the note to Beaucamp, who quickly unfolded it and began reading.

"McKeane, what the hell is this?" he asked, looking perplexed. "You call this information for Christ sake? There's nothing concrete here!" He pointed at the paper. "What's 'Early 19th Century' mean?"

Fletcher lifted his hands up in a gesture of innocent surprise. "We're sure it's the time period of my past life when everything occurred and…"

"What does 'Men' mean?" Beaucamp interrupted. "And who's Daniel Doherty?"

"That's part of the name of the pub, and the proprietor," Fletcher answered, becoming defensive. "I think."

Beaucamp inhaled and glanced back down at the paper. "Saw Buckingham Palace. Well, good! We at least know it's in London," he said sarcastically, folding the paper and shoving it in his suit coat pocket. "That narrows it down to a mere four or five thousand establishments. Jesus…"

Fletcher was offended and Beaucamp noticed, relenting. "I'm sorry, Fletcher. I lost it there for a minute. I suppose I was disappointed from expecting more. I guess I forgot what you're going through."

Fletcher appeared relieved. "Yeah, sure, I understand. I appreciate your support. I wouldn't be where I am without it."

"Look," Beaucamp said, looking thoughtful, "if the pub still exists we'll find it, and when we do I hope it leads us somewhere."

"Well," Fletcher replied, "if nothing else, it may trigger some more thoughts during my future sessions with Von Bruen."

Beaucamp nodded. "Okay," he said. "I'll call Julia this morning and give her this information. But I don't want you to worry about anything other than Jennifer right now. Go pick her up, okay?"

"I will," Fletcher agreed, "I'm leaving from here."

"Then what are your plans?"

"I thought I'd take her to see Von Bruen tonight," Fletcher answered, looking up toward the skylight. "However, we also both need a break. It looks like a nice day out there. If she's willing, maybe I'll take her sightseeing or somewhere to rest, like Regents Park."

"Good idea," Beaucamp agreed, glancing at his watch. "Okay, hey, we'd better get moving."

Fletcher waved over the waiter to sign the check.

"I'll call you if I need anything," Beaucamp said as they got up from the table.

They shook hands at the doorway of the coffee shop before Fletcher turned and headed for the elevator and his room. Beaucamp headed for the front entrance.

Catherine O'Grady, responding to the clanking rattle of the door-knocker, slowly opened the front door and stood in the doorway. The outside glare reflected a bedraggled, exhausted old woman who looked as though she'd had no sleep. Her clothes were disheveled and smudged from the soot of the fireplace and her thick graying bun of hair was unraveling. She squinted, attempting to identify the man at the door without her glasses.

Fletcher's cheerful spirits quickly changed to a stunned stare at her appearance. "My God, Ms. O'Grady!" Fletcher exclaimed, reaching for her arm, "What happened?" Gently backing her inside, he shut the door.

Her red and troubled eyes opened wider. "Mr. McKeane," she said, sounding strained but relieved, "'tis good you're here, surely 'tis."

His eyes expressed concern as he looked past her shoulder toward the reception room.

She put her hand on his arm. "Jennifer is in there," she said. "'Twas a tussle all right, most all of last night. But now she's calm. Let's step into the library. We need to chat before ya see her."

He followed her into the library and closed the door behind them.

"Ms. O'Grady," he said as they sat down at a reading table. "I can tell you've had a bad night. Please tell me what happened."

She laid her hand on Fletcher's and managed a smile. "Jennifer is unharmed but not at all fit. She writhed and fought all night. The evil has a strong hold, it does. It was a terrible clatter. She finally quieted about dawn, but she is still only a shell, battling to reach the Good Lord for help." She hesitated. "Surely though, I think she's getting closer to His hand."

Fletcher glanced around the room in an uneasy silence, looking for words. "I'm taking her to Von Bruen's tonight," he said, turning back toward her.

"Yes, very good," she answered, brightening. "Surely Madame will bring Jennifer out of her dreadful state, she will."

Fletcher's eyes were filled with worry. "Ms. O'Grady," he appealed. "I need to see Jennifer now."

"Yes, of course," she said. They rose from the table. She stopped him with a reassuring tug on his arm. "She indeed asked for you earlier. That's how I knew she is for the better."

Fletcher looked at her skeptically. "Did she really? Or are you just trying to make me feel better?"

"Yes, surely she did," she reassured, leading him out the door. "Now come along, but remember she has been through a lot. Do not be alarmed at her appearance."

When they entered the reception room, Fletcher saw the back of Jennifer's mussed hair. She sat on the couch, unmoving, and faced the fireplace. Catherine sat down at the dining table as Fletcher slowly walked around to the front of the couch. He noticed Catherine's smashed glasses lying in front of the fireplace before looking up at Jennifer. She turned toward him with an empty glance.

"Hello, Fletcher," she said simply, turning back toward the fire with a hollow stare.

Disappointed by her lack of emotion at seeing him, he sat down next to her and reached for her hand. Again, she turned back toward him. He took a deep breath at how she looked: pale and unhealthy, her face drawn and her eyes deadened. Then he noticed the crucifix still hanging around her neck and gave a thankful glance toward Catherine. Knowing what he was communicating to her, Catherine managed a weak smile.

He turned back to Jennifer. "Hello, Jennifer," he said softly. "How are you?"

"Okay," she answered, looking at him vacantly. "Have you come for me?"

"Yes," he answered, concealing his deep concern for her. He painfully realized that she was no longer consciously attached to him. He was now facing the ferocity of the evil one alone, and, worse yet, the evil one was fighting to possess her. He knew that he must find the answers soon before it was too late.

Putting his hand on her forearm, he gently urged her up. "Come," he said. "It's time for us to go."

Stopping on the porch, Jennifer turned to Catherine. "Thank you, Ms. O'Grady. Maybe I'll see you again before I go home."

"Yes, my dear," Catherine replied, tightly squeezing Jennifer's hand.

Fletcher then took Jennifer by the arm, led her down to the car and sat her in the passenger seat. He then walked back up to the porch where Catherine was standing, watching them. "Thank you, Ms. O'Grady," he said. "I can tell that she's better."

"Surely," she said, sighing. "I shall be happy when we can chat over tea again."

His face turned solemn. "But now I'm worried about you," he said in a serious tone. "You've been such a big help to us. Are you going to be all right?"

"You mustn't worry about me," she answered. "I'm a bit muddled, but I shall stoke the fire and sleep the rest of the afternoon. The day is certainly now fit for it." She looked up at the gradually blackening sky, then back at Fletcher. "We'll chat tonight, and discuss how ya faired with Madame. Cheerio."

"Of course," he agreed. "I'll call you right after we get back from Von Bruen's. Thank you for everything, Ms. O'Grady." He stepped off the porch and turned toward the car.

He was abruptly stopped by Catherine's alarming utterance: "Oh! Mr. McKeane."

He spun around and looked up at her.

"There is something I forgot to tell ya."

"What is it?" he asked, stepping back up on the porch.

"She had a frightful nightmare last night."

"Do you know what it was about?"

The old woman shook her head. "No, I surely don't. And Jennifer told me this morning that she didn't remember. But last night she screamed out the name of 'Annabella,' she did. Perhaps ya know of this Annabella?"

Fletcher stepped back, startled. "Ah…yes," he replied, astonished, recalling his last session with Von Bruen. "But I wasn't sure if Jennifer did." He reached over and squeezed Catherine's hand. "Thank you again, Ms. O'Grady."

"Surely, you're welcome," Catherine replied softly. She watched Fletcher jump into the car and pull away from the curb. "Surely you are," she repeated under her breath, stepping back inside and closing the door.

Wearily, she turned, making her way down the darkened hallway. She stopped to turn off the lights and close the library door before continuing toward the cold and oppressive reception room, unaware of the putrid smoky odor now filling the air.

Fletcher drove cautiously, preoccupied with thoughts about bringing Jennifer back into his world again and away from the grasp of the evil. He recalled Catherine's mention of Jennifer's nightmare about Annabella, proving that Jennifer somehow fit into the whole puzzle of his past life; not just his present. *But how could he discover where she fit in,* he wondered. *How was she linked to everything?*

Squinting with intense concentration, he thought about all of the events and places surrounding his past life that Von Bruen had recorded and relayed back to him. But he still couldn't piece it together. He realized that he had to pull Jennifer out of her current state to find out more? *I must find a way to get to her senses,* he concluded, glancing over at her. She sat expressionless, staring out through the windshield.

As an idea suddenly hit him, he abruptly pulled the car over to the far side of Cromwell Road and turned toward Jennifer. She looked at him as he gently put his hand on her shoulder, saying, "Jennifer, do you mind if we stop someplace before we go back to the hotel?"

"I don't care," she answered without emotion. "But don't we have to make our reservations to go home?"

"We have time," he answered, speeding away from the curb, heading for the eastern sector of London. Jennifer turned back without interest, again staring blankly through the windshield.

Fletcher stopped the car in the parking area at the top of Ludgate Hill and turned to Jennifer. She was nervously looking at the immense stonework building, looming majestically in front of them.

Fletcher took her hand. "C'mon," he said softly. "Let's go inside."

She appeared apprehensive, but got out of the car with him.

They stood for a moment, gazing up at the magnificent dome of St. Paul's Cathedral. He gripped her forearm lightly as they began to walk alongside the ornamental ironwork railings bordering the grassy churchyard. They reached the expansive flight of steps leading to the west entrance, stopped and looked up. The 'Great Paul' bell in the giant clock tower began its resonate clanging to announce the afternoon calling.

Fletcher tugged on Jennifer's arm as she began to shy away from ascending the steps, as if confused about where she was. She looked at Fletcher, fingering her crucifix. He remained silent but strengthened his grip on her arm, moving her forward. Entering through the enormous doors, they slowly walked past the Chapel of St. Michael. Jennifer's color began to return as she strained to scan the inside of the grand church.

Making their way through the vast length of the cathedral, disjointed thoughts from her past raced through Jennifer's mind. Yet she was unable to focus on the reason why the cathedral felt so familiar. She touched her face and hair, becoming cognizant of her appearance.

Fletcher noticed her sensitivity, her connection to reality, beginning to return. He stopped, let go of her arm and turned her around to face him. "Jennifer, you're safe now, with me," he said quietly. "God is with us and he will stay with us."

She remained silent, still focused on trying to take in every detail of the cavernous building. She left Fletcher's side and walked toward the open choir chamber, in front of the High Altar. Fletcher followed behind her.

When they reached the gleaming wrought-iron gates in front of the choir she knelt down and looked upward, searchingly, into the far apse. She paused, her eyes transfixed on the kingly portrait of Jesus Christ, which hung in the center of the Jesus Chapel.

Fletcher knelt down beside her, gently pushing her hair back away from her ear. He whispered, "Jennifer, sweetheart, please come back to me...I need you. Nothing matters anymore without you." When she didn't respond, he hesitated and turned his distressed eyes downward.

He then felt her hand on his and looked up to face her. As she tightly clutched his hand, tears began trickling down her flushed cheeks, falling off her lips now separated in a thin smile.

CHAPTER 36

Catherine's Fate, Mayfair

Fletcher grew increasingly concerned as he peered out the hotel window at the damp and bitingly cold evening. Dark and spectral, the fog had produced a tumbling shroud, sealing off the feeble light of the crescent moon.

He turned and walked hesitantly to Jennifer who was sitting on the couch, quiet but refreshed. She had showered, combed her hair and dressed casually in a denim pullover and jeans, sweat-socks and tennis shoes. She turned to him as he sat down next to her.

He shook his head. "I don't know," he said in a doubtful tone, "The drive to Von Bruen's tonight could be miserable." He paused. "How do you feel?"

"Much better after going to the cathedral today," she answered slowly. "But I'm still shaky. "

"I know," he responded, embracing her. "Don't worry, I know."

She tightened her embrace. "I must have treated you and Catherine very cruelly," she whispered into his ear.

He gently lifted her head. "Hey," he said tenderly, looking into her eyes, "I understand what happened and I know Catherine does too."

"I need to talk to her and let her know things are okay."

"How about later...after dinner. Let her get more rest."

"Okay," she agreed, smiling, "I can wait."

"Good," he replied, looking at her questioningly.

She noticed his change. "What is it?"

"I was wondering," he said carefully, "do you remember your nightmare last night?"

"Somewhat," she answered. "Not all of it, however."

"Do you remember the name Annabella?" he asked cautiously.

Jennifer looked upward, appearing uneasy as she answered, "Yes, but I'm sorry, darling, it's still all very confusing. Just like the visit to St. Paul's Cathedral today. It seemed that I'd been there before, like I knew my way around. But nothing was very clear." She shook her head, straining. "Oh, I'm just not sure."

Fletcher eased up, not wanting to take the chance of plunging her back into depression. He decided to drop the issue until after they had met with Von Bruen, who could probably help her remember. "Don't worry," he said, "it's really not important right now."

She glanced out the window. "Do you think we should go tonight?"

"I'm still not sure," he said, following her glance. "Von Bruen said she wants to see you but it wasn't that critical now that you seem better." He stood up. "Tell you what, I'm going to jump in the shower. Let's decide afterward."

"Sure," she agreed, "I'll rest for a while."

He reached down and kissed her before walking to the bathroom. She lifted her feet and stretched out on the couch.

He was beginning to relax as he stripped off his clothes and stepped into the steaming shower. While lathering and rinsing himself, he decided they should forget the drive to Von Bruen's. They would spend a quiet evening and enjoy a good night's sleep. Tilting his head back, he adjusted the spray-adjustment knob to allow the intense but soothing current to caress his neck and shoulders. He stood still, enjoying the calming flow when he heard the faint ringing of the phone. He arched his head, lifting his ear from the stream to listen, making sure that Jennifer answered the call. When he heard her muffled voice, he smiled, hoping that it was Catherine. He turned off the faucets and was reaching for a towel when he suddenly heard Jennifer's piercing scream: "Oh my God! Oh my God! No! No!"

Startled, he jerked upward and banged his crown on the shower head, momentarily stunning himself. He pulled open the shower curtain. "Jennifer? Jennifer?" he shouted in alarm. "What is it?" He received no answer.

"Jennifer, please talk to me!" he hollered again, grabbing the towel. He rushed from the bathroom, dripping a wet trail behind him. Scanning the main room, he noticed the entrance door was open and she was gone. He looked over at the bedside table and saw the phone receiver was off its cradle, dangling in the air. He picked it up and sputtered into the receiver. "Hello, hello?" He was greeted by only the buzzing of an empty phone line. "Shit!" He abruptly hung up the phone and rushed to the closet.

He hastily dried himself, threw on a sweatshirt, jeans and slipped on his loafers. He realized she hadn't taken the car when he saw the car keys still lying on the desk. He ran out the door to the elevators.

Reaching the main hotel entrance, he spotted the doorman standing just outside the doorway and rushed up to him. "Did you just see a woman run out of here?" Fletcher asked, panicky. "She had on jeans and a pullover."

"I certainly did, sir," he said, pointing into the billowing gray smoke across Park Lane. "That way sir, headed for the Queen's Gate."

Fletcher turned and looked into the fog, barely able to detect the obscured outline of Hyde Park. With his fear for Jennifer increasing, he ran across Park Lane, narrowly dodging the light traffic. "Jennifer? Jennifer?" he called worriedly as he trotted down the wide sidewalk toward the Queen's Gate. "Jennifer! Please! Jennifer!" he continued to call, "Where are you?"

He stopped when he came upon the shadowy figure, sobbing uncontrollably, kneeling against the gate and clutching it for support. Slowly he knelt down beside her and carefully gripped her shoulders, turning her toward him. The tears rolled down her cheeks amid the cold droplets of mist. Her hair, sodden from the damp air, was matted against her forehead, hanging down over her eyes. He moved it away with his index finger and pressed her head against his shoulder, comforting her and shielding her from the elements.

He moved carefully, recognizing how devastated she was. "Oh baby," he said softly. "Baby, please talk to me." He rocked her gently as she responded, clutching him tightly but still sobbing. "Sweetheart," he consoled her. "Sweetheart, I have you. I have you."

She managed to halt her weeping. "Catherine is dead," she mumbled into his shoulder, "Oh, God, Catherine is dead."

"Baby, I'm sorry," he said, his eyes becoming moist with sorrow for her. "I'm so sorry." Rising, he gently picked her up and began carrying her back to the hotel.

"I want to go home," she said weakly, her head resting on his shoulders "I can't take any more. Please, I want to go home."

"Yes," he answered, "we'll go home and pray to God it's over."

He reached the entrance of the hotel and met the concerned doorman hurrying toward him. "Please send a doctor to Fletcher McKeane's room, 1015, immediately."

"Straightaway, sir," the doorman answered quickly. "Straightaway."

Fletcher, exhausted from stress, leaned against the wall staring at Jennifer as she lay on the bed. A brisk, hard knock on the door jolted him forward. He shook his head to focus and walked over, opening it. He was surprised when Peter Beaucamp anxiously rushed in, asking, "How are you two doing?"

Fletcher was stunned, exclaiming, "Peter!"

Beaucamp looked around worriedly, repeating, "How's Jennifer?"

"She's all right," Fletcher answered. "The doctor left a few minutes ago. She's traumatized, so he lightly sedated her."

Beaucamp nodded, looking over at Jennifer.

Still puzzled at seeing Beaucamp, Fletcher asked, "Peter, how did you know there was trouble tonight?"

"I called earlier and talked to Jennifer. You were in the shower, and..."

"You called?" Fletcher interrupted. "I assumed it was Von Bruen who called."

"No, it was me," Beaucamp said. "I didn't realize Jennifer would take O'Grady's death so hard. I mean, after talking to you in the coffee shop this morning I thought she was okay. But when I heard her scream, I decided to get here as soon as I could."

"Yeah, she's totally distraught. She just wants to go home." Fletcher shook his head, adding, "It's hard to believe that O'Grady's dead."

"For sure," Beaucamp said, calming. "She's dead all right." He paused and wrinkled his face. "It was grim as hell, too."

Fletcher held his hand up, hushing Peter, and then glanced over at Jennifer who was still asleep but stirring. "I don't want her to hear," he said. "The sedative is mild because we may want to get out of here fast." He turned. "C'mon, let's talk over there."

Beaucamp followed Fletcher to the table.

"Okay, tell me what happened," Fletcher said quietly as they sat down.

"Scotland Yard actually found the old woman this afternoon. She had managed to dial the operator and ask for help just before she died. They traced the call back to the Association suite." Beaucamp paused and sat back, preparing Fletcher. "The find was quite gruesome."

"Go ahead," Fletcher said, unwavering. "Nothing bothers me any more."

"They found her lying face down, completely impaled on the log-fork." He paused and inhaled. "When she crawled to the phone she bled to death."

"How the hell did it happen?" Fletcher asked.

"They figure she accidentally slipped and fell on the tool while spearing logs for the fire. There was a trail of blood across the room that led to the fireplace."

Fletcher reflected on Beaucamp's statement, before abruptly exclaiming, "Bullshit! She never would've been that careless. Never! No one was as careful as she was around that fireplace. Bullshit!"

"Well," Beaucamp said, "that's what Scotland Yard told me. They found a rumpled throw rug on the outer hearth and assumed she must have tripped and…"

"Bullshit!" Fletcher interrupted, shaking his head firmly. "There were no throw rugs by the fireplace. I know because I worked on the fire once, and I was concerned about cinders catching something on fire."

"Jesus," Beaucamp responded with a blank look. "Okay, I believe you. What do you think then?"

"I don't know exactly, but it must be the work of the fucking evil thing that is after me and Jennifer…Catherine had helped us." Fletcher turned away, then looked back at Beaucamp, who still appeared baffled. "How'd you find out anyway?"

Beaucamp shook himself back to reality, re-gathered his thoughts and exclaimed, "Ah, as I said, just before she died she managed to drag the phone off the secretary. They found papers and my number on the floor and since I'm with the embassy they decided to notify me…" His voice trailed off.

"Peter, you really doubt all this, don't you."

"Well," Beaucamp wavered, "I believe it could be real, it's just that…"

Fletcher suddenly waved his hand in a yielding gesture, silencing Beaucamp. "It's okay, forget it," he said. "Anyway, that's it, we've had it. We're getting outta here tomorrow."

Beaucamp shot him a questioning look.

Fletcher noticed Beaucamp's look of surprise. "Dammit, Peter," he said in a distressed tone, standing up to pace. "How much do you think we can take? And you're wondering yourself if all this evil stuff is real."

Beaucamp nodded. "Okay," he said. "I admit that I'm skeptical, but I still want to help you and something new has come up since we last talked."

Fletcher looked back down at him: "What?"

"Julia Mitchell from the Brewer's Society may have located the pub," he said, quickly adding, "But, of course, she doesn't know for sure."

"Where is it?" Fletcher asked, sitting back down. "Where?"

"Not too far from here actually," Beaucamp answered, "She worked with the name 'Men' and found a pub called 'King O' Men' on Piccadilly Road. I understand the place has been there for well over a century."

"Shit!" Fletcher exclaimed.

"What's the matter?"

"Why now?" Fletcher said. "Just when we were planning to leave."

"Look, you can forget about it. I wouldn't blame you if you did. Hell, who knows, it may not even be the right place."

Fletcher pondered, then asked, "Are you familiar with where the place is?"

"Yes, I drove past it earlier, but I didn't go inside."

"Peter, is it close to Buckingham Palace?" Fletcher asked, swallowing hard.

"Yes, Fletcher," Beaucamp answered. "It is close to Buckingham Palace."

Fletcher looked worriedly over at Jennifer as she pulled the light blanket over herself and turned onto her side. Fletcher turned back toward Beaucamp.

"Fletcher, I know it's a tough decision," Beaucamp said. "However, I really think you shouldn't leave London without knowing for sure. It would eat away at you for life."

Fletcher again glanced at Jennifer, asking, "How long would it take us to get there?"

Beaucamp looked out the window. "Oh," he answered, "with the fog…probably twenty, twenty-five minutes, if we don't encounter any traffic problems." Beaucamp pointed toward Jennifer. "How long will she be out?"

"Probably not much longer. But if we do go, I want to do it without her. She's probably not strong enough to handle what we might find."

"Then you'll have to leave her here alone. You don't have any choice."

Fletcher hesitated, then quickly picked up a piece of paper and pencil. "I know," he said, anxiously writing a quick note for Jennifer. "Let's go, now."

Soon after they left, the phone began to ring. Jennifer tried to ignore it, but it wouldn't cease. Finally, she groped for the phone, fumbling with the receiver as she brought it to her ear. "Hello..." she mumbled groggily. "Yes, Madame Von Bruen, this is Jennifer." She sat up and blinked her eyes, desperately attempting to wake up. "Madame, please slow down…Madame, you're shrieking." Jennifer reached over to the table for her glass of water. "I can hardly understand you…What, come over now? I…I…don't know, I don't see Fletcher…Yes, I heard you. I understand the odor is present and it's cold in there." She hesitated and gulped down some water. "Yes, I know about Catherine...Yes, please calm down. Okay, I'll find Fletcher and come to your flat immediately. Please try to relax until we get there...Bye."

Hanging up the phone, she yelled for Fletcher, quickly realizing that he wasn't there. She felt woozy and unsteady as she got up from the bed. Turning on the overhead light, she noticed the note on the mirror:

Jennifer, be back soon. Please stay here if you wake up. Please don't go anywhere.

Damn! she thought as she wobbled into the bathroom and washed her face, thinking about how odd it was of Von Bruen to be so terrified and incoherent. *Why couldn't she just leave?* Jennifer wondered, brushing her hair back. Then she recalled Von Bruen shrieking something about confrontation being the only solution.

Beginning to feel steadier, Jennifer went back to the mirror and read the note again. She was reluctant to go but felt she had no choice. She quickly wrote down where she was going on the bottom of the same note.

She put on her trench coat, picked up her purse and walked out the door, wondering where she was really destined and what she would find.

Reaching the hotel entrance, she asked the surprised doorman—who recognized her from the earlier incident—to summon a cab. After the doorman whistled, the bright headlights of a cab emerged out of the thick gray air, pulling up next to the curb. The doorman opened the rear door for her, and she slid into the seat. The cabby turned toward her.

"Chelsea please," she said. "Chelsea Embankment Street, in Chelsea."

"Right, Ma'am," the cabby confirmed. "Chelsea Embankment Street, 'tis."

CHAPTER 37

King O' Men Pub, The Discovery

Fletcher and Beaucamp lifted their eyes to the high-pitched roof-peak where an almond-shaped wooden sign hung from the gable by thin chains. The hazy beacon of the outside floodlight faintly illumined thick black letters:

KING O' MEN

A vividly painted image of a bejeweled miter-crown and two scarlet-red roses were set directly beneath the name.

Beaucamp turned to Fletcher. "King O' Men. It must mean God."

"Right," Fletcher agreed, appearing awestruck.

"Tell me what you're feeling, Fletcher."

Transfixed by the sign, Fletcher answered, "Strange, the surroundings seem familiar but…" He spun around and gazed across the street, encountering only a thick layer of saturated gray. "Dammit!" he exclaimed, continuing his stare, but to no avail. "I can't tell if it's what I saw during my session with Von Bruen. It's too foggy."

"Come on then," Beaucamp suggested, leading him onto the porch stoop. "Let's go inside."

They entered and stopped just inside the doorway, scanning the room. There were a few patrons sitting at the tables and standing around a horseshoe-shaped bar. A small cluster of men was gathered in the corner competing in a dart game.

Fletcher quickly looked to the far side of the room, immediately struck by a scuffed wooden booth setting in the snuggery that was partially concealed by heavy satin drapes.

"I sense it, Peter," he said excitedly. "Yes! This must be the pub!"

A middle-aged graying man emerged from the back room. "Say there, gents," he greeted. "What can I do for ya?"

"Couple pints of Guinness, please," Fletcher requested as the two men sat down at the bar.

The bartender nodded, reached for two pint-mugs and filled them from the gaudy ornamental spigot attached to the bar-top. He set the mugs in front of them and started to walk away.

Fletcher put his hand on the bartender's arm, stopping him. "I'm looking for a man named Doherty, Daniel Doherty. Do you know anybody by that name?"

The bartender did an immediate double-take as he turned around. "Is this a lark, lad?" he asked with a half-smile.

Fletcher puzzled, replied, "No, I'm very serious."

The bartender shrugged, turned and pointed to the other side of the room. "There, lad," he said. "There's Daniel Doherty. My great-great-grandfather. I'm Michael Doherty, I am."

Fletcher and Beaucamp swung around on their stools, following the bartender's point toward the blazing fireplace. They spotted the painted portrait of the man, hanging on the stony chimney just above the mantle.

Fletcher eagerly hopped off the stool and walked to the fireplace, fixing his amazed stare on the portrait.

As the crackling flames created a warm shimmering glow, Fletcher caught his breath and leaned forward to read the inscription on the bottom of the portrait:

Christopher J. Wilkinson, July 15, 1833

Following closely behind Fletcher, Beaucamp watched with astonishment. He now knew that Fletcher had been right. *It could all be real,* he thought.

Fletcher's eyes inched downward to a smoked-glass cover, fastened to the chimney with hinges. It protected the oversized gaming darts and the glossy mahogany case that had once belonged to Christopher Wilkinson.

Fletcher then noticed the heavy yellow parchment paper, also covered by glass, attached to the mantle top. Text written in elegant sapphire-blue calligraphic script was titled:

The Fateful Legend of Christopher Wilkinson

Underneath the title:

Composed by Bishop Thomas William Thornton

May 10, 1835

Fletcher shivered with expectation as he read it. "Christopher," he recited in a low whisper as Beaucamp watched intently. Fletcher inched his finger down the glass while sporadically glancing up at the darts. His mind devoured every word. *Annabella,* the wife...*Melissa*, Annabella's sister...*Bernadette*, their friend. Fletcher then froze. "Peter, there he is!" he rasped, his eyes widening. "The husband, a surgeon! Sir Alec Drenton!"

He finished reading the legend, slowly backed up and turned toward Beaucamp with a look of satisfaction, silently telling him that he'd found his answer.

Nodding, Beaucamp firmly grasped Fletcher's shoulders, pleased at seeing his friend's expression of relief.

❖ ❖ ❖ ❖ ❖

Jennifer cautiously stepped out of the cab, feeling stronger yet still sluggish from the lingering effects of the tranquilizer. She handed the cabby his fair and he sped away, leaving her standing alone in the raw and swirling darkness. As she stood still, closing the top button of her trench coat, she heard the lapping of the waves against the rocky river shore.

She turned and looked toward the house, seeing there was no light coming through the windows of Von Bruen's flat. *It must be the shades,* she thought, as she made her way to the fuzzy contours of the porch. Although fearful about her situation, she knew that she had no choice. Von Bruen's flat was now the only security in this desolate, eerily-quiet neighborhood.

She stepped onto the porch, surprised to see the main entrance door standing wide open. Disregarding her wonder, she walked in. Pausing in the darkened hallway, she flipped the light switch and looked up, gripping the shoddy, splintered handrail. With the help of a dim lightbulb that hung from the stairwell ceiling by a frayed nylon cord, she carefully climbed the stairs.

Reaching the top landing, Jennifer was more puzzled at seeing the apartment door was ajar. She thought of Von Bruen's compulsion for locked doors. Although growing alarmed, she pushed the door open wide. She knew she had no choice but to continue.

The main rooms were dark except for the flickering gleam of a small candle sitting on the kitchen table. Using it as a guide, she entered the living room and closed the door behind her. It clicked shut and locked, shattering the fragile silence.

Startled, she jerked back, floundering for the doorknob. Catching herself, she took a deep breath and looked around. "Madame Von Bruen?" she called nervously. "Madame Von Bruen? It's me, Jennifer. Madame Von Bruen?"

Receiving no answer, she slowly proceeded into the hallway and was immediately drawn to a strange reddish-white glow flowing out from under the closed bedroom door. Filled with fear, she hesitated and listened for noises, but heard none. *Von Bruen must be in there,* she thought. *Then why doesn't she answer?* Jennifer swallowed hard, repressing her frightful thoughts.

A sense of threat hung in the air but she knew she must find out what's going on. Reluctantly, she walked down the hallway. With every advancing step the chill and offensive smoky odor seeping out from under the door grew more pronounced. Still she continued, knowing there was no turning back.

Fletcher glanced at his watch and fidgeted anxiously on the bar stool. Though worried about leaving Jennifer alone so long, he was unable to break away from the bartender's captivating details of Christopher Wilkinson's legend. He needed more answers.

"Aye," the bartender said, leaning forward on his arms in front of Fletcher and Beaucamp. "Ol' Daniel always asked that the pub be kept within our kin. 'Tis now in its second century with the Doherty clan, 'tis."

Fletcher leaned forward. "I'm interested in where the bodies are buried," he said impulsively. "The bodies of Christopher, Annabella and Sir Alec Drenton. Where are the graves located?"

The bartender, suddenly uneasy, abruptly stepped back. "The whole lot o' them," he said in a halting voice, "are buried in the churchyard at the ol' abbey in Lambeth, St. Mary's of Our Guidance."

Fletcher turned to Beaucamp but he shook his head. "Never heard of the place," he said calmly.

"Oh, ya wouldn't hear much of it," the bartender shot back. "The old abbey is abandoned and falling down from neglect. Only a few brave parishioners visit there now and again." He hesitated, appearing somewhat afraid. He scratched the stubble on his chin before adding, "Them and the ol' devoted churchkeeper, that is."

"What's the matter?" Fletcher asked, noticing the bartender's growing uneasiness.

The bartender bent down close to him. "It is bruited about that the churchkeeper is a true disciple of the devil," he answered in a hushed tone. "A depraved demon who roams the churchyard, keeping a wicked vigil over the graves. For sure 'tis a wretched place, for sure."

"Wretched?" Fletcher repeated.

Lowering his head as though protecting himself from being heard, the bartender whispered, "Long ago 'twas a fancy to be buried at the abbey. But over time many wicked deeds occurred there. They say that

Satan himself hand-picked the churchyard to defy the Lord."

The bartender backed away as Fletcher sat back, pondering. He glanced back toward the mantle and the legend. "Who was Bernadette Quinton?" he asked. "How'd she fit into everything?"

The bartender cast a quick look of concern toward the chimney. "Ah yes, Bernadette," he answered slowly. "A loose woman who'd worked at the 'King O' Men.' She became Sir Alec's mistress but turned against him in the end. She'd even become a good friend of Christopher's before he went to the gallows." He sighed and shook his head as he picked up their empty mugs. "'Tis a grisly tale of her passing, it is…a true victim of the churchyard."

"True victim of the churchyard!" Fletcher exclaimed. "What happened to her?"

The bartender set the empty mugs back down and again leaned on the bar as Fletcher and Beaucamp moved closer.

"Well," he began, "Bernadette was a repentant woman living at the abbey to tend the graves, till one day she turned up missing. No one knew what to think. Searched high and low for her, they did." His eyes widened. "That is until two abbey nuns walked up to the north end of the churchyard and spotted it."

"Spotted what?" Fletcher asked, becoming more intense.

"Her fresh plot right next to Drenton's. 'Twas Bernadette's grave all right, complete with a marker stone and all. Bernadette's friend, Bishop Thornton from the High Church, promptly had the authorities dig up the coffin."

"Jesus, man! How'd she die?" Beaucamp interrupted, unable to contain himself.

The bartender grimaced. "Carved up like a Christmas turkey, she was," he whispered slowly.

Beaucamp and Fletcher looked at each other, both matching the bartender's grimace.

"Yes sir, gents," the bartender continued. "They found her with 'er throat slit from ear to ear. And 'er heart had been cut out as perfect as could be. Tucked neatly in 'er clenched hand, it was."

"As perfect as could be?" Beaucamp repeated.

"Aye," the bartender confirmed. "Not a slice was wasted, they say. Must've been the work of a skilled surgeon. Much to the likes of Jack the Ripper."

"You mean that London butcher they never caught?" Fletcher asked.

Beaucamp looked at Fletcher, shaking his head, interrupting, "Yeah, but Jack the Ripper couldn't have done it, he came along much later in the century."

Fletcher nodded and turned toward the bartender asking, "Who did it?"

"Oh, they couldn't pin it on anyone," the bartender answered. "But it appeared to be a crime of revenge, and Drenton had been a brilliant surgeon."

"But Drenton was dead!" Fletcher exclaimed.

The bartender shrugged and backed away.

Fletcher glanced nervously at his watch as he thought about Jennifer.

The bartender again leaned closer to them. "Well," he said, "the next victim to perish from a ghastly deed was Bishop Thornton." He pointed toward the fireplace chimney. "'Twas right after he scribed and posted the legend, it was. He was walking alone in the churchyard one night..."

"Never mind, forget it," Fletcher interrupted throwing his hands up, suddenly filled to his limit with the bartender's baneful tales of graveyard lore. "Where is this church?" Fletcher asked. "I need to find it right away."

"Oh Gawd, ya can't be wantin' to visit there," the bartender answered flabbergasted. "Specially tonight, with no parish lantern available."

Fletcher looked puzzled, asking, "What's that mean?"

Beaucamp put his hand on Fletcher's arm. "It's a British expression," he said quietly. "Parish lantern refers to the moon. He's saying there's no moon."

Fletcher turned back to the bartender. "Please," he insisted. "Where is it?"

The bartender looked at him and shrugged. "Okay, suit yerself, lad," he said reaching for a napkin and pencil to jot down the information. "Suit yerself."

After rewarding the bartender with a sizable gratuity, Fletcher pocketed the directions to the church. He and Beaucamp then pushed away from the bar and headed for the front door.

Stopping on the outside porch, Beaucamp turned to Fletcher with a worried look. "I have to get home. It's late. Please don't go to the churchyard without me," he said. "Tomorrow we can scout it out together."

Fletcher peered into the dreary night. "Okay, it's too damn foggy and cold anyway. I can wait. I'd better get back to the hotel and stay with Jennifer."

"Good," Beaucamp said, hesitating. "By the way, are you going to tell her?"

"I dunno, depends on how she feels in the morning."

"Another good move," Beaucamp agreed. "Oh! Have you got your tools in case we find the grave?"

"Yeah, they're in the back of the car."

"And the acid?"

"Yeah, I've got that too."

Beaucamp turned for his car. “Excellent. I’ll call you in the morning.”

Fletcher reached out and grasped Beaucamp’s arm, stopping him. “Hey, be careful,” he said solemnly. “You’re really wrapped up in this mess too.”

Beaucamp looked back at him and paused with a sigh. “I know that, Fletcher. I know that well. But, I wouldn’t have it any other way.”

“Thanks,” Fletcher said, releasing his arm.

Beaucamp acknowledged Fletcher’s appreciation with a nod before they stepped off the stoop and walked separately to their cars.

Jennifer’s heart pounded wildly as she turned the doorknob and strained against the inside pressure, forcing open Von Bruen’s bedroom door. A nauseating stench and vapor gushed out causing her to step back and retch as she clutched her mouth. Overwhelmed, she pulled the large collar of her coat across her face and gasped for breath while focusing on the broad rectangular bed.

The flickering candlelight of a twelve-branched girandole attached above the headboard revealed Madame Von Bruen. She lay hovered on the bed under a heavy quilted bedspread, wide-eyed and speechless with panic. A celestial glow of soft white brilliance enclosed her quivering silhouette, protecting her from the deathly aura that filled the room.

Releasing her collar, Jennifer rushed in to help Von Bruen but stopped and whirled toward the crimson glow lurking in the far corner. Horrified, she stiffened at seeing the grotesque presence of a man, lacking an arm and a foot. It faced Von Bruen with a merciless, riveting stare. A greenish slime dripped off the torso, forming small noxious pools on the floor.

The deformed head, scorched bald, was covered with crusted peeling skin. Charred cheekbones protruded the putrefied flesh.

Slowly, the gruesome figure turned to face Jennifer, its yellowish eyes slit, casting a hideous look of evil gratification. Terrified and unable to move, Jennifer could barely recognize Frank Conklin's features through the ghastly deformities. Abruptly the creature began to transform into the shape of another man as the stench and cold began to subside.

"Jennifer!" Von Bruen cried hoarsely, flailing at a suffocating weight she suddenly felt inside her heaving chest. "Come over to my radiance for protection! Come over to me!"

Jennifer glanced toward the bed and Von Bruen's sacred refuge. Turning back toward the transformed figure of a man, Jennifer felt powerless to escape his mysterious lure. The air was becoming heavily laced with a sweetened fragrance. A warm sensation of rapture was building inside her.

"Ah, Bernadette, my beloved pub wench. We meet again," the figure said softly through an insidious grin, his jagged and rotting teeth showing clearly in the candlelight. "'Tis been a prolonged duration since we journeyed to Stratford-on-Avon together. I have missed you greatly. Please, come closer my love."

Attempting to reject him, Jennifer slowly backed up while reaching inside her coat to find the crucifix. Struggling to remain within present reality, Jennifer was incapable of sustaining her resistance—unable to convey any hallowed faith from within, rendering the amulet useless.

"But my love, do not struggle," he continued through a mellow tone. "You must relinquish your mortal existence. 'Tis time for you to join me again. Forever."

He moved to position himself between her and Von Bruen, who was now writhing and thrashing on the bed, gasping for air as the sanctuary of her radiant luminescence began to wane.

Weakening, Jennifer dropped her arms to her side and slowly backed against the wall. Transfixed by his commanding power, she remained motionless, mentally drifting out of physical existence into a subconscious realm from her past.

He moved closer, reaching for her.

Jennifer's eyes widened with terror. "Nought, Sir Alec! Nought, Sir Alec! Ya shan't do this," she screamed in a heavy British accent as she fiercely clawed at the wall.

Fletcher, eager to find Jennifer, unzipped his windbreaker as he rushed through the door of the darkened hotel room. Seeing the rooms were empty, he was immediately upset to discover she was gone.

"Damn it! What now?" he mumbled aloud as he instinctively turned toward the mirror. Noticing Jennifer's note beneath his, he pulled it down and scowled, reading that she had gone to Von Bruen's flat without him.

Crumpling up the note in his taut fist, he strode to the bedside table and fumbled through the stack of telephone numbers, finally finding Von Bruen's. He quickly dialed the number and listened to the unanswered, repeated ringing. Slamming the receiver down, he turned toward the door but then stopped. He went into his suitcase and retrieved his army bayonet, before rushing out the door. Heading for his car, he mumbled obscenities over his anger of not having his pistol anymore.

Fletcher brought the car to a screeching halt in front of Von Bruen's flat. Killing the engine, he jumped out and ran to the porch. He swung open the front door and bounded up the steps.

The door was halfway open as Fletcher barged into the darkened living room. He shone his powerful flashlight around the rooms seeing they were empty.

"Jennifer!" he yelled. "Madame Von Bruen! Where are you? Jennifer!"

Hearing nothing, he quickened his pace down the hallway, stopping at the open doorway of the bedroom. He grimaced at the fading but still pervading stench of rotting flowers and smoke. Regaining his composure, he scanned the room with his flashlight, suddenly stopping to focus the wide beam on the lifeless body lying on the bed. *Oh God, no!* He put his hand on the wall and felt for the light switch, flipping it on.

He stepped back in shock as he saw Von Bruen lying there. Her long slender body was still and her head was propped up on a pillow. The drip-pan of the girandole had been bent forward, allowing the molten candle wax to drip onto her narrow, ashen face. Her open, terror-filled eyes peered upward through the thin mounds of solid glistening tallow.

Tense, he looked around the room at the small pools of nauseous slime giving off a vile, steamy vapor. He nervously aimed his flashlight into the shadows of the corners, fearful at what else he may discover.

Alarmed, he abruptly froze the beam on Jennifer's crumpled chain and crucifix lying on the floor. Stepping around the mire, he picked it up and firmly grasped the silver cross while looking upward with a silent plea. He slipped the chain around his neck and hurried back into the kitchen. Pulling a piece of paper out of his wallet, he picked up the phone and dialed.

"Mrs. Beaucamp, this is Fletcher McKeane. I'm sorry to call so late, but it's an emergency. May I please speak to Pe…What? No, he's not with me. I left him earlier this evening!…Yes, Mrs. Beaucamp, don't wait any longer. He should've been home hours ago. Please call Scotland Yard," Fletcher requested, fearing the worst.…"Yes, I'm okay. I'm calling from Von Bruen's flat in Chelsea, but I'm leaving right now." He hesitated. "I'm sure Peter's fine, probably car trouble or something. I'll call you later, bye. Oh! Mrs. Beaucamp," Fletcher said, remembering Von Bruen lying dead in the bedroom. "When you call Scotland Yard, have them send someone to 3201 Chelsea Embankment, upstairs apartment…Thanks."

Fletcher hung up the phone, hurried out the door and down the steps, stopping abruptly on the porch. Distraught, he leaned against the railing. Looking into the smoky-gray horizon, he felt more alone than ever before. O'Grady and Von Bruen were dead and Beaucamp and Jennifer were missing, leaving no one to whom he could turn.

He walked to his car knowing that he must remain composed and collected. He opened the rear hatch-door and reached for the backpack, unzipping the pockets and checking their contents. Satisfied, he lifted the backpack out and closed the door.

Crawling in behind the steering wheel, he set the backpack on the front passenger seat and switched on the interior light. Anxiously, he pulled out the piece of paper with the bartender's directions to the abbey…the graveyard.

After carefully comparing the directions with the street map of London, he established his route and set the map on the floor. Pulling away from the curb to head for Lambeth, he knew he must somehow find and confront his enemy from another realm that had cruelly plagued him for his lifetime, and maybe even longer.

CHAPTER 38

Lambeth, Facing the Fear

Fletcher cruised along the deserted side street, occasionally stopping as he tried to make out the buildings through the stubborn fog. He finally spotted the shadowy outline of the tall church and brought the car to a stop. Lowering his head to look out the passenger side window, he attempted to scope the exterior of the complex and develop his plan. He quickly realized this effort was useless because of the poor visibility. He would have to plot his strategy after he'd entered the premises.

He straightened up and reached for his backpack, then paused. He grasped his forehead in a moment of distress as he thought about Jennifer and Beaucamp. *What could have happened to them?* Fighting to control his anxiety, he knew he had to concentrate on the task at hand.

He stepped out of the car into the stark pre-dawn darkness. Sliding into the backpack, he tightened the shoulder straps then turned for the church. He crossed the cobblestone road, avoiding the puddles, attempting to be noiseless. He was still uneasy about who or what he was hiding from and began thinking about the gruesome graveyard yarn the bartender had spun. He switched the flashlight to his other hand, allowing his free hand to toy with the handle of his bayonet, bouncing gently against his thigh. It provided him a moment of confidence as it brought back memories of his Viet Nam jungle prowls and how he had repeatedly used this formidable weapon for protection. He frowned, again disappointed at himself for being so careless about carrying his pistol yesterday, and losing it to Beaucamp. He knew he could use it now.

Crossing the rundown street corner, he approached the vaulted, Gothic-styled building and leaned back flat against the weather-stained wall. Hearing nothing, he rested his hand on the moistened yellow-brick for support and shone his flashlight upward. Observing the lofty ivy-clad towers, he wondered how anything could withstand this brutal weather for so many centuries. He lowered the beam to scan for an entrance into the interior, but all he saw was a high concrete wall attached to the end of the church building. It was capped with blockstone and extended the length of the complex. He felt thwarted, as the grounds appeared impenetrable.

Determined to get in, he dashed around the corner and bounced the flashlight beam along the face of the wall, seeing a narrow archway about halfway down the block. With new hope he ran on the balls of his feet until he reached the slender opening. Shining his light down the length of the pathway, he saw nothing but more high walls on either side. Then he saw an opening at the far end leading into pitch-blackness. He entered, creeping along the slate-stone path until he reached the end and stopped.

Scanning the inside of the dark perimeter with his flashlight, he saw that he had entered a large rectangular garden-cloister that bordered several darkened and seemingly empty buildings. All the windows were boarded up and the doors secured with padlocked steel bars. Shifting the light about the bemired cloister he saw it was unkempt, heavily vined and full of shriveled flower beds. An over-abundance of soggy wild thickets and bushes overlaid the crumbly walkway.

He was feeling more confident and began to loosen up, considering the probability that the complex was totally abandoned, while—unknown to Fletcher—dark intense eyes watched him from the adjacent wing of the cloister.

He continued his survey, shining the flashlight beam on another opening in the distant corner of the cloister. It didn't lead to a building, he excitedly determined. *It must lead to the churchyard! The graveyard!*

He moved cautiously toward the opening, deciding that he must remain prepared for anyone or anything that might be lurking in the darkness. Besides the abnormal dangers he might face, he would also want to avoid being caught in the illegal act of desecrating a grave. *Even the grave of the depraved Sir Alec Drenton,* he scoffed inwardly.

Pulling the crucifix out from under his sweatshirt, he remembered Von Bruen's words about how inner divine faith must truly be felt before the amulet could be effective. Faithfully, he prayed for guidance and support as he inched his way around the corner and shone his light toward the end of the walkway.

At last, his beam picked up a wide, wrought iron spear-pointed gate leading into the churchyard. Yet, again uneasy, he continued at a gradual pace as he kept the weather-eroded gate in the center of his trusty beam.

Reaching the gate, he put his hand on the steel top rail and pushed on it. The gate rattled noisily, but held fast. He quickly let go. Shutting off his light, he grimaced at his carelessness and stood still. Hearing nothing, he switched the flashlight back on, focusing on the heavy chain wrapped loosely around the gate end-post and the picket-rail, fixed by a huge rusty padlock.

"Dammit," he murmured as he shone the light between the pickets into the decrepit-looking churchyard. A creepy feeling enveloped him as the beam picked up the hazy outlines of graves and tombstones lining the yard. Chills raced up and down his spine as he waved the light outward across the grounds. The beam failed to reach the outlying edge of the expansive yard. Inhaling deeply, he backed up to survey the gate, considering the best way to enter.

Suddenly a waft of ice-cold air swept over his body as Fletcher felt a strange, paw-like grip on his shoulder!

Stunned, Fletcher spun around, slamming hard against the fence. Instinctively he grabbed his crucifix with one hand while focusing the light beam on the head of the figure with the other.

The man quickly turned his head away from the glare and slipped his hands into his wide pockets.

Still jolted from the encounter, Fletcher shakily scanned the tall figure from head to foot. His body was completely covered by a heavy woolen robe that reached the ground, drawn tightly at the waist by a rope belt. His face was almost hidden by an oversized cowl pulled far over his head. Long strands of sparse gray hair lay matted against his mist-dampened cheeks.

"I am the churchkeeper," he said in a low resounding snarl as Fletcher recoiled from his putrid breath. "What do you require here?"

"I, uh," Fletcher uttered incoherently. "I'm a visitor from the states and I understand that one of my relation is buried here. I…just…wanted…"

"You must go now," the keeper interrupted, oblivious to Fletcher's sputtering drivel. "You cannot enter the churchyard."

Fletcher looked up, aiming the flashlight at the keeper's mouth. He cringed, seeing the sharp-pointed incisors, surrounded by serrated, yellowed cuspids. He quickly recalled the bartender's lore about the demonic churchkeeper and held out his crucifix as he motioned toward the pathway entrance. The burly figure slowly stepped backward, letting him pass. Fletcher walked rapidly down the walkway as he heard the keeper rattle the gate, ensuring its security.

Fletcher, confused and frightened, stopped in the middle of the cloister and shut off the light to test the darkness. He could not distinguish anything around him as he heard sandals shuffling loudly on the flagstone coming toward him. *How in the hell can the churchkeeper see where he's going,* Fletcher thought, turning the beam back on and hurrying through the opening in the wall, back into the street.

He hustled to his car, got in and drove off, sensing that he was being watched. After turning the corner, he drove to the end of the block, pulled over to the curb and cut the ignition. He had to get back in there, he determined, but wondered what he was up against. He remembered how the churchkeeper had backed away after seeing the crucifix. *Damn! Was the bartender's lore accurate?* Was he truly up against something evil that protected the graveyard, and maybe even Sir Alec's grave? *Could the churchkeeper actually be Sir Alec's soul? Or maybe even a direct disciple of Satan?*

His thoughts turned to Jennifer, wondering where she was. And of his friend Beaucamp, what was his fate? Looking up, Fletcher fingered his crucifix, faithfully believing he had help. He had to ignore the apparent danger. *He must return to the churchyard and find the grave,* he decided.

He glanced at his watch, calculating that he had only a couple of hours before dawn. Then it would be too late. He'd never be able to violate the grave in the daylight. He inhaled deeply, grabbed his backpack and got out of the car. He took to the middle of the street and began walking toward the church. Soon he was trotting through the smoky mist, deciding that nothing—not even murder—would stop him from doing what had to be done.

Reaching the church, he crept along the wall until he reached the spot where he estimated the churchyard was located. He stared at the high wall that separated him from the completion of his mission. Pulling a nylon rope from the side-pocket of his backpack, he lassoed a fractured capstone. He pulled hard on the knot, ensuring that the loop was secure, and began to shimmy up the side of the wall. He grabbed onto the cold top-coping and grimaced as the jagged damp edge dug into his fingers. Undaunted, he pulled himself up and continued over the wall, dropping feet-first into the wet slippery mud of the churchyard. Managing to remain upright, he backed up and leaned against the wall while he oriented himself. Convinced that no one was around, he proceeded, using the stealthiness he'd learned from nighttime jungle patrols.

He pulled the flashlight from his pocket and switched it on, converting the light into a thin beam with the shielding sleeve of his windbreaker. After looking at his compass, he recalled how the bartender had told him the bodies were buried under a tall oak tree, facing East toward Jerusalem. All except for Sir Alec, who was interred on the north edge.

Cautiously, Fletcher threaded his way through the decaying foliage, careful not to step on anything that might make noise. Although the fog was beginning to lift, slightly increasing his visibility, he was becoming concerned over the approaching dawn and the possibility of being seen. Tramping anxiously past the weathered headstones, he suddenly stopped and fixed his beam on an ancient stone tablet, lighting up the lichen-covered wording. Feeling strange, as though he was looking at his own grave, Fletcher slowly bent down. He scraped away the heavy moss with his bayonet, revealing the inscription:

Christopher John Wilkinson
Born 1803 Died 1834

Swallowing hard, he slowly moved the light to the adjacent gravestone on the right and read *Annabella's* inscription, knowing that she was *Lainey's former self.* In awe, he slowly rose and shuffled past the grave of Annabella's sister *Melissa,* overwhelmed with the thought of having lived with and loved these people in an earlier life.

Stunned by his discovery, Fletcher forgot how carefully he had entered the graveyard and impatiently hurried past the seedy, deteriorating graves.

Meanwhile, the hulking churchkeeper crept quietly through the churchyard toward him, his narrowed eyes enraged by Fletcher's intrusion.

Reaching the northern rise, Fletcher stopped as he spotted the gleaming marble headstone of Sir Alec Drenton. *It's polished*! Fletcher marveled inwardly. He then saw the immediate area surrounding his grave was meticulously groomed. The oblong outline of his plot was decorated with neatly trimmed shrubbery and leafy plants. The grassy mound was closely cropped, adorned with two wide easels supporting wreaths of fresh flowers.

The bartender was right! Fletcher thought. *The churchkeeper must worship Sir Alec and maintain his grave site...the only grave site!*

"Well, fuck you Drenton!" Fletcher rudely said aloud as he began to mentally prepare for his task.

He slowly passed the light around the perimeter of the churchyard, spotting the lone grave just at the crest of the hill. He wondered if it was the one from the legend...*Bernadette's*.

Walking toward the grave, he shone the light on the headstone, seeing the inscription of Bernadette Quinton. He cringed, remembering the bartender's ghastly tale of her death. Then, freezing with dread, he spotted tennis shoes—Jennifer's tennis shoes. He focused the full beam of light on her exposed body, lying still behind the headstone. Her coat was unbuttoned; her clothes disheveled and muddy. Dropping the flashlight, he rushed to her, drawing her up by her shoulders. She hung limp in his arms. *Is she...? No!* he silenced himself inwardly, not letting himself think the unbearable.

Knowing he must remain composed, he picked her up and carried her back to the edge of Sir Alec's grave, gently lying her down. Slipping the backpack off his shoulders, he noticed the first ashy light of dawn began to lighten up the churchyard. He realized he must work quickly. He unzipped the main compartment of his backpack and pulled out the short-handled spade, followed by the canister of sulfuric acid, matches and a small bottle of holy water.

After setting them on the ground he angrily lurched toward the plot. He picked up the easels, uprooted plants and heaved them every which way to clear the grave site. "To hell with you, Sir Alec Drenton! You bastard!" he muttered through gritted teeth as he began to dig wildly for the coffin.

Without warning, a powerful yank on his shoulder sent him reeling backward, dropping the spade. Sprawled across the grave he looked up and saw his attacker coming at him. Fletcher wrenched sideways, pulled out his crucifix and appealed loudly, "Help me, God. Help me!"

Momentarily halting the brute with his hallowed gesture, Fletcher desperately grabbed the shovel and walloped it into the invader's broad stomach, sending him down. Fletcher then drew the spade back and swung with all of his strength, striking his foe across his temple. The brute turned, stumbled backward and fell hard to the earth.

Fletcher instantly pulled his bayonet and bolted madly toward the groggy figure. He raised the bayonet, then caught himself. *Is this murder?* He hesitated, turning back toward the grave. Seeing the still body of Jennifer sent him into an uncontrollable frenzy.

Fearing for both their lives, Fletcher turned and crouched down over the semi-conscious churchkeeper. As the churchkeeper's eyes flashed open, Fletcher fiercely jammed the bayonet deeply into the middle of his chest. With a deep gasp, the keeper's eyes slowly closed. Blood burbled through the heavy cloth robe where the long concaved blade remained plunged.

Unrelenting, Fletcher yanked hard on the grip, freeing the weapon from the body and bounded back to the grave, knowing he had no time to waste.

Fletcher continued to dig furiously with the spade until he hit the soft splintered top of the rotted wooden coffin. Sweating profusely, he cleared away the remaining dirt and pried off the lid, jerking back at the sight of Sir Alec. The body showed no sign of decay. The glassy-hard eyes were wide open and squarely facing him. His beard and thick sideburns still had strands of black bristly hair. Scores of slugs and worms slithered at the bottom of the coffin and all over the outside of the entire corpse, impatiently waiting to do their work.

Wild with revenge, Fletcher thrust the bayonet into Sir Alec's gullet and ripped downward with all of his strength, completely severing the upper torso. With the bloodless organs exposed, the worms and slugs started crawling into the body cavity, seizing their grisly opportunity. Immediately, a foul stench enveloped the area while a blaring shrill like that of a loon began to screech. Fletcher, oblivious to the maddening squeal and pervading odor, grasped the canister of acid. He carefully began unscrewing the cap, realizing the danger of the container's caustic contents.

He suddenly stopped when he heard rustling and a ferocious snarl emerging from the outer shadows. Fletcher looked up, facing the jaws of a powerfully built wolf dog. Its black flews were curled back, exposing razor-sharp incisors and extended canines.

Fletcher's eyes widened in astonishment when he saw the savage dog straddling the churchkeeper's empty robe. The side of its head was bruised and bleeding. Blood dripped steadily from a wound just below its neck. As it slowly slunk forward with attack in its eyes, Fletcher grew even more alarmed when he saw it was cloven-hooved.

My God, it has hooves! Fletcher exclaimed inwardly, now knowing this was no earthly beast. He carefully set the acid canister down, not wanting to risk getting any on himself. He reached for the spade and bayonet. Weary, Fletcher wondered how much more he could take as the beast began to move toward him.

Fletcher tightened his grip on the bayonet handle and glanced over at Jennifer. Again enraged at the sight of her lying motionless, he turned and glared back at the dog. He readied himself in a defensive stance.

"Come on you son of a bitch," Fletcher urged defiantly, as the beast's black eyes dilated, growing crimson. "Come on you son of a bitch!" Fletcher repeated loudly as he swung the spade with all of his strength into the coffin, shattering Sir Alec's brittle skull.

Frothing at the mouth, the beast raved and howled toward the sky while it continued its slow even gait around the grave, eyeing the crucifix and weapons that Fletcher waved crazily. The deafening shrill in the air grew louder as Fletcher drew back the spade and smashed the chest bones of Sir Alec. He then violently dismembered one arm and a leg with the pointed edge of the spade, keeping a watchful eye on the snarling dog waiting for its moment to pounce.

Losing strength, Fletcher knew he couldn't last much longer. Bending down, fumbling for the acid canister, he knew the end to all of this terror depended on destroying Sir Alec's remains.

Seeing its chance, the beast leapt with its broad jaws snapping and snarling. Fletcher jerked sideways, causing the mighty creature to careen into his shoulder, pounding him back into the grave and onto the coffin. Fletcher wildly grabbed for the pointed ears as the two rolled over, now both insane with rage.

The incised snout had Fletcher's arm, chewing and ripping through the windbreaker. It was drawing blood, slowly inching toward Fletcher's jugular!

Fletcher looked at his bloodied crucifix and once more appealed for celestial help. Although weakening, Fletcher maintained enough strength to keep the jagged jaws away from his neck. With his arm still caught in the dog's forceful jaws, he strained backward and found his bayonet. Crazed with anger, he swiped at the head, slicing off one of its ears. This only enraged the beast further, as Fletcher frantically rolled under the dog, smashing against the coffin only inches from the slugs and worms that were now feverishly feeding on the exposed organs.

His strength returning, Fletcher clutched the dog's midsection between its legs, maneuvering his bayonet to slit open the creature's soft belly. Bleeding heavily, the dog loosened his grip, allowing Fletcher to seize its head. He fiercely shoved the bayonet deeply into the shoulder crest, twisting and pulling it savagely downward. Choking on his spurting blood, the dog swung its head madly and slumped down, lying across the shattered remains of Sir Alec. It pawed futilely at the lengthy blade stuck into its neck. Fletcher pushed on the handle, driving the point of the bayonet into the wooden coffin bottom, stilling the beast, along with the mutilated corpse of Sir Alec. The slugs and worms moved toward the dog in anticipation of satisfying their feral appetite.

Fletcher tightened the sleeve of his windbreaker around his battered arm and crawled out of the fetid hole. Grabbing the acid canister, he unscrewed the cap and carefully emptied the contents over Sir Alec's corpse, along with the beast that was glaring up at him, strangely beginning to stir again.

Fletcher lay back as the raging foam threw off a strong sulfurous odor while instantly eroding the bodies in a seething froth. Fletcher threw the empty canister into the grave and reached for the matches as the shriek in the air intensified. With the deafening wail rising up around him, Fletcher lit a match and threw it into the coffin and rolled away from the edge of the hole. Lying on his back, he clutched his torn and bleeding arm and looked up at the sky, now brightly scarlet from the breaking sunrise and the roaring blaze.

As the fire quickly dwindled to a flicker, Fletcher reached for the bottle of holy water and rolled over, peering into the grave. He splashed the water onto the smoldering rubble of Sir Alec and the dog, then dropped the bottle into the grave. Gradually the stench dissipated and the screaming faded to a dead silence as Fletcher rose to his knees. Exhausted, he scraped and shoveled the dirt back into the hole, completing his task of casting Sir Alec's evil spirit and that of his beastly minion into the abyss of the damned.

With all that remained of his mortal strength, he crawled over to Jennifer. Taking off his crucifix, he hung it around her neck and drew her into his arms. He embraced her tightly, buried his head into her shoulder and stroked her hair. Frantically he rubbed her back, trying to warm her. He desperately needed her to respond, to come to life for him.

Totally sapped, he gave up his attempt to revive her and focused his teary eyes on the sudden sight across the churchyard. A brilliant light enveloped the graves of Annabella and Melissa. Fletcher knew this was the trusted celestial sign that their souls were ascending to the abode of God the Almighty.

But he wouldn't turn around and look at Bernadette's grave, now knowing that Jennifer had incarnated her soul. He was unable to bear what he feared the most, to see that same trusted sacred sign enveloping her grave. He laid back on the ground and drew Jennifer tightly against him. His moist eyes slowly closed as the dimming beam of the flashlight, lying next to the grave of his heinous archenemy, slowly faded out.

CHAPTER 39

Mid-Morning, The Churchyard

Clenching his teeth with determination, Peter Beaucamp gripped the long handles of the bolt-cutters and squeezed, closing the sharp jaws squarely on the eroded link. Snapping loudly, the chain unraveled and fell clanking in a heap beneath the heavy steel gate. Beaucamp dropped the cutters to the ground and began tugging on the latch-lock that was corroded onto the gate-post. Unable to release the catch, he drew his leg back and kicked the gate open. He burst into the churchyard and thrashed through the dew-covered foliage toward the north rise, followed closely by two bobbies from Scotland Yard.

"There they are!" Beaucamp yelled back to the trailing bobbies, picking up his pace as he ran toward the grave site. "Call for a paramedic unit. Wait! Make that two."

One of the bobbies turned and headed back to the patrol car while the other followed Beaucamp, who was already kneeling down next to Fletcher.

Peering out from under his helmet, the bobby examined Sir Alec's disturbed grave site. "What in bloody hell happened here?"

Beaucamp turned toward him and looked around, noticing that the grave was covered up and there was no obvious evidence to incriminate Fletcher in any serious crime. "Ah, I don't know," he lied, grabbing Fletcher's wrist, finding only a slight pulse. "But when I saw them last night they were partying quite heavily."

The officer nodded and looked down at Jennifer as Beaucamp placed his palm on her ashen face and then felt her icy neck. "They were probably robbed and beat up, or something like that," Beaucamp said, grimacing inwardly as he realized Jennifer had no pulse. "I didn't think they would really come here," he added, managing to continue his charade as he pushed up her eyelids, seeing her eyes were sunken and rolled back.

Beaucamp shook his head and stood up. When he heard the blare of the siren on the other side of the wall, he began walking toward the churchyard entrance. He soon met the paramedics as they raced into the yard, carrying their bags and portable stretchers.

"Where are they?" a paramedic asked excitedly.

Beaucamp, dispirited, waved his arm toward Sir Alec's grave site. "Over there," he replied, the paramedics turning to follow his direction. "He's bleeding badly but still alive..." He paused, then said sadly, "But I'm sure she's dead."

Somber, Beaucamp wandered around the east side of the churchyard, looking over the graves in the bright morning sun. He found the group that he was looking for and stopped, spotting a headstone that had been recently scraped clean.

Crouching down in front of the grave, he read the inscription of Christopher Wilkinson. He scratched his day-old chin stubble and lifted his head.

Thinking about Jennifer, Beaucamp looked upward. *Sir, Fletcher's had a rough go of it for a long time,* he appealed inwardly. *Now this. All I ask is that you give him the strength to face this last hurdle. Please.*

He wiped his eyes, stood and turned, seeing the paramedics clamoring toward the gate carrying the first stretcher.

"Hey, friend," Beaucamp heard as the paramedic reached him, "are you a doctor?"

Beaucamp shook his head. "No," he answered softly.

"I'm glad you're not, after hearing your earlier diagnosis," the attendant quipped. "She's alive and moving!"

The paramedics smiled as they hurried past Beaucamp.

Beaucamp stood with his mouth wide open at seeing Jennifer lying on the stretcher, twitching under the blankets. He quickly managed a smile of gratitude, and again looked upward. *Sir, I don't care about or need an explanation. But I owe you one. Thank you.*

Fletcher shakily lifted the coffee cup to his lips with his heavily bandaged arm and sipped the fresh brew as the nurse removed his tray of half-eaten breakfast. He leaned back against his propped-up pillows and was reaching for the TV remote when Beaucamp suddenly appeared at the foot of his bed.

"Damn!" Fletcher greeted, holding out his good hand. "Peter! How are you?"

Beaucamp shot him a wide grin. "Fine," he said, shaking Fletcher's hand. "Just fine."

"Where the hell you been?" Fletcher asked. "What happened?"

"Never mind about me. How's Jennifer?"

Fletcher appeared upbeat. "Recovering well, as far as I can tell," he answered. "She's had quite a time of it. They moved her out of intensive care and we were able to visit each other yesterday. She seems to be her old self again."

"Great!" Beaucamp replied, holding up his thumb, gesturing a victory.

"Yeah, but," Fletcher responded, quizzically, "I'm really confused. I was sure she was dead when I found her in the graveyard. I just don't understand it."

"Well, I guess that proves one thing," Beaucamp replied.

"What?"

"You're no doctor." Beaucamp smiled.

Fletcher laughed. "Yeah, I guess you're right."

"Anyway," Beaucamp said, "looks like it's only a matter of time before you're both outta here and on your way home."

"Yup, the doctor said it's only a matter of days. Now, what happened to you that night?"

"Ah, it's the craziest thing," Beaucamp answered. "When I left you I was running late so I took a shortcut home."

"A shortcut?"

"I know…I know it was a stupid move on such a miserable night. But I guess I was preoccupied with what we had discovered in the pub. Then without any warning I'm in the middle of heavy fog…couldn't see a damn thing. When I tried to steer clear of it my wheels locked and forced me into an embankment. I hit my head and was knocked unconscious. Just after dawn I woke up and drove my car off the train tracks and…"

"Train tracks!" Fletcher exclaimed, interrupting.

"Right," Beaucamp replied with an alarming glance. "And only about ten minutes before the commuter train raced through there."

"Jesus!" Fletcher exclaimed again.

Beaucamp nodded. "Yeah, damn scary huh? But anyway, I made it home and found the police there with my wife, concerned about me being missing. It was embarrassing but I explained everything to them."

"How'd you find me?" Fletcher asked.

"It was easy. When my wife finally calmed down and told me you'd called from Chelsea, I put two-and-two together and used the police for an escort. We went straight to Von Bruen's and found her…"

Fletcher shook his head, interrupting again, "She was dead when I got there."

"We figured she was," Beaucamp replied. "They didn't figure you'd kill her then call my wife and report where to find the body."

"What did they find out about her death?"

"The coroner performed an autopsy the next day," Beaucamp answered. "They ruled it death from natural causes, a massive heart attack." He paused and rubbed his chin in wonder. "Strange thing about the hardened wax on her face though. They think maybe she bent the girandole forward during her struggle with the attack."

"Natural causes? Heart attack?" Fletcher said, appearing skeptical. "Bullshit," he said adamantly. "It was…"

"I know," Beaucamp interrupted, smiling. "Another deed of the evil one."

"Wrong," Fletcher replied boldly. "The *last* deed of the evil one."

They both laughed heartily.

"Well anyway," Fletcher said, sobering, "I'm sure glad you knew where the church was."

"Like I said, it didn't take long to figure out where you'd gone when you weren't at Von Bruen's."

"Am I in any legal trouble?"

Beaucamp shook his head. "Nah. I talked to Scotland Yard and there was really no crime committed. They assume that you and Jennifer had been drinking and got yourselves into some macabre mischief. They didn't really push it. They figured you injured yourself with your shovel and Jennifer was a victim of the weather and maybe too much booze. Oh, there may be a small fine for trespassing or something like that. Regardless, I vouched for you. You're both free to leave London."

Fletcher suddenly thought about the grave site struggle. "What about the churchkeeper?" he asked slowly.

Beaucamp shot Fletcher a puzzling glance, asking, "Churchkeeper? What churchkeeper?" He hesitated, adding, "The bartender must have been wrong about that part of his story. Hell, we couldn't find anyone that even belongs to that parish any longer. The flock abandoned it long ago. In fact, I understand the whole complex is scheduled to be razed and the land will be turned into a gigantic parking lot."

Fletcher appeared mystified by Beaucamp's answer, but decided not to pursue it, not wanting to complicate things more. "Oh, I must have been delirious and dreamed that I saw him in the churchyard."

"Yes, you probably did dream that."

"Okay, whatever," Fletcher replied. "Anyway, thanks for your support."

"Sure," Beaucamp answered, turning toward the door. "Well I have to get to the embassy." He hesitated. "Incidentally, please plan on you and Jennifer having dinner with the wife and me on the night before you leave. We'll never forgive you if you don't."

"Sure, we'll look forward to it."

"Oh yeah, one more thing," Beaucamp said, waving his index finger. "You can take your pistol back home with you. The authorities have cleared it. I'll return it to you when we meet for dinner. See you soon."

"Thanks again," Fletcher called to Beaucamp, watching him walk away.

Fletcher laid back against the pillows thinking about Beaucamp's conversation, before falling into a deep restful sleep.

London quickly disappeared from view as the mammoth airliner sliced through the cinder-blue horizon. Fletcher put his hand on Jennifer's arm. She looked up from her newspaper.

"It's great to have you back," he said. "I mean, really back."

"It's wonderful to be back."

"What about Donald?" Fletcher asked with a pensive look.

She lowered her eyes, setting the newspaper on the floor. "It's over between us," she answered sadly. "I can't help how I feel. I sent him a letter asking him to meet me in L.A. I'll tell him then, though I'm sure he already knows."

Fletcher nodded as the flight attendant leaned in their row to adjust their trays and offer them champagne and hors d'oeuvre before serving their twilight dinner.

Jennifer pushed her empty dinner tray away, remarking, "That was great. I'm stuffed." She turned toward the porthole window. "I'm getting excited," she said, beaming. "We'll be in New York soon. I'm homesick."

He didn't answer but gently reached for her hand, the expression on his face troubled.

"What is it?" she asked tenderly.

"Do you remember what happened after entering Von Bruen's bedroom? I mean before I found you in the churchyard."

Suddenly uneasy, she swallowed hard. "Well," she replied slowly, "I remember that hideous looking fiend with the features of Frank Conklin transform into that other man. I remember Von Bruen frantically fighting for her life. And I remember he was coming toward me..."

Fletcher gripped her hand tighter.

She turned away, taking a deep breath. "I really don't know what happened after that, everything became dark and cold...very mysterious." She paused, then added, "I do remember feeling hopelessly drawn to him or it...whatever. I became weak as he touched me..." She looked down. "Then everything went blank. The next thing I remember is waking up in the hospital…" Frustrated, she shook her head, muttering, "I…I…"

"Never mind," he said, cutting her off. "All that's really important is that the doctors said you're fit and healthy, inside and out."

"Darling," she said, squeezing his hand. "Thank you."

They sat quietly for a few moments.

"Hey!" she blurted excitedly, turning toward him, her eyes wide. "I figured something out."

He grinned. "Now things are getting back to normal. Shoot."

"Frank couldn't have been just a possessed mortal," she replied. "He had to be an evil entity with the soul of the one in the legend, Sir Alec Drenton. He must have come from that third realm that Madame Von Bruen told us about. That's why he was able to transmogrify into something horrifying to coerce Lainey off the cliff, and to cause Chapman to jump from the plane at Catalina."

"Sure, that makes sense," he agreed. "And he didn't want any photographs taken because he didn't want to be identified or traced down."

She replied, cynically, "He probably wouldn't have materialized in the picture anyway."

He smiled at her quip, then furrowed his brow, asking, "But what do you think the missing mirrors had to do with everything?"

She thought for a moment. "Oh, I talked to Catherine about that. She told me that mirrors are common tools for dealing with supernatural evil. Demonic beings are repelled by mirrors—or by any shiny reflective surface, for that matter—because it's believed that a mirror reflects the soul. And they'd rather not see their souls." She paused, grinning.

"Remember the proverb that if you look in the mirror long enough, eventually you'll see the devil?"

He nodded, listening intently.

"I think in Frank's case he wouldn't have had to look very long." She chuckled.

"I see," he said, laughing with her. "I guess that answers everything. Right?"

She said nothing.

"Well, right?"

"Almost everything," she replied. "I want to know how I died before? I mean, as Bernadette."

"Really wanna know?" he asked, wrinkling his face.

"Yes."

"All the gory details?"

Her eyes widened. "Yes, now tell me."

"Okay," he replied. "Well, the bartender from the pub said that Bernadette ended up looking like one of Jack the Ripper's victims and they found her…"

She moved away from him, saying, "Forget it, just forget it."

"Hey," he said with a rousing laugh, "you wanted to know. By the way, your soul may be famous as the Ripper didn't come along until a lot later. Maybe he picked up his grisly habits after reading about Bernadette's death." He continued laughing.

"Thanks for that consolation," she answered sarcastically, reaching for the airline travel magazine. "You know what? I think we need a real vacation."

His face brightened. "Good idea. I agree!"

"How about the French Riviera?" she suggested. "I know, Monaco. It's beautiful there this time of the year." Her face clouded. "Catherine and I talked about it a great deal. She loved it there."

"Sure, we can go there," he said softly, leaning his head back, relaxed. "I've always wanted to see the French Riviera, especially the casino in Monte Carlo."

"Great," she said, setting the magazine down.

"I'll talk to Berkshire and Grahme when we meet with them next week," he added. "I'm sure they won't mind postponing the Colombian shoot after they learn what we've been through."

"Oh yeah, I forgot about Berkshire and Grahme," she said, sounding concerned. "Do you really think they'll believe our story? We don't have any pictures or substantial proof, do we?"

He thought a few moments while she stared at him, knowing his answer.

"Well, no, I guess not," he replied. "But dammit, they'll believe me. I mean, why wouldn't they?" he added firmly, wanting her to agree with him.

She only rolled her eyes upward. "Right," she said with a skeptical tone, laying her head back to catch a nap.

The landing announcement jolted Fletcher and Jennifer awake. Glancing past Fletcher, she looked out the window and smiled; delighted at viewing the vast skyline of New York City emerging on the sunny horizon.

Chapter 40

Geographic Unlimited, San Diego

The tense stillness within the grand office was finally shattered by the sudden tapping of Clifford Grahme's pencil against his desktop. Tom Berkshire glanced over at Grahme's desk, before looking back at Fletcher and Jennifer, sitting at the end of the long conference table.

"Fletcher, this is quite a report you brought back," Berkshire said as he looked down, leafing through the typed document sitting in front of him. "I've pored over it a couple of times."

"Yes, yes it is! Quite a report!" Grahme echoed.

Jennifer and Fletcher remained silent as they looked closely at the two men.

Berkshire looked back up at Fletcher and asked, "But, you say you weren't able to get any photographs or eyewitness reports of the paranormal events? Like when you were at the graveyard."

"No, sir," Fletcher answered, growing impatient over the increasing speculation of his report. "As I told you earlier, it didn't work out."

"I see, well…" Berkshire mumbled.

"Hmmm," Grahme added loudly.

"Gentlemen," Fletcher said, somewhat agitated. "I understand your reasons for doubting my story. But all I can tell you are the facts of what we know happened. It's very difficult to bring back proof of an alternate reality. They don't exactly sell postcards from a realm of another consciousness…" He paused, regretting his sarcasm. "Sir, I apologize for that remark."

"Forget it, I understand," Berkshire replied calmly. "Tell me, do you both think and feel that it's finished? This venture, I mean."

"Yes, we do," Fletcher answered, glancing at Jennifer, who nodded in agreement.

The hush in the room fell rigid as Berkshire again fingered the report, saying, "Fletcher, it's not that we don't believe your report. The data is well detailed and unusual. However, as we discussed in the beginning, we usually don't print stories of this nature. And without proof…well, frankly, it would be difficult for our readers to accept. Don't you agree?"

"Yes. I understand, Tom."

Berkshire, still unsure of any final judgement, looked down and opened to a section of the report tagged with a bookmark and, after scanning a few lines, said, "What about this Mr. Beaucamp from the American embassy you mention? I talked to him briefly a couple of times when you were in London. He seemed quite cooperative and reliable. Do you think he'd be willing to publicly offer support for your chronicles?"

"I don't know. We didn't really discuss it," Fletcher replied, shrugging. "I suppose it's all a matter of his perception. I do know Peter wasn't a witness to any of the paranormal incidents. But he was close to the whole situation."

Berkshire nodded, then quickly smiled at Fletcher and Jennifer as he closed the report. "Tell you what," he said in an upbeat tone. "If you don't mind, I'll contact Beaucamp at the embassy and get his personal account. Then I'll discuss the project further with Mr. Grahme and get back to you with our decision."

"Of course I don't mind," Fletcher agreed, reaching for Jennifer's hand. "And we'll accept whatever decision you make. We just want to get past all of this and get on with our lives."

"Sure, we understand, Fletcher," Berkshire replied casually, relieving the tension. "Now then, how long have you been back from London?"

"About a week," Fletcher answered. "We're staying at the Alpine Towers."

"Excellent," Berkshire replied. "We're pleased to have you here and eager for you to begin the Colombian assignment—back on full salary, of course. I assume you're going to move into your San Diego townhouse soon." Tom turned toward the wall calendar, adding, "I'll start making the arrangements with the consulate in South America. How about if you report here...Oh, let's say...the fourteenth. Does that give you enough time?"

Fletcher smiled nervously while Jennifer patted his arm. "Well, quite frankly, sir," he replied, "We were planning some time off. You know, sort of a vacation."

Berkshire quickly turned to Grahme who shrugged and sat back in his chair with his arms crossed. Seeing that it was his decision to make, Berkshire turned back to Fletcher and smiled. "Of course. How callous of me. I should've realized that."

"Thank you," Fletcher replied, relieved. "We'd planned to leave the day after tomorrow for the French Riviera. We want to spend some time in Monaco and Monte Carlo." Fletcher led all eyes toward the wall calendar again and continued, "When we get back I'll need about a week to move into my new place. So, if that's acceptable to you, I figure I can report for the Colombian shoot around the first of next month." He looked at Berkshire for confirmation.

Again Tom instinctively glanced at Grahme, who signaled his approval.

"Good! That sounds like a viable plan," Berkshire replied agreeably as he stood. "I'm sure that by then I'll have talked to Mr. Beaucamp at the embassy and we'll have made a firm decision about whether or not to publish your London adventure."

Fletcher and Jennifer stood and shook hands with Grahme before Berkshire ushered them from the plush office and out through the front lobby doors into the bright San Diego sunshine.

The skies over Monte Carlo were clear and calm as Fletcher and Jennifer sat on the patio of the Grand casino. They were relaxed and comfortable basking in the gentle Mediterranean night. Content and finally free of the burdens that had plagued them for so long, they were at the end of five fun-filled days. They had enjoyed the bliss of each other's love amid the tranquil and exciting surroundings.

Finishing their champagne, they rose, leaving the empty flutes on the table and began a flower-scented walk through the gardens, toward the sea. Coming upon the harbor, they sat on a seaside bench and took in the captivating view. Multi-colored yacht lights ornamented the port like Christmas trees, with the magnificence of the great castle of Roquebrune providing the backdrop.

Slowly Jennifer turned toward Fletcher, saying, "Darling, everything appears so beautiful and serene now. I'm glad the situation in London is over."

"Yes," he answered softly, looking out at the sea. "For the first time in my life, I really feel at peace."

She turned, following his gaze. "It all seemed like a crazy fantasy, like some kind of a horrible fairy-tale."

He smiled, remarking, "And, as always, good triumphed over evil."

She paused, her face turning serious over his statement. Then, impulsively, she began to laugh.

"What…what's so funny?"

"Well, do you think we'll live happily ever after?"

He stared into her eyes, suddenly moved by her beauty, wit and strength, yet soft womanly ways. He gently reached over and stroked her long flowing hair.

Speechless, she felt a rush of joy, knowing something special was coming by the electricity of his touch and the expression of adoration in his eyes.

"Jennifer, I'm very much in love with you," he whispered tenderly. "I didn't tell you before because I didn't understand it at first. I felt guilty because of Lainey's memory, but now I know she'd want it to end this way. Yes, I think we'll live happily ever after."

She stroked his cheek, matching his passionate gaze. "Don't worry, darling," she replied lovingly, as her eyes welled with tears. "Lainey knows your love for her was real. And I know she'll always be with us. To share our lives and watch over us."

"Thank you, sweetheart," he said as he drew her close and kissed her.

They stood. Hand in hand they began the slow stroll back to their hotel.

The large round bed was soft and warm as the early morning sunlight and crisp breeze streamed through the bellowed lace curtains of the open French doors. Fletcher and Jennifer lay wrapped in the bed-coverings when the phone abruptly shattered their deep sleep.

Fletcher groggily shifted himself away from Jennifer and drew the satin sheet over her naked body. She crankily cracked one eye and pulled the sheet over her head to escape the persistent ring.

"Hello," he answered sleepily, sitting up. "Oh, hello, Tom. How'd you find us?...Right, I see..." Fletcher's conversation began to arouse Jennifer's curiosity. "What? Jesus!" he continued. "Really? Fill me in, I'm awake..." Jennifer stuck her head out from under the sheets and squinted up at him.

After a few minutes of patiently listening to his caller, Fletcher broke his silence. "Sure, of course I'll investigate it...Huh, do it there? Leave right from here, Monte Carlo? But we're planning to come home tomorrow...Okay, I understand. I'll leave here as soon as I can...Umm, not sure, I'll have to ask her...Okay, I'll contact you when I check into a hotel so you know where to ship my equipment...Yeah, bye." He hung up the phone, shaking his head, attempting to fully comprehend the conversation.

Jennifer crawled out from under the sheet and propped herself up on her elbows. "Who was it?" she asked.

"Berkshire," he answered, gathering his thoughts.

"Berkshire! How'd he find us?"

"It wasn't hard," he replied with a vacant look. "He called all the hotels. There aren't many of 'em in Monte Carlo."

"Well, what did he want?" she asked impatiently.

"I guess when Berkshire finally got a hold of Beaucamp in London he gave Tom some stunning news."

"About what?" She was becoming irritated at having to press him for the answers.

"The 'King O' Men' pub was burned down last week," he replied, rubbing the sleep from his eyes. "And the authorities know it was arson."

"Couldn't it be a coincidence?"

He looked at her. "Maybe, but remember the pub bartender, Michael Doherty? The one I told you about."

"Sure."

"They found him hanging in the ice closet behind the pub—murdered."

"Murdered!"

"Yeah, his throat had been slit and his tongue cut out and…" He grimaced.

"And what?"

"It was stuffed into his hand."

She gasped.

He glanced at the clock. "Anyway, I guess I need to go to London."

"They don't suspect that you had anything to do with it for God's sake, do they?"

"No, but Berkshire wants me to photograph and chronicle the investigation. He thinks it'll help validate our story, maybe even promote its publication."

She grew nervous as she thought things through. "Damn, here we go again," she said, now fully awake.

Fletcher shook his head. "Nah, I don't think so. A lot of people were familiar with the bartender's gruesome stories. It was probably robbery or something. The killer probably wanted to create a sensation to throw Scotland Yard off the track."

"Do you really believe that?" she asked skeptically, thinking about what Fletcher had said last night at the harbor about good always triumphing over evil. "Maybe there's more to it than meets the eye. Maybe it's something more that only we could understand."

"Oh, shit, I don't know," he answered curtly, rubbing his forehead, trying to rid himself of the fog the champagne had left. "But let's not read anything into it right now, okay?"

"Okay," she relented. "So what's your plan?"

"Berkshire wants me to fly immediately to London and meet with Beaucamp and the authorities at Scotland Yard."

"To London? From here?"

"Yes," he replied. "Berkshire is going to ship my equipment there."

Stunned, she went silent.

He reached for her hand. "C'mon, I'll arrange for the airline tickets."

"Tickets?"

"Right. Aren't we a team?"

Unsure of his hasty plans, she facially balked.

"Baby, I want you along," he appealed.

"I know, darling," she replied gently, gazing up at him. "But it's so sudden. Umm…how far do we have to go with this thing anyway?"

He thought for a moment. "Oh, about as far as our minds will take us."

Her eyes widened as the excitement began to well up insidc hcr.

He smiled, knowing he'd won her over with that answer. "Let's go, we've got to get moving. We're going to need some new clothes. I have a feeling we'll be spending the fall in England."

"Yes!" she answered eagerly, wrapping the sheet around her.

They jumped out of bed and headed for the bathroom.

"Hey!" she exclaimed, stopping them at the foot of the bed. "Let's rent a plane and I'll fly us to London. It's a short trip."

"Yeah, why not?" he answered. "Hell, I'll even pilot some of the way."

"Hmm," she quipped, "On second thought, maybe…"

"C'mon," he said, laughing and tugging on her arm as they hurried into the bathroom.

"Damn! Wait!" she exclaimed again, abruptly stopping him at the shower door, letting the sheet fall to the floor.

"What now?" he asked, rolling his eyes.

"I told them at the FAA office that I would report back to L.A. next week. How am I going to tell them I won't be there?"

He grinned. "Easy, we'll have our trusted intermediary from the embassy in London send them a message."

She smiled widely as he pulled her into the shower with him.